THE THIRD SECRET

VOLUME I

MARCO DE SIO

ISBN 978-1-63814-422-9 (Paperback)
ISBN 978-1-63814-423-6 (Digital)

Covenant Books, Inc.
11661 Hwy 707
Murrells Inlet, SC 29576
www.covenantbooks.com

The Godfather meets *Da Vinci Code*! This multi-generational story is lightning in a bottle.

—*The New York Times* best-selling author Daleen Berry https://www.daleenberry.com

PART I: THE IMMIGRANT

(THE STORY OF BIG AL)

The Doomsday Clock

On January 23, 2020, former four-term California Governor Jerry Brown participated as the Bulletin of the Atomic Scientists moved the hands of its symbolic Doomsday Clock closer to midnight, indicating that the likeliness of a human-caused apocalypse had increased since the prior year. It also meant that the Earth was inching closer to disaster.

The Bulletin adjusted the clock to reflect looming threats from nuclear weapons and accelerated global warming. The clock was set at one hundred seconds to midnight, the closest it had ever been to symbolic doom and the first time the hands had been within the two-minute mark.

"Thus, I make it known to you that from the end of the nineteenth century and from shortly after the middle of the twentieth century...the passions will erupt, and there will be a total corruption of customs. The Devil will work to persecute the ministers of the Lord in every way, working with baneful cunning to destroy the spirit of their vocation and corrupting many.

"The pope will be persecuted and imprisoned in the Vatican through the usurpation of the Pontifical States and through the malice, envy, and avarice of an earthly monarch.

"Unbridled passions will give way to a total corruption of customs because Satan will reign through the Masonic sects, targeting the children in particular to ensure general corruption..."

—A little-known, Vatican-approved prophecy delivered by the Madonna to Mariana de Jesus Torres in Quito, Ecuador, in 1594

(The prophecy came true, as now told.)

Chapter 1

LITTLE AL

Italy, 1881

Ten-year-old Alfred sat in the back of the boat as his father, Rocco, and a hired man rowed the oars. His dad was a fisherman at Costiera Amalfitana, otherwise known as the Amalfi Coast, a stretch of coastline on the southern coast of the Salerno Gulf on the Tyrrhenian Sea, located in the Province of Salerno.

Rocco owned a small traditional Maltese boat, called a *frejgatina*, which he used every day. The boat was equipped with traditional fishing equipment, including a variety of traps, fishnets, and long lines.

The type of fish he caught was determined by the fishing season. Today, he and the hired man were after octopus.

"Papa, I hear that some frejgatinas have a spritsail that propels the boat with wind power," Alfred commented. "Wouldn't that be great? So much easier than rowing!"

Rocco dramatically shifted his head from left to right and then looked back at his son.

"Alfred, there's no wind today," Rocco said. "How would a spritsail help us?"

Alfred's shoulders dropped.

"The water looks like glass," his father continued. "Besides, oars build muscles. At the end of the day, tired arms remind the fisherman that he's done real work."

Alfred watched as seagulls darted in and out of the water, doing some fishing of their own.

"The problem is that you don't yet appreciate the value of tired arms," Rocco kept on. "Trade places with me, Son. You row for a while."

Alfred's heart raced at the opportunity. This was not the first time his father had asked him to row, but each time he felt like pumping his fist in the air.

I am so lucky! he thought.

Alfred rowed and rowed, but after a while, his young arms ached. He struggled to keep up with the hired man, but he simply couldn't.

"*Andiamo, andiamo!*" Rocco shouted. "Let's go, let's go!"

It was no use. Alfred's heavy arms bent like noodles. Pain shot down his shoulders all the way to his fingers. "Papa, I am sorry, but I'm not yet as strong as you."

"When I was your age, I experienced the same problem," Rocco said. "Do you know how I solved it?"

"No, Papa, how?"

"By eating more pasta!" Rocco laughed. "Then I grew."

"If I eat more pasta, will I grow?"

"Yes! Then, instead of Little Al you will become Big Al."

The older men put out their steel octopus pots while Alfred watched the sun climb over the cloudy horizon. Brilliant rays of light shone brightly and warmed the cold November air.

"I feel bad for Margie," Alfred said of his sister, who was the closest in age to him out of seven siblings. She was just two years younger than him.

"Why do you feel bad for Margie?" Rocco asked.

"Because she is at home cooking and cleaning with Mama and I get all the fun out here with you, Papa!"

Rocco took his son's head in his giant hand and playfully shook it. At six-foot-five and two hundred seventy-five pounds, his father looked more like a lumberjack out at sea than a fisherman.

"Let's not tell Margie how much fun we have out here, okay, Alfred? If she knew, she might want to come along next time!"

Alfred pursed his lips. He definitely didn't want anyone else crowding in.

"I won't tell," the boy said.

The men rowed to another location, where they'd put out octopus traps earlier in the week, which they now pulled up.

"They're full!" Rocco cheered. "This spot never disappoints."

Rocco had fished these waters as a boy with his own father, so he knew the best places.

"Papa, when we get back to the docks, do we have to sell *all* the octopuses? Can we keep a few?"

"Are you hoping your mother will make her famous dish?" Rocco asked.

"Yes! Italian stewed octopus." Alfred grinned from ear to ear.

"Let's hope John Marino gives us a fair price," Rocco said, his voice trailing off.

For months, the manager of the Port of Salerno had been paying far less for the catch than ever before. The fishermen suffered mightily, but what could they do? Marino ran things down at the docks, and he set the prices.

"Papa, you should open your own fish store."

"And why would I do that?" Rocco questioned.

"Because Mr. Marino needs competition. As long as he has none, he can pay whatever he wants for our catch."

"Not a bad idea," Rocco said.

"When I grow up, I am going to have my own fish store." Alfred puffed out his chest, feeling important at the thought.

"Is that so?"

"Yes, it is so," Alfred continued. "I am also going to own a bunch of fishing boats."

"Sounds like a great plan," Rocco said.

"Mr. Marino is a middle man," Little Al continued to explain. "If I own a fish market, I can cut out the likes of him."

"I see. Did you know Marino isn't the one actually setting the prices?"

"He's not? Well then, who is?"

"The rich business owners who operate the restaurants and produce stores. They pressure Marino to sell our fish cheap to them. Therefore, Marino pays us less, that way the business owners can still make a profit when they re-sell our fish."

"Hmm. Well then, I am going to own my own restaurant one day too!" said Alfred.

Rocco chuckled.

"Operating fishing boats, a fish store, and a restaurant is a lot of work, Alfred. How will you find your workers? Have you considered that?"

Alfred rubbed his chin and looked off at the ocean.

"Well, there's an answer for that too," the boy replied.

"Which is?"

"I will have a lot of children, and they will be my employees."

"I see," Rocco said with a sideways grin. "And how will you feed all these kids of yours?"

"I plan to own many boats and catch lots of fish."

Several hours later, the men rowed to another spot, where thirty-five octopus pots had been set out several days ago. Once again, the traps were full.

"We are going to need a bigger boat, Papa!"

On days like this, when the catch was good, Rocco inflated a large, heavy-duty raft and put the excess fish in it. Today, Rocco put the octopus inside the contraption and dragged it behind the frejgatina.

The men rowed to several more locations. When the sun dropped below the ocean, the men rowed back to the docks. When they arrived, Rocco paid the hired man.

The Port of Salerno was bustling at this time of the day as longshoremen offloaded fish from the boats. Alfred loved the action.

"Son, stay here, please, and wash down the boat. I will see Old Man Marino about getting paid for today's catch. There's a long line at his office door, but I shouldn't be gone too long."

Alfred was cold. He worked up a sweat scrubbing the boat, but after he was done the boy was even colder. His clothes were wet, so he shivered.

Alfred wrapped his arms around his chest and hopped up and down to stay warm. An hour passed, but Rocco still hadn't returned.

What is keeping Papa?

Concerned, Alfred scrunched his brows together. His stomach was twisted in knots. In the distance, he heard a noise. Alfred tilted his head to one side and listened.

Waves crashed against the docks as the high tide came in.

Then he heard faint yelling from the direction of Mr. Marino's office. He sprinted to the port manager's office. As he got closer, Alfred could see an angry mob. Fishermen were yelling. Police officers protected Marino.

"Your prices are not fair," said Cosmo Ricci, a fisherman who grew up with Rocco in the nearby village of Cava de' Tirreni, where they both still lived.

"Step back," warned a member of the Polizia di Stato. He pulled a baton club from his belt. The other police officers did the same.

"Oh, I see," said Rocco. "That's how it's going to be, Marino? You intend to beat us up?"

"If I have to, I will," said the port manager, whose back stiffened. "You do not make the rules around here, Rocco."

Cosmo Ricci took a step forward, meeting Marino nose-to-nose. His fists clenched and his face flushed. But before Cosmo could do anything, a police officer struck him in the knee with his club. Cosmo fell to the ground and groaned in pain.

The other police officers lashed out with their clubs too. Cosmo and the fishermen were defenseless. Tears streamed down Alfred's face as he watched helplessly.

A sharp tingle ran down his spine. He tried to scream, but the only thing that came out of his mouth was a soft whimper.

Alfred attempted to run, but his feet felt cemented to the ground. When the beating was over, twenty-four fishermen were on the ground. Cosmo suffered a broken jaw and a fractured skull. He would never be the same again.

Rocco was out of work for six months due to his own injuries. His hips and left shoulder suffered permanent damage.

In order to feed the family, Rocco's wife, Mary, took over as the breadwinner. She picked up an extra shift at the fish-packing plant at the Port of Salerno.

Now, instead of working nine hours a day, she worked eighteen, even though she was four months pregnant.

The conditions at the fish packing plant were unsanitary and unsafe. Flies congregated around the fish heads, fins, scales, and bones.

The workers, mostly women, often hurt their hands while shucking and packing fresh shellfish. There was dried blood everywhere, especially on the walls and floors.

Nonetheless, no one complained because jobs were so hard to come by. The number of people on the waiting list for fish-packing work was too many to count.

Mary made ten cents an hour, netting her $1.80 a day. That came out to $10.80 during a six-day workweek. At home, she raised sheep, chickens, and grew a vegetable garden to supplement the family's food source.

While her mom was gone at work, nine-year-old Margie became the woman of the house, because she was the oldest daughter. She liked being the one in charge.

Margie cooked all the family meals, bossed around her younger siblings, and ran the house in the way that Mary had taught her.

Margie was a carbon copy of her mother. They were take-charge people.

"If there's a will, there is a way," Mary would say, which Margie coined in her own words as, "Determination will overcome any obstacle!"

Margie's cheekbones were set high, like her mother's. Their eyebrows were full and matched their dark hair, which both wore at shoulder length. Her lips were thin, also like Mary's.

Both Margie and her mother had a habit of pursing their lips when something displeased them. In contrast, their smiles lit up a room.

Even at her young age, you could tell Margie was going to be beautiful, just like her mother.

While Rocco was home with his injuries and Mary was working a double shift, Margie didn't go to school. She studied at home, which was no big deal because she was the smartest kid in her class.

Alfred took up working at the Port of Salerno each day after school for Mr. Marino.

Alfred liked his job at the port, just not the man he worked for. He unloaded fishing boats and washed down boats. Alfred was lanky but strong.

On Saturdays, he cleaned the offices and stores at the port, which meant sweeping the floor of the main office where Marino worked. He was a mean boss, particularly to women.

Marino yelled at women and, quite often, looked for reasons to fire them. For example, one day Marino fired Mrs. Lombardi because she arrived ten minutes late to work from Naples, some thirty miles away.

"But the bus got a flat tire," the woman protested.

The real reason Marino fired her, however, is that he thought the beautiful Mrs. Lombardi refused what he perceived to be advances toward her by a wealthy customer, Supremo Pasquinelli, who owned a restaurant in Salerno.

"Get your things and leave," Marino yelled at Mrs. Lombardi.

"But, Mr. Marino, I need this job. My family cannot afford to live without it."

"How's that my problem? Get out!"

On his thirteenth birthday, Alfred received word that Marino wanted to see him in the manager's office. Alfred's shoulders tensed, and there was a knot in his stomach.

He is the reason my dad was injured and Cosmo Ricci's head and jaw are permanently messed up, Alfred thought.

When he arrived, the port manager pretended to be interested in Alfred and his dad.

"How is your dad?" Marino asked.

You are a jerk, Alfred thought.

Despite his thoughts, he answered politely. "He is doing well, sir. My papa is fishing again. His shoulder isn't as good as it used to be, and it probably never will be, which makes it hard for him to row."

Marino's face was blank. His eyes glazed over. He couldn't have cared any less.

"Yes, well, anyway, I have something I'd like to discuss with you, boy," Marino said. "Mr. Pasquinelli needs a worker at his restaurant on the weekends, both days, Saturday and Sunday."

That is the man who got Mrs. Lombardi fired, Alfred thought.

"You may have seen Mr. Pasquinelli around here before. He's the giant-looking man who buys a lot of fish, a really good customer.

"The restaurant pays well," Marino continued. "You'd be a dishwasher there. Are you interested in working for him?"

"I need to talk with my priest, sir. Normally, we do not work on the Sabbath, as you know. You and I attend the same Church parish, so you know what Father DeBenedetti thinks about that."

"Given the fact that your dad has injuries, I think Father DeBenedetti will allow you to work on Sundays after early morning Mass," Marino countered.

Alfred ran his hands through his thick hair.

"Go ahead and check with him," Marino said, picking up on the boy's hesitation. "Remember, though, Mr. Pasquinelli is a special customer. We don't want to disappoint him."

That evening, Alfred listened as seventy-five fishermen crammed into Rocco's home and voiced their complaints about Marino.

"We're still not getting fair prices for the catch," a fisherman complained. "That's not right!"

Rocco took control of the meeting.

"Cosmo Ricci is my best friend," Rocco noted. "A lot of you are friends with him too. But look at how he is. He can barely talk. His mind is all scrambled. Cosmo did not deserve the beating he took. Shall we avenge him?"

Silence.

"I asked, are we going to defend Cosmo's name?" Rocco repeated.

"Look, let's face it, if we step out of line again, we may all die," said Bobby Piziali, a recent high school graduate who took over his family's fishing business because his father had severe arthritis.

"We should all just leave and go to America," added Rocco's brother-in-law Michael Piazza.

"He's right, the fishermen there get better prices because they belong to a union," said Piziali.

"Why not create your own union here?" asked Luigi De Sio, a coal worker and Rocco's long-time friend.

Luigi was at the meeting with his coal coworker, Freddy Boyardee.

"Decades ago, the coal miners had a problem with their bosses," said Freddy. "The Carbonari took care of it. They protested and set fire to businesses."

"The Carbonari? You mean the charcoal burners?" Rocco asked.

"Yes. They got the name because they burned charcoal in the forests of the land barons," Freddy said. "They were effective as secretive freedom fighters. The Carbonari were a covert force that raised hell."

"You guys need to set fire to businesses and go nuts like the Carbonari did," Luigi chimed in.

"Go back to your coal mines," countered an older man standing in the corner.

"And who are you?" thundered Freddy Boyardee.

"I am 'General Valentino.' I own Valentino Vineyards. Ten years ago, I led the Carbonari in a war for full Italian unification. I'm here to tell you that Marino is ruthless. I've done business with him. You have no idea the kind of person you are dealing with."

"Yeah, I heard he fired a woman at the fish packing plant just for showing up a few minutes late," said Frankie Ricci, Cosmo's young son, who also happened to be Alfred's best friend.

"Marino will think differently when we go on strike and he has no fish to sell around town," Rocco countered.

"You want to strike?" General Valentino asked. "I have been organizing strikes and protests in southern Italy for a long time. Are you prepared to sit it out for weeks? Months?"

"However long it takes," said Rocco.

"You are at the mercy of Marino," General Valentino warned. "His job is to negotiate with the restaurant and store owners. They are his concern, not you. They have the money, not you. Am I right?"

"You are right," Luigi agreed.

"So, that means you guys need to negotiate directly with the restaurant and store owners yourself. Cut Marino out," General Valentino asserted.

That is what I was telling Papa on the boat, Alfred thought.

"So, if I am following you correctly, you think we should sit down with the business owners ourselves and negotiate directly with them for the prices we want?" asked Bobby Piziali.

"Yes," said General Valentino. "Go around Marino. He's nothing but a middleman."

My point exactly! Alfred thought.

"What if the restaurant and store owners don't agree to our demands?" Bobby Piziali asked.

"Then go on strike," General Valentino replied.

"Rough people up," Luigi De Sio added. "Blackmail them."

"Set fire to their businesses," said the general. "Put all kinds of pressure on them to accept your prices."

"I like it," said Bobby.

"Then it's settled," Rocco exclaimed. "I will go down to the manager's office tomorrow morning and give Marino one last chance. I'll tell him our demands. If he balks, we go on strike."

"Fair enough!" the men cried out.

Alfred watched the men leave. His stomach did flip-flops at the idea of his papa confronting Marino the next day.

Old Man Marino is not going to take it well. Not at all, Alfred thought.

The next morning, activities at the Port of Salerno came to a grinding halt after Rocco talked to Marino. No fishing boats went out. Marino had refused Rocco's ultimatum and shut down all operations at the port, including the fish packing plant, which put Alfred's mother out of work.

"I'll not be bullied," Marino declared. "Have your strike. Let's see how long that lasts."

For the first week, the fishermen walked around town with their chests puffed out. As the impasse dragged on, however, they were not so cocky. The men fell on hard times. Local businesses struggled too.

"Rocco, how much longer will this go on?" complained Joe Molinaro, the owner of Molinaro's Market in Cave de' Tirreni. "No one is buying anything."

"Not much longer," Rocco reassured him.

Privately, though, Rocco wasn't as confident as he let on. Mary was now nine months pregnant. Their family was without much money, and he was feeling the pressure of a growing family.

With his injuries healing, Rocco passed the time by adding on a new room to the house for the baby. He'd learned carpentry from his own father, just like fishing. His father had been a jack-of-all-trades who died out at sea when Rocco was nineteen. Caught in an unexpected storm, his father never returned home.

These days, the only money Rocco and his family had coming in was the little bit that Alfred made at the docks after school and at Pasquinelli's Seafood Restaurant on weekends. Father DeBenedetti had given the youth "special dispensation" to work on the Sabbath due to the injuries Rocco had suffered.

The strike was taking its toll at the restaurant, too, though. Without fish on the menu, there were fewer customers.

"Alfred, has your dad told you if the fishermen plan to go back to work soon?" Mr. Pasquinelli asked one day.

"I really don't know when the strike is going to end, Mr. Pasquinelli."

"I have been serving steaks and veal, but the customers want fish!" the owner complained.

"My papa says the fishermen have a backup plan. He calls it their 'Plan B' if the strike continues much longer," Alfred replied.

"What is Plan B?" Pasquinelli asked.

"The fishermen plan to negotiate directly with the store and restaurant owners who buy their catch from Mr. Marino."

"Is that so?" said Pasquinelli. "No one has talked with me yet."

"Probably because they are still in Plan A. Plus, you are a giant."

"Excuse me?" Pasquinelli asked. "What does my size have to do with anything?"

"You are so big, they're probably afraid of you."

"You are one to talk, Al. You have been growing like a weed lately. What are you now, six feet tall?"

"My dad says I'm growing a lot because I eat lots of spaghetti," Alfred replied.

Pasquinelli clapped his hands.

"Well, anyway, you only have five more inches to grow until you catch me!"

Alfred dropped his head. His back stiffened.

"Mr. Pasquinelli, I am afraid the fishermen are going to get hurt."

"Why do you say that?"

"As part of Plan B, they intend to shake business owners down."

"You mean, bully them?" Pasquinelli asked.

"Yes. If they don't get the prices they want from the store and restaurant owners, the fishermen say they will protest and burn down buildings."

"I see," replied Pasquinelli. "Thank you for telling me. Alfred, please come to my office later tonight after you finish with the dinner service. I'd like to discuss this issue with you some more."

Three hours later, after he'd cleaned and dried all the dishes, glasses, and coffee cups with a dish towel—along with help from Patty, the lead server—Alfred went to see the owner. His heart fluttered. Perspiration built on his forehead.

I wonder if I said too much earlier today. Maybe he is upset with me?

When Alfred entered Pasquinelli's office in the back of the restaurant, he plunged his hands deep into the pockets of his pants. He didn't want the restaurant owner to see them shaking.

Pasquinelli was seated behind a large desk, dressed in his customary silk suit with a handkerchief in the breast pocket. He wore a fedora hat, from which a dove's white feather stuck out of the band.

Pasquinelli dressed nice every night because he was the greeter at the front door during the dinner service. He loved talking to people and telling them stories.

"Do you know why I have called you here?" the owner asked.

"No, sir."

"I see you are sweating, Alfred. Are you afraid of me?"

"I know that you are an important man and a very tall person. Like a giant."

Pasquinelli chuckled.

"Earlier today, we talked about the strike. I know your father has told you his version as to why the fishermen are holding out."

Alfred nodded in agreement.

"I just want to be sure you see both sides, the entire picture."

"Okay."

"Alfred, do you understand how our government works?"

"I don't understand what you mean," the young teenager replied.

"The Kingdom of Italy is ruled by a constitutional monarchy, meaning we have a king who exercises his power through appointed ministers."

"We studied that in school, yes, I know."

"Okay, good," said Pasquinelli. "In your studies, did you learn that landlords in Italy have called the shots for centuries?"

"Um, maybe. Are you talking about feudalism?" asked Alfred.

"Yes. The feudal system in Italy has continued into the nineteenth century. As common people buy pieces of land, the lord, or land baron, retains certain rights over its use. Are you following me?"

Alfred nodded his head that he was.

"Feudalism still defines the relationship of those who control or work the land, whether for its agricultural value or for minerals, timber, or water."

Alfred looked down at the floor. Then he scratched his head.

"So, if I am following along correctly, what you are saying is that feudalism influences the rights that common people have?" Alfred asked.

"Correct," Pasquinelli clarified. "Laborers like fishermen and farm workers are at the bottom of the hierarchy. What you shared with me today is disconcerting because it goes against the system."

"You mean the part I told you about fishermen negotiating directly with owners?" Alfred asked.

"Yes. That is not how the system works. In Mr. Marino's case, he caters to owners because they outrank the laborers. He will never concede to the fishermen for that reason. That's just not how it's done."

Alfred stared deep into Pasquinelli's eyes. The boy nodded to show that he understood.

"Alfred, your father and his fellow fishermen won't even get an audience with the owners."

"I get it now," Alfred stated.

"If the fishermen try to negotiate directly with the business owners, I guarantee you, they will not be successful. In fact, they will probably get hurt, just as you fear."

Alfred rested his chin in his hand and furled his forehead and eyebrows.

"Who speaks for the laborers, then?" Alfred asked.

"I do," said Pasquinelli.

"What do you mean?"

"The working class pays me money to make sure their needs are considered," said Pasquinelli. "We call it protection money. It's my job to make problems go away."

"I still don't understand," Alfred said.

"Someday you will," said the grizzly bear-sized restaurant owner. "But for now, I need to take care of this strike."

A tingle shot down the back of Alfred's neck.

There is something more to this man than meets the eye, he thought.

"Mr. Pasquinelli, if I can be so blunt, why did you get Mrs. Lombardi fired if you are so worried about people and their jobs?"

The restaurant owner's face fell. He turned his head sideways.

"What are you talking about?"

"Mrs. Lombardi worked with my mother at the fish packing plant until she was fired by Mr. Marino," Alfred responded. "You flirted with her but she didn't flirt back, so Mr. Marino fired her."

The owner ran a giant hand through his coarse black hair. Then, he tapped his pencil on the ledger in front of him. His face turned bright red.

"Is this true, she was fired?"

"Yes."

The massive man stood up to his full-sized frame and shot his cuffs, exposing twenty-one-karat gold cuff links.

"Alfred, have you heard the expression, 'there are bigger fish to fry'?"

"Yes, sir."

"And what does that expression mean to you?"

"I take it to mean, don't get slowed down by the small things when there are bigger things to worry about."

"Bravo," said Pasquinelli, who picked up his things to go.

"This meeting is over, Alfred. I have bigger fish to fry."

***

The next day news quickly spread throughout the region that the strike was over. Alfred replayed over and over in head his conversation the night before with Mr. Pasquinelli.

"It is my job to make problems go away," he'd said.

Down at the docks, the fishermen went back to work, as did Mrs. Lombardi.

Chapter 2

STORMY SEA

Italy, 1885

Big Al's family took up an entire pew at Church. With the new baby, there were ten of them.

"This had better be our last child," Mary whispered in Rocco's ear, "or else we will take up two pews!"

Rocco grinned. Although the injuries he sustained from the attack on the docks limited him and probably always would, he was getting back in the swing of things. Rocco was fishing again, which made him happy.

In contrast, the once free-spirited and outgoing Cosmo Ricci was angry at the world. His injuries were much more severe. He would never be able to work as a fisherman again.

Cosmo seldom talked with people anymore, and he always gave them a sideways, suspicious look.

Father DeBenedetti focused his sermon on the plight of laborers like Cosmo and the other fishermen who had been beaten and gone on strike.

"The Vatican believes that social conflict has risen in the wake of capitalism and industrialization and that it has led to the rise of socialism and communism as ideologies," the priest said.

Cosmo, sitting with his wife and three children in a pew directly behind his best friend, Rocco, forcefully nodded his head in agreement.

"Pope Leo XIII believes there needs to be improvement between the owners of land and laborers. The Holy Father says there needs to be an improvement of the misery and wretchedness pressing so unjustly on the majority of the working class."

"Amen!" yelled Cosmo Ricci.

People in the congregation turned to look at Cosmo. From his seat in the back of the church, the port manager, Marino, shook his head in disagreement. His entire body stiffened, and his jaw locked tight as Father DeBenedetti continued.

"Laborers should not be oppressed by landowners or businesspersons," said the priest. "People should reject socialism and push back against unrestricted capitalism."

"Hallelujah!" shouted Cosmo Ricci.

"The role of the state should be to promote social justice through the protection of rights," said Father DeBenedetti, who was getting more and more animated.

"The pope says the Church must speak out on social issues in order to teach correct social principles and ensure class harmony rather than class conflict."

A fanabla! Go to hell! Marino thought. The port manager got up and walked out.

After Mass, Alfred ran home. He saddled his father's scooter and rode to Pasquinelli's Seafood Restaurant for his priest-approved job of washing dishes on the Sabbath.

"God expects you to help out your family," the priest said. "Christ says not all labor on the Sabbath is condemned. Priests work on Sundays, do they not?"

"I guess that is true," replied a wide-eyed and surprised Alfred.

"Have you heard the story where Christ and his disciples were passing through a grain field on a certain Sabbath?" the priest asked.

"No. What is the story?"

"The disciples, being hungry, plucked ears of grain and husked them with their hands," the priest told Alfred. "The Pharisees saw the Lord's men doing this and questioned Jesus as to why his disciples did that which was 'not lawful' on the Sabbath."

"What did Jesus tell them?" Alfred asked.

"He said the purpose of the Sabbath was to allow people a respite one day a week to rest the body and refresh the soul with religious exercises. The Sabbath is not a slavish regulation, however."

"Does that mean I can work at the restaurant?"

"Yes, you can work there. Help feed your family. Christ allows it, just as he allowed the disciples to pluck ears of grain and husk them."

Alfred liked washing dishes. He stood all day in front of the double sinks. It was his post for ten hours. He'd put extremely hot, soapy water in one sink. In the other sink he put even hotter, clear water.

He washed dishes in the one and rinsed in the other. Alfred felt relaxed when his hands were in hot water. The hotter the better.

"Here you go," said Patty, the head server, as she brought him the day's first tray of dirty dishes, left over from breakfast service.

"Hey, Patty, look at this," Alfred said as he pulled his hands out of the hot water. Steam came off of his gloves like heavy smoke.

"You are a nut," Patty said. "No one can ever say you don't sanitize the dishes. Honestly, I don't know how your hands don't melt."

The corners of Alfred's lips turned up in a wide grin.

"Nothing bothers him," said Pasquinelli.

Patty turned around and gave the owner a wink. He did a double take.

"Hey, what's this?" the owner asked.

Pasquinelli grabbed Alfred by the arm and pulled him in close. "It's been a month since I last checked. How tall am I, Patty?"

"Um, I don't know? Giant," she answered Pasquinelli.

"I am six foot five," Pasquinelli replied. "And look at this kid, he's now up to my nose. Soon he's going to be taller than me!"

"Let's call him 'Big Al' from now on," Patty said.

"Big Al!" exclaimed Mr. Pasquinelli. "I like it. From now on, that's how we will address you. Big Al it is."

The restaurant owner took a step back and looked down at Alfred's feet.

"They are perfect!" he exclaimed.

"What are perfect?" Alfred replied. "My feet?"

"Yes, your feet. Next Sunday after Mass, I am going to teach you how to stomp grapes. Bring your sister Margie. You come too, Patty. I will teach you all how to make wine!"

"Yippee, I can't wait!" Patty exclaimed. "That will be so much fun."

Big Al finished washing the breakfast dishes. He went out of the kitchen and into the dining room to see if there were any more dishes out on the floor to be washed. That's when his eyes landed on Marino.

The manager of the port sat with his back to Big Al at a large table with twenty-five other business owners, all of whom were dressed in their Sunday best.

They were having a private meeting. Big Al crept in closer to listen.

"This Rocco, he's a problem," Marino said. "He got the fishermen all riled up, and they went out on strike."

"The fishermen had no business getting involved in our pricing," a business owner complained.

"That was out of line!" another exclaimed.

"Something must be done about it!" said a third person.

Big Al felt the room spin. He thought he was going to faint. There was a ringing in his ears. Perspiration rolled down his back.

"Rocco cut into our profits with that strike," Marino declared. "He needs to be taken out."

The business owners all voiced their hearty agreement.

Big Al could not breathe. Oxygen was not getting to his lungs. The room spun even more. He braced a hand against the wall to keep from falling over.

"Okay, okay," said Marino. "Then we agree. I'll take care of this matter. Now, eat up. *Mangia!*"

Big Al hurried through his work and then rushed home. That evening, Marino visited Rocco's house and knocked on the front door.

"Mr. Marino, come in," Mary said. "This is unexpected."

Big Al could hear the conversation from his bedroom.

"Mr. Marino, how may I help you?" Rocco asked as he came into the room.

"There is a last-minute request by a business owner for cod," Marino said. "I need you and one of my men to go out fishing tomorrow morning."

"But the weather is supposed to be bad tomorrow," Rocco objected. "It's not safe to go out on the ocean. High winds and possibly even rain are expected."

"I'll make it worth your while," Marino said with a grin. "I will pay you double."

Mary caught her husband's eye and shook her head no.

"I can't let this person down," Marino pleaded. "He's very important, and his daughter is getting married. This is the dinner where the families of the bride and groom meet for the very first time before the wedding. It is an arranged marriage, you see, but a very special occasion nonetheless."

"If I go out, I'd prefer to bring my own man with me," Rocco said.

Mary threw her hands to her side, balled up her fists, and stomped out of the room.

"Your guy would eat into my profits," Marino whined. "I have to make money too, Rocco. I'll already be paying you double."

"No good," Rocco replied.

"Look, my man has a boat with a motor," the port manager argued. "His boat can hold more fish than your skiff. I promise you will be on and off the water before the storm hits."

Rocco lowered his head and folded his arms across his chest. The port manager's argument made sense.

"Okay, I will take the job!"

"Wonderful!" Marino called out. "Be at the pier at six a.m. My man will be ready, and he'll go out with you. *Grazie!*"

Big Al climbed into bed.

What is Marino up to?

The teen decided to go to the pier in the morning too.

I need to see what's really going on.

The next morning, Big Al dressed early and left before his father. He found a place to hide at the pier between some large commercial fishing boats.

Soon, his dad arrived. Rocco walked along the pier toward a stocky man with a bald head and an unshaven face. Even with his heavy stubble, a nasty scar on the left side of the man's neck was exposed.

The man's scar stretched up to his face and across his left eye, which was covered with an eye patch.

He looks like a pirate, Big Al thought.

Marino greeted Rocco and walked the two men over to a steam-powered fishing boat, where the captain was waiting. The captain also looked like a rough person. His rounded shoulders gave him a bull-like appearance.

The two strangers moved slowly and deliberately. Their every move seemed calculated.

When they spoke, the man with the eye patch did not look at anyone. His head was down the entire time. Despite being only around five foot nine inches tall, the man with the eye patch was obviously not someone to be messed with.

"Isn't she a beauty?" Marino said of the boat. "And see those nets protruding out both sides of the boat? They are for a trawl system of fishing. There are also lines and drift nets."

Lightning flashed in the distance and thunder roared. The storm was coming.

"Mr. Marino, are you sure this is a good idea?" Rocco asked. "I bet your client would understand that, for safety's sake, a few cod are not worth taking such a risk."

"Like I said, he is planning a huge dinner tonight," Marino said. "I cannot disappoint him. Besides, this beauty will get the job done before the rain starts to fall."

Rocco, the captain, and the man with the eye patch got on the boat.

"See you after lunch," Marino said. "Happy fishing!"

The men did not return after lunch, however.

At around one p.m. the sky turned pitch-black, and the wind swirled with such force that trees doubled over. Seagulls frantically sought shelter from the storm, their eyes wild and frenzied.

By three p.m., the rain was falling in a heavy downpour. The ground was covered with water. An hour after that, small streams flowed through the streets of Salerno. Rocco did not arrive for dinner that night, nor any other night for that matter.

On the night of the big storm, Mary had put the children to bed and cried by the living room window. The men were officially declared missing the next day, presumed dead. Down at the docks, Marino avoided eye contact with Alfred.

***

Two weeks after the men presumably drowned, Father DeBenedetti presided over a celebration-of-life ceremony for Rocco. Four hundred people from the village attended, pretty much the entire population.

There was not much to celebrate, though, without a body to bury. The priest gave his blessing:

"Forasmuch as it hath pleased Almighty God of his great mercy to take him unto himself the soul of our dear brother here departed, we therefore commit his memory to the ground; earth to earth, ashes to ashes, dust to dust."

The women cried and comforted Mary, who was inconsolable. Cosmo Ricci was the only other person besides the priest to speak at the service for Rocco. "He was my best friend. A great confidant, father, and husband."

Cosmo stepped back. His body tightened. His face flashed hot and his fists clenched. Shouts replaced his soft-spoken voice.

"Rocco was pressured into going out on the sea that day," Cosmo continued. "Not fair! Our unbalanced labor system, endorsed by the government, forces people to work in unsafe conditions. The king will answer one day for Rocco's death. You can count on it!"

Later that evening, at dinnertime, Pasquinelli stopped by to see Mary, with baskets of food. She invited him to stay and eat dinner.

"I admired your husband," Pasquinelli said to Mary. "He saw injustices and wanted to fix them. He and I were a lot alike in that way."

"Thank you for your kind words, Supremo. They mean a lot."

Pasquinelli continued.

"Rocco was a fighter. He did not want people to suffer, nor do I. Sometimes you have to fight for what you believe in. Rocco did that, and I respected him for it. I'm sorry this happened."

Tears were in Mary's eyes. Her lips trembled.

"How am I going to take care of this family? There are so many mouths to feed."

The restaurant owner pushed back in his chair, stood, and walked around the large wooden table and stood next to Mary. He squatted down. His large legs resembled tree trunks.

"You don't know what I am, but that doesn't matter," Pasquinelli said softly. "What does matter is that you know that your family will be taken care of."

Big Al covered his mouth with both hands. Mary's eyes flew wide open.

"How can you promise that?" Mary asked.

"That's my job. I take care of the people in this region who need my help. I do not let them suffer.

"On Monday, come to the restaurant, Mary. I will have a job ready for you there. Bring the baby. I will also have people ready to help you with that. They will babysit so you can work."

Tears flowed like rivers out of Mary's eyes. It was as if someone had turned on a water spigot full blast.

"I hear you are an excellent cook," Mr. Pasquinelli continued.

"She's a fantastic cook," Big Al said on her behalf.

"There's always a need for a good cook in the restaurant business," Pasquinelli said.

"First, I'll start you out as a waitress, so you have the opportunity to learn our menu. Patty, my head server, will teach you how we prepare the different foods. Then, after a short period of time, when you are familiar with everything, I'll move you into the kitchen."

Mary's head dipped completely over the table. She laid it on the table, beginning to sob. Her crying got so violent, Alfred got up and consoled her.

"As for all these mouths to feed," Mr. Pasquinelli said, looking around at the children with a crooked smile, "don't worry."

The giant restaurant owner winked at the kids.

"Everything will be taken care of, you guys," he said to them all.

Then he turned to Big Al.

"I still want you and Margie to come to the restaurant on Sunday. Bring Cosmo Ricci's oldest kid, Frankie, with you. I'm going to teach you all how to make wine. It's not for kicks. Winemaking is an important skill to know. I use only the best grapes, from Valentino Vineyards in Amalfi."

***

The next Sunday, Father DeBenedetti delivered a sermon on the brevity of life. Afterward, Big Al, his best friend, Frankie, and Margie met up with Pasquinelli and Patty at the restaurant. He took them downstairs to a cellar.

"The foot is the perfect, natural machine for crushing grapes," Pasquinelli instructed. "The pressure from human force is gentle enough so that the seeds won't break, except maybe in your case, Big Al, because you are so big.

"If the seeds break, an unideal astringent taste ruins the wine. Humans, however, have the intuitive control over when to stop so the seeds won't break."

"What about his stinky feet?" Margie said, punching her brother playfully in the shoulder.

"Very doubtful Big Al or any of you will spread bacteria during our grape-stomping process," Pasquinelli replied. "Stomping grapes with your feet is perfectly sanitary, thanks to the delicate balance of acid, sugar, and alcohol that prohibits human bacteria from surviving in wine."

"But will it taste like his foot?" Margie asked.

Pasquinelli burst out in laughter. "No. My wine tastes like nectar from the gods. When the fishing is not so good, I sell wine. We also serve my wine at the restaurant, and it is almost as popular as my turtle soup—almost!"

He showed them the white grapes and black Mission grapes, which were in lug boxes.

"These cost two hundred dollars a ton, which makes over one hundred gallons of wine," said Pasquinelli. "But between fermentation and evaporation, you might get eighty gallons, which is a year's worth of wine."

Pasquinelli walked over to a large lot of Concord grapes.

"I use the Concord grapes to make dark wine. Father DeBenedetti prefers this kind. So do the other priests in the area. They serve it during communion.

"The only problem with the Concord grapes is that once in a while the barrel blows up when there is too much fermentation. Don't worry, though. That usually only happens when I forget to put a little vent in there for air. What a mess!"

"Well, don't forget today!" Patty warned.

"Show us how to do this," Margie exclaimed. "I'm so excited."

"Okay, all of you take off your shoes and then wash your feet under that water nozzle over there," Pasquinelli said.

"Can I wash your feet, Boss?" Patty asked Mr. Pasquinelli, giving him a wink.

His face flushed.

"Um, I won't be stomping grapes today."

Big Al, Margie, Patty, and Frankie washed their feet. Then, Pasquinelli led them over to two barrels, each one big enough for only one person.

"There's twelve pounds of grapes in each," he explained. "Margie, you are the stomper for this barrel over here. Big Al, you will be her swabbie."

"What's a swabbie?" he asked.

"That's the person who scoops aside the stomped grapes and directs the juice down the drain into a jug."

"Do I get to eventually have a turn as the stomper?" Big Al asked.

"Oh, yes. Don't worry. The two of you are going to take turns throughout the day. Believe me, it's exhausting work."

Pasquinelli led Patty and Frankie to another barrel.

"Patty, you will start out as the stomper, and Frankie will be your swabbie."

"I'd rather work with you," Patty said to Pasquinelli with a pouty face.

Again, he blushed.

"How do you stomp?" Margie asked, rescuing Pasquinelli from his awkwardness.

"For the first minute or so, you stomp all the grapes to smithereens," Pasquinelli said. "Then you use your feet to move the squashed grapes to the rear of the barrel, while continuing to stomp them. Your swabbie, meanwhile, also pushes the grapes to the rear, while scooping the juice toward the drain."

The giant-sized restaurant owner watched for a little while as the foursome stomped and swabbed away. Then, he retreated to the backyard. Pasquinelli warmed up an oven with newspaper and wood. For the next several hours, he made bread.

When the grape stomping was over, Pasquinelli served them fresh bread with Italian meats, olives, cheese, and mineral water. After they ate, he called Big Al over for a private conversation.

"Big Al, you're now the man of the house. Unfortunately, that means you need to work full-time. No more school."

Big Al's face went slack.

"You are big, a bit lanky, but strong. Trust me, you'll grow into your height. I've arranged a good-paying job for you as a dockworker at the port in Praiano."

The ancient fishing village was located on the Amalfi Coast.

"My friend Lorenzo Pirelli Sr. runs things there. Take Frankie with you. Cosmo Ricci will never be able to work as a laborer again because of his head injuries, so Frankie needs to work full-time too."

"Praiano is far," Alfred said.

"You can get there in just over an hour. I am sorry, but it's time to leave your childhood behind. You're fifteen years old, and your family is counting on you now to step up."

***

The next day, which was Monday, Big Al and Frankie started their new job as longshoremen, loading and unloading fishing boats. They hauled fish to a weighing station, where Mr. Pirelli set the prices and paid the fishermen. He was a lot nicer than Mr. Marino at the Port of Salerno.

"Did you hear the king has started an aggressive campaign for the occupation of African land?" Pirelli said to Big Al and Frankie one day as they worked. "He is setting his sights on conquering the Horn of Africa."

"Why does the king want to invade another country when he can't even take care of the Italian people?" Frankie replied.

"The reason he's eyeing the less desirable territories in Africa is because Italian colonization would improve our trade with other countries," Pirelli explained.

"That's crap," said Cosmo's son. "All the king wants is more power. My dad says all leaders want more power. That's why they attack other countries. Simple as that."

"If the king can establish trade markets in other countries, it will make Italy stronger," Pirelli countered. "Colonization is all the rage. Even America is doing it. Italy is actually late to the game."

"Colonization is nothing more than a land grab," Frankie insisted. "No government can be trusted."

Chapter 3

BACK FROM THE DEAD

Italy, 1888

Big Al leaned against the railing outside the port manager's office. Frankie sat next to him on a long bench. With the sun setting, the two eighteen-year-olds were anxious to off-load the boats that were making their way back in.

Big Al, now six foot six inches tall, was no longer lanky. His body was filled out, and he weighed two hundred forty-five pounds with no body fat to hide his impressively big muscles.

Pirelli stepped outside his office and took a pack of cigarettes from his pocket. He sat down next to Frankie, lit the cigarette, and took a long drag. In the three years they had worked for the forty-two-year-old port manager, Alfred and Frankie had never been treated poorly by him.

"You know what you guys need?" he asked them.

"No, what do we need?" replied Big Al.

"A bicycle."

The corners of Big Al's mouth lifted. He let out a chuckle.

"Is that so?"

"Yes. All the ladies would love you guys if you owned a bicycle," Pirelli said.

"The ladies already love me," Big Al played back, running a hand through his coarse black hair.

Frankie shook his head in fake disgust. "That's not what I hear."

"Have you gentlemen heard of Giovanni Battista Ceirano?" Pirelli continued.

"No, who's that?" Frankie queried.

"He's an Italian entrepreneur."

"Like I said, never heard of him, but why do I have a feeling I am going to hear about him now?"

Pirelli ignored the comment.

"Giovanni Battista Ceirano spent eight years as an apprentice at his father's watchmaking business," said the port manager. "He left the watch business this year to build Well-Eyes bicycles."

"Well-Eyes bicycles?" Big Al asked. "What kind of Italian name is Well-Eyes?"

"It's not Italian," Pirelli replied. "English."

"What's up with that? I thought you said this guy, Giovanni, is Italian?" said Big Al, shaking his head.

"Yeah, Giovanni is an Italian name," Frankie agreed with his best friend.

"English names have more clout with the public than Italian names," Pirelli reasoned. "That's why Giovanni and his two brothers are building the bicycles under the name Well-Eyes. They call it 'marketing.'"

"I call it selling out your Italian heritage," Frankie countered. "If you're Italian, be proud of it."

Pirelli shook his head side to side. "No, no, no. You don't understand. This guy is smart, unlike you two *stunods*."

"So now we are stupid?" Frankie remarked.

"Just listen up," Pirelli continued. "Giovanni and his brothers are also planning to build the Well-Eyes motorcar."

"Now that's what I need, a car!" said Big Al.

Frankie nodded in agreement. "Women would rather ride in a car than on a bicycle."

"Not with you," Big Al joked.

"Ha-ha." Frankie walked over to his friend and punched him in the arm.

"Well, boys, thanks to the industrial revolution, you now have many choices," Pirelli said. "Italy is now among the modernized world powers. Take your pick: either a bike or a motorcar. Or you can have them both."

"A car," Big Al repeated.

"The industrial revolution can't do anything to improve that face of yours," Frankie said to Big Al.

"No need," Big Al replied, striking a pose. "Why mess with perfection?"

In northern Italy, extensive industrialization and the building of a modern infrastructure was underway. The media was calling it "The Miracle."

Alpine railway lines connected Italy to the French, German, and Austrian rail systems. Two south-going coastal lines were also completed.

Most of the larger industrial businesses started out with considerable investment from Germany, Britain, France, and others. Subsequently, the Italian state decided to help initiate heavy industry such as car factories, steelworks, and shipbuilding, adopting a protectionist trade policy from the 1880s onward.

"Under our king, Italy is thriving," Pirelli said. "We're just as competitive as America."

"Northern Italy is thriving, but not so much here in the south," Frankie disagreed.

"Don't worry, boys," Pirelli countered. "As I told you before, the king is wisely looking to grow our markets by expanding into other countries. Once he establishes new trade markets, all of Italy will prosper."

"That's a fancy way of saying the king intends to invade other countries," Frankie replied.

"Don't be all high and mighty, Frankie," said the port manager. "All advanced countries look for new markets and opportunities."

"They do?" Big Al asked.

"Yes, sir. The United States is also attempting to expand its influence in foreign countries as we speak, for economic reasons," Pirelli stated. "Our king is wise to do the same."

"Last Sunday, Father DeBenedetti talked about America's advancing industrialization during his sermon," Big Al pointed out. "He said industrialization has increased America's need to find new trading markets."

"As it has in Italy," retorted Pirelli. "Just as America is looking for more land for factories and trading, so is our king."

"What land are the Americans looking to take?" Frankie probed.

"Hawaii, Cuba, Puerto Rico, Guam, and the Philippines."

"I didn't know that," said Big Al.

"Yes, that's why our king wants to colonize Africa," Pirelli expounded. "He's copying America's playbook for economic growth."

Big Al nodded in agreement. "Father DeBenedetti said that too, during his sermon."

"One day when you are in the boss's shoes like me, Frankie, you will see that economics drives everything," Pirelli chided.

"Economic expansion is the reason why governments invade other countries and go to war," Frankie shot back.

"Are you always such a downer?" Pirelli asked Frankie.

"I am a realist."

"Look, Frankie, countries have to expand their economic power or else they become second fiddle to everyone else. Do you want Italy to be a second-rate country?"

Frankie shook his head in disagreement. "I am telling you, as countries become more industrialized, there will be big wars, just you wait and see. There might even be world wars."

Pirelli took a final puff from his cigarette and dramatically crushed it out with his foot.

"If countries want trade markets—and I'm telling you that they do—they sometimes have to fight for it," Pirelli argued. "That's how it's been since the beginning of time. Just read your Bible. Big wars were happening even then."

"In the meantime, people are leaving southern Italy because we're not like the north," Frankie pushed back. "People are starving here."

"Then let them go," Pirelli argued. "Those people are selling out the king and our unified country. We don't need them. Besides, you just said it, 'if you're Italian, be proud of it.' In my book, that means staying in Italy and not leaving because times are hard."

***

The next evening, Frankie hung on every word as Cosmo Ricci complained at dinner about the poor living conditions in southern Italy. Cosmo's wife, Valentina, had cooked a fabulous five-course dinner with the help of Rocco's widow, Mary.

Every Sunday, people in the village got together for dinner. They rotated which house they would go to from one week to the next.

"Salerno and other towns in southern Italy are not experiencing the kind of industrial boom as northern Italy," Cosmo said. "Our Campania region is suffering from high poverty."

"Cosmo is right," agreed Luigi De Sio. "The rich and middle class are keeping laborers down. They call us peasants."

"Why would they purposely do that?" asked a doubtful Father DeBenedetti, a regular at their Sunday dinners.

"Because of a thing called 'class warfare,'" Cosmo replied.

"The workers in southern Italy need to rise up like the Carbonari did and fight," said Luigi De Sio.

"There will be no fighting, Luigi," Mary cautioned. "Especially you, since you want to enlist in the military. Keep your nose clean."

Luigi's face flushed.

"Oh, all right," he replied sheepishly.

Cosmo, however, was just getting started. He'd built up a head of steam.

"Every morning I pick out a business and go there," he said. "When the workers arrive, I hand them leaflets about how the government is keeping them down."

"You do?" asked the priest. "Don't the business owners get mad at you?"

"Yes, but who cares? When the workers leave at the end of the day, I'm out there again."

"What do you tell them, exactly?" asked Big Al.

"I tell them to unite against poor wages! Take a stand against poor working conditions! Speak up! Demand better!"

"And the police don't arrest you?" asked the priest.

"Oh, I've been arrested," Cosmo said. "But that doesn't stop me. Eventually, my message is going to get through. People will rebel against the government one day. Everyone has a breaking point."

After the men ate, Cosmo approached Big Al.

"Tomorrow morning, before you and Frankie go off to work, come down to the Port of Salerno with me."

"Why?"

"Tomorrow is the fifth anniversary of the beating Marino and his goons laid on us," Cosmo said. "I have a few things I want to say. Your father would want you there."

**

The next morning, Big Al joined Cosmo, Frankie, and seventy-five fishermen at the Port of Salerno.

"Look at those ungrateful peasants," Marino chortled from inside his office. "I conceded to their demands during the strike, but did that end it? No. Here they are, back for more, protesting against me."

Marino turned to one of his henchmen. "Let's teach them a lesson. Go get some men and meet me out back."

Fifteen minutes later, Marino's henchman returned.

"Ready with some men, sir."

They numbered more than one hundred people, but this time, the attackers with knives and clubs were met with resistance. The fishermen fought back.

Unlike five years earlier, when he could not even manage a scream, this time an enormous Big Al crushed the attackers.

The riot went on for forty-five minutes, until the Polizia di Stato arrived from Naples, some thirty miles away.

Marino's men clearly got the worst end of the fight.

"Go home," shouted the police captain.

"His men started it," Cosmo yelled back, pointing a finger at the henchman whose back was turned away from the fishermen. "That's the instigator right there."

The henchman spun around, exposing a long, nasty scar that stretched from his neck to his left eye. He wore an eye patch.

"You!" shouted Big Al through clenched teeth. "I thought you were dead!"

The burly henchman sneered back.

***

That evening, as was his custom, Big Al waited for his mother to finish cooking at Pasquinelli's Seafood Restaurant. He walked her home every night. While he waited, he asked Patty if she could arrange for a private meeting between him and Pasquinelli.

"What's so important that you asked for a formal meeting?" Pasquinelli inquired as they sat down in his office.

"Did you hear about the fight today down at the pier?" Big Al probed.

"I know everything that goes on in this town," said Pasquinelli.

"What do you know about Mr. Marino's henchman?"

"What henchman?" Pasquinelli asked.

"He is rough-looking; has a bad scar that runs from his neck up to his deformed left eye, which he covers with an eye patch."

"I have never seen a guy like that," said Pasquinelli.

"I've seen him before," replied Big Al.

"Where?"

"At the port, on the day my papa died," said Big Al.

Just then, Mary arrived.

"I am all done," she said. "Ready to go, Alfred?"

"Just a minute, please, Mary," said Pasquinelli, who turned his attention back to Big Al.

"You say this man has a bad scar and wears an eye patch?"

"Yes."

"And you saw him the day your father, Rocco, went missing?"

Mary gasped. She stumbled for a chair.

"Yes, I saw him that day," Big Al continued.

Pasquinelli folded his hands together on his desk. They looked like giant bear paws.

"Sir, the night before Papa disappeared, Mr. Marino came to the house. Do you remember that, Mama?"

Mary nodded her head.

"I was in my room, but I overheard Mr. Marino tell Papa that he needed him to go out on the ocean the next morning."

"Why?" asked Pasquinelli.

"Mr. Marino said a special client needed cod. He said he would pay my father double to go out with one of his men and a ship captain."

"Rocco protested because bad weather was expected," Mary added. "But Mr. Marino would have none of it."

"His request is not so odd, though," Pasquinelli countered. "I am sure Marino gets last-minute orders from time to time."

"Yeah, maybe, but what I heard earlier that day *was* odd," Big Al replied.

"What did you hear?"

"I was washing dishes at the restaurant and went out to the dining room to see if there were any remaining trays from breakfast."

"And?"

"A group of business owners were meeting," said Big Al. "A few of them complained that Papa had stirred up too much trouble."

"Stirred up trouble, how?" Pasquinelli asked.

"With the strike," Big Al replied.

Pasquinelli stood up. He was massive.

"This meeting in the restaurant bothers me," said the owner. "Are you sure they were complaining about the strike?"

"Oh, they were talking about the strike, all right," Big Al said. "They hadn't let it go. Marino said he would take care of the problem."

"Wait, Marino said that? Those were the words he used?" Pasquinelli asked.

"Yes, and then that evening Mr. Marino showed up at our house."

"What then?" asked Pasquinelli, his face tightening.

"I got up early the next day and went out to the docks before Papa arrived. I hid there."

"You went to spy on them?" Pasquinelli asked.

"Yes. I wanted to see what Mr. Marino was up to."

"And what did you see?"

"Mr. Marino and the man with the eye patch met my papa."

"Same man as the one you saw today?"

"Yes."

Mary gasped for air.

"Patty, Patty," Pasquinelli shouted. "Please bring Mary a glass of water, quick."

Within seconds, Patty had poured a glass of water and brought it to Mary in Pasquinelli's office, spilling some of it as she entered.

"Here you are, Mary. Drink this. Take your time," Patty said as she took Mary's hand in hers.

Big Al was pretty sure Patty had been listening outside the door the entire time.

"Go on, Supremo," Patty said, nodding to him.

Pasquinelli looked at Patty with momentary uncertainty. Rarely did anyone call him by his first name.

"Tell me about the captain," Pasquinelli continued.

"Older. Fat. He wore a captain's outfit, which I thought was strange because none of the fishermen around here dress like that."

Pasquinelli's jaw clenched. "Why did the henchman make it off the boat, but not Rocco?"

"And why did Mr. Marino claim that all three men died at sea?" Mary mumbled through her sobs.

"Good point," Pasquinelli replied. "This conversation stays in this room with us. Are we all agreed on that?"

Everyone nodded, including Patty, who was both pleased to have worked her way into the conversation but also flushed by the restaurant owner's commanding demeanor.

"Come on, I will take you all home," Pasquinelli said. "Do not let your heart be troubled tonight, Mary."

***

The next morning Big Al and Frankie accompanied Mary to the restaurant, as they did every day. They would drop her off and then go on to the port at Praiano.

When they got near the Port of Salerno, Frankie noticed a crowd had gathered.

"What's going on over there?" he asked.

"Let's go and find out," Big Al replied.

They walked down a paved road on a steep hill. As they got closer to the Port of Salerno, the crowd noticed them and parted out of the way, revealing the cause of the commotion.

Hanging from a big oak tree were three men; one was wearing an eye patch, the other had on a captain's uniform, and the third man was Mr. Marino. Under their feet was a sign:

"This is what happens to vigilantes around here."

Chapter 4

COMING TO
AMERICA

Italy, 1891

Twenty-year-old Big Al hung on every word as King Umberto I spoke to the crowd from a railroad platform at Napoli Centrale, otherwise known as Naples Central Station. Ordinary people loved the second king of the united Italy, who was nicknamed il Buono (the Good).

King Umberto I had won the respect of ordinary people because of the way he conducted himself during his military career and as a result of his marriage to a royal and the subsequent birth of their son, who was to later become King Victor Emmanuel III.

Radical leftists, known as anarchists, did not feel the same way about the king, however. They didn't agree with his harsh ways of dealing with civil unrest. That was the knock that Cosmo Ricci had against the king, anyway.

"I can see why that cook tried to assassinate the king," Cosmo muttered while standing at the train station next to Big Al, his son Frankie, and Luigi De Sio.

"Shh, be quiet. I am trying to listen," Luigi insisted.

The king had been attacked thirteen years earlier by a cook who was also a proclaimed anarchist. He jumped on Umberto's carriage and tried to stab him, but the king warded the blow off with his saber. It was the first of three attempts on his life.

"This guy and his imperialist policies," complained Frankie, shaking his head. "He's full of crap."

Cosmo nodded in agreement.

"Silence," demanded Luigi, who was wearing his new military uniform. "I can't hear with you guys talking."

Naples Central Station, which opened in 1867, was the primary rail terminus and station for Naples. The place was also a favorite stop for politicians, like the king, to make speeches.

"During my first year of reign, in 1878, an anarchist attempted to assassinate me with a dagger during a parade right here in Naples," the king said. "Thankfully, today, there are no such protesters."

Cosmo's face turned beet red.

"The country of Italy was a mess before my father, King Victor Emmanuel II. My father turned things around. He unified us as a country! It is my duty to make Italy an even greater nation and to lead the Italian people to a place of prosperity and greatness."

Cosmo muttered to himself some more as the crowd chanted, "Umberto the Good! Umberto the Good!"

"Let me see a show of hands," the king roared. "Who remembers the flooding of 1882, when Verona and Venice suffered massive damage?"

Hands shot up throughout the crowd.

"I personally gave from my own funds to aid those who were displaced," said the king.

Loud applause.

"The following year, when the massive earthquake struck Ischia, I ordered rescue operations to continue on five days longer than planned, which resulted in many lives being saved."

Even louder applause.

Big Al looked over at Cosmo, who was now cursing. The veins on his head were popping out. Similarly, his son Frankie swung his fists against the air.

"Diseases and natural disasters have swept through Italy, and the government hasn't brought real aid to the people," Frankie grumbled.

"In 1884, when the cholera epidemic struck here in southern Italy, I didn't turn my back on you," the king continued. "I'll never turn my back on you."

"You have!" Cosmo shouted.

The station got instantly silent.

The king and his guards shifted their gaze to the fifty-year-old unemployed fisherman.

"Shut that man up," the head guard said to one of his men.

"Oh, I stand corrected," the king said. "We do have a protester with us today. That's okay. I know this region has been suffering. But I assure you, colonial expansion will pull southern Italy out of these hard times!"

"Why expand when you cannot take care of your people at home!" Cosmo yelled. "Feed your people, Umberto. Give them decent-paying jobs. Give them respectable working conditions."

In the next moment, the guards were on Cosmo. They knocked him to the ground. Frankie tried to help his dad, but a guard wrestled him to the ground too.

They dragged Cosmo out of the station by his arms and beat him unconscious several blocks away in the town square. They left him there for everyone to see.

"That will shut you up, anarchist!" a guard yelled before spitting on Cosmo.

Big Al ran over to his papa's best friend and put a hand on his back. He was out cold.

"Oh, Lord, why couldn't Cosmo have just kept quiet?" said Big Al, gazing up to the heavens. When he looked up, Big Al noticed a billboard directly above his head. *America Wants You*, said the billboard.

When Frankie and Luigi arrived, Big Al pointed up.

"It's an omen," he said of the billboard. "I am supposed to go to America."

"What are you talking about?" asked Luigi.

"Time for me to leave," Big Al said.

"That's a quitter talking." Frankie folded his arms across his chest and glared at Big Al.

"This is not the land of opportunity. America is," Big Al countered. "They will even pay you to go there."

"Who will pay you?" Frankie asked.

"American coal and steel and construction companies. Haven't you seen the other billboards around?"

"He's right," Luigi said. "They advertise steamship tickets, to be paid for in advance. In turn, companies hire the ticket-holders when they arrive on US shores."

"They deduct the ticket's price from the immigrant's wages," corrected Cosmo Ricci, who had regained consciousness. "Not like it is free."

"But it's worth it," replied Big Al.

Transatlantic transportation was indeed becoming more affordable. As word of American prosperity came via US recruiters, Italians like Big Al were finding it increasingly difficult to resist the call of "L'America."

"I've heard the stories of American labor recruiters traveling through southern Italy, spinning their tales of a Streets of Gold America," said Cosmo, shaking his disbelieving head.

"What they don't tell you is that when you get to America, you're expected to sweep those streets of gold and clean them."

"You guys get Cosmo home," Big Al said to Frankie and Luigi. "I've got to go to the restaurant."

A short time later, Big Al arrived and took a seat in Pasquinelli's office with his arms wrapped across his chest. He rocked back and forth in his chair as he waited for the owner to come in.

"Is there something wrong, Big Al?" Pasquinelli asked when he arrived.

"I want to leave Italy and go to America."

"Why?"

"More opportunity."

Pasquinelli sat in his desk chair, which barely managed to hold his massive frame.

"Are you not satisfied at Praiano? Is Lorenzo Pirelli not treating you well?" the restaurant owner asked.

"That's not it," Big Al corrected. "Mr. Pirelli is a wonderful boss."

"Then what is it?"

"I want to be a fisherman like my papa."

"You can be a fisherman here," Pasquinelli said.

"The pay is much better there," Big Al retorted.

Pasquinelli interlocked his hands behind his head.

"What about your mother and siblings?" the owner asked.

"I will send money home to them," Big Al stated.

"The grass isn't always greener on the other side of the fence."

"In America, they have unions that fight for the workers."

"The Mafia does that here."

Big Al's head snapped back. "What?"

"Remember years ago, I told you that one day you'd come to realize why I'm a powerful person?" Pasquinelli asked. "I told you I was sort of like the unofficial mayor around here."

"I remember."

"That's because I run the Camorra here."

"You run the Mafia?"

"Yes."

"In Sicily, the Cosa Nostra has a reputation for being very violent. Same with the 'Ndrangheta of Calabria," said Big Al.

"The Camorra is different."

"How so?"

"We're not a centralized organization like the Cosa Nostra or 'Ndrangheta. The Camorra is a loose confederation of different, independent clans, groups, and families. We're like a mutual aid society. Each Camorra group takes care of its own businesses, and it protects the working people in its territory."

"Is that why you were so interested in the fishermen's strike?"

"Exactly. The Camorra acts as the go-between with local politicians, public officials, business owners, and workers."

"And that works?"

"Very much so. Local politicians and public officials have a grip on communities, and the Camorra has a grip on them. We often put forward our own political candidates."

"Interesting."

"If a contract is needed to build a road, we make sure that our workers are the ones to build it, not laborers who aren't from around here," said Pasquinelli.

"We provide jobs for our people; take care of our own. If a thief takes the blacksmith's tools, we return them. No need to wait on the police to come from Naples or a lengthy investigation.

"If there's a property dispute, we resolve it. The Camorra grants privileges to residents, such as protection and intervention, in return for their silence and support against local authorities and the police."

"How long has this been going on?" Big Al asked.

"The Camorra dates back to the seventeenth century."

Big Al looked down at the floor.

"If you represent the working class, why didn't the Camorra protect the fishermen during the strike?"

"I protected both sides. The fishermen got the prices they wanted, but I helped the business owners absorb the loss in profits."

"How did you do that?" Big Al asked.

"Have you happened to notice that the business owners have bought less fish from the fishermen at the Port of Salerno ever since the strike?"

Big Al's mouth fell open.

"I didn't notice."

"I made a deal with Lorenzo Pirelli at the Port of Praiano," said Pasquinelli.

"What kind of deal?"

"Pirelli would provide more fish to Marino. So, you see, the fishermen in Salerno thought they won, when the truth is that no one really came out a winner in that strike."

Pasquinelli stood up and rolled his massive shoulders toward the ceiling. He shook his huge neck back and forth.

"The strike would have continued if I hadn't arranged a supply deal between Pirelli and Marino. Eventually, businesses would have gone under. Then, workers would have lost their jobs. Who wins in that scenario?"

"No one, I suppose."

"Even worse, you told me that the fishermen planned to go to Plan B, become vigilantes. I don't tolerate bullying and blackmailing. The owners were already stressed out enough during the strike. Therefore, I put a stop to it.

"That day, when I said there were bigger fish to fry, that's what I meant. I was looking at the bigger picture, the entire region."

Big Al stared down at his hands.

"Economics is a delicate balance," Pasquinelli said. "So, tell me, Al, what's the moral of my story?"

"I guess it would be that everyone suffers if the businessman doesn't make a profit," Big Al replied.

"Bingo."

Pasquinelli slapped Alfred on the knee.

"But this does not resolve the more important issue tonight, which is that you want to go to America."

"I want to go out on my own, yes."

"You want to be an adult, have an adventure. I get it. No one is stopping you. I was young once too."

"I have a dream of owning my own boats, my own restaurant, and my own fish store."

"Then go to America. However, don't settle for less than your dreams, Big Al. Don't be content being in the middle of the pack or, even worse, at the bottom. Make it your goal to be the person on top. Be the boss, like me, the one in charge. Be big, Al."

"Okay."

"Once you get to the top, take care of your people."

Pasquinelli leaned over and put a massive hand on Big Al's chest. "It starts and ends here, with heart."

His one-way ticket cost thirty-five dollars, which Pasquinelli paid "as an advance on your future, which undoubtedly will be a success."

New York 1892

When Big Al saw the Statue of Liberty in the New York Harbor, he jumped up and down like a kid and danced with delight.

A better life awaits.

His legs wobbled slightly as he got off the steamship. Most of the people on the boat had gotten sick crossing the Atlantic, but not Big Al.

They arrived at Ellis Island on January 1, the first day the immigration center officially opened. Big Al was the first person off the boat when it docked.

He was at the head of the line to be processed, but at the last minute, being a gentleman, he let the woman directly in line behind him go before him. *The New York Times* would run a story on the front page about seventeen-year-old Annie Moore from County Cork, Ireland, being the first immigrant to be processed at Ellis Island.

After he was processed at Ellis Island, Big Al made his way to Italian Harlem with Joe Molinaro, the grocer from his village who also happened to be on the ship.

From East 96th to 125th Street in East Harlem, the Italians who lived there re-created the traditional village life of Italy. It was full of Italian restaurants, barbershops, bakeries, and meat markets.

The Italians had also built churches. Even the architecture emulated their homeland.

"If I didn't know any better, I would think we were in Italy," said Molinaro.

"Why did you come to America, Joe?"

"When people are starving, they don't need a grocer," he replied.

Molinaro's wife and children stayed behind in Italy, as was the case with most Italian men who came to America.

"Mr. Pasquinelli told me we should go to a certain area of East Harlem, where there are other Italians from Salerno," said Big Al.

"Where would that be?"

"On East 115th Street."

The men noticed that the immigrants grouped themselves by the different regions of Italy. From one street to the next, Big Al could tell which part of Italy the residents were from just by the Italian dialects spoken.

For example, on East 100th Street between First and Second Avenues, there were Sicilians from Santiago; on the next street were Northern Italians from Piscento; and on East 109th Street they encountered a large settlement of immigrants from Calabria.

"Those people over there are from Sarno, near Naples," Big Al called out as they ventured on East 107th Street between First Avenue and the East River.

When they got to East 112th Street, Big Al called out, "They are from Bari!"

"What are you going to do for work, Big Al?" Molinaro asked as they continued walking.

"I've been working as a longshoreman in Praiano, so I figured I'd try to get a job at the Port of New York, which includes the harbors of Brooklyn and Hoboken."

"I hear that line of work is dominated by the Irish Americans," said Molinaro. "They're not receptive to the new Italian immigrants."

The grocer was right. Up until 1880, 95 percent of the dockworkers in New York were Irish, but that was changing because Italians were willing to work for nearly any wage and under any working conditions, unlike the Irish Americans, who were fighting to improve both.

"Mr. Pasquinelli told me to seek out a guy named Paolo Vaccarelli," Big Al said.

"Who is this guy Vaccarelli?" Molinaro asked.

"He's only sixteen years old. The son of Italian immigrants from Sicily. Mr. Pasquinelli knows the family really well."

"He's so young," Molinaro commented. "How can he be of any help to you?"

"Apparently, he's a big deal," Big Al replied. "He's a well-known bantamweight boxer."

"He fights?"

"Yes. He recently changed his name from Paolo Vaccarelli to Paul Kelly, which is Irish sounding. I guess he figures he can gain more fights if he doesn't have an Italian last name."

"Well, that sounds a bit like discrimination to me," Molinaro complained.

"Italians are considered in America to be of low class," said Big Al. "So Vaccarelli changed his name. According to Mr. Pasquinelli, this kid is very intelligent. He has knowledge of three languages, is liked by everyone, and is well dressed."

"I want to meet this guy!" declared Molinaro.

"Come with me tomorrow morning and you will," said Big Al.

That night the two men slept on the basement floor of a tenement that housed several families. Pasquinelli had arranged it.

They were bitterly cold because there was no heat. A baby cried all night, probably from the cold and hunger.

***

The next morning Big Al and Joe Molinaro drank coffee and ate dry toast before dressing and heading out on a long nine-mile walk from East Harlem to Paul Kelly's athletic club in Lower Manhattan.

"Tell me some more about this boxer," Molinaro said.

"He has invested his boxing earnings in brothels in the Italian immigrant district east of what is called the 'Bowery.'"

"What is that?" Molinaro asked.

"The Bowery is a street and neighborhood in the southern portion of the New York City borough of Manhattan," said Big Al. "Paul Kelly has also added athletic clubs to his properties, which I am told he operates as fronts for a street gang that he controls and consolidates."

"He controls a street gang?" asked Molinaro.

"He runs the Five Points Gang."

"The Five Points Gang? That's a strange name."

"The name is a play on geographic boundaries. The Five Points is an area of Lower Manhattan where four streets converge."

"So, the gang operates in Lower Manhattan?" asked Molinaro.

"And Harlem and Brooklyn."

When the men reached the athletic club, they noticed that it was surrounded by run-down immigrant housing made up of wood-frame and brick dwellings, warehouses, and commercial enterprises.

"This area looks like a slum," Molinaro said.

Big Al looked around. Mostly poor English, Eastern European, Jewish, and Irish refugees populated the area. There were gambling dens and brothels in the Five Points area.

"I'm glad I am with you, Big Al," said the diminutive Molinaro. "This is a rough area. I see some Italians around, but not a lot."

A pack of young men stood outside of the gym. They spoke in a heavy Irish dialect.

Molinaro glanced sideways and took a handkerchief from his pocket. He wiped his forehead, which was drenched in perspiration even though it was a cool morning.

"Let's go in," Big Al said.

Inside, they saw the baby-faced boxer sparring with a much bigger opponent. Big Al and Molinaro watched as the smaller man landed several jabs with lightning speed.

"To the body, kid," his trainer called out. "Work the body."

Paul Kelly connected several hard shots to his opponent's ribs.

"That's it, kid," the trainer shouted. "Now double up!"

He threw a left-right combination to his opponent's face that sent the bigger man crashing to the ground.

"Time!" yelled the trainer.

Paul Kelly backed away from his fallen opponent and hopped up and down waving his arms in the air. Then, he ducked in between the ropes, came out of the ring, and made his way over to Big Al and Molinaro.

"You're really good!" Molinaro exclaimed.

"That's how you get it done, all right," bragged the teenager, who looked extra diminutive next to the six-foot-six Big Al.

"You really punched that guy out," Molinaro continued to marvel.

The boxer looked Molinaro up and down.

"What do you want?" he asked suspiciously.

"Supremo Pasquinelli sent us," Big Al said.

"Supremo, ah, yes! Now there is another big man, just like you," Paul Kelly said to Big Al, sizing him up.

"I've got an inch on him now, finally," Big Al said with a chuckle, hoping lighthearted banter would put the wound-up boxer at ease.

Paul Kelly quit moving around just long enough for his trainer to remove his boxing gloves. But once they were off and the tape around his hands had been cut off, he was back to moving at hyper speed.

"What are your names?" Paul asked as he pumped his fists and moved his feet in a manner of fighting against oneself called shadow boxing.

"I'm Alfred Tedesco. My friends call me Big Al."

"Joe Molinaro."

"A couple of dagos," the boxer growled.

A puzzled look shot across Big Al's face. He put his hands on his hips, then scratched his head.

"Now wait a minute. Your family is from Sicily. Why are you insulting Italians?"

Paul smiled broadly. "You got me!"

"How come you changed your name?" Molinaro asked.

"For business reasons. People don't like Italians around here, if you haven't learned already."

"Smart move," Molinaro said, trying to get on the boxer's good side.

"You look like the smart one," Paul Kelly replied to Molinaro. "Are you good with numbers?"

"I was a businessman and ran a grocery store for twenty-two years, so, yeah, I am good with numbers."

"I could use a numbers guy," Paul Kelly said.

The boxer pounded a fist into his other hand.

"What about you, big guy. What do you do?"

"I come from a long line of fishermen. But I'm hoping to get work as a longshoreman."

"When did you guys get in?" Paul Kelly asked.

"We both arrived yesterday," Big Al replied.

"Fresh off the boat," the boxer quipped while wiping the sweat from his muscular chest with a towel.

All of a sudden, the boxer spun around in a circle and bounced up and down, for twenty seconds.

"I like Supremo," said Paul, picking up a jump rope. "If he sent you guys to me, then you're good."

"How do you know him?" Big Al asked.

The boxer whipped the jump rope over his head and then under his feet, talking as he went.

"My dad and Pasquinelli were childhood friends," he said. "Later on, when Pasquinelli became the leader of the Camorra, he helped my dad out a couple of times. When my dad ran short on money for his fishing operation, Pasquinelli lent him cash."

"That sounds like Mr. Pasquinelli," Big Al noted. "He is the helping type."

"So, I'm going to help you," Paul Kelly offered.

"Both of us?" Molinaro asked.

"Hey, I said I was going to help," the teen thundered. "Now, listen up, here's the plan. Al, go see my friend Jimmy 'the Frog' Bianchi over there in Italian Harlem. Tell him I sent you. He will set both of you up with a place to live."

Big Al nodded his head in agreement.

"Joe Molinaro, numbers guy, I need a smart money man to help run my businesses. You interested?"

"Will I get hurt?"

"Not if you do your job right. You'll be protected."

"Then I'm in," Molinaro said, blowing out a huge sigh of relief. "Thank you so much!"

"And you, big guy, you don't want to be a longshoreman."

"I don't?" Big Al replied.

"Forget about it. Dream bigger. Go see Antonio Colombo down at the pier tomorrow. Tell him you want a boat. Use my name. The plan is for you to catch me fish— lots of fish."

"Okay, I can do that."

"Work your tail off," Paul Kelly ordered. "If you eventually need more boats and more men, we'll expand the business. Understand?"

"Yes! What do I do with the fish?"

"Take them to Gambino's Fish Market in East Harlem. Tell Giovanni Gambino there that you are working for Paul Kelly."

Big Al's mouth fell wide open.

"You will do all that, really, Paul?"

"I may have changed my name from Paolo Vaccarelli to Paul Kelly, but I'm still a proud Italian. We need to stick together. Plus, like I said, Supremo Pasquinelli is my dad's friend. Out of respect, I'm going to do this."

Big Al and Molinaro looked at each other as if they had just won the grand prize in a contest.

The boxer continued, "I know people. I can read their eyes. Your eyes look hungry, Big Al, and I have a big appetite for success."

***

Weeks later, at a bakery just down the street from Big Al's tenement building, he met his future wife, Carmelita. She was working as a server at her uncle's bakery.

She stole his heart from the moment he saw her in a colorful embroidered skirt and bodice over a puffed, frilly blouse with a lace collar and broad ribbon tie. Her S-bend corset thrust her athletic hips backwards and forced her sizable chest forward in a fashionable pouter-pigeon shape.

Big Al ate at the bakery every morning for a month before he worked up the nerve to ask Carmelita's uncle for permission to take her out on a date. She was just eighteen, and he was twenty-two.

On their first date, they went on a picnic in Jackson Square Park, situated along Greenwich Avenue in Manhattan. They walked the two and a half miles to the park from Harlem. Her entire extended family followed them twenty paces behind.

Carmelita packed a picnic basket with Italian sandwiches, grapes, Asiago cheese, and *pizzicati* cookies.

Big Al, looking dapper in a fedora hat, tan three-piece suit, and freshly shined wing-tipped shoes, brought his favorite bottle of wine from Valentino Vineyards.

They all played bocce ball together. Big Al knew Carmelita was the woman for him and ended their first date with the words *"Conquistiamo il mondo insieme!"* (Let us conquer the world together!)

They married six months later. Over the years, Big Al and Carmelita had seven children—four boys and three daughters.

***

Later that same year, twenty-five-year-old Giuseppe Morello came to the United States from Italy. He was a member of the Corleone Mafia faction in Sicily commanded by Paolino Streva, who was also a friend of Paul Kelly's father in Sicily.

Back home, Morello was a wanted criminal. He shot down a Sicilian police official named Giovanni Vella, who was going to prosecute Morello.

A witness reported seeing Morello, who was born with a badly deformed right arm, in the area when the police officer was murdered. The witness was shortly thereafter found dead of gunshot wounds.

Fearing prosecution, Morello left for the United States and settled in the Italian Harlem area. His associates back home fixed things so a political opponent of the murdered police official took the fall, not Morello.

Later, an Italian court tried and convicted Morello in absentia for counterfeiting and fraud. He received six years and forty-five days in solitary confinement and a fine.

However, Morello was on the other side of the Atlantic establishing himself as one of the first street-gang leaders in America, along with Paul Kelly.

Morello and his enforcer, Ignazio "The Wolf" Lupo, who was also from Sicily, established a new model of Cosa Nostra in America. Their alliance came to be known as the Morello-Lupo Gang in East Harlem.

New York's criminal marketplace was already an arena of ferocious street-gang competition. The tenements of Manhattan where they operated were a patchwork of territories of sharp-dressed hoodlums.

Paul Kelly and his Five Points Gang controlled the streets of Italian Harlem.

***

One cold winter day, Morello and Lupo asked to meet with Paul Kelly in an effort to establish a pact between them. They met at Veniero's Pasticceria & Café, an Italian bakery. Paul Kelly asked Big Al and Molinaro to join him.

"You may speak in your Sicilian dialect, Morello. I understand the language," the leader of the Five Points Gang said.

"Thank you," said Morello. "I respect that your family is also from Sicily."

"We have that in common," replied Paul Kelly.

"I realize that I am late to the game," said Morello. "I cannot dominate the streets here like I want. But I would like a bigger territory and to coexist with you."

"What do you have in mind?"

"I would like to carve out a competitive slot from the Sicilian communities in New York and leave the rest of the turf to you," Morello said.

Paul Kelly nodded his head in agreement.

"The Corleone Mafia faction in Sicily, commanded by Paolino Streva, were good to my family back home," the boxer said.

"We can all get along in New York, Morello. However, I do not trust the Irish. So, I would prefer that you and I are on the same side and stand united against them."

Paul Kelly and Morello shook hands.

New York, 1893

Seventy thousand Italians, mostly men bearing wooden suitcases, left fishing villages and poverty-stricken farms in southern Italy for America. Many were Italian criminals from the Mafia who engaged in the "Black Hand" racket.

These criminals forced Italian immigrants to pay protection money, or "insurance," for their shops and families.

Black Hand extortion letters were signed with a handprint in black ink, giving the practice its popular name.

Morello was a master of the Black Hand racket. The Morello-Lupo Gang killed people who ignored the Black Hand letters they received.

The city logged multiple "barrel murders" that year with victims who refused to pay protection money.

The victims, usually Italian immigrants, would be stuffed inside a barrel after being shot, stabbed, or strangled to death. The barrels would be left on a random street corner or back alley, or shipped to a nonexistent address in another city.

The barrel murders alerted authorities to the existence of Italian Mafia practices in America. In response, cops from the New York Police Department walked the streets, keeping an eye out for thugs.

"There's a lot of heat on the streets," Big Al said to Molinaro one evening as they ate spaghetti and meatballs at a local restaurant.

"I'm glad Paul Kelly isn't involved in the Black Hand or barrel murders," Molinaro replied.

"That's good to hear," Big Al said. "Do you like working for him?"

"He treats me very well. Funny thing is, when we are in private, he asks me to call him Paul Vaccarelli."

"I guess you can take the man out of Italy, but you can't take the Italian out of the man. That makes me happy," said Big Al.

Molinaro burst out in hearty laughter. "He fancies himself a sophisticated guy. And he does have legitimate businesses, I'll give Paul that. I manage them and keep the books. You know, do the accounting."

"It's all on the up-and-up?" Big Al asked.

"Well, there is one little noncompliance."

"Which is?"

"He uses his legitimate businesses to 'wash money,'" Molinaro said.

"What do you mean, 'wash money'?" asked Big Al.

"We call it money laundering."

"And what is that?"

"The process of concealing the origins of money obtained illegally by passing it through a sequence of banking transfers or commercial transactions. The overall scheme of this process returns the *clean* money to the launderer in an obscure and indirect way."

"Sounds complex," Big Al noted.

"I'm the money launderer. That's my job."

Big Al's breathing quickened.

"Joe, let's find you a different job. This one sounds too risky."

"No way. I love it," Molinaro shot back. "Money laundering brings out my creativity. I find it challenging—almost an art—to launder money so there's no trace."

"What if you get caught?" Big Al asked.

"I won't get caught, I'm too smart. The amount of money I wash is ridiculous. I'm getting rich!"

"Well, I'll stick with fishing," Big Al replied. "Fish can't kill you."

"Ever read the story about Jonah in the Bible?" Molinaro asked.

"You mean the fisherman who gets swallowed up by a large fish, in whose belly he spends three days and three nights?"

"Yep, that's the one," Molinaro replied. "Don't tell me fishing doesn't have its dangers."

Big Al rolled his eyes. Now twenty-three, he was also doing quite well under the arrangement with Paul Kelly. His number of boats had gone up from one to three. Each

boat was thirty feet long and eight to ten feet wide—much bigger than the frejgatina that his father, Rocco, had owned.

Things were going so well for Big Al that he sent for his two eldest brothers, eighteen-year-old Adolfo and seventeen-year-old Leonardo. He also sent for his best friend, Frankie, who surprisingly arrived in America with his father, Cosmo Ricci.

Cosmo got a job in a weaving mill and resumed running the anarchist newspaper that he'd started a few years ago in Italy called *La Questione Sociale*. All of Cosmo's spare time and extra money was devoted to his newspaper.

Big Al, Adolfo, Leonardo, and Frankie fished every day, except on Sunday, the Sabbath. They would take the boats out in deep water.

"The bigger fish are in the deep water," Big Al would say.

***

One day while they were fishing for cod, Frankie shared the news that Supremo Pasquinelli had recently gotten married, at the age of forty-five.

"Whom did he marry?" Big Al asked.

"You're not going to believe this. Patty!" Frankie said.

"The lead server at the restaurant?"

"Yep. And they're expecting a baby next month!"

"Wow, miracles never cease to exist," said Big Al. "How about Father DeBenedetti? Is he doing well?"

"Most of his congregation has left Cava de' Tirreni for America. He's threatening to come here too," Frankie replied.

"You should've heard his last sermon," Adolfo interjected. "He railed against corruption and dark influences."

"What corruption?" Big Al asked.

"The Italian banking crisis. Have you heard about it?" Adolfo questioned.

"No," said Big Al. "News from Italy doesn't travel here very quickly. What happened?"

"Earlier this year, a scandal surfaced over the bankruptcy of Banca Romana," Adolfo explained.

"A commission issued a report in January that revealed politicians have been receiving money to finance their election expenses and to run or bribe newspapers."

"That is definitely a scandal," Big Al agreed.

"Yes, but there's more to the story," Frankie interjected.

"What?"

"Banca Romana had been the official bank of the Papal States since 1851," Frankie said. "About twenty years ago, it was made one of the six national banks authorized to issue currency in Italy. A man named Bernardo Tanlongo, who had made his career in the bank, was promoted to governor ten years after the unification of Italy.

"Tanlongo had a remarkable ability to secure friendships and protections through corruption and loans to cover up secrets."

"What kind of secrets was he covering up?" Big Al asked.

"It was discovered that Tanlongo provided illicit entertainment to Vatican officials."

Chapter 5

A MOST VIOLENT TIME

New York, 1896

Mass was underway at All Saints Roman Catholic Church, located at 47 East 129th Street, at the corner of Madison Avenue, in the Harlem neighborhood of Manhattan.

Built in 1879 by predominantly Italian laborers, the brick church had a Venetian Gothic design with terra-cotta trimming, and an elegant oil-based mural.

Big Al sat in a pew with his brothers Adolfo and Leonardo. Joe Molinaro joined them.

Cosmo Ricci sat in the pew directly behind them, as was his custom in Italy, to have Rocco's back. Frankie joined his dad in the comfortable hand-carved pew.

On the altar, Father Brady, a young Irishman, gave a sermon about the world's new economic order, which he said had "resulted in the growth of an impoverished working class who have increasing socialist sympathies."

Cosmo Ricci stirred in his seat.

"Pope Leo XIII is trying to reconcile the Church with the working class," said Father Brady. "His papacy is moving the Church back to the mainstream of European life."

Cosmo Ricci jumped to his feet, fists clenched.

"And just how is he doing that, Father?" he shouted.

The entire congregation let out a collective gasp.

"He is improving relations with Russia, Prussia, Germany, France, Britain, and other countries," replied Father Brady.

"Why doesn't the pope start by addressing the anti-labor policies of King Umberto I?" Cosmo shot back. "Why is the pope silent about that?"

Father Brady stepped from the altar and marched quickly down the long center aisle toward the interrupter.

"Oh, I know all about you, Cosmo Ricci. You own the newspaper that incites people with its anarchist views," the priest shouted.

"I educate people," Cosmo countered.

"You incite," corrected the priest.

"People deserve to know the truth!"

"Then tell the truth, not lies," said the priest, his face flushing.

Father Brady glared face-to-face with Cosmo, then he turned and walked back to the altar. Once there, he spun around so hard that his shoes squeaked like fingernails dragging across a chalkboard.

"The truth is that ever since the fall of the Pontifical States after the unification of Italy, Pope Leo XIII considers himself to be a prisoner in the Vatican and insists that Italian Catholics should not vote in Italian elections or hold elected office."

Cosmo sat back down.

"Pope Leo regards King Umberto I as presiding over a climate hostile to the Church. Did you hear what I just said, Cosmo Ricci?"

Cosmo's face fell.

"In his relations with the king, Pope Leo XIII defends the freedom of the Church," the priest continued. "The pope stands against what we consider persecutions and attacks against the Church, which culminated in an attempt to throw the body of the deceased Pope Pius IX into the Tiber River in July of 1881!"

That triggered the nuns seated in the front row, and they burst out in tears.

"Pope Leo XIII has even considered moving his residence to Austria. Therefore, Cosmo Ricci, do not mistake the pope's silence for apathy.

"Just because he is not radical in theology or politics, as you clearly are, it does not mean the pope agrees with the king's policies."

After Mass, parishioners milled out in front of the church. Street vendors served sausages with onions and peppers in a French roll, meatball sandwiches, and gelato.

"Man, the priest really let Cosmo have it," Adolfo said.

"He deserved it. Cosmo shoots from the hip," replied Leonardo.

"Cosmo is a passionate person. I respect that," said Big Al.

"The thing about my dad is that he can be reasoned with," Frankie replied.

"He can?" Big Al questioned.

"Did you notice that he sat back down?" Frankie replied. "He knew Father Brady was right. Had my dad disagreed, there would have been some real fireworks, trust me."

Molinaro came over to the men. He was dressed in a short-cut sack jacket that ended at the hips, a vest, starched shirt with a stiff stand collar, and a silk tie worn short. His pants had a high waist, cut slim with a flat front, with no pleats.

Like his friends, Molinaro wore a low, soft-felt fedora and laced shoes made popular by Thomas Jefferson.

"Gentlemen, I have some news," Molinaro said.

"You've found a way to make Morello even richer?" Adolfo joked.

"Well, yes, that I have," Molinaro said. "But that's not my news."

"What is your news?" Big Al asked.

"The Morellos have gone to Louisiana to visit family," Molinaro said. "I think they're really scouting the place out to see if they want to relocate their business there.

"Anyway, they may not come back. There are farming opportunities in Louisiana, apparently."

"Farming?" Big Al questioned. "How is Morello going to farm with just one arm?"

"I don't know and I don't care," said Molinaro. "What it means for me is that I'm headed home. I am going back to Italy."

"What?"

"I've always said my plan was to be in America for five years and then go back home. It's been five years. Now that the Morellos have left, I'm leaving. The timing is perfect."

"But you are doing so well," Big Al objected.

"I've gotten rich, yes. But America is not my home, Italy is."

"What's waiting for you in Italy?" Frankie asked. "The country is a mess."

"My wife and kids are waiting."

"Send for them," said Big Al.

"I don't want to stay," Molinaro stated. "Americans look down on us. They don't want us here, so I'm going. Why tilt at windmills?"

"Who cares what they think of us?" said Big Al. "As long as you are making money, it doesn't matter."

"Matters to me," Molinaro replied. "They say we're taking away their jobs. Americans look down on us like they do black people."

"Well, we are taking away their jobs, that part is correct." Frankie laughed.

"The media calls us 'Mediterranean types' and says Italians are dark-skinned like African-Americans and inherently inferior to people of European heritage," Molinaro continued.

"Okay, so? Northern Italians look down on southern Italians. Prejudice is everywhere," Big Al pushed back.

"Have you heard of the Ku Klux Klan?" Molinaro asked.

"Yes," the men answered.

"The KKK is attacking Italians. They've lynched nearly twenty Italians so far," Molinaro reported.

"I heard the KKK is also vandalizing and burning churches," said Leonardo.

"In New Orleans, the police chief ended up dead," Adolfo added. "The mayor blamed Sicilian gangsters and rounded up more than one hundred Sicilians.

"Eventually, nineteen went on trial but were found not guilty. That night, before the Italian prisoners were set free, a mob of ten thousand people broke into the jail and dragged eleven Sicilians from their cells and lynched them."

"For heaven's sake," Molinaro said. "See what I mean?"

"Joe, are you worried about your safety?" Adolfo asked.

"With the Morellos gone, yes, I am."

"Paul Kelly will protect you," Big Al said. "No one will touch you."

"That's not the point," said Molinaro. "If I go home to Italy, I won't be worried about my safety. Financially, I'm well off too."

"What will you do in Italy?" Big Al asked.

"I want to be a politician. Maybe Pasquinelli will help me out. The Camorra likes to put their own people in government positions."

Italy, 1897

La Questione Sociale

King Umberto I Survives Another Assassination Attempt
By Editor Cosmo Ricci

Rome—A brave nationalist, whom I personally know and can attest to, attacked

King Umberto I near Rome with the intention of putting an end to his life. He wasn't successful in that effort.

The attacker was Bobby Piziali, who stood with me and other fishermen at the Port of Salerno sixteen years ago, when the port manager ordered the police to beat us.

Mr. Piziali fell on hard times during the now-famous strike by the fishermen. He left the vocation and tried to make a living as an iron worker and then as a blacksmith, but his lot did not improve.

On April 20, 1897, Mr. Piziali closed his blacksmith shop permanently. He soon learned of the king's appearance at the derby horse track outside of Rome on April 22nd.

Aware that King Umberto I was traveling along the Via Appia Nuova, Mr. Piziali waited for him near the Porta San Giovanni, armed only with a homemade dagger. The royal carriage arrived at 2:00 p.m.

Mr. Piziali attacked the carriage and attempted to murder the king, although he failed and was subsequently detained.

Who can blame Mr. Piziali for the attempted assassination? One only has to look at the trials of the Fasci Siciliani leaders that took place in Palermo in April and

May of 1894 to determine that the king's government is unjust.

The Fasci Siciliani was a popular movement by the working class to restore equity to the distribution of land and labor.

The king treated the unrest the way he always does, with over-the-top resistance. He is too heavy-handed with protesters.

Many former adherents of the Fasci Siciliani movement have left the country for America. After the failure of the rebellion, many peasants had no choice but to vote with their feet and opted for emigration.

Italy, 1898

It had been seven years since Big Al came to America, and he'd achieved great success. So, early that summer he sent for the rest of his family—his mother, Mary; his sisters Margie, twenty-five, Louisa, nineteen, and Olympia, seventeen; and, his brothers Diego, fifteen, and Filippo, thirteen.

"This deserves a toast!" he said when they arrived.

They all held up their glasses of sambuca, an Italian liquor served flaming hot—literally on fire—and coffee beans.

"*Salute!*"

Also arriving in New York was the Morello family. They'd returned after traveling to Louisiana and staying with a cousin. However, after contracting malaria, the entire family came back to New York to reestablish their street-gang operation.

With Molinaro now gone, Morello needed someone to run the money for him. Frankie was his choice.

"You there, can I have a minute?" Morello called out one day to Frankie, who was washing down a boat at the docks.

"What do you want, Mister?" asked Frankie, recognizing Morello by his deformed arm.

"Come work for me."

"Doing what?"

"Counterfeiting money."

"I don't know how to do that," Frankie replied.

"I will teach you."

Frankie quit his fishing job with Big Al and went to work for Morello the next day. His personality became darker after that, and he grew violent.

Six months later he was arrested for counterfeiting. The police chief, an Italian, got word to Big Al to come down to the jail to get Frankie. Big Al went immediately, grabbing his coat and storming out the door.

When he arrived at the jail, he found Frankie in a cell with Morello.

"What happened?" Big Al asked.

"The police raided our place," Frankie replied. "We're each being held on five thousand dollars' bail."

The jail warden overheard the conversation and came over.

"Our arrests grew out of a Secret Service investigation that started with counterfeit five-dollar bills discovered in Brooklyn and North Beach," said the warden. "Morello and Frankie are thought to be suppliers of the money."

"What makes you think it was them?" asked Big Al.

"The money was printed on very poor paper with crude workmanship," the warden continued. "We got a tip and found a bunch of fake five-dollar bills on Frankie."

In the months that followed, however, the police could not make the charges stick against the men, even with the money Frankie had on his person, so the charges were dropped.

"You are playing with fire," Big Al warned his best friend. "Next time, Frankie, you may not be so lucky."

New York, 1900

Cosmo Ricci had been missing for about a week. At first, Frankie just assumed his dad had gone on a drunken bender, but then the receptionist at the anarchist newspaper office called him to report that money was missing from the safe.

Soon after, they learned the full story. Cosmo Ricci had gone back to Italy and assassinated King Umberto I. He told the police that he murdered the king to avenge the death of Rocco and the attack on the Fasci Siciliani.

"Did you know your dad was going to kill the king?" Big Al asked Frankie.

"No. He never said a word about doing that."

Big Al's mother, Mary, served them breakfast consisting of eggs, sausages, melon, and coffee. The entire family ate with them.

"He was my husband's best friend, as you know," Mary said. "He was never right in the head after the beating he took at the Port of Salerno that day by Marino's men. It permanently changed him."

After the incident, Frankie withdrew altogether. He stopped hanging out with Big Al. A counterfeiter by day, Frankie became a thug by night. He participated when the Morello-Lupo Gang shook people down for money and beat them up. And Frankie liked it.

The New York Times reported that the Morello-Lupo Gang was on the rise, gaining dominance in the streets of East Harlem by defeating its rival gang, the Neapolitan Camorra of Brooklyn.

New York, 1901

President William McKinley was the scheduled speaker at an upcoming luncheon, and Paul Kelly had two extra tickets.

"Come with me, and bring Frankie," he said to Big Al.

"Frankie might not be the best company," Big Al replied. "He is really withdrawn these days."

"All the more reason for him to come."

In his most persuasive way, Big Al convinced Frankie to join them.

***

On the day of the luncheon, New York Mayor Robert Anderson Van Wyck introduced President McKinley.

"The president's foreign policy is creating an overseas empire and putting America on the world's list of major powers!" the mayor declared.

Frankie shook his head in disgust.

"In 1898, our president led the nation into war with Spain over the issue of Cuban independence," the mayor continued. "The brief and decisive conflict ended with the US in possession of Puerto Rico, the Philippines, and Guam."

Frankie turned to Big Al.

"Remember when we talked about this at the Port of Praiano?" Frankie said to Big Al. "I told you then that territories would be seized in the name of colonialism and that it could lead to wars."

"Shh," Paul Kelly said.

The mayor continued with his introduction.

"In general, President McKinley's foreign policy has opened the doors for the United States to play an increasingly active role in world affairs."

"Sounds just like something King Umberto would say," Frankie griped.

President McKinley took to the podium.

"Colonization has been good to America. Thanks to our victory over Spain, the country has new trade markets."

Frankie got up from his chair and walked out. Big Al followed him from the building.

"Hey, Frankie, why did you walk out?"

"Remember how King Umberto talked about colonization that day at the rail station, when my dad was beaten up by the king's guards?"

"Yes, I remember."

"McKinley is a carbon copy of King Umberto."

***

In the weeks that followed, Frankie could not let it go. Every morning, he passed out leaflets at rail stations as people were going to work. In the literature, Frankie called upon the president to resign.

"Feed your people, Mr. McKinley. Give them decent-paying jobs. Give them respectable working conditions," Frankie wrote.

***

In September, Frankie went to jail again—this time for the murder of President McKinley. Frankie shot President McKinley at the Pan-American Exposition in Buffalo, New York. McKinley was just six months into his second term.

The president was shaking hands with the public when Frankie shot him twice, once in the abdomen and another in the shoulder. The president did not die right away. He died several days later of gangrene caused by the wounds.

"Anarchist kills the president!" screamed the headline in *The New York Times*.

Frankie died in the electric chair the following month.

New York, 1902

Big Al and Paul Kelly were betting on horses at the new Yonkers Raceway. Kelly loved going to the horse track, and it seemed like he always won. At the moment, his horse was in the lead.

"And down the stretch they come," the announcer called out. "It will be 'The Galloping Ghost' by a nose."

"Yes!" shouted Paul Kelly as he waved his winning ticket in the air.

The leader of the Five Points Gang was slowly moving away from street life and into politics. He'd established close political ties with the Tammany Hall political machine, which controlled New York City and State, including Democratic Party nominations and patronage.

Tammany Hall did many things for many people, especially in the nineteenth century, when there were no government programs in the US for anything at that time.

Tammany and other political machines around the country provided services and jobs, paid people's doctor bills, and brought turkeys to working-class families on Christmas.

The only thing they wanted in return was a person's vote. They recognized this was how democracy worked; whoever got the most votes won.

Tammany Hall very shrewdly capitalized on that. Paul Kelly gladly paid these Tammany politicians, who, in turn, protected his operations, which were becoming increasingly sophisticated.

"Say, Al, there's something I'd like to talk with you about."

"What is it, Paul?"

"I'm building a name for myself down at the docks. The International Dockworkers Union is fertile ground. However, an Irishman named T. V. O'Connor has a lock on things right now. He's the union president."

"How can I help you?"

"I need two men full time, guys I can trust," Paul Kelly said. "I'm thinking that your brothers Adolfo and Leonardo could work down at the docks for me instead of the boats for you."

"What would they do?"

"Mostly, they'd be my eyes and ears. I need to know what O'Connor is doing.

"The Irish workers have been getting the bulk of the work down at the docks for years, but I want to change that. Italians are better workers."

"My brothers would be helping to put other Italians to work?" asked Big Al.

"Yes. You see, it's for a good cause," Paul Kelly replied.

"They would be totally out of the fishing business, then?"

"Yeah, but you would still have your other brothers, Diego and Filippo. Plus, your sons are getting older and should be able to help you out more and more."

"To be honest, I think Adolfo and Leonardo could use a change of scenery," Big Al replied. "Fishing isn't in their blood. I will miss them, but they will enjoy working at the docks and helping other Italians to get work."

Paul Kelly patted Big Al on one of his massive shoulders.

"Perfect. Thank you!" he said.

"My pleasure, Boss."

"There's one more thing."

"Another request?" Big Al asked.

"There's this incumbent politician that Tammany Hall does not like. He votes the wrong way. They have been bugging me to run him out. I've been dragging my feet on it, but it's time to act."

"Why?" Big Al asked.

"Last week the guy told the local newspaper that he wants to keep brothels out of his ward, which would hurt my brothel businesses. So, it's time to take him out."

"You mean, kill him?" Big Al stammered.

"No, take him out, clean. At the ballot box. Get your brothers and your sons together. We're going to knock the incumbent out."

"Paul, you know I don't like violence."

"I'm not asking you to carry a gun or anything like that," he replied. "I plan to unleash more than a thousand of my street-gang members against the incumbent.

"We'll ensure the incumbent's defeat by blocking polling booths and by voting early and often for our own candidate."

***

Several weeks later, the incumbent soundly lost. The plan worked.

New York, 1903

The barrel murders continued in New York with the discovery of the body of a Brooklyn grocer in a barrel floating in the water. The grocer's tongue was slit, presumably for talking to the police and breaking the Mafia code of silence.

A second person ended up dead in a barrel too. The deceased was a Morello-Lupo Gang member, Benedetto Madonia, who was the brother-in-law to a police informant.

The informant had been a Morello-Lupo Gang member as well, but he was in jail. He'd been giving information to the police. Because Morello and Lupo couldn't get at the informant, they killed the brother-in-law, Madonia, who'd been brutally tortured. His body was discovered in an old sugar barrel, on East Eleventh Street in the East Village.

In a search of Madonia's house after his murder, the police found an incriminating letter regarding the Morello-Lupo Gang.

With this evidence, the police arrested several gang members, including Morello, Lupo, Tommaso "The Ox" Petto, and restaurant owner Pietro Inzarillo, as well as several other members.

After witnesses changed their statements, police dismissed the charges, and none were convicted. But the story didn't stop there.

The informant who was in jail, Giuseppe DiPrimo, swore he would avenge his brother-in-law's death when he was to be released in three years.

DiPrimo let everyone know that his sights were set on the four men he believed were involved in his brother-in-law's death—Morello, Lupo, Tommaso Petto, and Pietro Inzarillo—along with four others.

Unnerved that DiPrimo was going to be coming for them, Morello and Lupo requested a meeting with Paul Kelly, who brought Big Al with him.

"We need your help," Morello said to Paul Kelly.

"What kind of help?"

"Protection," said Morello.

"You want me to protect you?" Kelly asked with surprise.

"DiPrimo is going to come hunting us."

"I can make sure you both aren't touched, but it's going to cost you, Morello," Paul Kelly said.

"Let's make a deal," Morello suggested.

"What kind of deal are you thinking?" Kelly asked.

"My gang has connections back in Sicily, our mutual homeland. We have people there who ship us black-market goods, such as drugs, weapons, and other types of contraband."

"And?"

"These shipments come into the Port of New York," Morello said. "The deal I'm offering is this: we give you a cut of our profits in exchange for protecting me and Lupo."

Paul Kelly looked up at the ceiling. His eyes darted back and forth. He was thinking about the deal.

"How safe are your shipments?" Kelly asked.

"What do you mean?" Morello replied.

"Do you have your own people at the port making sure no one messes with your cargo?" Kelly asked.

"Well, no," Morello answered.

"See, that's a problem," Kelly pointed out. "Why would I agree to be your partner at the port when there is a risk that we will be busted? That rat O'Connor would love to see me take a fall, especially now that I'm second-in-command under him in the dockworkers union."

Morello and Lupo looked at each other.

"We never thought about that," Morello said.

"That would explain why your crew keeps getting arrested," Paul Kelly said sarcastically. "You guys don't think about the little details."

"What do you suggest?" Morello asked.

"I want fifty percent of your profits from the cargo coming in and out of the port," Kelly bargained. "I have men at the docks who will clear your paperwork without any hassles. They'll sign off on the cargo as being legitimate."

Morello and Lupo were delighted with the deal.

"Done!" they exclaimed.

New York, 1905

Big Al's uncle, Michael Piazza, arrived from Italy. He was a fisherman in Salerno who'd struggled to make ends meet, so he came to America to be near his older sister, Mary. She prepared a huge dinner in celebration of his arrival.

"Ladies, do you like your job?" Michael asked during the meal.

Like most Italian women in New York, they all worked in the garment industry, also known as sweatshops.

"My hands hurt every day from sewing," said Big Al's eldest sister, Margie.

"The work is very hard," said Big Al's wife, Carmelita. "None of us like our job, Michael, but it is necessary. Price-cutting often leads to the number of garments increasing over time, and workdays extending far into the night. This is called the task system."

"Sounds like the 'rip-off system,' if you ask me," Michael quipped.

"It is not uncommon for us to work fifteen to eighteen hours a day, six days a week, but only be paid for four days' work," said one of Big Al's other sisters, Olympia.

"I don't like that child labor is used," commented Louisa, another of the three sisters. "Children are used to carry goods to and from shops and to perform simple operations, such as removing basting threads."

"None of what you are telling me is okay," said Michael, who reached for his second helping of lasagna. "Are you required to have tailoring skills?"

"Many garment workers came to the United States with some tailoring experience, but most are unskilled or have only the sewing skills they learned at home," Carmelita answered.

"How are *you* liking America, Michael?" Margie asked.

"It's hard because I am finding out quickly that Americans look down on Italians," he replied. "They think we are ignorant, insular, superstitious, lazy, prone to crime, ignorant of the law, ignorant of democracy, and prone to righting wrongs with personal vendettas and acts of violence."

"That's a long list." Big Al chuckled.

"He's right, though," Margie said. "They even attack our form of Catholicism because Americans see our Mediterranean faith as unusual."

Like most Italians, their faith blended with other kinds of beliefs, some of them pre-Christian, such as belief in the evil eye, and in good and evil spirits. The annual public celebrations and parades of the saints—known as Italian *festas*—were also glaring novelties at the time.

"Italians have to do a better job assimilating," Big Al countered. "Too many of our people come to America with the idea that they are going to leave in five years or so, like Joe Molinaro.

"They do not bother to learn the English language. They do not try to learn American ways. They just stick to themselves and do not broaden themselves. Can you see how this looks to Americans?"

"Why bother?" said Michael. "They don't want us here."

Mary stood up and walked over to her brother. She wrapped him up from behind and squeezed him tightly in his chair. "I want you here!"

Michael immediately softened. "Tell me more about this job of yours, Sister."

Mary's face tightened. She went back to her chair and sat down.

"In the garment industry, manufacturers provide contractors like us with bundles of cut cloth," she said.

"We are paid to assemble the pieces into clothing. Payment is for completion of a certain number of garments per day."

Big Al's brother Adolfo saw the logic in how the garment businesses operated and decided to explain it to everyone, although the women didn't really want to hear it.

"Contracting gives clothing manufacturers tremendous flexibility to quickly increase or reduce their output as the market requires," he reasoned. "It also lets them search out the cheapest means of production."

"Spoken like a true Mafia spokesman," Margie criticized. "The Mafia has no problem ripping workers off if it means more profits for them."

Adolfo blushed. He was having more Mafia contact these days working down at the docks, but he didn't know his sister knew about that. She was also right; the garment industry was something the Mafia favored and was moving into because of the opportunity to take a hefty percentage of the profits.

"I'm just giving you the economic reason why the manufacturers do what they do," he replied. "Their business model is set up like that for a reason, which is to make money.

"With manufacturers and contractors all competing against their counterparts, wages stay low."

"And the business owners get richer," Margie continued to argue. "The working conditions are awful."

Leonardo came to his brother's defense.

"A contractor can set up a shop for as little as fifty dollars," he said. "All it takes is a couple of sewing machines, a few tables and chairs, and a place to work.

"To compete against factories with modern equipment, contractors must pay meager wages and locate shops where rents are low. With their profit margins razor thin, most shops last only a few years."

Carmelita stood up to get espresso from the kitchen.

"Most of the contractors are recent immigrants themselves," she said. "The only thing controlling how they treat their workers is social pressure."

"What do you mean by that?" Michael asked.

"My boss is Irish," Carmelita replied. "He does not like Italians. Therefore, he treats us poorly but is nice to the Irish women."

***

The next evening, Big Al and Paul Kelly met for dinner at the Flatiron building, built three years earlier. The restaurant was located in the basement of the building and was huge, accommodating up to fifteen hundred guests.

"How are things going these days?" Paul Kelly asked Big Al.

"My mom's brother, Michael, is working with me now. I am his 'padroni,'" he replied.

The padrone system was a contract labor system utilized by Italian immigrants to find employment in the United States. The padroni, or sponsor, provided communal housing and eating arrangements, controlled the allocation of pay, and essentially was responsible for the immigrant.

"Did you hear Joe Molinaro has returned to America?" Paul Kelly asked.

"No, I hadn't heard!" exclaimed Big Al.

"This time he brought his wife and kids with him. They arrived today."

"Really? I thought he planned to be a politician in Italy and live the rich life with all the money he made working for Morello," Big Al said.

"Apparently, it didn't work out," Kelly replied. "Pasquinelli said Joe wasn't needed in public office. The positions were already filled with Supremo's Mafia people. The social and political unrest wore on Joe, so he decided to come back."

"What is he planning to do here?" asked Big Al.

"I've heard he's going back to working the books for Morello."

Big Al shook his head in disbelief.

"How about you, Paul? Things good?"

"Very good. I've taken on new help. Johnny Torrio recently came over from Italy. I call him 'The Brain' because he is an unusually smart person.

"Then I have some solid young people like Lucky Longo, Bugsy Siegel, and a brash kid named Al Capone, who is just a teenager. Capone works as a bouncer in my brothels. He's caught on fast to street business."

"Have things cooled down since your nemesis Monk Eastman went to jail last year?" Big Al asked.

Kelly's jaw tightened. "That guy! I am glad he's out of the way. I couldn't fart without him wanting a whiff of it."

Eastman was the longtime leader of an Irish street gang that was in direct competition with Paul Kelly. The two street gangs often fought it out.

Tammany Hall had worked closely with both Kelly and Eastman to mobilize their members in elections and patronage schemes. Nevertheless, its officials grew tired of the feuding between the two gangs and the bad press generated with civilians killed or injured in the gangs' cross fire.

The warfare between the two gangs had reached a fevered pitch in September of 1903, with a protracted gun battle among dozens of gangsters. One gang member died, and a police officer was fatally wounded. Numerous innocent civilians were injured. Eighteen members of the Eastman Gang were arrested.

Then, in 1904, Eastman tried to rob a young man on Forty-Second Street and Broadway in Manhattan. The police caught him.

Tired of all the bad publicity from Eastman, Tammany Hall refused to help him after the robbery attempt. Eastman received ten years in prison for attempted assault.

"What about the Morello-Lupo Gang?" Big Al asked. "You still partnering with them down at the docks?"

"Oh yeah. I got the better end of that deal. We get fifty percent of the profits from the shipments that come in from Italy, big money, and DiPrimo is still in jail. Easy money."

"Are Morello and Lupo still into counterfeiting money?" Big Al asked.

"Yeah. He has a new man, Giuseppe Fontini, who just arrived off the boat from Italy. He's been working for them down at the docks. I don't trust him."

"Why not?" Big Al asked.

"He's a very bad guy. Fontini is a Mafia tough guy who was acquitted of killing the mayor of Palermo."

Big Al's eyes flew open wide.

"Tell me that story," he said.

"While on a train journey between Caltanissetta and Palermo, the Palermo mayor came under attack," said Paul Kelly. "He was stabbed to death and his body flung from his carriage into a field."

"Pretty brutal."

"Like I said, Fontini is a bad guy. He has a deadlier way of doing things, and it's bringing the heat down on all of us."

Big Al grimaced. "How so?"

"The New York Police Department has stepped up its response," Kelly said. "The Board of Aldermen of New York City has formed a squad of exclusively Italian policemen."

"An all-Italian police force? I've never heard of such a thing."

"Yup, and the man in charge is a Salerno-born cop, Joe Petrosino. He's on a personal mission to catch Fontini and smash the Black Hand and Italian street gangs."

"Tell me more about Petrosino."

"He joined the NYPD in 1883 after emigrating from Italy," Kelly said. "He soon realized that American law was unable to deal with Italian crime in an effective way. Therefore, he investigates the Italian underworld in his own way."

"What way is that?"

"Not by the book. In 1895, he was promoted to sergeant of detectives by the president of the Police Commission Board, Theodore Roosevelt.

"Petrosino hunts criminals, day and night, harassing their friends and family for information and frequenting their hangouts."

***

A few months after Big Al and Kelly's dinner at Flat Iron Restaurant & Café, Petrosino came calling down at the docks. Big Al and Michael were scrubbing down boats when the cop arrived.

"Are you Big Al?" he asked.

"Yes. Who are you?"

Petrosino took out his badge and showed it to Big Al.

"I'm the cop who's going to put the bookkeeper behind bars."

Big Al scratched his head. "Who's the bookkeeper?"

"Don't play coy with me or I'll throw you in jail too," Petrosino snapped. "Tell me where I can find Joe Molinaro, the bookkeeper for the Morello-Lupo Gang. I'm going to arrest him."

Big Al stared into Petrosino's eyes. He could see determination in them.

"I'm going to put your brothers in jail too."

Big Al jumped back. "My brothers? They have done nothing wrong. They have legitimate jobs down at the docks working for Paul Kelly."

"Oh, really?" Petrosino scoffed. "Signing off on shipments for the Morello-Lupo Gang is not legitimate, and you know it."

"They don't work for Morello," Big Al countered. "They work for Paul Kelly doing work on his behalf for the International Dockworkers Association. They find jobs for Italians."

"Is that what they've told you?" Petrosino said.

Big Al's eyes went blank. He was completely confused.

"Your two brothers Adolfo and Leonardo are helping Morello and Lupo," Petrosino explained.

Big Al's mouth fell open.

"Kelly has made a pact with Morello and Lupo to clear their contraband in exchange for protection against Giuseppe DiPrimo. Your brothers are the ones doing the clearing."

Big Al had been with Paul Kelly when the deal was made with Morello and Lupo, but he never would have guessed that his brothers were a part of the scheme. But then again, they worked down at the docks, so it was possible the cop was right.

Petrosino leaned in close to Big Al, so close that their noses touched.

"Check your sources, Big Al. You don't have the full story. Your brothers are helping Morello and Lupo, who are behind most of the barrel murders."

Big Al's entire body tingled.

"I will talk to them."

"Look, I like you," Petrosino said. "We both come from the same area of Salerno. We both know Supremo Pasquinelli, and he's a good man. For that reason, I will cut your brothers some slack. They'll walk if you give me what I want."

"Which is?"

"Morello, Lupo, and the bookkeeper."

Big Al's heart was beating fast. He was having trouble getting air into his lungs. He was swallowing constantly.

"Think about it," the cop said. "I'm going to get them eventually. If you want what's best for Adolfo and Leonardo, you'll help me."

***

That evening, during a game of poker at home, Big Al confronted his brothers.

"A cop named Petrosino came to see me today," he said.

Joe Molinaro, who was visiting, bit his lip. He looked down at his cards.

"Hey, Al, let's play," Molinaro demanded.

Suddenly, Big Al shot out of his chair, which went crashing into a wall behind him. He put both brothers in a headlock, one in each arm.

"Ow, let go!" they protested.

"What are you doing for Morello and Lupo down at the docks? Answer me!"

Adolfo and Leonardo were turning blue.

"Let them go," Molinaro protested. "They can't breathe."

Big Al slammed their heads together. They hit so hard, it sounded like a cannon blast. The brothers crumpled to the floor, both unconscious.

Hearing the noise, Big Al's mother, Mary, came running into the room from the kitchen. She discovered her oldest son lifting Molinaro off the floor by the collar of his shirt.

"Put him down," she screamed.

"Not until he tells me what my brothers are doing for Morello and Lupo!"

"Okay, okay," Molinaro agreed. "Just put me down first."

Big Al lowered Molinaro to the ground.

"Talk."

"Your brothers are the eyes and ears down at the docks for Paul Kelly," Molinaro said.

But before Molinaro could finish explaining, Big Al had lifted him back up in the air.

"I know that already," Big Al barked. "I'm asking what they are doing for Morello and Lupo, not Paul Kelly!"

"Put me down," Molinaro begged.

Mary positioned herself in between Big Al and the other man.

"Alfred, I demand you stop this right now!" she screamed.

Big Al jolted.

He put Molinaro back on the ground, as his mother had asked.

"Talk!" he demanded.

"Like I said, they are looking out for Kelly's interests down at the docks. They find work for Italian immigrants."

Big Al coiled back his fist and was about to strike when Molinaro realized he was a moment away from being knocked out.

"Stop, stop, stop," Molinaro pleaded. "All right, okay. They make sure Morello's cargo from Italy is unloaded and moved out of the port without being flagged for illegal contraband."

Big Al took two steps back.

"Is that all they do? Are they involved in the Black Hand or the barrel murders? Anything like that, Joe?"

"No! They are falsifying cargo records. That's it."

"That's it?" Big Al shouted. "That's it, you say!"

The walls shook under the power of Big Al's giant voice.

"What they are doing is illegal," Big Al stated. "I don't want my family involved in anything illegal!"

"Selling your fish to Gambino's Fish Market in East Harlem at exaggerated prices is wrong," Molinaro shot back.

Big Al balled up his fists.

"You hold your tongue, Joe. What I do is not illegal."

Big Al looked down at his brothers on the ground. They'd regained consciousness.

"Talk!"

"Joe is right," Adolfo said. "We are helping Morello and Lupo."

"Did Paul Kelly put you up to it?" Big Al asked.

"No. He doesn't know anything about it. Morello is the one who pays us."

"So that I understand," Big Al said, "you left my fishing business to help Paul Kelly provide work down at the docks for Italians."

"Yes, and we do that," Adolfo said. "Then one day, Morello came to me and Leonardo and asked if we wanted to make some money on the side by protecting his cargo ships."

"That's right," said Leonardo.

"Why didn't you tell me?" asked Big Al. "I was under the impression Paul had other men to do that."

"Because we knew you wouldn't approve."

Big Al looked at Molinaro. "Did you know?"

"Yes."

Big Al could feel his blood boiling.

"You two are not to work for Morello and Lupo anymore, you hear me?"

The brothers nodded.

"As for you, Joe, you are not welcome here anymore. Get out!" Big Al ordered.

***

The next day, Big Al went down to the police station to straighten things out with Petrosino. Paul Kelly pulled out of his deal with Morello and Lupo when he heard the news.

"Our deal is off," he growled at Morello. "You went behind my back and involved Big Al's brothers."

***

A week later, two of Paul Kelly's former henchmen, Razor Riley and Biff Ellison, shot Kelly three times inside one of his nightclubs on orders from Morello and Lupo as payback.

Paul Kelly recovered from the injuries, but Tammany Hall ordered him to tone it down.

***

That November, Petrosino wrote the following letter requesting federal funding to help with the eradication of New York street gangs:

> Unless the federal government comes to our aid, New York will awaken some morning to one of the greatest catastro-

phes in history. You may think I am foolish making this statement, but these Black Hand blackmailers are growing bolder every day. In a little while, they will turn their attentions to the American people and pursue the same tactics and methods they now employ in dealing with the Italians.

Not even in Italy does such a bad condition of affairs exist as in New York at the present day. Only the national government can save this situation for us.

As the law stands at present, we are helpless largely against these desperadoes. They know the penal code from end to end.

I have information that there are not less than thirty thousand members of the Camorra in this country, working under twelve leaders stationed in the principal cities.

New York, 1906

Giuseppe DiPrimo was out of jail, and one of his first orders of business was to avenge his brother-in-law's barrel murder, as promised.

First, he killed Tommaso "The Ox" Petto, who was in hiding in a mining town in Pennsylvania.

A month later, Girolamo Mondini was lured with a letter to an East Harlem address, and shot in the street.

Another of the gangsters, Nicola Nera, was killed in Palermo.

Vito Laduca, Morello's most prominent lieutenant, met his end in Carini a few months later.

Morello and Lupo, no longer protected by Paul Kelly, went into hiding.

DiPrimo was eventually caught and deported back to Italy. Only two men on his list of eight survived his vengeance—Lupo and Morello.

Chapter 6

MIRACLE OF THE SUN

New York, 1908

Big Al and Paul Kelly sat in a booth at Lombardi's Pizza in Manhattan. Two of Kelly's bodyguards stood at the front door.

"I'm sorry to hear about the death of your wife," Big Al said.

"Thank you."

"You've been going through a bit of a rough patch lately," Big Al commented. "First you got shot, then you lost Minnie."

"Hey, any day above ground is a good day," Kelly said, trying to downplay it.

"Well, Paul, I guess it helps to have a positive outlook. Good for you! Have your wounds healed from the shooting?"

"Pretty much. I got lucky."

"I heard you have retired from street life."

"After I was shot, I swore it off," Kelly said. "I shut down my Lower East Side gambling, strong-arm, and prostitution rackets."

Big Al pumped his fist. "Good! We want to keep you around. So, what will you do now?"

"I'm going to be an honest businessperson now," Paul Kelly replied.

"Doing what?"

"I'm a registered junior associate in my brother's real estate business."

"Are you really on the up-and-up, Paul, or is this a trick, rebranding yourself as a legitimate businessman so that you can continue doing rackets on the down-low?"

"It's on the up-and-up."

"My brothers Adolfo and Leonardo say you are becoming more powerful every day with Tammany Hall and the International Dockworkers Association."

"Your brothers are correct."

"They also say you are now into union strong-arming and strikebreaking," Big Al pressed.

Kelly slapped his thighs and threw his head back.

"Okay, okay. You caught me. I'm off the streets. However, I haven't given up my work at the docks."

"Is it true that you hired fifty strikebreakers to clash with strikers of White Star shipping line and that there were casualties?"

Kelly rolled his eyes.

"Al, can we focus on the positive?"

"Which is what, exactly?"

"I'm the new manager of the Scow-Trimmers' Union," Kelly said. "It has six hundred members."

"Congratulations! What the heck is a scow trimmer?"

"They sort and load garbage onto barges."

"Sounds like trashy work," Big Al joked.

The fisherman then leaned in closer to his friend and whispered, "What did you do with your gambling, strong-arm, and prostitution rackets?"

"I divvied them up among other street gangs."

The waitress interrupted their conversation with their pizza.

"Do you plan to divvy up our fishing operation too?" Big Al asked when the waitress was gone.

"Ah, you are worried about your job. Don't be. You've always been a special project of mine. I like you, Big Al. There is something respectable about a man who makes his living fishing.

"I see it as honest work. I admire you for it. I'm living vicariously through you. Call it osmosis."

Big Al let out a huge sigh.

"How's the fishing going, anyway?" Kelly asked.

"Really well," said Big Al. "We have five boats going out every day."

"That's terrific," said Kelly. "Our business is growing. Let's see if you can't bump it up to ten boats by the end of the year. I want to get more fish to the market."

"You know, Paul, we could make more money if we cut out the middle source—Gambino's Fish Market."

"You want to open our own fish market?" Kelly asked.

"Why not?" Big Al replied.

"Gambino's is a legitimate way to launder money."

Big Al's face flushed at the mention of laundering money.

"I thought you said you had given up the rackets?"

"I have, but not the ones that involve our fishing business."

Big Al gave his friend a sideways look.

"After I got shot, Tammany Hall told me to take a lower profile," Kelly said. "So, I relocated to Italian Harlem, where I carry out my old line of work to a certain, toned-down point.

"Plus, as vice president of the International Dockworkers Association, I have to keep my nose clean."

"You're really a new man?"

"Or, a man simply going back to his old self," Kelly said. "Depends how you look at it."

"What do you mean?"

"Well, for one thing, I am changing my last name back to Vaccarelli."

"Ah, I get it," said Big Al. "You're going back to your old self by being Italian. I like it!"

"I'm making other changes too," Paul Vaccarelli said.

"Like what?"

"I am buying the Stag parking garage at 234 West Forty-First Street and a private social club, which I'm going to call the Club Room."

"Are these legitimate clubs or are they brothels?"

"They're legitimate. I'm tired of being chased around by the police."

New York, 1909

The top story in *The New York Times* that day was the murder of Petrosino, the NYPD cop. According to the story, he'd been murdered outside a restaurant in Palermo called Café Oreto by two men who shot him four times.

Petrosino was the first and only NYPD officer to be killed on foreign soil while on duty.

Big Al put down the newspaper he'd been reading over breakfast. He wasn't sure if he was saddened by the news or relieved for his brothers Adolfo and Leonardo, since they had been in the cop's crosshairs.

"What was Petrosino doing in Italy in the first place?" asked Big Al's wife, Carmelita.

"He was investigating gangsters," answered Big Al. "But that's like going straight into the hornet's nest."

According to *The New York Times*, Petrosino went to Palermo after convincing his boss, the police commissioner, to let him travel to Italy to collect accurate intelligence from contemporaries about the Italian criminals who were creating so much mayhem in New York.

"He was researching a counterfeiting ring in Italy that was a cause of concern for the US Treasury and linked into the activities of the Morello-Lupo Gang," Big Al continued.

"*The New York Times* said Petrosino planned to set up an espionage ring in Sicily to gather information."

"Who shot him?" Carmelita asked.

"Word on the street is that Giuseppe DiPrimo did it because he blamed Petrosino for being deported before he could finish off his killing spree," Big Al explained. "Morello and Lupo were still on his to-do list."

"Really?" Carmelita asked.

"Yes, he believed Petrosino got in the way of justice," said Big Al, who picked up the newspaper and continued reading:

"Petrosino tried to camouflage his presence in Italy, but the Mafia in Italy were tipped off and knew he was coming. Even though he traveled under the alias of Simone Valenti di Giudea, his arrival in Palermo was known to his enemies even before he stepped off the boat."

***

In the days that followed, news of Petrosino's murder spread fast. A wave of Italian hatred traveled through New York. Petrosino's murder was seen as an act of public execution, a lesson and a warning to others not to come meddling in the affairs of the Mafia in Italy.

The Palermo police headquarters received an anonymous letter from New York claiming that it wasn't DiPrimo who killed Petrosino, but rather, it was the Morello-Lupo Gang with its newest member, Fontini, as the trigger man.

After Petrosino's murder, the NYPD was more determined than ever to get the Morello-Lupo Gang. The police raided a building in November of that year that the gang was using as a front for its counterfeiting operation.

The police recovered a large amount of American and Canadian counterfeit bills. They also found letters by Black Hand victims from New Orleans and New York.

Police arrested fifteen Morello-Lupo Gang members, including Morello and Lupo themselves, Fontini, and Joe Molinaro, who had in his possession one thousand dollars' worth of counterfeit money. Each person received a twen-ty-five-year jail sentence.

***

Later in the year, Father DeBenedetti arrived in America. He showed up at Big Al's door with a wooden suitcase in hand.

"Father, what a surprise! What are you doing here?" Big Al exclaimed.

"Practically my entire congregation left to America," the priest replied. "So, I thought I might as well come too. What's it they say? Oh yes, 'if you can't beat them, might as well join them.'"

"Are you retired?"

"No. The Vatican assigned me to Our Lady of Mount Carmel Church in East Harlem. I am replacing Father Brady. No sense in the priests from Ireland getting all the good jobs here in America!"

Big Al's mother, Mary, rushed over and hugged the priest.

"Father, you must stay for dinner," she insisted.

***

That evening, Mary cooked while people crammed into Big Al's home. They almost didn't have enough space for everyone to eat.

They set up folding tables designated as "kids only," although several aunts cheated midway through dinner and came over to sit with the children.

In total, there were eighteen children. Big Al sat back in his chair during dinner and watched them with a fixed gaze.

"God has blessed you," Father DeBenedetti whispered to his friend. "America has been good to you."

Seated next to the priest, Mrs. Molinaro's eyes filled with tears. She tried hard to quiet her sobs with her hand.

"There now," said the priest. "I heard about Joe, and I know you miss him. He's a good man. All he ever wanted was a better life for you and the kids. Things will get better in time."

The woman sniffled hard, as if attempting to suck the tears back into her eyes. Mary came around to the sad woman's side of the table and softly pulled Mrs. Molinaro out of her chair.

"Olivia, come with me to the kitchen. We need your help," said Big Al's mother.

In the kitchen, Big Al's sisters were putting the final touches on dinner.

"I'll serve the antipasto," Margie bossed. "The rest of you, take out the clams, bread, salad, wine, and lemonade. We'll start with that."

Every one of Big Al's sisters was in a serious relationship, including the thirty-six-year-old Margie. No one ever thought Margie would find a man because she was so bossy.

All of the sisters were planning to be married soon, each to an Italian-American man.

"Start eating, everyone," Mary called out above the many conversations that were going on at the same time. "Olivia and I will get the rest of the food while you get started."

"First, we need to say a dinner prayer," said Father DeBenedetti.

The younger kids shot their hands up, hoping to be chosen to say grace.

"Okay, you, Paula," the priest said, calling on Big Al's four-year-old daughter.

Little Paula made the sign of the cross, clasped her hands together in prayer, and then spoke at the top of her lungs: "Bless us, O Lord, and these, Thy gifts, which we are about to receive from Thy bounty. Through Christ, our Lord. Amen."

"Amen!" everyone followed.

A few minutes later, Mary and Olivia brought out broccoli, pasta, and braciole, which is a rolled-up beef flank steak basted with tomato sauce.

"*Buon appetito!*" Mary called out.

For the next several hours, they talked, laughed, and exchanged stories. Father DeBenedetti updated them about certain people they all knew in Italy.

"How is Mr. Pasquinelli?" Big Al asked.

"He's doing very well," said the priest. "He married Patty and they now have four children, all girls. He is so cute around them. They definitely bring out his softer side."

"How is Luigi De Sio?"

"He's also good. Still in the military."

After dinner, they drank espresso and ate amaretti, an almond-flavored biscotti. After that, the men, with the exception of Father DeBenedetti, went for a walk and smoked cigars.

As was the custom, the women stayed behind—they laughed and talked about plans for the future while washing dishes and putting things away.

"I can't wait for me and Paulie to be married," Margie said. "We're going to have a beautiful wedding."

"I never thought you would get married," said Louisa, now twenty-eight. "You and Paulie need to hurry up and tie the knot so that Tommy and I can have our turn!"

"Then it'll be my turn after that," said Olympia.

While the ladies talked about weddings, Big Al's mother pulled the priest aside for their own conversation.

"How's the pope doing?" Mary asked Father DeBenedetti.

"Pope Pius X is an amazing man."

"How so?" Mary delved.

"I have many friends who work with him in the Vatican. They say he doesn't waste a day. He's a hard worker."

"Tell me more about him," Mary continued.

"Pope Pius X grew up in a very poor family," explained the priest. "They immigrated to Italy from Poland, where the family received political asylum. Now that he's the pope, he hasn't forgotten his roots."

"What do you mean?" Mary asked.

"After the great earthquake in Messina, Pope Pius X opened up his residence, called the Apostolic Palace, for the refugees and homeless to take harbor. That was very unusual."

"Tell me more," Mary encouraged.

"Do you want to hear about the great scandal he has caused?" Father DeBenedetti proposed.

"I love scandals," said Margie, coming over to her mother and the priest. Her sisters followed.

"Pope Pius X has ceased dining alone at his residence," the priest said with a decidedly unpriestly giggle. "He invites his friends and people he meets to eat with him. The elite do not like this.

"He's broken the mold on papal dining habits. He is, in many ways, just an ordinary guy who rose to the papal throne."

"I've heard he's done miracles," Mary said. "Is that true?"

"During one papal audience, Pope Pius X went to hug a paralyzed boy," said Father DeBenedetti. "During the hug, the boy suddenly broke free and ran around the room in joy that he was healed."

"No way!" Margie shouted.

"Yes, it's true. Another time, a couple he knew had a son with meningitis. They wrote a letter to him asking for his help.

"The pope wrote back telling them to hope, fast, and pray. Two days later, the child was cured."

"Amazing!" said Olympia.

"He goes out and shares religious teachings with the homeless and makes many friends among them in Rome and elsewhere, as he did while a bishop and earlier."

"He sounds like a lovely man," Mary said.

New York, 1911

Twenty-four-year-old Vincent Mangani stepped off the ocean liner *San Guglielmo* and pulled up his collar against the cold wind.

Snow flurries swirled all around him, so he pulled a scarf over his medium-sized forehead, his small mouth, round chin, broad nose, and oval face.

"Taxi!" he called out to one of the gasoline-powered taxicabs that started operating in the city in 1907.

"Where to, Mister?"

"Sixty Union Street, to my mother's house," he lied.

Stuffed in his pocket was one thousand dollars. When they reached the destination, he paid the driver.

However, rather than go to the house, the five-foot-six Mangani walked a few more blocks away, to an important meeting.

"Give me a beer," he said to the bartender, rubbing a hand through his hair.

"Is it snowing out?" the bartender asked.

"Spitting snow showers out there."

"You just get off the boat?"

"Yeah. I'm from Palermo. Here on business."

"What's your business?" the bartender pried.

"I'm an exporter."

Mangani was not keen on conversation. He was suspicious of people and did not like them knowing too much about him, so the mobster paid the bartender and moved to a table in a darkly lit corner of the bar.

A few minutes later, another gangster joined him.

"How was the trip?" the grim-faced visitor asked.

"Awful. Very stormy. I puked the entire time," Mangani replied.

Salvatore "Tito" D'Aquila, the new leader of the Morello-Lupo Gang, shot Mangani a concerned look.

"Forget about it," Mangani said. "Everything is good, Tito."

When Morello and Lupo were sent to prison, D'Aquila took over. He'd been one of Lupo's chief captains on the streets.

With Fontini also in prison, the Mafia dons in Italy worried about the safety of their shipments. So, they sent Mangani to New York as Fontini's replacement.

He was the person the Mafia in Palermo trusted to handle the cargo between Italy and New York.

"We have a little problem down at the docks," D'Aquila said.

"What is it?" Mangani replied.

"Two guys were helping Morello and Lupo clear the paperwork on our cargo down at the docks. Their names are Adolfo and Leonardo, but they quit."

"What do you mean they quit?" Mangani asked. "Can they do that? In Italy, we wouldn't let that happen."

"Their older brother, an influential guy named Big Al, found out and went nuts," answered D'Aquila. "The entire arrangement fell apart after that."

"Who's clearing the cargo now?" Mangani asked.

"Nobody."

Mangani slammed his fist on the table. Then, just as suddenly as he'd lost his temper, he regained his composure.

"Forget about it," Mangani said. "I will take over that job. For the time being, though, we need to consolidate our waterfront operation to just one location, Brooklyn."

"That works," D'Aquila replied. "Albert Anastasia, who runs Murder, Inc., has a solid connection there—his brother. He's the president of Brooklyn Local 1814 of the International Dockworkers Association. We'll be safer in Brooklyn. Good call, Mangani."

From that day on, Mangani controlled all of the cargo being loaded or unloaded at the Brooklyn docks. He required a "tribute," or "payment," from the ships that went in and out of the docks.

Mangani took it upon himself to personally clear all of the paperwork associated with the cargo.

Eventually, D'Aquila and Mangani were doing so well that they left the Morello-Lupo Gang and started their own gang. They were tired of explaining to everyone that Morello and Lupo were in jail and not around anymore, so the gangsters decided to go out on their own.

D'Aquila established dominance of what became his own Palermitani crime family in East Harlem. Mangani was his enforcer.

They used their ties to other Mafia leaders in the United States to create a network of influence and connections. Soon, they were a powerful duo in New York.

Joe Masseria took over the Morello-Lupo Gang. He went to war with D'Aquila over control of the streets in New York. They were constantly at war.

D'Aquila became so obsessed with fighting Masseria, that he became almost blinded to everything else.

Mangani, however, kept his eye on the big picture. He watched Big Al and his brothers as they went out early every morning on their fishing boats, and then as they came in at the end of each day.

They were hard workers. Loyal. No-nonsense.

Mangani wanted them.

"Adolfo and Leonardo know how to run things down at the docks," Mangani said to D'Aquila one afternoon. "I want them on our side."

"Good luck," D'Aquila replied. "Have you seen the size of their older brother? They call him 'Big Al' for a reason."

But Mangani wouldn't be discouraged. Whenever he saw the two brothers, he made it a point to court them, giving them gifts like tickets to boxing matches, Yankees games, and Broadway plays (for their wives)—all aimed at building trust with them.

Mangani considered the real prize, however, to be Big Al's four sons: Alfred Jr., fifteen, Alessandro, thirteen, Maximo, eleven, and Francesco, nine. They were young and could be groomed.

"Hey, you two," Mangani called out to Alfred Jr. and Alessandro one day as they were walking home from school. "Do you each want to make a couple of bucks?"

The boys looked at each other like deer caught in headlights.

"Is it illegal?" Alfred Jr. asked.

"No, just looking for information."

"I, uh, I don't know that we should," Alessandro stammered.

"Shut up!" said Alfred Jr. "What kind of information?"

"Where does your dad sell his fish?"

Alfred Jr. and Alessandro narrowed their eyes and tilted their heads.

"Really, that's the kind of information you want to know, Mister?" asked Alfred Jr., who slowly approached Mangani.

The boy was impressed by the gangster's fancy clothes. Mangani wore a double-breasted brown sack suit with three buttons. The coat went down to his mid-thigh. His wing-tip shoes were also brown and nicely polished.

"Gambino's Fish Market," Alfred Jr. blurted out. "That's where he takes the catch."

Mangani smiled. "Here you go, that's two dollars for both of you."

"That's it?" Alessandro asked.

"What's the rub?" Alfred Jr. replied, massaging his chin.

"There's no trick," Mangani replied. "I just wondered. Easy money, right? You didn't even have to think too hard, did you?"

The boys quickly stuffed the money in their pockets, afraid the man would change his mind.

"What else do you want to know?" Alfred Jr. replied.

"That's all for today," said Mangani.

"You sure?" Alessandro asked in a more confident tone. "We know a lot, Mister."

"Just keep your ears open. From time to time, I may come around asking questions. Pay attention to what your father says and does, where he goes, and whom he talks to."

"Why are you so interested in my dad?" Alfred Jr. asked.

"He is an important guy, boys. I like to know what important people are doing, so I can support them."

"Why don't you just ask him?"

"Come on, kids. Important people don't have time for people like me. They're too busy. Your dad cannot waste his time. Give me a break. You think President Taft talks to just anyone? Wise up."

Alfred Jr. and Alessandro scratched their heads as they watched Mangani walk away.

"Who was that guy?" Alessandro asked.

"I don't know, and I don't care. We just made easy money."

New York, 1914

The gangster who used to call himself Paul Kelly but was now going by Paul Vaccarelli stood on a street corner. He looked at his pocket watch, then up and down the street.

Seconds later, Big Al arrived.

"Right on time," Vaccarelli said. "You're never late."

"I know your time is valuable, Paul."

Each man was dressed to the nines in a jacket and tie.

"Sorry we have to meet on the street, but I don't have time to eat or have a drink with you even," Paul Vaccarelli replied. "Walk with me."

"I understand, Paul. You're a man on the go," said Big Al.

"In my role with the International Dockworkers Association and Tammany Hall, I deal a lot with politicians, as you know," Paul Vaccarelli explained. "They keep a tight schedule, so I do too."

Big Al nodded.

"There's a guy from the Midwest my folks like. His name is Warren Harding. He's from rural Ohio."

Big Al listened quietly, but his head was on a swivel. His senses were always heightened whenever he was with Vaccarelli.

He never knew who might open fire.

"This guy Harding was a newspaperman who ran for office in Ohio. He seemed to be a rising star. Had dreams of going to the White House."

"Big dreams," Big Al repeated.

"Harding ran for a seat in the Ohio State Senate in 1899 and won. Then he went on to serve as lieutenant governor."

"A rising star, all right."

"Yes; however, he ran for governor in 1910 and lost," said Vaccarelli.

Big Al nodded his head. "I am following you."

"Harding is trying for office again. This time he's thrown his hat in the ring for US Senate.

"My associates want him to win, but they say Harding needs a lot of help. I've got connections and all that, but you're the one who can really make a difference."

"Me? How?" Big Al asked.

"By helping me raise money for Harding," Vaccarelli replied.

"I don't know anything about politics," said Big Al. "You have the wrong guy."

"It's going to take everyone I know to get Harding elected," Vaccarelli explained. "You know a lot of rich Italians, and don't tell me that you don't."

Big Al looked up toward the sky. He was counting in his head the number of people he knew who would contribute.

"Yes, you're right. I know quite a lot of people," he agreed.

"I'm not asking you to shake people down or resort to Black Hand tactics here," Paul Vaccarelli said with a laugh.

"But I do need you to get after it, Al. Talk with people and make them understand how important this is."

Big Al snapped his fingers.

"I have an idea," he said. "Let's do something a little different."

"Different how?"

"Rather than pressure people for money, let's make it fun," said Big Al. "Why not hold a fundraising event?"

"What do you have in mind?"

"A bocce ball tournament! People will pay to play, eat good Italian food, and drink some vino. You okay with that approach?"

Vaccarelli slapped Big Al on the back. "Love the idea."

"Can you get your boy Harding over here from Ohio?" Big Al asked.

"Sure, I can. Let's do it in two weeks, on a Sunday after Mass?"

"Perfect. I will ask Father DeBenedetti to join us," Big Al continued.

"The padre loves bocce ball, although he's terrible at it. He likes to drink the vino, but it messes up his coordination. I'll make the wine. Before we play, Father DeBenedetti can give the blessing."

***

Several days later, on Sunday, Big Al approached the priest before the start of Mass and invited him to the fundraiser.

"Of course! I would love to be there!" he exclaimed. "I was the lawn bowling champ in Cava de' Tirreni."

"No, you weren't," Big Al replied with a grin. "I was there."

"You'll see," the priest clowned.

Father DeBenedetti gave a solemn sermon that day. He broke the news that, on the previous evening, a Serbian nationalist had shot and killed Archduke Franz Ferdinand, heir to the Austro-Hungarian Empire, and his wife.

The assassination was done in protest of Austro-Hungarian rule over Bosnia and Herzegovina, including a town located in the southwestern area called Medjugorje.

"My brothers and sisters, years ago at my parish in Cava de' Tirreni, I shared with my parishioners a vision by Pope Leo XIII," said Father DeBenedetti.

"He saw events of the twentieth century, which included war, immorality, genocide, and abandonment of religious belief on a large scale. I believe those events are unfolding."

***

A few weeks later, on the very day of the bocce ball tournament for Harding, Russia joined with Serbia, which was under attack by Austria-Hungary. Belgium, France, and Great Britain joined with Serbia and Russia too. Germany aligned with Austria-Hungary. World War I was underway.

Despite the grim world news, Harding was in a good mood during the bocce ball tournament.

"After I lost my bid for Ohio governor in 1910, my path to the White House was doubtful," Harding confided to Big Al.

"Judging by the turnout today and the amount of money you raised, Alfred, I am more confident I'll win this time."

"Big Al knows how to get things done," said Father DeBenedetti. "He also makes good wine, although today it is a bit too strong for me!"

Father DeBenedetti wobbled and struggled to roll when it was his turn. His rolls came nowhere near the smaller pallino ball he was aiming at.

"I just can't seem to get coordinated," the priest complained.

"I thought you said you were a champion?" Big Al replied.

"A champion complainer," Harding said with a chuckle.

Harding and Big Al instantly hit it off. Harding saw in the Italian immigrant qualities that he valued: the immigrant was hardworking, a family man, ambitious, and he believed in God.

"Alfred, you came to America with practically nothing more than the shirt on your back, and look at you now," Harding said.

"You're a success. When people talk about America being the land of opportunity, they're talking about you, Alfred!"

"I came to America to achieve my dreams," Big Al replied. "You are also chasing your dreams. This beautiful country allows people from all walks of life to do just that, be their best."

In Harding, Big Al also saw an answer to his growing problem with the increasing number of restrictions being placed on business owners. Congress was instead passing laws that were friendlier to labor. Big Al hoped his new friend, Harding, could help change that, if he were elected to the US Senate.

Eventually Harding was elected, and he introduced business-friendly legislation that President Woodrow Wilson signed into laws. This helped Big Al become very rich, and he gained the reputation for being a kingmaker.

New York, 1917

For more than two and a half years, the country's new president, Woodrow Wilson, tried to keep the United States out of the war.

However, when Berlin shot down five American merchant ships in March, the country was enraged. Wilson asked Congress for a declaration of war on April 2, and he got it.

Vincent Mangani, the strong-armed gangster working with D'Aquila, went off to war. Lady Luck smiled on him as he went.

Mangani had the good fortune of ending up in the same infantry division as all four of Big Al's sons and also with the sons of Big Al's two oldest brothers, Adolfo and Leonardo.

A huge number of Italian Americans, 10 percent of all US soldiers, fought in World War I. Tens of thousands of Italians swept into the armed forces and shipped out to the trenches of France.

Every morning, Big Al's wife, Carmelita, and his mother, Mary, went to Mass and prayed for the safe return of the boys. They lit a candle for each one, every day, and offered up prayers for them.

***

Pope Benedict XV made repeated pleas for world peace, but they were ignored. So, he directly appealed in May of that year to the Madonna (Mother of Jesus) to intercede.

Just over a week later, the Madonna appeared in Fatima, Portugal, to three shepherd children, ages ten, nine, and seven. The oldest child, Lúcia dos Santos, and her cousins, Francisco and Jacinta Marto, saw a bright flash of something like lightning, followed by another flash in the clear blue sky.

They looked up to see the Madonna clothed in white, brighter than the sun. The children would see her more than a half dozen times that year. They were given three secrets.

One month after the final apparition, a Masonic sect from a neighboring town to Fatima rallied against the reported sightings.

They attacked a makeshift shrine where the Madonna had brought together seventy thousand people on Her final appearance. A local newspaper wrote the following account of the incident:

> With an ax, they cut the tree under which the three shepherd children stood during the famous phenomenon of the thirteenth of this month. They took away the tree, together with a table on which a modest altar had been arranged, and on which a religious image (of the Madonna) had been placed.

***

One Sunday during Mass, Father DeBenedetti shared with his church congregation the story of the three children in Fatima.

"The oldest child, Lúcia, was the only one of the three with the ability to speak with the Madonna," said Father DeBenedetti. "The Mother of Jesus told the children that she would reappear to them for six months on the thirteenth day.

"The children told their parents, and while some in the village didn't believe them, others did.

"As the weeks and months passed, more and more of the faithful made pilgrimages to Fatima. No one else could see the Madonna except the children.

"The gathered adults would stand riveted as Lúcia took the lead and described her visions.

"On the Madonna's final appearance on October 13, an estimated seventy thousand people attended the site. The Madonna urged repentance and the building of a chapel at the site.

"She lifted her hands to the sky and called to the crowd to look at the sun, upon which people reported a silvery disc emerged from behind the clouds. They experienced 'the Miracle of the Sun.'

"Not everyone reported the same thing; some present claimed they saw the sun dance around the heavens; others said the sun zoomed toward Earth in a zigzag motion that caused them to fear it might collide with our planet or burn it up.

"Some people reported seeing brilliant colors spin out of the sun in a psychedelic, pinwheel pattern, and thousands of others present didn't see anything at all. The whole event took ten minutes."

***

That same year, Masonry celebrated the two hundredth anniversary of its first grand lodge opening in London by openly declaring war on the Church through a series of protests in the city.

They littered Rome with posters showing the archangel Pietro defeated on the ground, trampled beneath a triumphant Lucifer.

One person reported witnessing banners with slogans written on them that said, "Satan must reign in the Vatican. The pope will be his slave."

Chapter 7

THE BUSINESS OWNER

New York, 1919

An influenza pandemic, labeled the Spanish Flu, erupted the year before and was gripping the country.

Caused by the H1N1 influenza, the pandemic was unusually deadly and lasted more than twelve months, from spring 1918 to early summer 1919, infecting five hundred million people—about a third of the world's population at the time.

"Don't forget to wear your mask," Carmelita called out to her husband as he left one morning to go fishing.

"I can't breathe in that thing," he complained.

"I don't care," Carmelita insisted. "Put it on! I'd much rather you be uncomfortable than not breathing at all."

"The fish won't get me sick."

"On the boat, do what you want," she insisted. "Wear it everywhere else."

Big Al shrugged his shoulders and put on his mask. Wearing it was mandatory. Law enforcement officers doled out five-dollar fines for anyone who went without a mask in public. Hundreds of people in New York found themselves carted off to jail if they failed to comply.

"Carmelita, I will be home a little late today. After we are done fishing, I have to stop off at the church and talk with Father DeBenedetti. He wants to see me."

"Okay, but don't be too late. I am making your favorite dinner, homemade ravioli."

Big Al did a little dance at the news. He hugged his wife and then walked out the door humming a tune.

After a productive day of catching black bass, Big Al went to see Father DeBenedetti. He found him out in front of the church, planting flowers.

"Al, I always know when you're coming, from a mile away," the priest said.

"And how is that?"

"You smell like fish!"

The two men slapped each other on the back and took a seat on a bench out front.

"What did you want to see me about, Padre?"

"I'm going to Rome at the request of the Vatican. I want you to come with me," Father DeBenedetti replied.

Big Al's head rocked backwards. "Why do you want me to go to Rome? For that matter, why are you going to Rome?"

"I've been asked by my superior to assist him with the very first meeting between a sitting president and a reigning pope. The two world leaders are going to talk about the next steps toward peace now that the war is over."

"That sounds important, but why do you want me to go?"

"I need an assistant," the priest said. "My boss, who is a cardinal, will not be doing any heavy lifting for the event. That's just how it goes. The big shots are there for a news story only."

"I see," said Big Al. "You are the one, then, who will be doing all the work."

"Bingo. I need a dependable assistant, someone who knows how to speak Italian and who's a Catholic."

"What type of work would we be doing?" asked Big Al.

"We'd be taking care of all of the coordination between the White House and the Vatican—the little details. I need your help with that."

"Do I seem like a detail kind of guy to you?" asked the burly fisherman.

"You take orders well, and that's what counts," Father DeBenedetti replied. "I've seen Carmelita order you around, and you do what she tells you really well." Big Al pretended to laugh.

***

That afternoon, Big Al told Carmelita about his conversation with Father DeBenedetti.

"You should go," she said. "Being asked to assist the pope and the president is a really big deal."

"Who is going to take care of the fishing business?" Big Al asked.

"The boys are back from the war. They can do it. You also have Michael. He knows what to do."

"That is true," Big Al replied, though he was a bit hesitant.

He wasn't so certain his sons were up to the task. They'd returned from World War I as changed men—and not for the better.

Flamethrowers had hit Alfred Jr. and Alessandro during trench warfare. Both men had been badly burned. Maximo and Francesco also were injured in a tank explosion. The allied tanks of World War I were unpredictable and often broke down, which is what happened to the one Maximo and Francesco had been in.

A grenade hit their stalled tank, and each of them had suffered the loss of several of their fingers and toes. Their skulls were also cracked.

"Do you think they can handle it?" Big Al asked about his sons temporarily running the fishing business.

"I know Maximo and Francesco seem to be a little off in the head since the bombing," Carmelita replied. "And Alfred Jr. and Alessandro are resentful of the scars on their faces.

"But the boys need to be pushed. They can't keep moping around and doing nothing."

"So then, you think it will do them some good to work again," Big Al paraphrased.

"Yes, I do. Adolfo and Leonardo should go back to work too," she said. Big Al's brothers had lost their sons in the war, which had sent their wives over the edge.

Both women had suffered nervous breakdowns and ended up in a mental health sanitarium.

"I suppose you are right," Big Al agreed. "It's time to get this family back on its feet."

***

A few days later, Big Al told Father DeBenedetti that he'd travel with him to Vatican City.

"There you go!" said Father DeBenedetti. "Then it's settled."

"When do we leave?" asked Big Al.

"Tomorrow."

"Wait, what? I cannot possibly be ready to travel by tomorrow."

"We'll take a nice boat, not like the one you and Joe Molinaro came across the Atlantic in," said Father DeBenedetti.

"Our boat will be carrying the president, so you can bet your bottom dollar it'll be top of the line."

"I don't know much about the new pope who has replaced Pius X," Big Al said. "What is he like?"

"Pope Benedict XV," said the priest. "He is a hard worker. He was only in his job a month when the Great War started. Now that the war is over, he is committed to alleviating the suffering and hunger that has resulted."

"And what about President Woodrow Wilson, what's he like?" asked Big Al.

"Well, let's just say the two men are very different."

"How so?" questioned Big Al.

"President Wilson wants to create a new world order on his terms, as he sees it. Wilson was only president for one year when the war started. He was jealous that the Vatican came out before him with a prospective peace plan.

"The president felt that he could do better, so he subsequently issued his Fourteen Points peace plan, which was four points better than the Vatican's."

Big Al stared blankly at the priest. "How is this going to work, Enzio? The president and the pope sound like two alpha dogs; really competitive with one another."

"Both are high-minded men who are statesmen, and they know the world will be watching them," said Father DeBenedetti.

"Now's the time for them to put forward ideas for the world, and they know it. In the end, they'll shine together in the spotlight. Both are keenly aware of the stakes and of their reputations."

Big Al and Father DeBenedetti set out on their trip on the USS *George Washington*. They traveled for nine days.

Convoyed by the battleship *Pennsylvania* and ten destroyers, the transport's voyage brought her near Brest, France.

A large force of US Navy battleships and destroyers were in European waters and ceremoniously escorted the ship into the port. From there, the president disembarked to Paris by rail.

Big Al and Father DeBenedetti traveled instead to Vatican City, where they worked long hours—day in and day out—organizing the upcoming event.

The local newspaper ran the following story:

The New York Times

President Gets Warm Reception on Way to Vatican; Meets with Pope

Rome—Today, on his way to the Vatican, great crowds greeted President Wilson with wild cries of "Vive le President Wilson!" He seemed to bask in the adulation.

Cardinal Daniel O'Reilly of the Catholic Archdiocese of New York accompanied the president, along with Father Enzio DeBenedetti of New York and Alfred Tedesco, an American businessman.

A platoon of Swiss Guards met President Wilson this morning at the Vatican as a band played the American national anthem.

The president and pope spent about a half hour together, during which time the pope quizzed Mr. Wilson about conditions in the different countries he has recently visited.

When their meeting ended, the pope offered the president a prayer.

Either he misunderstood, or he was acting as the prickly Presbyterian that he was, but President Wilson wanted clarification. Pope Benedict XV reassured him that the blessing was for everyone in the room, not just President Wilson; he did not discriminate in invoking God's blessing upon people.

Nevertheless, President Wilson turned around and barked out: "Are there any Catholics here?"

While the Catholics in the group knelt, the Presbyterian president bowed his head.

After the prayer, Pope Benedict XV expressed that he wanted to be involved in the upcoming peace discussions at Versailles, but President Wilson disagreed with this.

The Holy Father presented President Wilson with a copy in mosaic of one of the masterpieces of Guido Reni, while the Vatican's Secretary of State, Cardinal Gasparri, offered him two sumptuously printed and bound copies of the New Canon Law, one for the president personally, the other for the University of Princeton.

The American president immediately headed for the American Episcopal Church in Rome, where he received delegations from Protestant denominations.

President Wilson is on a months-long trip in Europe. His ultimate destination is the peace conference in Paris, but he has decided to see Europe for himself. Italy was one of the first stops on his itinerary.

No sitting president has ever left the continental United States for such an extended period.

Wilson's European sojourn is history-making in and of itself. Leaving the country will not be as history-making as what he just did: met with a reigning pope.

From Rome, President Wilson traveled on to Paris and the peace conference. Pope Benedict intends to continue his efforts for peace among nations.

Big Al and Father DeBenedetti did not immediately sail home after the meeting at the Vatican. Instead, they took a train to Naples, where the seventy-one-year-old Supremo Pasquinelli and his wife, Patty, were waiting for them at the station.

"Supremo, you look like you haven't aged a bit," Big Al lied.

Time had not been kind to Pasquinelli. He no longer looked like a grizzly bear, but rather like a broken tree.

Pasquinelli was permanently hunched over due to a back condition. His hair was whiter than snow, and his eyes no longer glimmered their former ocean-blue color.

"You are full of crap," Pasquinelli joked with Big Al. "I know I look bad, but I still make a mean loaf of bread!"

The old friends embraced, and then Patty led them to the car. She drove them to their home in Salerno, where the visitors stayed for a week.

During that time, Big Al and Father DeBenedetti were startled by the widespread civil unrest and political strife in the immediate aftermath of World War I.

On the day before they were to return to America, Patty sat down with Big Al at the kitchen table while he was eating crackers and homemade cheese.

"Supremo isn't well," she said.

Big Al's head bowed. "I sort of figured. He looks like a shell of himself."

"He has cancer of the colon."

Big Al's lip quivered. "How long have you known?"

"Only a few months. Came on fast. The doctor says he has maybe a few months to live, but likely only weeks."

Big Al took Patty's hand.

"What can I do for you?" he asked.

"Oh, I'm going to be fine. You know Supremo, he takes care of everyone, and he certainly has taken care of me. There's plenty of money. My children live close by, so I won't be lonely.

"But I'll miss my husband terribly. He's like my great big teddy bear."

"He has been my role model," Big Al replied. "He taught me to be kind to people. Supremo once told me to treat people the way you want them to treat you. He modeled that behavior, and I've tried to live by it."

"He has a big heart," Patty replied.

"His style of running a Mafia clan was so much different than how it is in America," Big Al pointed out.

"How so?"

"With the Camorra here in this region of Italy, he took care of people. Supremo used his own belief system as his guide for how justice and compassion should be carried out. It was a fair and balanced approach.

"However, in America, with the exception of Paul Vaccarelli, the gangs are vicious. They're only out for themselves."

"Supremo isn't involved with the Camorra anymore," Patty said. "He's too old and sick."

"Nevertheless, I can tell you that the Camorra has changed in Italy too. They're more violent as well. I guess as people became dissatisfied with their living conditions, they lashed out, both here and in America. We're living in rougher times."

"What will happen to the restaurant?" Big Al asked.

"Oh, I'm still going to run it. I love that place. The restaurant is my second home. I'll never sell it."

Big Al and Patty hugged. They knew it was probably the last time they would ever see each other. Tears streamed down Big Al's face.

He couldn't remember the last time he was so sad.

***

After a week, Big Al and Father DeBenedetti set sail to return home. When they arrived in America, Big Al was informed that Supremo had died while they were out at sea.

He also learned that President Wilson, who had recently suffered a stroke, agreed to an early prison release for Morello, Lupo, and Joe Molinaro.

New York, 1920

Big Al and Vaccarelli sat at a local café drinking espresso in the outdoor patio area.

"Would you say you've accomplished your dreams, Al?" the former boxer asked.

"This afternoon, as I finished cleaning the boats, I knew I'd made the right decision coming to America," Big Al replied.

"Why? What makes you say that?" asked Vaccarelli.

"I have a good life. I am a fisherman. I get to do what I always wanted to do, and they pay me to do it. How can I not be happy?"

"But you have not answered my question. Have you accomplished all of your dreams?" Vaccarelli repeated.

Big Al looked down at the floor. His shoulders fell forward.

"Hey, wait, you haven't!"

"Well, not entirely," Big Al responded in earnest.

Paul Vaccarelli tensed his jaw. "What haven't you accomplished?"

Big Al tapped his fingers on the bar, and then he turned and looked directly at his boss.

"My dream, ever since I was a young boy, was to have *my own* fishing boats. What I have today are your boats, not mine."

"I get it," Vaccarelli said. "What else?"

"When I was ten years old, I remember being out on the ocean with my papa, Rocco. He was setting out octopus pots. And I told him, one day I would like to have my own fish market and a restaurant."

"You want to be a business owner, like me," Vaccarelli replied.

"I want that, yes," Big Al agreed.

Vaccarelli rubbed his chin.

"These are your dreams."

"Indeed, they are."

"Al, how many boats do we have now?"

"Twelve."

"They're yours," Vaccarelli replied. "All of them."

"Really?" Big Al exclaimed as crocodile tears welled in his eyes.

"Yes," Vaccarelli answered. "Now, about that dream of owning a fish store. You don't know this, but I own Gambino's Fish Market."

"You do? You're right. I never knew that."

"Sometimes it's better for people not to know too much," Vaccarelli said with a chuckle. "I'm giving that to you too. The fish store is now yours."

Big Al put his head down on the bar and sobbed. Then he reached out with his massive right arm and put it around Vaccarelli. He squeezed them together.

"Hey, hey, take it easy, big fella," Vaccarelli joked. "You're going to wrinkle my nice suit."

Big Al sat up and shook his friend like a tree.

"Why are you doing this, Paul?"

"Remember a few years back when I told you I parceled out most of my illicit businesses to other gangs?"

"Yes."

"You asked me if I was ever going to parcel out the commercial fishing business and I said 'no' at the time. But, the time has come for me to let the rest of the stuff go.

"You've earned the right to have them. Besides, like I told you then, I like you, Al."

"I am so grateful to you."

"No, Al, I'm grateful to you. All these years, with the bullets flying all around me, I always knew I could count on you. You've never once let me down."

Big Al trembled like a child.

"Now, as for a restaurant," Vaccarelli continued. "I don't have one to give you. However, I do know that old Johnny Boy Tomasso has a nice place just two blocks from the fish market. He's old and looking to retire. I'll talk to him."

"You can't be serious?"

"As serious as a heart attack, Al. You come up with the money and I'll make sure you get a fair price on Tomasso's restaurant. Deal?"

Big Al stood up from his bar stool and gave Vaccarelli a bear hug.

"You and Mr. Pasquinelli are the greatest men I have ever known, besides my own papa."

***

The following evening, Big Al called a family meeting. He invited Michael and the Molinaros to attend as well, including Joe, whom he'd forgiven after he served his time in prison.

"A very special thing happened today," he said to open the conversation.

"What?" asked Big Al's mother, Mary, who, at the age of sixty-nine, seemed to have more energy than most people half her age.

"Paul Vaccarelli turned over his fleet of boats to me, as well as Gambino's Fish Market, which I was surprised to learn that he owned."

Big Al's sisters, seated with their husbands, jumped out of their chairs and shrieked with joy.

"Now you have your own boats and a fish market to sell your catch!" exclaimed Margie.

Big Al turned to Michael.

"Continue being my right-hand man with the boats?" he asked.

"Absolutely," Michael replied.

Next, Big Al addressed his four sons.

"Boys, I need you to work with me on the boats," he said.

The sons nodded in agreement.

Big Al then turned to the seventy-year-old Joe Molinaro and his wife, Olivia.

"Can you and your kids manage the fish store?"

"Be happy to," replied Molinaro, fighting back the tears. Ever since being released from prison, he'd struggled to find a purpose with his life.

"Okay, there's one more thing, for the women," Big Al said slowly, letting the anticipation build.

"Spit it out!" Margie exclaimed.

"Paul says old Johnny Boy Tomasso's restaurant is for sale. He wants to retire. Therefore, we have an opportunity to buy it at a fair price. Does the family want to put our money together and purchase a restaurant?"

"Yes!" the women enthusiastically exclaimed.

"All right. You can quit your jobs at the garment factory. I would like for you and your husbands to come to work at the restaurant."

Each of the women shouted a happy, "Hooray!"

"Carmelita, you are a wonderful cook," said Big Al. "Your mother taught you well in Amalfi. Will you be my head cook?"

"Oh, Alfred," she said with tears in her eyes. "You are the best husband ever. Of course, I will."

"And, Mama, you were Mr. Pasquinelli's best cook. Will you help out?" he asked Mary.

"Yes! Yes! I miss those days at Supremo's restaurant so much. I'd be more than happy to work there as cook or whatever else you need me to do."

"What'll you call the restaurant?" Margie asked.

"How about Big Al's Restaurant," Carmelita replied.

The corners of Big Al's mouth rose.

"Sounds perfect."

"Can we make wine at the restaurant like we did at Mr. Pasquinelli's place?" Margie asked.

"With the prohibition on alcohol, you need to be careful," cautioned Molinaro, who was overly careful about everything since serving hard time.

"Yes, we can make wine," Big Al declared.

"Maybe we can even sell a little bit under the counter," Margie said with a wink.

"And we will bake bread in an outdoor oven too, like Mr. Pasquinelli used to do," Big Al continued.

He turned to his younger brothers, Diego and Filippo.

"Paul Vaccarelli wants to talk with the two of you about a new project he has coming up," Big Al shared. "I'll set up a meeting with him."

They nodded in agreement.

***

Several nights later, Mary insisted on cooking a special dinner for Paul Vaccarelli as her way of showing appreciation for his kindness. She made a huge meal.

The first course was a turtle soup, followed by ravioli, tripe, veal, and a side dish of broccoli with freshly squeezed lemon. They had salad at the very end, followed by homemade gelato ice cream for dessert.

"The meal was exceptional, Mary!" Vaccarelli said after they had finished eating.

"I'll cook for you any time you like," Big Al's mother replied.

"You have a deal!" Vaccarelli howled.

While the women cleaned up in the kitchen, the men sat at the dining room table and smoked cigars.

"I talked to old Mr. Tomasso today," Vaccarelli said. "He was so delighted to hear a solid family was interested in buying his restaurant. He wants to practically give the place away to you because he knows you'll be a good owner."

"Really?" asked Big Al. "He'd do that?"

"Oh, yes," said the former boxer with the crooked nose. "The restaurant is like his baby. He's more interested in it being run by good people than in the money."

Big Al's eyes teared up again.

"Then we have a deal!"

Big Al poured the men a shot of anisette, and they raised their glasses for a toast.

"Salute!"

"Paul, you said there is something you want to talk to my younger brothers about?" Big Al asked. "Is now a good time, since we are all here?"

"Yes, it is," Vaccarelli replied. "I am working with Lucky Longo and his pals to start a construction company. Diego and Filippo, would you be interested in joining us? You too, Al?"

"Join you, how?" Big Al asked.

"For starters, I need you to help us finance the business," Vaccarelli answered. "Specifically, we need start-up money to get involved in the concrete business."

"You want me to be an investor in concrete?" asked Big Al, raising his eyebrows.

"Yes," Vaccarelli replied. "The City of New York is launching a massive public works program. Someone has to provide the concrete for these projects. Why not us? What do you say, Diego and Filippo? I need two full-time guys to dedicate to it, that way we can manage things our way and keep an eye out for the bad actors."

"What do you think?" Big Al said, looking at his younger brothers.

"Sounds great," they agreed.

Vaccarelli leaned across the table and shook their hands.

"Congratulations, you're now in the construction business!"

Big Al shook his head and smiled. "Paul, you're too much."

***

Down at the Brooklyn dock, someone else was not as happy. The NYPD had confiscated one of Vincent Mangani's shipments from Italy, and he was furious with himself for the screwup.

Mangani had gotten so busy lately with other rackets that he'd been ignoring the waterfront. No one had cleared the now-confiscated shipment when it came in.

"What are you going to do about it?" asked his partner, D'Aquila.

"Our new gang is growing so fast that I can't keep up," Mangani complained. "I need help! Let's hire two guys to work down at the Brooklyn docks to clear our shipments."

"Whom do you have in mind?" D'Aquila asked.

"Big Al's brothers Adolfo and Leonardo," Mangani said. "Now that Paul Vaccarelli is getting away from most of his businesses, I hear the brothers are available."

"Yeah, but I also heard they went slightly mad—along with their wives—after their kids died in the war." D'Aquila was clearly not comfortable with the idea.

"They're angry, not nuts," Mangani said. "Angry makes for good Mafia soldiers. Besides, I've been making nice with them for years. They like me.

"I was in the same infantry division as their sons and Big Al's four boys. That sort of makes me like family."

"You have a few screws loose yourself, Mangani," D'Aquila replied. "But if you think you can make it happen, go for it."

***

The following week, D'Aquila did a double take when the forty-five-year-old Adolfo and his forty-three-year-old brother Leonardo showed up for work at the Brooklyn docks with Mangani.

"I told you so," crowed Mangani.

The brothers walked carefully and cautiously. They sized everyone up and down.

Adolfo and Leonardo were definitely different men since their sons died in the war. To them, the world was a bad place. Everyone in it was their enemy.

Both men were also angry with God and had stopped going to Church.

"You will find dockworkers today are a real pain in the rear," Mangani told the two of them. "They want to unionize, but we won't let them."

"Why do they want to be in a union?" Adolfo growled.

"They see so-called 'landmark' advances coming out of the White House to protect the rights and safety of American workers," Mangani replied. "They feel like dockworkers are somehow being left behind."

"That's total crap," Leonardo jeered. "They're just being greedy."

"Young people today didn't have it hard like us," Adolfo said.

"You got that right." Mangani nodded fiercely. "These dockworkers today want more and more."

In truth, however, the United States was the only country with a large foreign commerce without any laws to protect the safety of its dockworkers.

Even the celebrated Clayton Antitrust Act of 1914, which legalized strikes, boycotts, and peaceful picketing, did little to improve actual working conditions for dockworkers.

"You'll see what I mean soon enough," Mangani said to the brothers. "I want you guys to do the hiring and firing down here at the Brooklyn docks.

"Plus, I need you to clear the paperwork for our shipments coming in from Italy. We don't need any problems with customs agents. The bankers are already bad enough to deal with."

"What's up with the bankers?" Adolfo asked.

"They're levying too many fees on the shipments," Mangani replied. "The bankers are always finding a way to tax us."

***

Two days later, the headline in *The New York Times* read, "Bomb Goes Off in a Horse-Drawn Wagon at the Corner of Wall and Broad Streets in the Financial District of New York."

The Wall Street bombing occurred at 12:01 p.m. on Thursday, September 16, in the financial district of Manhattan. The bomb killed thirty people immediately, and another eight died later of wounds sustained in the blast.

"You think the bankers got the message?" a snarling Adolfo asked Mangani that afternoon at the docks. Mangani staggered backward, clearly dazed by the unexpected comment.

"Did you guys have something to do with the bombing?" he asked.

"Maybe the bankers will wise up," said Leonardo, who winked at his older brother.

Mangani was at a loss for words. He'd always considered himself a tough guy, but he knew he didn't have the guts to blow up a building with people still inside it.

Leonardo put an arm around the weak-kneed Mangani.

"You let us know if anyone else is giving you problems, Boss."

***

Over in East Harlem, Paul Vaccarelli stood in the afternoon sun as Big Al and Michael cleaned the decks of their boats with a mop. Big Al's sons worked along with them.

"Hey, Al, can I have a word with you?" Vaccarelli called out.

"Sure thing. What's up?"

"Remember a few years back when we blocked the polling booths and voted early and often against the incumbent who wanted to shut down my brothels in the Ward?" Vaccarelli asked.

"How could I forget?" Big Al replied.

"We need to do it again."

"What! What are you talking about?"

"Remember Warren Harding?" Vaccarelli asked.

"The lousy bocce ball player?" Big Al recalled. "I liked the guy a lot, for a politician."

"I like him too," Vaccarelli said. "And you're right, he stunk at bocce ball. But I don't think he cared about the game because we raised a ton of money for his US Senate bid."

"He won. That was the important thing," Big Al said with a satisfied grunt.

"Well, now Harding is running for president," Vaccarelli said. "He's a real long shot to win. We need to help him. Tammany Hall wants me to send some people to the Republican convention in Chicago to make sure he gets the party's nomination."

"That's impossible," Big Al replied.

"No, it's not," Vaccarelli objected. "Al Capone, who was with me when I was head of the Five Points Gang, runs the Mafia in Chicago now. Bugsy Siegel, another one of my kids, is Capone's right-hand man. They'll help us."

Big Al scratched his head. "I don't think we can pull it off."

"Come on," Vaccarelli pushed back. "You don't know until you've tried. Let's go down there and mix it up. Bring your boys."

Big Al rolled his eyes.

"There's never a dull moment with you, Paul."

With help from Big Al and his boys, Harding won the Republican Party nomination on the tenth ballot.

Later that year, Harding won the presidency.

Chapter 8

THE WEDDING

New York, 1922

A teenager who'd protested King Umberto I's government so many years ago was the new prime minister of Italy after leading an organized mass demonstration. Benito Mussolini's March on Rome resulted in the king firing his existing prime minister.

"Mussolini and his National Fascist Party have ascended to power in the Kingdom of Italy," Big Al told Father DeBenedetti one day after Sunday Mass.

"We anticipated his rise to power, didn't we?" the priest countered.

"I guess we did," replied Big Al. "I didn't entirely see it coming, though. A massive march on the capital. The government resigning. So crazy!"

In addition to the change in government, a new pope was in charge of the Vatican. Pope Benedict XV passed away unexpectedly from pneumonia at the age of sixty-seven.

"What do you know about the new pope, Pius XI?"

"He was born in Desio, Italy," said Father DeBenedetti.

"Hey, that's Luigi De Sio's last name!" Big Al exclaimed. The two men chuckled.

"Spelled a little differently," the priest pointed out.

"Any word on what initiatives the new pope will be working on?" Big Al asked.

"Officials from the Vatican recently wrote to me," said Father DeBenedetti. "They're going to hold a secret meeting with Mussolini and Pope Pius XI in the next few months."

"Why?"

"In his maiden speech, Mussolini spoke of the historical importance of the Church," said Father DeBenedetti. "Pope Pius XI believes he has a politician with whom he can finally work. As you know, the monarchy was not on friendly terms with the Vatican."

"Yeah, I know," Big Al replied. "It's been that way ever since the Papal States were conquered and made part of the Kingdom of Italy."

Big Al leaned back in his chair and looked up.

"Why does the pope think he can trust Mussolini?"

"Neither Mussolini nor the new pope have any love for parliamentary democracy," the priest replied. "Top officials in the Vatican also believe their interests can be easily served by a direct link between the pope and Mussolini.

"They'll support Mussolini and Fascism, and in return, Mussolini will grant favors to enhance the role of the Church in Italy."

Big Al frowned. He wasn't so sure.

That evening, Big Al greeted guests at his restaurant, just as he did every night. Dressed in a fancy suit, Big Al addressed them with a warm, "Ciao, paisano!" as they walked in.

The fisherman loved interacting with people, being the center of attention, and putting on a show.

He stood by the front door and, despite Prohibition, handed out small cups of wine to his customers who were waiting for an empty table.

Dimly lit candles were on every table, which were adorned with red tablecloths. Fresh sawdust was on the floor. A large portrait of the pope hung above the entryway to the kitchen.

I am a blessed man, Big Al thought happily.

New York, 1925

Lucky Longo sat next to his mentor, Paul Vaccarelli, and across from Big Al in a booth at Big Al's Restaurant.

"You guys want to hear a story?" asked Lucky, who matter-of-factly flipped a skeleton key in between his fingers.

"Do we have a choice?" Vaccarelli joked.

Lucky ignored the comment. "There's a ghost in this story!"

"Sure," said Big Al. "I love a good ghost story."

"Well, this isn't the kind of ghost story you tell around a campfire," Lucky clarified. "It's a Mafia ghost story."

Vaccarelli rolled his eyes. "Get on with it, Lucky!"

"Three years ago, I was hired by Mob boss Joe Masseria to be his bodyguard."

"You mean he hired you to be his gunman," Vaccarelli clarified.

"No," said Lucky, giving his mentor a crossways look. "Like I said, I was hired to be his bodyguard. Big difference."

Vaccarelli shook his head.

"Masseria was at home on the Lower East Side, and I was outside keeping watch," Lucky said. "Just after midday, two men pulled out front of his house and stepped out of a blue Hudson car. They walked across the street to a restaurant. One of them was Umberto 'The Ghost' Valenti, who was a veteran hit man.

"The Ghost was an associate of one-armed Morello, who wasn't happy that Masseria had taken over his gang while he was in prison. For about an hour, The Ghost and his accomplice waited and watched Masseria's house from the restaurant across the street.

"Next thing I know, Masseria comes out of his house in a straw hat and light summer suit and decides to take a stroll."

"What happens next?" asked Big Al.

"Before I could get in position to protect him, I see the two thugs from across the street get up and follow Masseria. The Ghost pulled out his weapon.

"Masseria saw them and tried to duck into a hat shop, but he got caught in front of a women's clothing store."

"What happened next?" asked Big Al, leaning forward.

"The Ghost fired three shots, missing Masseria each time at point-blank range. Masseria ran home while I made my move.

"The Ghost and his accomplice saw me and ran to a waiting car with running boards along the sides. They jumped on the running boards, and the car started to drive away. I opened fire.

"There were guns blazing all around. I injured the would-be assailants."

"Four innocent men and two women also got hit," Vaccarelli interjected. "You left that part out of your story."

Lucky gave his mentor another sideways look. "Who's telling the story here?"

"Go on," Big Al encouraged.

"The police later found Masseria sitting on his bed inside the house, with two bullet holes in his straw hat. After that, Masseria was given the nickname 'The Man Who Could Dodge Bullets.'"

"What a crazy story!" said Big Al, who reached into his pocket. "Say, I have a letter from Luigi De Sio. You guys want to hear it?"

"Sure!"

Big Al unfolded the letter and read it to them.

Dear Al,

The military discharged me because the local Fascists suspected I have Socialist leanings. This suspicion has caused me to be unemployed for a long time.

These were the circumstances on the day I went down to the railroad station in Naples to meet the train that carried Mussolini and his party members.

The train was destined for Reggio Calabria, where Mussolini was to inspect a recent landslide devastation. A huge crowd filled the railroad station by the time I arrived. Occasionally, I would hear a person call out, "Hey, Luigi, what are you doing here?"

However, I would not answer. I knew what I was going to do, and small talk with an acquaintance would only divert me from my plan.

I climbed a ladder that someone placed on the roof so people could watch from up there with Il Duce's supporters.

Once I sat down on the roof, I felt inside my coat pocket for my military discharge papers. Those documents represented my many years of military service.

I was convinced that there was not any work in civilian life that I was qualified to do. That's why my plan to go to America had to work.

Just the other day, a group of local Fascists came to the house, beat me senselessly, and told my wife and oldest daughter to take and swallow a laxative they gave them or I would receive more severe punishment.

The laxative was a symbol that a good bowel movement could eliminate the former Italian regime.

Then there was the recent legislation passed by Mussolini's politicians that emigration would cease immediately.

No one was to leave the country for overseas residence without express approval from Rome, which I knew was an obstacle to my plan.

How would I get to America now?

I was depressed. My chances for success appeared slim. What else could I do that I'd not already done?

I had taken on odd jobs to bring some money home for my wife, four sons, and two daughters. However, that wasn't enough.

As I waited on the roof, I heard the whistle of Mussolini's train.

The people on the station platform started to stir. The local band played a patriotic song. I moved toward the edge of the roof.

The train slowly made its way into the station and then stopped.

Suddenly, I noticed that the rail car that was the center of attention, the one Mussolini occupied, just so happened to be directly below me!

In my haste to drop down onto the platform, I landed on the back of a local Fascist who was moving toward the rail car.

That was a mistake.

Other Fascists, thinking that I was trying to inflict some kind of harm, hit and kicked me. I never was able to get to my feet.

The Fascists seemed to take pleasure in beating me. The commotion got the attention of Mussolini in the plush rail car.

Soon, the curtain over one of the windows pulled to the side and the window opened. One of Mussolini's aides asked what was happening.

A local Fascist party member in the crowd asked me why I was there. I stated that I was a veteran in the military whose services as a soldier were not wanted.

"He's unemployed at the moment," the local party member shouted out. "He says he was a soldier."

"Does he have identification?" asked the aide in Mussolini's rail car.

Some men on the platform raised me to my feet, searched me, and found the discharge papers in my pocket.

"He has discharge papers here!" the local party member said.

After a few moments, Mussolini's aide commanded, "Bring him to me!"

"Why are you here?" he said after he retrieved the papers.

"I have no work," I replied. "The only work I can get is cleaning tables at the university cafeteria."

The man asked me other questions and then ducked back into the rail car to talk to Mussolini.

A short while later the aide once again stuck his head out the window. He asked me one last question, and this time he was quite formal.

"Luigi De Sio, do you have relatives overseas?"

"Yes, sir!" I replied.

"Where?"

"In America."

"Whom do you have in America?"

"Two brothers-in-law."

"Do you want to go to America?"

"Oh, yes. But I thought—"

"Send your papers to this address in Rome that I have written on this pad. A letter of sponsorship must accompany them from one of your brothers-in-law in America. Do you understand?"

"Yes, sir!"

A short while later, Mussolini stuck his head out the same window to address the crowd and express the purpose of his trip. However, by then I was on my way home to announce the good news.

I will see you soon, Big Al, my dear friend. I am coming to America!

Sincerely,
Luigi

New York, 1928

"You may kiss the bride," said the sixty-seven-year-old Father DeBenedetti after the hour-long wedding ceremony.

Tears streamed down the faces of Big Al and Carmelita as the groom, a handsome Italian American, leaned in and kissed their youngest daughter, Paula, twenty-one.

The crowd of nearly 125 people threw rice at the bride and groom as they walked down the aisle of Our Lady of Mount Carmel Church in East Harlem.

"Paula looks so beautiful in her white dress," said her sister Giovanna, twenty-three, who had gotten married two years earlier.

"Almost as beautiful as you did," said Francesca, twenty-five, with a wink. "Her bouquet is gorgeous."

In keeping with southern Italian tradition, the mother-in-law gave the bouquet to the bride as she departed the altar after the ceremony.

The bride and groom went out the front door of the Church and into a waiting limousine, which took them to Big Al's Restaurant, where tables were beautifully arranged for the outdoor dinner reception that would last until one a.m.

On every table, wrapped in lace, were sugared almonds, known as *confetti*.

There were also more bags of rice, which the guests would toss at the wedding couple when they left for the night. Mixed with the rice were rose petals, which came in small bags personalized with the date and names of the wedding couple.

"The rice is a symbol of an abundance and wealth," Carmelita explained to one of her non-Italian friends.

During the cocktail hour, which lasted about an hour and a half before the sit-down dinner, people dropped by who hadn't attended the wedding, many of whom were Mafia members who wanted to pay their respects to Big Al.

Even though he was not a Mafia member, everyone liked Big Al and recognized that he was an influential person in many ways.

"Where's the beautiful bride?" asked Albert Anastasia, one of the founders of Murder, Inc.

"Paula, come on over here, please," Big Al called out.

The new bride came over quickly with her mother, Carmelita.

Anastasia handed the bride an envelope with cash inside.

"Grazie," she said.

Other Mafia men came forward—Joe Adonis, Vito Genovese, and Frank Costello. All were future Mafia kingpins. Lucky Longo joined them.

"Why, don't you men have impeccable timing!" Carmelita exclaimed.

"When we go out in public, we usually travel together, for our safety," Anastasia explained. "We're friends, so we watch each other's back."

Each man gave Big Al's youngest daughter an envelope with cash in it. As they turned to leave, Masseria showed up. The man who had taken over the Morello-Lupo Gang constantly looked over his shoulder as he walked toward the bride.

"Joe 'The Boss,' how are you today?" asked Lucky of the mob boss he'd protected years ago against D'Aquila and The Ghost.

"Glad to see you here, Lucky," Masseria replied. "I came to pay my respects, but I get nervous whenever I'm out in public."

"Don't worry, Joe, I got your back," Lucky replied.

But before Masseria—also known as "The Man Who Could Dodge Bullets"—could take out the envelope from his pocket, D'Aquila showed up with his hit man, "The Ghost" Valenti. Mangani was with them.

Lucky's mouth dropped when Big Al's brothers Adolfo and Leonardo ran up to greet the men. He had no idea they were now secretly working for Mangani and D'Aquila at the Brooklyn docks.

From across the football-sized lawn, where he was standing next to an outdoor bar, Paul Vaccarelli also noticed the men arrive.

The storm that has been brewing between Masseria and D'Aquila is here, he thought.

"This is going to get ugly," Lucky whispered to Big Al.

"You're not welcome here," Masseria shouted at D'Aquila and The Ghost.

Lucky stepped up next to Masseria and stood beside him, his fists clenched.

Paul Vaccarelli raced across the lawn to intervene.

"Stand down, boys," he yelled.

"You shut your mouth," The Ghost shouted back at Paul, which got Big Al's blood boiling.

"Back off," Lucky said to The Ghost.

Carmelita stepped in between the men as the bride watched it all unfold in horror.

"This is my daughter's special day. Let there be a twenty-four-hour truce," the bride's mother proposed.

"Not today," said The Ghost, who pulled out a knife and charged at Masseria, stabbing him in the shoulder.

That triggered Big Al's four sons, who, at the sight of a knife, flew into military mode.

They ran full steam across the lawn from the bar and rammed into The Ghost, sending him flying.

D'Aquila pulled out a gun from under his coat. But as he fired, Lucky caught his arm and swung it upward. The shot went into the air. A full-on fight erupted.

"Grab them!" Anastasia called out to his friends.

Joe Adonis grabbed Mangani, and Vito Genovese pulled D'Aquila to the ground. Frank Costello restrained The Ghost.

Big Al's brothers Adolfo and Leonardo came to the defense of D'Aquila and The Ghost, but Big Al put each one of them in a tight headlock.

Tears streamed down the bride's face.

"Oh, Mother, they've ruined my wedding!" the bride wailed. Beyond distraught, she ran to the restaurant, with Carmelita chasing after her.

"I told you there was a storm brewing," Vaccarelli shouted.

With the fight over, Vaccarelli turned to D'Aquila and The Ghost.

"What's the matter with you guys?" he chided. "Who pulls a knife and gun at a wedding? Have you no respect?"

"Get your hands off me," The Ghost screamed at Costello.

Vito Genovese made the mistake of releasing D'Aquila, who took out yet another gun, from a holster around his ankle. He took dead aim at Masseria.

As D'Aquila squeezed off a round, Big Al hit him across the face with one of his massive fists. The errant gunshot hit his pal The Ghost, who fell to the ground with an injured leg.

Lucky stepped in and sorted out the mess.

"Everyone, clear out!" he ordered.

A short time later, with calm restored, Big Al went inside the restaurant, where he found Carmelita consoling the bride.

"Your special day hasn't been ruined," he said to Paula. "It was just men behaving like a bunch of schoolboys."

After the tumultuous cocktail hour, the wedding soon got back on track during the two-hour dinner, which included two "first dishes" (pasta and rice), and two "second dishes" (fish with vegetables, and meatballs with sausages).

Afterward, there was the cutting of the wedding cake, and other typical Italian sweets and fruits.

"Let the dancing begin," Big Al called out after that.

Paula danced with her father and was happy again.

An Italian band played traditional songs to an accordion, clarinet, violin, and small drum adorned with bells. Before the dancing ended that night, the married couple handed out small gifts to their guests called *bomboniere*, which contained *confetti* and beautifully printed ribbons.

"Thank you for attending," the bride and groom said as they handed out the gifts, a symbol of family life.

D'Aquila was found shot to death the following day. He had been without his injured bodyguard. People widely speculated the triggerman was Joe "The Boss" Masseria. There would never be any convictions, however.

New York, 1929

Big Al sat with Paul Vaccarelli at a private table in the very back of his dimly lit restaurant. The head server, Rosemary, brought them their main course, veal parmigiana and linguini.

"Is there anything else I can get for you at this time, gentlemen?" Rosemary asked in her usually attentive manner.

"Only one thing," Paul Vaccarelli commented.

"What do you need, Paul?" she asked with a frown.

"I need to know, are you an angel?" he asked flirtatiously.

Rosemary blushed.

"Paul, what would your late wife say?"

"I'm not flirting," he replied. "I want facts!"

"Oh, Paul," Rosemary said, smiling and shaking her head as she walked away.

"That one's a winner," Vaccarelli said.

"When it comes to women, you are beyond the pale," Big Al said.

"I'm Italian," Vaccarelli said. "Can we help it if we appreciate beautiful women?"

Big Al spooned Romano cheese on top of his veal and linguini.

"Never forget, Paul, Romano cheese is better on pasta than Parmesan!"

"I'll make a note of that," Vaccarelli replied. "Say, I have a business proposal for you."

"Another one?" Big Al asked. "Last time, you talked me into starting a concrete company."

"And look how it's worked out," Vaccarelli replied. "I made you rich with that one."

"What is it this time?"

"There's a big construction project being planned called the Empire State Building," said Vaccarelli.

"The what?" asked Big Al.

"A huge Art Deco skyscraper in Midtown Manhattan," Vaccarelli explained. "Going to be one hundred and two stories. The name is derived from 'Empire State,' which, as you know, is the nickname of the state of New York."

"What do you know about this project, Paul?"

"Tammany Hall is behind it. The elected officials want it built. What else is there to know?"

"So, how would I be involved?" Big Al asked.

"I want to expand our construction business," said Paul Vaccarelli. "Let's get in on a piece of this action."

"More than providing the concrete?" Big Al quizzed.

"Yes, I want to also provide the iron," said Vaccarelli. "I'd like to put your brothers Diego and Filippo on the job. They've been doing great with the concrete projects."

"Done," said Big Al.

Vaccarelli was right, putting Diego and Filippo in charge of the concrete business a few years back had been a smart move. They were good at that kind of work.

However, unbeknownst to Big Al and Vaccarelli, Mangani had gotten to Diego and Filippo and convinced them to join the "Concrete Club."

More and more, the Mafia regulated the distribution of cement and concrete for large-scale construction projects. The Concrete Club extorted club "dues" and a 2 percent cut of the value of contracts.

The Concrete Club also monopolized the ready-mix concrete business in New York City.

Unlike cement sold in bags, which required significant preparation before application, ready-mix businesses did the hard work for their customers—they mixed cement with water, sand, and desired aggregates, and clients simply dictated where the mixture was to be poured.

The Mafia-owned ready-mix businesses supplied the material to multiple projects and ensured that their product be regularly used, and in excess, even when the design did not demand it.

With their infiltration of the labor unions and control of the material supply, the Mob put the city in a stronghold.

By eliminating access to workers and concrete, the Mafia could literally stop new and continuing construction of highways, housing, schools, hospitals, and government buildings.

New York, 1930 No problem with the Depression?

Big Al stood at his customary spot by the front door of his restaurant. There was an overflow crowd of guests, as usual.

The guests drank wine as they waited, and he entertained them on this evening with the following story about fishing:

There once was a businessman who was sitting by the ocean in Praiano. As the businessman sat there, he saw an Italian fisherman rowing a small boat toward the shore, who had caught quite a few big fish.

The businessman was impressed and asked the fisherman, "How long does it take you to catch so many fish?"

The fisherman replied, "Oh, just a short while."

The businessman was astonished. "Then why don't you stay longer at sea and catch even more?"

"This is enough to feed my whole family," the fisherman said.

The businessman then asked, "So, what do you do for the rest of the day?"

The fisherman replied, "Well, I usually wake up early in the morning, go out to sea and catch a few fish, then go back and play with my kids.

In the afternoon, I take a nap with my wife, and when evening comes, I join my buddies in the village for a drink—we play guitar, sing, and dance throughout the night."

The businessman offered a suggestion to the fisherman.

"I am an expert in business management. I could help you to become a more successful person. From now on, you should spend more time at sea and try to catch as many fish as possible.

"When you have saved enough money, you could buy a bigger boat and catch even more fish. Soon you will be able to afford to buy more boats, set up your own company, your own production plant for canned food and distribution network.

"By then, you will have moved out of this village and to Rome, where you can set up headquarters to manage your other branches."

The fisherman tilted his head and looked at the businessman. "And after that?"

The businessman laughed heartily. "After that, you can live like a king, and when the time is right, you can go public and float your shares in the stock exchange, and you will be rich."

"And after that?"

"After that, you can finally retire. You can move to a house by the fishing village, wake up early in the morning, catch a few fish, then return home to play with kids, have a nice afternoon nap with your wife, and when evening comes, you can join your buddies for a drink, play the guitar, sing, and dance throughout the night!"

The fisherman was puzzled. "Isn't that what I am doing now?"

The audience of restaurant goers nodded their heads in agreement.

One of the customers, Babe Ruth from the New York Yankees, was among those who agreed. He sat with a young woman and several teammates, who were also with lovely women.

"How much money do you need to be happy?" Big Al shouted out to the crowd.

"Perhaps not nearly as much as we are led to believe," Ruth replied.

"Correct, Bambino," said Big Al. "Obviously, we do need some money in this life to cover the basics. Without that, we will likely be miserable.

"However, you can certainly be happy without much else beyond the basics. When you recognize this, you can quickly become free."

People clapped loudly. While they did, Rosemary grabbed Big Al by the hand and led him away in a hurry.

"You are needed," she said, pulling him through the dining room. She pushed open the swinging doors leading into the kitchen.

"What is so urgent?" Big Al asked.

Rosemary led Big Al through the kitchen and out the back door, where they found fifty-five-year-old Carmelita slumped in a chair. Big Al's daughters were crowded around their mom.

"What is wrong, Carmelita?" Big Al cried out.

His wife gasped for air.

"Carmelita had a bad coughing fit," Rosemary said. "She couldn't get enough oxygen into her lungs."

Big Al held his wife in his arms. Even at fifty-nine years old, he was strong as a bull. Just a few weeks earlier, he had climbed six flights of stairs with a refrigerator on his back to help a friend.

"Call the doctor," said Big Al. "I will take her home."

They received bad news a few hours later. Carmelita had contracted tuberculosis; she didn't have much longer to live.

"We conquered the world together," Carmelita said to Big Al. "I am the luckiest girl alive. I married the man of my dreams and had seven wonderful children. We built a great life in America."

Carmelita passed away several days later.

***

In the months after his wife's death, Big Al walked around in a daze.

I lost my best friend.

In the evenings, after the restaurant closed, Big Al sat alone at the bar and drank.

"And here you are again," Rosemary said one night after she had set up the tables for breakfast the next morning. "How long is this going to go on, Alfred?"

"I don't really know," he answered.

"There are a lot of people counting on you," she replied.

"Like who?"

"Your daughters need their father. As a daughter myself, I can tell you no one is more important to a girl than her dad."

Big Al shrugged his shoulders and poured himself another shot of Jack Daniels.

"Your boys need you too," Rosemary continued. "Your grandchildren do as well."

Big Al dropped his head and cried, hard. He could not remember the last time that happened.

"You are the rock of your family," said Rosemary, who at five foot two was tiny next to the six-foot-six fisherman.

The lead waitress put her arm around Big Al and pulled him close.

"I need you, Alfred."

Big Al wiped the tears from his face with his massive paws.

"When you hired me years ago, I was just an eighteen-year-old kid who left Italy with nothing but the clothes I was wearing," she said. "You gave me a job. Because of you, I have been living my dream of being in America."

Big Al laid his head on her shoulder.

"You have a powerful impact on people. Don't lose your power, Al."

He could smell Rosemary's perfume. His head swirled. For thirty-seven years, he'd been with only one woman, his Carmelita.

This was literally the first time since then that he was close enough to another woman to smell her perfume, and he liked it.

Rosemary stroked Big Al's coarse black hair.

"You're a tough man, Alfred, and a kind man too. You take care of other people. Right now, while your heart is on the mend, why don't you let someone else take care of you?"

By the end of the year, they were married.

Chapter 9

PROHIBITION

New York, 1931

In his blue silk suit, black wing-tip shoes, and fedora, Lucky Longo stood out among the blue-collar workers on the Brooklyn docks.

Mangani was talking with Adolfo and Leonardo, but he came right over when he noticed Lucky.

"How are you doing today, Lucky?"

"Doing really good."

"That's a sharp suit you got on."

"Never hurts to make a good impression," Lucky replied. "Dress for success!"

Lucky turned to Big Al's brothers, Adolfo and Leonardo. "How about you two? Everything good?"

They gave half-hearted shrugs.

"Forgive them, Lucky," Mangani said. "They don't talk much."

"I thought we are friends?" Lucky asked the brothers. "Your brother and I are pals, anyway."

"Doesn't matter," Mangani replied. "They are distrustful of people."

"You don't trust me?" Lucky said, leaning in toward the brothers.

"Joe 'The Boss' Masseria hired you to be his bodyguard," Adolfo said. "That means you are with him. That *coglione* killed our friend D'Aquila."

"Not to mention the scene Masseria made at our niece's wedding," Leonardo added. "The man is rude."

"Yeah, no class," agreed Adolfo.

"I thought you said they don't talk much?" Lucky chided Mangani.

"There is a code of honor, and Masseria crossed it," continued Adolfo, who stepped forward and shoved his face into Lucky's. "Masseria got away with the stunt he pulled at the wedding. There has been no justice. Where is the Mafia code of honor? He walks around like he's untouchable."

"No one is untouchable," Lucky said.

"I think you are full of crap, Lucky Longo," Adolfo challenged. "I don't sweat you."

Mangani moved in between the two men.

"Okay, take it easy, Adolfo. Lucky, let's you and me take it inside. We have some business to discuss."

The following day, *The New York Times* reported the death of Mob boss Masseria in the following way:

> Masseria was seated at a table playing cards at a local bar with two or three unknown men when he was fired upon from behind. He died from gunshot wounds to his head, back, and chest. No witnesses came

forward, though two men were observed leaving the bar and getting into a stolen car. No one was convicted in Masseria's murder, as there were no witnesses.

***

Down at the Brooklyn docks, Big Al was scrubbing down his boats at the end of a long day. His favorite boat was called *The Dreamer*, named after him.

"The Empire State Building opened today," said the seventy-nine-year-old Molinaro, who was waiting for the longshoremen to offload fish into his delivery van so he could take it to the market.

"I heard there was a ribbon cutting," Big Al replied. "Vaccarelli told me yesterday that he planned to go."

"I saw him there. I went too," said Molinaro.

"How was it?"

"Really impressive. All the big shots were there, including the mayor," Molinaro replied.

"I can't believe it only took one year and forty-five days to build," said Michael, who was also scrubbing down the boats.

"There was a big race to get it done," Molinaro noted.

In the late 1920s, as New York's economy boomed like never before, builders were in a mad dash to erect the world's largest skyscraper.

The main competition was between 40 Wall Street's Bank of Manhattan building and the Chrysler Building, an elaborate Art Deco structure conceived by car mogul Walter Chrysler as a "monument to me."

Both towers tried to best each other by adding more floors to their design. The race really heated up in August 1929, when General Motors executive John J. Raskob and former New York Governor Al Smith announced plans for the Empire State Building.

Upon learning that the Empire State Building would be one thousand feet tall, Chrysler changed his plans a final time and fixed a stainless-steel spire to the top of his skyscraper.

The addition saw the Chrysler Building soar to a record 1,048 feet, but unfortunately for Chrysler, Raskob and Smith simply went back to the drawing board and returned with an even taller design for the Empire State Building.

When completed in May of 1931, the colossal Empire State Building loomed 1,250 feet over the streets of Midtown Manhattan. It would remain the world's tallest building for nearly forty years, until the completion of the first World Trade Center tower in 1970.

"When they came up with the idea to build the Empire State Building, it was supposed to be a symbol of the Roaring Twenties," Molinaro continued. "I find it ironic that it was completed during the Great Depression."

The Empire State Building was to house corporate offices, but it got off to a rocky start thanks to the 1929 stock market crash and the onset of the Great Depression.

When it opened, less than 25 percent of the building's retail space was occupied, earning it the nickname the "Empty State Building."

"The economy of the Roaring Twenties just couldn't last," Molinaro noted. "The stock market was well above par, and the industrial output was more profitable than ever, but the country was overdependent on its production industries, including ship-building docks and automobiles."

Big Al, now sixty years old, was in a hurry to get going. His four sons—Alfred Jr., thirty-six, Alessandro, thirty-four, Maximo, thirty-two, and Francesco, thirty—no longer worked with him. That meant he and Michael did everything, so it took longer to finish.

His sons now worked full time for Mangani, who teamed with the leader of Murder, Inc., Albert Anastasia, down at the docks in Brooklyn and Hoboken after the death of D'Aquila. Adolfo and Leonardo also worked for Mangani.

Big Al's younger brothers, Diego and Filippo, managed the family's construction business. They were also doing business with Mangani and the Mafia, though Big Al didn't know it.

***

The following evening, Big Al's entire extended family ate dinner together at his restaurant after closing hour, their nightly custom.

The Molinaros joined them, along with Lucky and Paul Vaccarelli.

"The Great Depression is really dragging on," said Molinaro.

"A lot of people are hurting," added Vaccarelli.

"As long as there's prohibition on alcohol, our family will be okay," said Alfred Jr.

"You got that right, Brother," said Alessandro with a smirk. "We can't keep up with the demand."

Hardened by the war and the burns they had suffered through, Alfred Jr. and Alessandro had eyes that were permanently dark and squinted. They very seldom showed any emotion. Their disposition was mean and somber.

"Bootlegging has been a game-changer," said Alfred Jr. "Guys like Capone are able to rake in up to one hundred million dollars each year thanks to illegal booze. We ship a lot of it to him."

Since Prohibition, criminal gangs ran amok, but they were mostly bands of street thugs involved in minor extortion and loansharking rackets in predominantly Italian, Jewish, Irish, and Polish neighborhoods.

In fact, before the passing of the Eighteenth Amendment in 1919 and the nationwide ban that went into effect in January 1920 on the sale or importation of "intoxicating liquor," it wasn't the Mobsters who ran the most organized criminal schemes in America, but corrupt political bosses, which is why Paul Vaccarelli and Tammany Hall were so successful.

New York, 1932

After the death of Masseria, who died of a heart attack, Lucky set up high-level networks of the Mafia, with five families in charge. He inserted Mangani as the boss of the Gambino crime family (which he would go on to run for twenty years), and he named Albert Anastasia as Mangani's underboss.

supposed to be LUCIANO

Lucky became the father of modern organized crime in the United States. He established the Commission, which is the governing body of the five Mafia families in the US.

Big Al's two oldest brothers, Adolfo and Leonardo, were initiated as "made men" in the American Mafia, meaning they were now full-blown members. So were their younger brothers, Diego and Filippo. Big Al's four sons were initiated as "made" members too.

"All my brothers and sons are now made men in the Mafia," Big Al complained one day over dinner to Lucky and Vaccarelli. "I don't like it, and I am worried."

"Listen," Lucky replied. "Remember how Pasquinelli did things? He did them the right way. He ran the Camorra like a mutual aid society. That's how I am going to go about it."

Big Al objected some more. "The Mafia in America is way more violent."

"That is absolutely not true," Lucky shot back. "The Mafia in Italy is just as brutal. However, under me, it will be controlled and even sanctioned."

Big Al half-heartedly nodded in agreement.

"Our friend Paul Vaccarelli here taught me how to set up legitimate businesses," Lucky continued. "That's how I want the Mafia in America to conduct itself. Like a business."

"What about when Mafia members step out of line?" Big Al asked.

"The purpose of the Commission is to oversee all Mafia activities in the United States and serve to mediate conflicts between families," Lucky said.

"But if that fails, Albert Anastasia will continue to run the enforcement division. The bottom line is that I can't have Mafia members running around town shooting people. Things like that give the Mafia a bad name."

Big Al sat back in his chair. His tense muscles relaxed.

"Lucky sounds like Supremo Pasquinelli when he talks like that," he said to Vaccarelli.

"You do know that Anastasia is one of my boys too?" bragged Vaccarelli.

Big Al stared at Vaccarelli. "You are just like a proud papa."

"I have been told," Vaccarelli said with a laugh. "They'll always be my boys."

"Who are the five Italian-American families, Lucky?" Big Al asked. *They weren't called these then*

"Mangani runs the Gambino Family, like I mentioned. The other families are Bonanno, Colombo, Lucchese, and Genovese, which I run."

The three men ate their dessert, which was spumoni, a molded gelato made with layers of different colors and flavors, containing candied fruits and nuts. After that, they smoked cigars.

"Don't worry about your brothers and sons," Lucky reassured his old friend. "Mangani will be good to them, and I'll keep an eye out as well. We believe in the old Mob customs that Pasquinelli practiced: honor, tradition, respect, and dignity."

Big Al crushed out his cigar stub in an ashtray on the table.

"I still wish they hadn't joined the Mafia." He stood up and put on his fedora.

"Look, I have to get home. Rosemary is very pregnant. Our baby could come at any time now."

As Vaccarelli and Lucky stood up too, one of Lucky's young associates charged into the restaurant.

"Big Al, I have an urgent message!" cried the associate. "Your wife, Rosemary, is in labor. You're needed at the hospital right away."

"I'll drive you," Lucky said.

Minutes later, Big Al blinked several times as he held a crying baby in his huge hands.

"It's a boy!" the doctor exclaimed.

"It's a miracle!" said Big Al's mother, Mary. "If only your father, Rocco, could have been here to see this day!"

At his age, no one, including Big Al himself, thought he'd be a father again.

Rosemary looked like her full heart was going to burst.

"I love you so much, Alfred. He is beautiful, just like his papa!"

"Do you have a name in mind?" asked Margie.

"I think we should name him after your father, Rosemary," said Big Al, who leaned down and kissed his wife.

"Really? That would be such an honor."

"Then it's settled. His name is Giuseppe!"

Big Al's daughters jumped up and down on their feet.

"A baby brother, I cannot believe it!" said Francesca.

"May I hold him?" asked Mary.

"Of course you can," Rosemary replied.

The nurse handed baby Giuseppe to Big Al's eighty-one-year-old mother, and she cradled him tenderly in her arms.

"Yes indeed, Rocco would be so proud," she said.

Big Al put his arm around his mother. He knew she missed his papa every day, even though decades had passed since the day he went missing out at sea.

Father DeBenedetti came into the room.

"Bravo, Rosemary and Alfred," he said, putting his hands together in prayer.

Mary walked over to the priest, who put his right hand on the baby and said a blessing. He ended the prayer with, "And thank you, God, that Giuseppe looks like his mother."

Big Al rolled his eyes.

"It's our turn to hold him now, Mother," Margie said as her sisters, Louisa and Olympia, continued to jump up and down.

Father DeBenedetti turned to Big Al.

"Let's go for a walk; give the ladies some time alone with the baby."

The two men walked outside and sat in a courtyard with neatly trimmed hedges and a rose garden.

"It's a wonderful day," said the priest. "How are you feeling?"

"Blessed."

"Missing Carmelita?"

"A little, yes. I never thought I would be starting over, but Rosemary is an exceptional woman."

"You're lucky to have found love twice, Alfred. Some people never find it."

Father DeBenedetti took two cigars from the pocket of his shirt underneath his priestly robe. "A vice or two never hurt anyone," he said and winked.

"Let's celebrate," said Big Al, reaching for one of the cigars.

"Giuseppe has been born into a suffering world," said the priest. "There's nothing great about the Great Depression that we're experiencing."

"You got that right," Big Al replied. "Business at the restaurant has definitely fallen off, but we do better than most because of our alcohol sales. The fishing is still good.

"We have had to cut back on the amount of fish we take in so nothing goes to waste at the market or restaurant. Our real moneymaker these days is the construction business."

"I heard," said Father DeBenedetti. "Seems the city fathers are pushing out construction contracts as a way to put people to work."

"Well, it's a great strategy," Big Al noted. "My brothers are very busy. In fact, they have added Luigi De Sio as a part-time worker."

"I heard Luigi recently sent for his entire family to come here from Italy," said the priest.

"That's true," Big Al agreed. "Once his sons arrive, the plan is to put them to work in the construction business."

"Excellent news," said Father DeBenedetti.

They puffed quietly on their cigars for several minutes, each thinking about how much better their lives were since coming to America.

"They say Hitler may soon run all of Germany," said Father DeBenedetti, breaking the silence.

"I am not so sure that would be a good thing," Big Al replied. "He seems possessed with hate."

"Hitler has been complaining a lot lately because the United States and other countries ended their aid to Germany, due to the Great Depression," said the priest.

"Our president was correct to do that," Big Al explained. "He has to take care of his people at home first."

"Well, Hitler says Germany has been one of the countries most affected by the Great Depression, because it was already suffering in the aftermath of the Great War, and that cutting off aid is like an act of war," the priest continued.

Big Al exhaled. "Hitler was a soldier in the war, and to him, all defeats are compounding."

"He'll likely seek retribution," Father DeBenedetti predicted.

"What does the Vatican have to say about that?" Big Al asked.

"Pope Pius XI met with Mussolini in the pope's study a few weeks ago," said Father DeBenedetti. "The subject of Hitler was discussed."

"What was said?"

"Hitler sees Mussolini as his role model. He keeps a bust of Mussolini in his office. A reporter mentioned this to the pope, who asked Mussolini if he feels the same way."

"And?"

"Mussolini said he sees himself as Hitler's big brother," said the priest.

"Hmmm," replied Big Al. "Not sure I'd claim Hitler as my brother."

"Do you remember Cardinal Daniel O'Reilly of the Catholic Archdiocese of New York?" asked Father DeBenedetti.

"He's your superior, the one who traveled with us to Italy for the meeting with the president and pope," recalled Big Al.

"He didn't do much work, just showed up for the photo opportunities."

"That's him," said the priest with a laugh. "He and I are traveling to Vatican City again next month. The pope is convening a meeting of people he trusts to talk about tensions in the world and people we need to keep an eye on, like Hitler."

"Smart idea," said Big Al.

"There's something else," said the priest.

"What?"

"The pope wants me to permanently relocate to Rome," shared Father DeBenedetti.

"Why does he want you to return to Italy?" asked Big Al.

"He wants me to be his aide in the Vatican."

Big Al's eyes flew wide open. "That's a promotion!"

Father DeBenedetti smiled. "Yes, it is."

"I think that is wonderful news!" said Big Al. "What a great way to cap off your superlative career."

"I'm excited but also sad."

"Why?" asked Big Al.

"You and your family are the closest thing I have to being my own family," said the priest. "I'll miss everyone."

"And we will miss you, but you have to take this promotion. The pope needs you. That is a very high calling."

The two men embraced.

"We will stay in touch, Enzio," said Big Al. "Do not worry about that. You cannot get rid of me that easily. Now, let us go back inside. I haven't held my baby son enough yet!"

New York, 1933

Big Al and Rosemary slowly walked to Central Park from East Harlem. Their baby was asleep in his wooden stroller.

"Have you seen the *New York Tattler*?" Rosemary asked.

"What in the heck is that?"

"It's a new tabloid newspaper."

"What's a tabloid newspaper?"

"A magazine that reports gossip about movie stars and other celebrities," Rosemary replied. "Sometimes there are odd stories about UFOs and stuff like that. Tabloids can be sleazy too."

"I see," said Big Al. "Any stories you want to share?"

"There was one I found fascinating, about a creature."

"A creature?" asked Big Al. "What kind of creature?"

"It's called the Loch Ness Monster," she said. "The creature was recently sighted in the Loch Ness Lake in Scotland."

Big Al burst out laughing. "What is the Loch Ness Monster?"

"Loch Ness is said to look like a dragon or a prehistoric monster," Rosemary said in a matter-of-fact manner. "Eyewitness reports date back to ancient times, but the recent sighting was the first in modern times."

"And the *New York Tattler* got the scoop," said Big Al, continuing to laugh.

"Yes, it did," said Rosemary. "The first written account of Loch Ness was in 565 AD. According to that long-ago report, the monster is a big swimmer."

"See, that's why I never learned to swim," said Big Al. "I am afraid of creatures in the water."

Rosemary playfully hit him with her shoulder.

"Every fisherman should know how to swim," she chided.

"Tell me more about this recent sighting," said Big Al.

"Last month, a road adjacent to Loch Ness was built, offering an unobstructed view of the lake," said Rosemary.

"A couple saw an enormous animal, and after crossing their car's path, it disappeared into the water.

"The incident was reported in a Scottish newspaper, and then retold in the *New York Tattler*."

"Which means it just has to be true," Big Al said with a smile. "Tabloid news. Very interesting stuff."

"Yes, it is," said Rosemary as she and Big Al sat down on a park bench.

"You say tabloids report on space aliens too?"

"Yes, but I don't believe in those," Rosemary said, leaning in and putting her head on Big Al's shoulder.

"So, you believe in sea dragons but not Martians. Makes perfect sense to me."

Rosemary playfully socked Big Al in the leg.

"There was another interesting story in the *New York Tattler*," Rosemary continued. It was about the new federal penitentiary out in California on Alcatraz Island."

"Now that one I have heard of," said Big Al. "The penitentiary is built on a rock in the middle of the ocean."

"Yes," said Rosemary. "The *New York Tattler* says Alcatraz is intended for prisoners who continuously cause trouble at other federal prisons, a 'last-resort prison' to hold the worst of the worst, who have no hope of rehabilitation."

"I know a lot of people who fit that description," said Big Al.

Rosemary stood up, leaned over the stroller, and took Giuseppe in her arms.

"I received a letter today from Father DeBenedetti," said Big Al. "Would you like me to read it to you?"

"Oh yes, please do share!" Rosemary exclaimed as she wrapped the baby tightly in a blanket.

Big Al took the letter from his coat pocket and read:

Dear Alfred,

My new position at the Vatican is great. I am an assistant to the pope and work on political matters.

We are keeping a close eye on Adolf Hitler, the new Chancellor of Germany. Hitler has banned all other political parties, turning Germany into a one-party state. He seems particularly against Jewish people and Catholics.

The pope is also concerned with Hitler's friendship with Mussolini.

Their friendship troubles the Holy Father because he has been working for several years to have a relationship with Mussolini. Now the pope wonders if that was a mistake.

Germany has quit the League of Nations, which is causing concern over

German intentions toward France and other European countries.

Hitler has also established something called the "Gestapo," which is a secret state police. We do not yet fully know what the Gestapo will be doing.

We have received intelligence that Hitler opened a concentration camp at Dachau, in southern Germany.

Dachau is a camp for political prisoners. The Vatican has received intelligence that Dachau could be a death camp where Jews are tortured and executed.

In addition to Jews, the camp's prisoners include members of other groups Hitler considers unfit for the new Germany, including artists, intellectuals, the physically and mentally handicapped, and homosexuals.

The population of Germany is around sixty million, of which almost all consider themselves to be Christians. There are forty million Protestants and twenty million Catholics.

At first, many Protestant Church leaders under German rule supported Hitler because he seemed to share their conservative values, but that changed when the German government prevented Jews from serving as clergy.

It also changed when the liberal fringe group within German Protestantism, the so-called German Christians, advocated for an Aryan, non-Semitic Christianity with Hitler's support.

The Nazi leadership urged Protestants to unite all regional Churches into a national Church under the centralized leadership of a well-known pastor and Nazi party member, who was appointed as Reich bishop.

We are also closely monitoring the Great Depression, which is a global problem. Across the globe, people are withdrawing their money from the banks.

One in four people are unemployed in America. Tens of thousands of people travel the road and rail in America, looking for work.

As I am sure you know, the continuing drought in the Midwest has turned the land into dust bowls.

Due to soil erosion, millions of people are leaving the Great Plains states because they can no longer earn a living from the land. The Vatican is concerned about this problem.

This is a dire time, Alfred. Hugs to Rosemary and Giuseppe.

Enzio

Chapter 10

THE PEACE ROSE

New York, 1935

That evening, Big Al sat with Luigi De Sio, Paul Vaccarelli, and Lucky Longo at the Madison Square Garden Bowl. They were attending a boxing match between heavyweights James Braddock and Max Baer.

"Does watching the fight make you miss boxing?" Big Al asked Vaccarelli.

"Not at all. I have to protect this handsome face," he joked.

"I've got five hundred dollars on Braddock," Lucky noted.

"That man can punch," replied Vaccarelli. "I think you'll win your bet, Lucky."

For fifteen rounds, the two American boxers beat up on each other. In the end, Braddock was the new champion, making Lucky a big winner.

"Steaks on me!" he exclaimed.

"Let's go to Rao's," said Vaccarelli.

Not Rao's for steak

At the restaurant, the men talked about world affairs and dined on osso buco, which is roasted veal shanks with vegetables and white wine.

A waitress took their picture, framed it, and put it on the wall.

"I see where Mussolini has gone to war with Ethiopia," said Luigi.

"It's true," Big Al answered. "Mussolini invaded Ethiopia to show the strength of his regime. The ill-equipped Ethiopians were no match for Italy's modern tanks and airplanes.

"Italy quickly captured the capital city, Addis Ababa. Mussolini incorporated Ethiopia into the new Italian empire."

"Now we know why Mussolini signed an agreement earlier in the year with France, in which neither would oppose the other's colonial claims," said Luigi. "He was laying the groundwork to attack Ethiopia."

"Tripoli and Cyrenaica saw the handwriting on the wall and got out," said Big Al. "The two Italian colonies joined together to become Libya. They wanted no part of Mussolini."

"Both Mussolini and Hitler are making calculated moves," Lucky noted.

"What kind of calculated moves?" Luigi asked.

"Hitler reinstated the German air force, rearmed his troops, and brought back the country's draft," Lucky clarified.

Italy/New York, 1936

Father DeBenedetti sat in a wingback chair in the study of the pope's apartment. He and Pope Pius XI sipped their tea.

"I am sending the Vatican's Secretary of State, Eugenio Pacelli, to the United States to meet with the president," the pope said. "He'll be the highest-ranking Catholic official ever to visit the US."

"What'll they discuss?" Father DeBenedetti asked.

"Eugenio will talk with President Franklin Roosevelt about the threat of communism, for starters," the pope replied. "I've also instructed him to discuss efforts to achieve diplomatic recognition of the sovereignty of Vatican City."

"How can I help?" Father DeBenedetti asked.

"You and Big Al proved yourselves to be invaluable when President Wilson visited the Vatican," the pope said. "Can you guys do it again?"

"Consider it done, Holy Father," Father DeBenedetti replied.

pretty unbelievable as the whole book

***

Cardinal Pacelli left Naples on October 1 aboard the Italian liner *Conte di Savoia*. He arrived in New York seven days later and was met by Father DeBenedetti, the Italian ambassador to the US, and the secretary of the embassy.

He delivered a brief statement to reporters, then went to the East Harlem home of Big Al and Rosemary, who hosted him for several weeks.

"What a beautiful view," said the cardinal as he looked out the big dining room window after dinner one evening.

"Thank you," Big Al replied. "We just bought this house last year. That view of the Harlem River was a major selling point."

Just then, young Giuseppe bounded into the room.

"Well, hello, little one," Cardinal Pacelli said. "What is your name?"

"Giuseppe," he replied. "I am four."

"You don't say. Four years old!"

"I am big now."

"Yes, you are," replied the cardinal. "Do you help your mother around the house?"

"Uh-huh."

"And do you help your father sometimes on his fishing boat?"

"Oh yes! I am the first mate. He's the captain."

Cardinal Pacelli rocked back and forth on his feet, the corners of his mouth turned up in a broad smile.

"Tell me, Giuseppe, have you heard of heaven?"

"Yes. That is where Mr. Molinaro went. He died."

"Ah, I see."

"My grandma Mary is there too. She died."

"Then you know two people in heaven."

"Yes. Papa says they are angels now."

"He is right," said Cardinal Pacelli.

"Do you know anyone in heaven?" the boy asked.

"Why, yes. God is in heaven. Have you heard of him, Giuseppe?"

"Yes."

"And who is God?

"Mama says God created everything. The stars. The moon. The Earth."

"You're a smart boy!" Cardinal Pacelli replied.

***

The next day after dinner, Cardinal Pacelli sat with Big Al on the balcony overlooking the river. They drank espresso and ate cannoli.

"Father DeBenedetti speaks highly of you, Alfred."

"Enzio is a good man. We go back a long time. He was my parish priest in Cava de' Tirreni. How is he doing in Vatican City?"

"He is a big help to the pope. His knowledge of American politics and Italian history is very important given how the world is today."

"He and I used to talk a lot about world politics," said Big Al. "But now that Enzio is gone, I don't really have anyone to talk with, certainly not Paul Vaccarelli."

"Who?"

"Paul, a former boxer and street gang leader, although he prefers to be regarded as a businessman."

Rosemary came out on the balcony and refilled their espresso.

"Dinner was wonderful, Rosemary," Cardinal Pacelli said.

"We're just so delighted you are here with us, Eugenio."

When she pulled the door shut behind her, Big Al stood up from his chair and walked over to the railing. He stared hard at the Harlem River, but his mind was someplace else.

"They say you are next in line to be the pope," said Big Al.

"Maybe, but Vatican politics are anything but predictable," Cardinal Pacelli replied.

"With the world possibly headed into a second war, who wants that headache?" Big Al probed.

"We're all called to put our talents to good use," said Cardinal Pacelli.

"I don't understand."

"Jesus once told of the Parable of Talents. Have you heard it?"

"No. Tell me this parable."

Cardinal Pacelli closed his eyes and recited it from memory:

> "For it will be like a man going on a journey, who called his servants and entrusted to them his property.
>
> "To one he gave five talents, which is a form of money, to another two, to another one, to each according to his ability. Then he went away. He who received the five talents went at once and traded with them, and he made five talents more.
>
> "So also he who had the two talents made two talents more.
>
> "But he who received the one talent went and dug in the ground and hid his master's money.

"Now, after a long time, the master of those servants came and settled accounts with them.

"He who received the five talents came forward, bringing five talents more, saying, 'Master, you delivered to me five talents; here, I have made five talents more.' His master said to him, 'Well done, good and faithful servant. You have been faithful over a little; I will set you over much. Enter into the joy of your master.'

"He also who had the two talents came forward, saying, 'Master, you delivered to me two talents; here, I have made two talents more.' His master said to him, 'Well done, good and faithful servant. You have been faithful over a little; I will set you over much. Enter into the joy of your master.'

"He also who received the one talent came forward, saying, 'Master, I knew you to be a hard man, reaping where you did not sow, and gathering where you scattered no seed, so I was afraid, and I went and hid your talent in the ground. Here, you have what is yours.'

"But his master answered him, 'You wicked and slothful servant! You knew that I reap where I have not sown and gather where I scattered no seed. Then you ought to have invested my money with the bankers, and at my coming, I should have received what was my own with interest. So take the talent from him and give it to him who has the ten talents.

"'For to everyone who has will more be given, and he will have an abundance. However, from the one who has not, even what he has will be taken away. Moreover, cast the worthless servant into the outer darkness. In that place there will be weeping and gnashing of teeth.'"

Big Al clasped both of his massive hands behind his head and leaned back.

"I get it," he said. "The moral of the story is that we all must invest our talents and put them to good use and not waste them."

"Well done, Alfred!" Cardinal Pacelli exclaimed. "Now, I must go to bed. I need my rest."

Rosemary showed the cardinal to his room.

"Is there anything you would like before turning in?" she asked.

"Perhaps a glass of milk?" he asked with a boyish grin.

"Of course!"

***

In the days and weeks that followed, Big Al was with Cardinal Pacelli nonstop.

They toured New York, where Cardinal Pacelli met with the president of Columbia University and celebrated a Pontifical Mass in St. Patrick's Cathedral. Then they went on to Boston, Philadelphia, and Washington, DC.

On November 5, Cardinal Pacelli, flanked by Big Al, met with President Roosevelt. They met at the home of Roosevelt's mother in Hyde Park, New York. Cardinal Pacelli asked Rosemary to accompany them because First Lady Eleanor Roosevelt would be joining them.

"The president will be in a wheelchair," Cardinal Pacelli cautioned them when they arrived at the Hyde Park home. "Don't be surprised. He hides his condition from the public."

Big Al and Rosemary were more stunned, however, when the First Lady answered the front door. They didn't have a butler. The Roosevelts were just like regular people.

"Greetings!" Eleanor said when they arrived. "Please, come in."

The First Lady had a commanding presence. She stood five feet eleven inches tall. Her dark-blonde hair and deep blue eyes were emphasized by the colorful afternoon dress she wore, made of rayon crepe, with puff sleeves, belted waist, and a large collar.

"Your dress is so pretty," said Rosemary.

"Thank you! I sewed it myself," Eleanor replied.

The president greeted them in his wheelchair.

"Ah, Cardinal Pacelli. It's a pleasure to meet you!"

"The pleasure's mine," said Cardinal Pacelli. "First, let me congratulate you on your reelection yesterday."

"Thank you. There is a lot of work that still needs finishing. The Great Depression isn't making my job very easy."

"I bet not," said Cardinal Pacelli. "The economy is simply awful everywhere. Mr. President, please allow me to introduce you to Alfred Tedesco, whom everyone calls Big Al, and his lovely wife, Rosemary."

"How do you do?" the president asked.

"Fine!" came the reply.

"Alfred and Rosemary are my hosts here in America," the cardinal continued. "They've been very gracious and accommodating. Big Al is touring with me too, helping with my arrangements."

"I like your dress," the First Lady whispered to Rosemary while the men exchanged pleasantries.

Rosemary wore an afternoon dress made of silk with decorative buttons, bows, and trapunto, a method of embroidery using quilting techniques to create puffy shapes and patterns.

"Why, thank you." Rosemary blushed. "I've only seen pictures of you before, Mrs. Roosevelt, and let me just say you're even more beautiful in person."

"Please call me Eleanor! While the men do their business before we eat, can I show you the rose garden?"

"I'd be honored," Rosemary replied.

So, as the men discussed world affairs, the two women walked outside to see the roses.

"I understand your husband is quite a successful businessman," the First Lady said.

"He's done very well since coming to America," Rosemary replied.

"Are you involved in those businesses?" asked Eleanor.

"I manage our fish store and the restaurant," Rosemary answered. "Alfred is an investor in many different things, including a construction business."

"I admire you for being involved," said the First Lady. "So many women cannot find their own purpose. They support their husbands but lose themselves in the process. Having one's own identity is important."

The First Lady stopped in front of a row of roses. They had light-yellow to cream-color petals. "This is the Peace Rose, formally called the Rosa 'Madame A. Meilland,'" she said.

"So beautiful!" Rosemary declared.

"Do you see how it's slightly flushed at the petal edges with crimson pink?" Eleanor asked.

"I've never seen this type of rose before." Rosemary looked at the delicate flower in awe.

"It was developed last year by French horticulturist Francis Meilland, who recently sent cuttings to friends in Italy, Turkey, Germany, and the United States to protect the new rose in the event of war."

"Ugh, the prospect of a second world war scares me," Rosemary replied.

"My husband will try everything he can to keep the United States out of it," Eleanor promised. "He's working hard to get us out of the Great Depression. A war would mess up his recovery plan."

"Does it look like the Great Depression will end anytime soon?" asked Rosemary.

"Eventually," replied the First Lady. "The president is creating new construction jobs. You may already know this since your husband is in the construction business.

"We've been building city parks, dams, bridges, anything and everything. Construction puts people to work."

Rosemary's face tightened, and her jaw became rigid.

"Is Hitler as horrible as they say?" Rosemary asked.

"He was devastated by Germany's defeat in the last war and would like nothing more than to avenge that loss," Eleanor replied. "There are credible reports that he's targeting Jewish people for extermination, which makes him horrible, yes."

"Our priest, Father DeBenedetti, used to say Emperor Napoleon I was a Devil on Earth because of how he persecuted the Church and literally dragged the pope from Rome."

"I've heard that story," answered the First Lady. "In the late spring of 1812, Pope Pius VII was a prisoner of Emperor Napoleon I, since 1809.

"They dragged him over the Alps, in precarious health, to Fontainebleau in France. The pope arrived at the gates of Fontainebleau Castle nearly a corpse."

"My husband says Hitler is even worse than Napoleon," Rosemary replied.

"Napoleon Bonaparte was only five feet six inches tall. Hitler claims to be five feet nine inches tall, but like his ego, that's inflated," Eleanor noted.

"Both of these short men overcompensate for being small, in my humble opinion."

Rosemary chuckled.

"Don't worry about Hitler. There's a big lady in the White House to make sure the big man in charge thinks logically, if you get my meaning?"

"I do, yes," Rosemary replied.

"Good!" Eleanor explained. "Now, let's go have lunch."

They ate for two hours. During their conversation, Cardinal Pacelli secured from President Roosevelt a promise to appoint a US envoy to the Vatican by 1940.

No such diplomatic link had existed since 1870, when the last envoy was killed during an Italian raid on the Pontifical States.

"For now, Father DeBenedetti is unofficially serving in that role, and he is doing a fantastic job," Cardinal Pacelli said.

"But we need to prepare his successor, someone who can work with both the president and the pope."

***

The next day, Cardinal Pacelli, Father DeBenedetti, and Big Al embarked on a five-day coast-to-coast air tour covering seven cities—South Bend, Indiana; Chicago; St. Paul; San Francisco; St. Louis; Syracuse; and New York City.

Meanwhile, in Spain, Fascism was getting its first real test as Francisco Franco and his Nationalist Party rose to power, touching off a Spanish civil war.

The two big-name Fascist dictators of the period, Mussolini and Hitler, decided to send supporters to help Franco.

The Church also fully supported Franco in the military uprising of 1936 against the Spanish Second Republic. Publicly, it was a nod to Mussolini by Pope Pius XI and their alliance.

A young man named Licio Lastra volunteered for the Blackshirts expeditionary forces sent by Mussolini in support of Francisco Franco's rebellion in the Spanish Civil War.

Lastra enrolled under the assumed name of Livio Gommina. He even enrolled in the Falange, the Spanish Fascist party.

Lastra fought with the Spanish foreign legion, the famous Tercio, which gathered the most violent elements of the international Fascist groups.

***

Later that year, Paul Vaccarelli died of a heart attack. His protégé Lucky Longo was arrested and successfully convicted for compulsory prostitution and running a prostitution racket. His sentence was thirty to fifty years in prison.

New York, 1937

"A letter came in the mail today for you, my dear," Rosemary said when Big Al arrived home after a long day of fishing.

"Who is it from?"

"Cardinal Pacelli. Open it!"

Big Al carefully took the letter from its envelope and read it out loud:

Dear Alfred,

I wish to thank you and Rosemary for your hospitality while I traveled in the United

States. We accomplished a great deal. There is much more yet to do, however.

Your understanding and appreciation of world affairs is remarkable. You have a keen sense of the politics at play in the world and the ramifications of certain actions should they occur.

The American people were smart to re-elect President Roosevelt for a second term. He is a wise man.

The Vatican still has a major problem with Benito Mussolini.

The Vatican has acted as a pillar of the Fascist regime while the pope frequently has called on the Fascists to serve the moral, social, and religious interests of the Vatican.

The support of the Vatican for Fascism was not weakened by the imposition of Mussolini's one-party dictatorship in 1925, when Pius XI still encouraged clerical support for the regime.

As I mentioned to you on your balcony in New York, Italy's relationship with Germany now threatens the continuing relationship between Pius and Mussolini.

When Hitler became German chancellor four years ago, in 1933, the pope secured a concordat with Nazi Germany.

However, Hitler was less accommodating than Mussolini was, and the Nazis frequently and deliberately violated the concordat.

A closer relationship between Germany and Italy developed this year. The pope fears that Italy might emulate Germany in persecuting the Church.

The pope has warned the Italian dictator against close links with Germany.

Early this year, Pope Pius XI decided that Nazism was a greater threat to Christian society than communism and issued a papal letter critical of Nazi Germany.

In particular, the following two actions this year by Hitler troubled the Vatican:

- He rearmed the nation and signed strategic treaties with Italy and Japan to further his ambitions of world domination.

- He held a secret meeting in which he stated his plans for acquiring "living space" for the German people. This means he plans to invade other countries.

We are trying to track everything that is going on.

However, our task is more difficult because Father Enzio DeBenedetti is suffering from colon cancer. The disease will eventually kill our mutual friend.

I am sorry this letter is so negative. Typically, I am an upbeat person, but these are unprecedented times.

We cannot afford to ignore the wrongs we see in the world or be afraid to shed a light on them because they make us uncomfortable.

Now is the time for good men to step up and meet the moment. A battle is taking place between good and evil.

Sincerely,
Cardinal Eugenio Pacelli

Big Al stared at the letter for several moments. He scratched his head and then cocked it sideways to look at his wife.

"Wow. That is a lot to digest," he said.

"That was something else, all right," Rosemary replied.

"Enzio's health sounds bad."

"Yes, it does." Rosemary lowered her head, sad to hear about their friend's health plight.

Big Al stood up and paced the room for several moments.

"Sounds like the Vatican made a bad deal in getting close with Mussolini."

"Mussolini sounds like he is Hitler's puppet," Rosemary replied.

Big Al sat heavily in a chair.

"When you and Eleanor were talking in the rose garden, Cardinal Pacelli told us some things."

"What did he tell you?"

"He said compromise with the Nazis would be out of the question. Cardinal Pacelli has strong opposition to the Nazi regime."

"Sounds like the Vatican isn't going to tolerate Hitler."

"You are right about that," replied Big Al. "Cardinal Pacelli called Hitler a 'fundamentally wicked person' and an 'untrustworthy scoundrel.'"

"That's definitely not mincing words," said Rosemary.

"Cardinal Pacelli went on to say that he is not a Nazi sympathizer and is convinced that the Nazis are a threat to the Church and the stability of Europe."

"Hey, I have an idea," Rosemary said with a smile. "Why don't I get Giuseppe up from his afternoon nap and then we take a stroll? Let's get some zeppoles!"

Zeppoles are Italian doughnuts made from pate a choux dough, the same one used for cream puffs and eclairs. These doughnuts also use water or milk with butter, flour, and eggs. Then, the dough is fried.

"You always have the best ideas," Big Al said. "But let's be clear, for me, the real treat isn't the zeppoles, it's getting to spend time with you and Giuseppe."

"Oh, Alfred," she exclaimed, grabbing his hand. "You say the sweetest things. How'd I get so lucky?"

Italy, 1938

The year got off to an ominous start when Hitler abolished the country's war ministry and created a new body with nominal oversight over the German army, navy, and air force.

In truth, Hitler now controlled the German military. In addition, Hitler dismissed political and military leaders considered unsympathetic to his philosophy or policies.

"He is gearing up for war," Big Al declared one morning over breakfast with Rosemary. He held a piece of toast in one hand and *The New York Times* in the other.

Rosemary poured them each a cup of coffee.

"Will you be fishing today? The weather looks really bad outside."

"No, not today. Too risky. Hey, here is a troubling story, Honey. Hitler met with the chancellor of Austria and threatened to invade. The chancellor yielded to German demands for greater Nazi participation in the Austrian government."

"Hitler is an insufferable bully." Rosemary sighed deeply.

"Hitler proclaimed that he plans to invade Czechoslovakia by October first," Big Al continued to read out loud.

"Winston Churchill, a member of the British Parliament, says his country and France will defend Czechoslovakia against Nazi aggression. He suggested that Britain may want to set up a broad international alliance, including the United States and the Soviet Union."

"Wait, he said that?" Rosemary asked.

"Yes," Big Al replied. "Why?"

"When I was talking with Eleanor in the rose garden, she said quite clearly that her husband would avoid being drawn into the war. His focus is on the economy at home."

"Well, clearly, this news article in *The New York Times* gives the impression that President Roosevelt is receptive to the idea of an international alliance against Germany," Big Al said.

Rosemary shook her head and pursed her lips.

"Something isn't right with that story," she said.

***

The next day, *The New York Times* reported that during a ceremony marking the unveiling of a plaque at Pointe de Grave, France, celebrating Franco-American friendship, American Ambassador William Bullitt said, "France and the United States are united in war and peace."

This led to much speculation in the press that if war did break out over Czechoslovakia, the United States would join the war on the Allied side.

That evening, during one of his "Fireside Chats," a series of evening radio addresses given by the president, Roosevelt said the news accounts were "one hundred per-cent wrong."

He declared, "The US will remain neutral."

"That sounds more like what Eleanor told me," Rosemary said.

"Mussolini made a speech today, in which he indicated that Italy is supporting Germany in the Sudeten crisis," Big Al said.

"Forgive me, Alfred, but what exactly is the Sudeten crisis?"

"The Sudetenland is the German name for the northern, southern, and western areas of Czechoslovakia that is inhabited primarily by German Bohemians, also known as Sudeten Germans," Big Al explained.

"These are ethnic Germans living in the Czech lands of the Bohemian Crown, an integral part of Czechoslovakia. Hitler very much wants to invade the Sudetenland.

"Churchill warned of grave consequences to European security if Czechoslovakia comes under attack. Soviet Foreign Commissar Maxim Litvinov made a similar statement today to the League of Nations."

"War is coming," Rosemary warned.

***

Several days later, in a vitriolic speech, Hitler defied the world and implied war with Czechoslovakia would begin any day. In response, the Polish army backed Germany by collecting along the Czech border.

That prompted the Soviet Union to warn Poland that if it crossed into Czechoslovakia, the 1932 nonaggression pact between the two countries would be void.

"Any day now," predicted Luigi De Sio.

"Yesterday, Hitler invited Mussolini, the French premier, and the British prime minister to one last conference in Munich," said Big Al. "We are just days away from Hitler's self-imposed October first deadline for his invasion of Czechoslovakia."

Rosemary served them coffee and *esse di Raveo*, traditional Italian cookies made with butter, sugar, eggs, flour, baking powder, and baking soda. Shaped in the form of an *S*, the cookie dough is baked until golden brown.

"Were the Czechs invited to this conference?" Luigi asked.

"Nope. The Italian, British, and French leaders agreed to Hitler's demands regarding annexation of the Sudetenland in Czechoslovakia," said Big Al. "They called it the Munich Agreement."

The Munich Agreement provided "cession to Germany of the Sudeten German territory" of Czechoslovakia. Most of Europe celebrated the agreement, because it prevented the war threatened by Hitler, by allowing Nazi Germany's annexation of the Sudetenland.

Hitler announced that the region of western Czechoslovakia, inhabited by more than three million people, mainly German speakers, was his last territorial claim in Europe.

***

On October 1, as promised, Hitler's troops and those from Poland marched into the Sudetenland.

The Polish government gave the Czech government an ultimatum: turn over the region within twenty-four hours, per the Munich Agreement, or suffer an attack.

The Czechs complied.

Polish forces occupied the region.

The agreement handed over to the Nazi war machine 66 percent of Czechoslovakia's coal, 70 percent of its iron and steel, and 70 percent of its electrical power.

In Nazi Germany, Jews' passports were invalidated, and those who needed a passport for emigration purposes were given one marked with the letter *J* (for "Jude" or "Jew").

Big Al and Rosemary—like most people in America—huddled around their radio at night to hear the latest news.

Winston Churchill of Britain, in a broadcast address to the United States, condemned the invasion of the Sudetenland.

"America and Western Europe need to prepare for armed resistance against Hitler," Churchill declared.

***

Two days later, *The New York Times* reported that the German government expelled twelve thousand Polish Jews living in Germany.

The Polish government accepted four thousand and refused admittance to the remaining eight thousand, forcing them to live in the no-man's land on the German-Polish frontier.

The New York Times reported the incident in the following way:

> The Munich Agreement, which according to British Prime Minister Neville Chamberlain purchased 'peace in our time,' was actually a mere negotiating ploy

by Hitler, only temporarily delaying the Fuhrer's blood and land lust.

***

On October 21, *The New York Times* reported that Hitler, "in direct contravention of the recently signed Munich Agreement," circulated among his high command a secret memorandum stating that they should prepare for the "liquidation of the rest of Czechoslovakia."

***

On November 9, the "Night of Broken Glass" occurred in Germany. Nazi activists and sympathizers looted and burned Jewish businesses.

During the all-night affair, Germany destroyed 7,500 Jewish businesses, burned 267 synagogues, killed 91 Jews, and arrested at least 25,000 Jewish men.

Chapter 11

DEVIL ON EARTH

Italy, 1939

White smoke emanated from a special chimney placed atop the Sistine Chapel. The voting was over, and a new pope had been chosen.

White smoke meant there was a successor to Pope Pius XI, who had passed away.

A large crowd gathered outside the chapel. People were buzzing over the speed in which the College of Cardinals had named Cardinal Pacelli as the new pope.

He took the papal name Pope Pius XII. His selection came after only one day of deliberation and three ballots, the fastest vote ever.

"New Pope Selected," screamed the headline of the *la Repubblica* newspaper.

Seventy-four-year-old Father DeBenedetti was the first person to greet Pope Pius XII when he arrived at the Apostolic Palace, his new residence.

"Congratulations, my friend!" the priest declared.

Tumorous growths had developed in Father DeBenedetti's large intestine and were taking a toll. He was frail, and his face was ghostly white.

"Thank you, Enzio. I cannot believe how fast it happened," said Pope Pius XII. "I made them vote again because I didn't believe they got it right."

"The College of Cardinals couldn't have picked a better person," said Father DeBenedetti.

He took out a handkerchief from inside of his black robe as he began to cough. Bent almost double, he coughed some more into it, leaving a red bloodstain behind when he pulled it away from his lips.

"That's not good," said Pope Pius XII, pointing at the handkerchief.

"I know," said the priest. "Lately, I've been in bed most of the time. But today, I wanted to be here to greet you on this special occasion."

"Thank you, but we need to get you back to bed."

"First, I have something to give you," said Father DeBenedetti. "Before he died, Pope Pius XI asked me to pass along this letter."

The priest handed Pope Pius XII an envelope affixed with the papal seal. The new pope cocked his head back and looked at the envelope for a moment.

He didn't expect anything from his predecessor because he'd died unexpectedly of a heart attack in the Apostolic Palace.

Slowly, the new pope opened the envelope and pulled out a handwritten letter. He quietly read it to himself:

To my successor,

Behold, you have assumed a noble place within the Church and its rich history. Congratulations!

However, know this: Danger awaits you.

I warn you, keep your guard up. Unwittingly, I made a pact with a Devil.

In developing ties with Benito Mussolini, I opened the door for a dark prince to enter. His name is Adolf Hitler, and he is a Devil on Earth.

Several months ago, Hitler paid me a secret visit. He demanded to know the three secrets of Fatima.

Hitler believes that at least one of the secrets is a foretelling of the future ruler of the world, and that it has to do with him.

Why Hitler believes this, I do not know.

Much to his ire, I told Hitler that the three secrets of Fatima were unknown to anyone but Sister Lúcia, who has not yet revealed them.

I said she plans to eventually write them down in a memoir. That really upset him.

Recently, I received a letter from José Alves Correia da Silva. He is the bishop of Leiria, Portugal.

He said Nazi soldiers have been in the municipality of Tui, Spain, just across the northern Portuguese border, where Sister Lúcia lives in a convent.

He believes they're after the secrets of Fatima.

Upon learning about the Nazi soldiers, I instructed that Sister Lúcia use extreme caution. She should limit leaving her convent, and restrict her visitors to just immediate family members.

Given that we do not know what the three secrets of Fatima say, I strongly recommend that you make it a priority to find out during your papacy.

If another world war occurs, which I believe will happen at any time, it would be nice to know what those secrets have to say.

Sincerely,
Pope Pius XI

Pope Pius XII made the sign of the cross. "I will dispatch three Swiss Guards immediately to Tui and post them in front of Sister Lúcia's convent," he said to Father

DeBenedetti. "She must be protected, for the good of the Church."

***

Two days later, Father DeBenedetti died. Also dying was Licio Lastra's older brother, Raffaello, who was a soldier in the Spanish Civil War, just like Licio.

His death upset Licio and left him even angrier for the rest of his days.

***

World War II broke out six months later.

Italy, 1940

In Rome, Mussolini and Hitler secretly met. Licio Lastra was with them and listened as they planned their strategy in the aftermath of the Germans occupying France.

"In October, Italy will launch an invasion of the Kingdom of Greece from Albania," Mussolini reported.

"Sounds good," said Hitler. "Invading the Kingdom of Greece will send a positive nationalist message to the Germans living in the Balkans that I support them. Germany has a growing influence there."

"Then it is agreed!" Mussolini exclaimed.

The two men shook hands.

Even though Mussolini thought Hitler and Nazism were uncultured and simplistic, a budding alliance was in place between the two men regardless.

"Is there anything else we need to discuss?" Mussolini asked.

"Yes," said Hitler, looking over at the twenty-one-year-old Lastra.

"Let's send this young man to find that nun who knows about the three secrets of Fatima. Time for her to break her silence."

"You believe the secrets are a foretelling of the future?" Mussolini asked.

"I do, and let me tell you a story that explains why, Benito. When Napoleon Bonaparte was a small boy, the Madonna appeared in the tiny village of Pontmain, France, during the height of the Franco-Prussian War in 1871, which, by the way, was also around the same time as Italian unification.

"Two brothers, ages twelve and ten, saw the Madonna, from their barn. She was wearing a blue gown covered with golden stars and a black veil under a golden crown. Their sisters, ages eleven and nine, joined the boys and were also able to see the Madonna.

"Soon, other village children were able to see the Madonna, but not the adults. That evening, ironically, the Prussian forces stopped their advance. They retired the following morning. The war inexplicably ended."

"What had happened?" Mussolini asked.

"The commander of the Prussian forces said he felt as if he should no longer continue," Hitler replied.

"I believe the spirit of the Madonna came over him, and that it was related to Her appearance to the children."

"I understand now," Mussolini concluded. "You believe the three secrets of Fatima might say something

235

about this current war, just as Her appearance during the Franco-Prussian War probably played a part."

"Exactly," Hitler agreed.

"I'm ready to go!" Lastra told them eagerly.

Hitler walked over to the young man and put his hand on his shoulder.

"Get those secrets, Licio. Our future depends on it, I'm certain of that."

***

In Vatican City, Pope Pius XII desperately needed an aide after Father DeBenedetti's death, someone he could trust. The priest had been a valuable asset to the Vatican.

The pope reached out to President Roosevelt.

"Mr. President, when we dined together several years ago at your mother's house in New York, you promised to appoint a US envoy to the Vatican."

"Yes, I did."

"Can we do that now?" Pope Pius XII asked.

"Absolutely," said the president. "With the war raging, I need a person in the Vatican to give me intelligence."

"Thank you. Would you mind asking Big Al if he's interested? He knows the Italian language, understands the ways of the Church, and is astute in world affairs."

"I cannot argue with any of that," said President Roosevelt. "Besides, Eleanor adores his wife, Rosemary. I don't want to get on Eleanor's bad side."

The two men chuckled.

"I'll call Big Al tonight and let him know the country needs him right away!" Roosevelt said.

***

The following week, Big Al arrived in Rome with Rosemary and eight-year-old Giuseppe.

Chapter 12

THE THIRD SECRET OF FATIMA

Rome, 1941

On a dark and stormy night, Adolf Hitler's men came to the pope's residence in search of the Third Secret of Fatima, which they believed had been delivered several days earlier to Pope Pius XII on behalf of Sister Lúcia. Rain pounded Rome.

The Milizia Volontaria per la Sicurezza Nazionale, commonly known as the Blackshirts or *squadristi*, knocked on the door and waited for it to open. When it did, the soldiers pushed their way inside.

"What is this? I must object," said the bespectacled Pope Pius XII.

A shadowy figure dressed in a trench coat and wearing an officer's uniform stepped forward from the darkness.

Licio Lastra was now a liaison officer between Hitler and Mussolini.

"Give me the Third Secret," Lastra demanded.

The pope gazed into the hateful eyes of the shadowy figure.

"The Vatican is neutral in this war. There's no cause for this," said the pope.

"Give me the Third Secret of Fatima, now!" Lastra repeated.

"I don't have it," insisted the pope. "The nun hasn't written it down yet."

"I don't believe you."

"But it's the truth."

"Sister Lúcia was told three secrets by the Madonna in 1917," Lastra insisted. "My sources tell me you recently received her memoir."

"She only had two of the three secrets of Fatima delivered to me," the pope countered. "I do not have the Third Secret of Fatima."

Lastra took a cigarette out of his trench coat and lit it. Slowly, he took a long, deep drag.

"All right, Pope. I will be back, soon. Have the Third Secret of Fatima in your possession when I return, or there will be hell to pay."

And with that, Lastra and the Blackshirts slipped back into the tumultuous night.

The pope turned and went directly to his study. He typed an urgent telegraph to Big Al, whom he had dispatched a week ago to the nun's convent in Spain to convince her to share the Third Secret.

Dear Big Al,

I'm afraid we are out of time. You must get Sister Lúcia to tell you the Third Secret of Fatima right away or mankind may never recover. Hitler has made obtaining it a cornerstone in his war effort. We cannot let him get to it first!

Sincerely,
Pope Pius XII

***

A week earlier, when the two secrets had been delivered to Pope Pius XII as part of the nun's memoir, he had reviewed it with Big Al.

The First Secret of Fatima was a vision of hell. The nun wrote about it in the following way:

> As the Madonna was finishing a prayer, She opened her hands and a mysterious holy light radiated out. The light seemed to open the earth, and it revealed a very terrifying scene.
>
> Only for a brief moment, we saw the fires of hell, the ugliest demons, and the poor charred and transparent burning souls of people suffering tremendously.

Beads of sweat had built up on Big Al's forehead, and the room spun a little. Both he and the pope remained quiet for several minutes as they thought about the First Secret of Fatima.

"I talked to the bishop who brought the memoir to us on behalf of Sister Lúcia," the pope said. "He told me the three children who encountered the apparition were extremely thankful that the Madonna promised they would go to heaven, otherwise, they felt they would have died of fear and terror."

The pope then made the sign of the cross, pushed back his glasses, and let out a heavy sigh. He read the Second Secret of Fatima out loud:

> "You have seen hell, where the souls of poor sinners go. World War I is going to end, but if people do not cease in offending God with their nonbelief, a worse war will break out during the pontificate of Pius XI."

The pope turned to Big Al.

"We know that already happened," he said. "In 1938, Hitler began his aggressive quest for more living space. A second world war began with Nazi Germany's attack on Poland the following year."

Pope Pius XII looked back down at the Second Secret and finished reading it. "Our Lady calls for a blessing of Russia to Christianity; otherwise, Russia will spread her errors throughout the world."

The pope got up from his chair and paced back and forth.

"There's another problem," he said.

"What can be worse than what we've already heard?" Big Al asked.

"This isn't all of it," the pope replied. "Sister Lúcia didn't write down everything."

"You mean there is more?"

"She left out the Third Secret of Fatima."

"Why?"

"She said the final secret is too disturbing."

"She thinks people can't handle knowing it?" Big Al furrowed his brow in concern.

"That's correct."

"What do you think it could be about?" asked Big Al.

"The Third Secret of Fatima is probably a foretelling of the future," the pope predicted.

"Hitler wants it and has been ransacking Church property searching for it because he doesn't believe Sister Lúcia didn't write it down. He thinks the Vatican has hidden it."

In Polish territories that the Nazis had annexed to Greater Germany, Hitler systematically dismantled the Church in his pursuit of the Third Secret of Fatima—arresting its leaders, exiling its clergymen, and closing monasteries, convents, and churches.

Many clergymen were tortured for information and even murdered. Polish clergy were killed in concentration camps.

"You must go right away to Spain and convince Sister Lúcia to write down the final secret," the pope had instructed Big Al, who packed a suitcase with warm clothes, because it was December and very cold. Big Al also packed a handgun.

***

When he'd arrived in Spain, Big Al went directly to see Sister Lúcia, who'd had an urgent request of him. She wanted the pope to perform a blessing of the Soviet Union.

"Why?" asked Big Al.

"The Madonna wants it done because Russia has turned its back on Christianity," she said.

The pope, however, declined the request. He was too busy dealing with problems being created by the budding relationship between Hitler and Italian leader Benito Mussolini.

***

Five days later, on December 7, 1941, the Japanese bombed the American fleet at Pearl Harbor, and the United States officially entered World War II.

Spain, 1942

Big Al was doing everything he could to convince Sister Lúcia to write down the final secret, but she was resisting. The US envoy had been in Spain for a year now, trying to convince her.

Another person was also in Spain trying to get his hands on the Third Secret of Fatima—the shadowy underworld figure Licio Lastra.

Every day, he watched as people came in and out of the nun's convent, but he couldn't figure out a way to get to Sister Lúcia. She never left the place.

One afternoon, however, much to Lastra's surprise, Sister Lúcia made a rare excursion out of the convent. His eyes flew wide open when she walked out the front door and to a grocery store just a few blocks away.

The nun smiled warmly at the grocer when she entered the store. When she reached for two ruby-red apples, a hand grabbed her wrist.

"Got you!" yelled Lastra.

Sister Lúcia started to cry out for help, but the shadowy figure placed his other hand over her mouth.

"If you want to live, you will come with me."

But before the thug could make another move, three Swiss Guards stepped in.

"Let her go!" they commanded.

Lastra released his grip on Sister Lúcia, who turned and ran back to the convent, never looking back.

"Mother Superior, help!" she cried out.

The convent's stout head nun opened the front door.

"What is wrong, child?" the Mother Superior shouted.

"A bad man just tried to abduct me! If it weren't for the three Swiss Guards that Pope Pius XII sent to protect me, I'm sure I wouldn't be here."

The Mother Superior slammed the door shut and bolted it.

Minutes later, Licio Lastra had returned and was hiding out in front of the convent again. He, too, had run when the Swiss Guards approached him.

Now what am I going to do? he wondered.

The shadowy man crouched behind a tree and watched for several hours as nuns and priests entered the convent.

He perked up when an exterminator showed up. Lastra had an idea.

***

The next morning, Lastra knocked on the front door of the convent.

"Who is it?" asked the Mother Superior.

"Exterminator," the shadowy figure replied.

"Oh, I am glad you're back," said the Mother Superior, opening the door. "We saw three mice yesterday running through the kitchen. The nuns screamed something fierce!"

Lastra quickly scanned the place, but he remained quiet.

"Come on in," invited the Mother Superior. "Let me take you to the kitchen."

Once there, Lastra observed three women preparing breakfast. Two nuns were mixing batter in a bowl while another was cooking eggs, sausages, and bacon.

"Sister Jacinta's famous pancakes are on the menu this morning," said the Mother Superior. "I will not let any mice ruin that occasion!"

The shadowy man noticed when Sister Lúcia entered the kitchen. She went to a cupboard, got out a glass, and poured herself orange juice.

The nun was short, standing no taller than five feet. A large cornette covered her jet-black hair.

"Good morning, Sister Lúcia," said the Mother Superior. "I see you are the first one for breakfast, as usual."

Sister Lúcia smiled and left the kitchen. Lastra followed her. The thirty-four-year-old nun took a seat at a table in the empty dining room.

"Excuse me, sir," the Mother Superior called out to the impostor. "You haven't put out any mouse traps."

In the next instant, Lastra came up from behind Sister Lúcia and put her in a headlock.

The Mother Superior cried out and dropped the pitcher of orange juice that she was holding.

"Someone, help!" the stout woman cried out.

"Everyone, remain calm," Lastra demanded. "The nun is going to tell me about the Third Secret of Fatima. You, Mother Superior, are going to help. Go get a piece of paper and a pencil. Write down what she says."

The Mother Superior stood frozen. Her head was spinning so fast that she could not get her feet to move.

"Go, now!" Lastra howled. The head nun raced into the kitchen and then came back, huffing and puffing, with the items in hand.

"Now, talk!" Lastra said to Sister Lúcia, who was turning blue from the force of his arm against her neck.

"Please, release your pressure. I cannot breathe," said Sister Lúcia.

Lastra realized the nun was right; he was choking her too hard. He relaxed his grip and looked around the room. The three nuns who had been preparing breakfast were now huddled in a corner, sobbing.

In a dark corner of the room, Lastra thought he saw a tall shadow move. He blinked several times.

Are my eyes playing tricks on me? he thought.

When he turned away, Big Al emerged from the darkness and pointed his pistol dead aim at Lastra.

"Let her go," he said.

"Who are you?" the shadowy man replied.

"I am a person you should not mess with," said Big Al. "If I can carry a refrigerator on my back up six flights of stairs—which I can, by the way—Lord knows what I can do to your scrawny body."

Lastra stepped back. He pulled Sister Lúcia up from her chair by her neck. They both walked backward toward the front door. Big Al slowly kept pace, with his gun still pointed at the shadowy man.

"My papa taught me how to use this pistol, and I am deadly with it, Mister," he warned.

"Is that right?"

"Yeah, that's right. I can shoot the eyes out of a squid from forty yards away."

"Who even does that?" Lastra replied as they inched closer to the front door. Just then, Lastra released Sister Lúcia and pushed her toward Big Al, who stepped sideways so that they wouldn't crash into each other.

The thug bolted out the door. Big Al tucked the pistol inside his pants and gave chase.

Lastra was small and slender, only 140 pounds. Nevertheless, what he lacked in size, he more than made up for in speed.

After two blocks, he left Big Al far behind.

Big Al walked back to the convent, where he found a defiant Sister Lúcia telling the Mother Superior what she would do if Lastra showed his face around there again.

"I'll stick his nose in a mouse trap!"

The Mother Superior, visibly shaken, would have none of it.

"Oh no, you won't, Sister Lúcia! You are lucky he did not hurt you. Oh, sir, thank you so much! If it weren't for you, who knows what would have happened!"

Big Al pulled up a chair at the dining room table and sat down. He motioned for Sister Lúcia to do the same.

"Look, this goon is not going to stop until you have written down the Third Secret of Fatima.

"I am begging you, please, write it down and let me give it to the pope. Once you do that, I will let the word slip out that the Vatican has all three secrets. That will get the thug out of your life."

"I can't do that."

"Why not?" replied Big Al, burying his face in his large hands.

"The Madonna told me not to share the Third Secret of Fatima yet. There is a date in which I'm to tell the world, but it isn't now."

Big Al shook his head.

"I can't leave here, Sister Lúcia, until you write down the Third Secret of Fatima."

"Well, you are going to be here a long time, then," she replied.

***

Soon, it was Christmas. During his Christmas Day sermon, the pope strongly denounced the growing Holocaust. Giuseppe and Rosemary attended Mass in the Sistine Chapel when Pope Pius XII delivered his fiery message.

The New York Times supported the sermon with an editorial that day that read,

> The pope cried out for the hundreds of thousands who, without any fault of their own, sometimes only by reason of their nationality or race, are marked down for death or progressive extinction. The voice of Pius XII is a lonely voice in the silence and darkness enveloping Europe this Christmas. He is about the only ruler left on the continent of Europe who dares to raise his voice at all.

In Germany, the *Gestapo Report* interpreted the pope's Christmas message differently, saying,

> In a manner never known before, the pope has repudiated Nazism. It is true, the pope does not refer to Nazism in Germany by name, but his speech is one long attack on everything we stand for. Here he is, clearly speaking on behalf of the Jews.

At the same time as the news reports, Sister Lúcia became deathly ill with a lung issue.

"Sister, if you die, the Third Secret of Fatima dies with you," Big Al reasoned. "Surely, that was not the intent of the Madonna."

Sister Lúcia looked up at Big Al from her bed.

"Alfred, you are persistent," she said. "Of all the people in the world, I find it interesting that God would send *you* to retrieve the Third Secret of Fatima from me."

Big Al reeled at the comment.

"What do you mean by that?" he asked.

"Alfred, you are a fine man. However, we both know that you have Mafia connections."

Big Al dropped his head. He tried to explain, but she cut him off.

"Alfred, no one is more determined than you," she said with a smile. "You have a big heart. So, in that regard, God sent the perfect person to me."

***

In the final days of December, Sister Lúcia agreed to write down the Third Secret of Fatima. She put the single sheet of paper in an envelope, sealed it, and handed it to Big Al.

"Take the secret to my local bishop," she instructed. "He will go with you to Vatican City to deliver it to the pope. Tell the Holy Father not to read the Third Secret of Fatima until closer to 1960, at which time it will become clearer."

Chapter 13

ENEMY ALIENS

Italy, 1943

As if tensions weren't already running high in Rome during the war, five hundred American bombers dropped 1,168 tons of bombs on railway yards on the entire working-class district of San Lorenzo in July.

Three thousand Italians died in the raids.

The recent Nazi surrender at Stalingrad marked Germany's first major defeat, and an Allied victory in North Africa enabled an invasion of Italy.

Mussolini was on the brink of being driven out of power.

"We are losing the war," Mussolini complained to his aide, Licio Lastra. "The Italian people are losing faith in me."

Hitler increasingly gave inflexible orders whereby German armies stood their ground in tactically hopeless positions. Surrender was not allowed, under any circumstance.

On the Eastern Front, the cold, snowy weather was aiding the 5.5 million Soviet troops, which outnumbered the three million German forces.

"How can I help?" Lastra asked Mussolini.

"Go see Hitler and find out how he plans to turn this mess around!"

**

On July 25, while Lastra was away in Germany, Allied Forces ousted Mussolini. General Pietro Badoglio replaced him. The general wanted peace so the fighting could stop.

"General Badoglio is a sellout," Lastra complained to Hitler.

"No matter," Hitler replied. "Benito will be back. This is just a temporary setback."

**

On October 13, Italy signed an agreement to officially become part of the Allied Forces. The next day, Big Al walked from his residence in Rome to Vatican City, a four-mile trek that was part of his daily routine.

People screamed and cheered and waved flags in the streets.

"The Italian people are happy," Big Al said to Pope Pius XII when he arrived for work at the Vatican.

"Joining the Allied Forces has brought them joy because they believe that the war will be over soon," the pope replied. "But the public is misinformed."

Big Al was wide-eyed. "How so?"

"Italy will not be a neutral party and stop fighting," said Pope Pius XII. "The country will have to continue fighting in the war, except the Italians will now be fighting for the other side."

The pope was right. Later in October, Italy declared war on Nazi Germany. In response, Hitler decided Germany would have a hostile takeover of Rome.

There were already German soldiers stationed in Italy before the switch in loyalty, so the Führer held the upper hand. Italian soldiers and civilians tried to defend the city against the Germans in a battle at the Porta San Paolo, but they failed.

In all, 597 Italian men and women died trying to save Rome from the invasion.

The Germans took over Rome, beginning a nine-month occupation that included hunger, deprivation, and oppression.

People were tortured and imprisoned. Others were sentenced to death.

Big Al, his wife, Rosemary, and his young son, Giuseppe, fled to the Vatican, where Pope Pius XII took them in and made certain they were protected.

The Nazis imposed a seven p.m. curfew on citizens and hung posters around the city with new rules that were punishable by death.

The gestapo took over a former apartment building called Via Tasso and used it as the Nazi headquarters and prison. The headquarters was a place where Italian people died.

The Via Tasso was directly next to a boys' boarding school, and the children could hear the screams of tortured prisoners through the walls.

Hitler also had a plan to force the new Italian government's hand by starving citizens from food and much-needed supplies.

The plan stumbled, though, when forty-six-year-old Lucky Longo, who had been deported back to Italy from the US, saw a German soldier push an elderly Italian woman to the ground one day while she was carrying groceries.

"They might as well have pushed my own mother," Lucky fumed to Big Al, who had to restrain the Mafia leader from going after the offending soldier.

Lucky's answer was to use his Mafia connections to smuggle food to Italian residents.

But he had no answer when Big Al's three daughters were arrested shortly thereafter in New York and placed in an internment camp.

***

Late one night, Big Al turned to the pope for help.

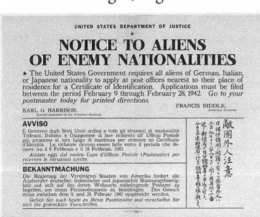

"The US government has taken my daughters!" Big Al informed Pope Pius, who was dressed in a long flannel nightgown with a night cap.

The pope rubbed the sleep from his eyes.

"What's the reason?" asked the Holy Father.

"They have been designated as enemy aliens," complained Big Al.

"What?"

Big Al handed the pope a letter that he'd received only a few hours ago. It said the envoy's daughters—Francesca, Giovanna, and Paula—had been taken into custody by the US Office of Navy Intelligence.

During World War II, Italian and German agents were entering the United States through New York, making the docks susceptible to sabotage.

In response, the US was arresting people thought to be responsible and putting them in internment camps.

"Darn it, I just got through dealing with a similar issue," said Pope Pius XII.

"You did?" asked Big Al. "What do you mean?"

"Have you heard of a baseball player named Joe DiMaggio?" asked the pope.

"Who hasn't?" said Big Al. "He is a superstar for the New York Yankees."

"Joe recently wrote me a letter," the pope said.

"The American government confiscated his dad's fishing boat in San Francisco. Commercial fishing is a big part of his dad's livelihood, so Joe was very upset."

"Why was his dad's boat confiscated?" Big Al asked.

"Joe DiMaggio's dad was born in Italy and immigrated to America. The US Customs and the Immigration and Naturalization Service was worried he could be a spy."

"What? A spy? His son is one of the greatest ballplayers in America! That's nuts."

"The US government is worried about all Italian Americans who work around the docks," said the pope.

"They don't want people counting military and cargo ships at anchor or monitoring their sailings. Italians like the senior DiMaggio—and now your daughters—are seen as possible spies."

"That's a load of crap," countered Big Al.

"So even though Joe DiMaggio's father has been a fisherman for decades, just like me, he is no longer allowed on San Francisco's ocean?"

"That's right," the pope replied. "He's also confined to a small area of travel within San Francisco."

"His son has a restaurant in San Francisco that overlooks the bay!" Big Al exclaimed. "It makes absolutely no sense."

"Thousands of Italian-American, Japanese-American, and German-American citizens are being harassed, imprisoned, and denied their rights as citizens merely because of their heritage," said Pope Pius XII.

Big Al clenched his fists and punched the air. His long, jet-black hair fell over his eyes.

"The government is really worried about spying, which is why they cut a deal with Lucky," the pope continued.

"What deal?" Big Al narrowed his eyes.

"Lucky was in prison, right? Did he ever tell you why he was released and deported back to Italy?"

Big Al shook his head.

"He cooperated with US officials," said the pope.

"They wanted to know what goes on down at the docks, and Lucky told them from his prison cell."

"That's why he was deported?" Big Al asked.

"Yes! The US Navy contacted Lucky because of his Mafia connections at the ports. He provided the names of Sicilian Mafia members, among other information. In exchange for his intelligence, the Navy suspended Lucky's prison sentence and deported him back here, to Italy.

"The feds even gave Lucky's intelligence a name—Operation Underworld."

"I had no idea," said Big Al. "But this is different. All three of my daughters were born in America! They are US citizens! How can the US government put them in an internment camp?"

"Hey, I'm not saying I agree with it," the pope replied.

"What's the difference between what the Nazis are doing—putting its own people in concentration camps—and what the American government has done to citizens like my daughters?"

Big Al raked his hands through his hair in frustration.

"From my intelligence, there's a big difference," said the pontiff.

"Nazi concentration camps are actually death camps. In America, people aren't being killed in internment camps."

"But they are being held against their will, and that's not right!"

Pope Pius called out to his butler.

"Dante, please bring me the telephone and dial the number for President Roosevelt."

A minute later, the president was on the phone.

"Holy Father, how may I help you?" the president asked.

"Hello, Franklin. We have a problem. Big Al's daughters have been arrested and put in an internment camp."

"What?"

"Can you please do something right away to remedy this situation?" asked the pope.

On the other end of the line, the president lost his cool. When Britain and France declared war on Germany, he'd asked J. Edgar Hoover to create a Custodial Detention List.

The FBI director had included people he deemed to be pro-communist, anti-Fascists, pro-Nazis, and even some Jewish refugees.

There were a lot of complaints with the list, however.

"That Hoover," the president muttered to himself. "I warned him after the DiMaggio fiasco to take better care about checking the list. How in heaven's name did Big Al's daughters get on there?"

After venting, the president came back on the line and calmly addressed Pope Pius XII again.

"Your Holiness, this issue will be corrected immediately."

"Thank you, Franklin," the pope replied. "That's a relief. We can't have our envoy distracted. There's too much work to do. By the way, can I suggest that all American-born Italians, such as Big Al's daughters, be removed from the list?

"I think you'll agree that a blanket classification of Italians as 'subversives' is blatantly unfair."

"Oh, I agree with you, all right. There's going to be hell to pay for this slipup."

***

In Europe, Lastra was also fuming.

"I cannot believe Italy has switched sides in this war!" he exclaimed.

Lastra responded by switching his personal allegiance from Italy to Germany.

Hitler, still believing Germany would eventually win the war, took Mussolini out of Italy and gave him rule over his own German puppet state, called the Italian Social Republic, popularly and historically known as the Republic of Salò.

German troops helped maintain the territory.

Hitler then named Lastra as the official liaison in Salò between the Fascists, the secret police of Salò, and the Schutzstaffel, a major paramilitary organization under Hitler and the Nazi Party.

The shadowy figure, Lastra, established himself as a torturer, a skill he learned from the Nazis in Germany.

***

Several months later, while eating cannoli—tube-shaped shells of fried pastry dough filled with a sweet, creamy filling, usually containing ricotta—Big Al and Lucky watched as another German soldier shoved a young Italian girl and her mother.

The soldier took their bags of food and tossed them to a pack of wild dogs roaming the streets.

Lucky's face flashed hot. He stood up, fists clenched. Big Al rose with his friend. He put his massive hands on Lucky's shoulders and pushed him back down.

"Wait," Big Al said.

A young man came running out from the grocery store to help the mother and her daughter after the soldier walked off. Lucky watched the soldier go, never taking his eyes away from him.

"Let it go, Lucky. Let it go."

Lucky twisted his face, smoothed out wrinkles on his jacket that were not even there, and adjusted the fedora on his head that wasn't in need of adjusting.

"If this were New York, I'd pop a cap in that jerk. You don't treat women like that."

"You have to bite your tongue for now," said Big Al.

"I don't see why." Lucky glared at the now-empty street.

"Did you hear what happened to the people in Porto who fought back?" Big Al raised his eyebrows.

"The rural farming village? What happened?" Lucky asked.

"A group of partisans got mad, just like you, and they killed a small number of German Nazi soldiers who were raiding the farmers and stealing their property," Big Al said.

"Good for them!"

"The partisans believed they were far enough away from the city for the Nazis to never figure out who was to blame for the soldiers' deaths.

"However, Italian Fascist sympathizers knew, and they told one of Hitler's henchmen, a guy named Licio Lastra. He hung the partisans in the center of Porto for everyone to see."

Lucky's eyes narrowed to slits.

"If I ever come across that guy Lastra, I will knock him out."

"No!" Big Al replied. "The Nazi resistance in Italy has to work quietly, and in secret. That's how it works.

"We use secret code words and meet in the shadows, passing along secret information that will help the Allies win the war."

"Who are some of the resisters?" Lucky asked.

"Many of the leaders in the resistance movement are priests. For example, Father Maurizio from the Fatebenefratelli Hospital on the western side of the Tiber Island in Rome is busy all day intercepting the radio signals of the Germans in his secret room in the basement of the facility."

"Wow," Lucky said. "The Mafia could use a guy like him."

"Father Maurizio takes the German information and passes it along to the leaders of the Italian Air Force."

Lucky took off his hat and wiped away the perspiration that had built on his forehead. Even though it was March, the weather was unusually warm.

Then he pulled a skeleton key out of his pocket and flipped it in between his fingers, a nervous habit.

"Why do you always play with that thing?" Big Al said, eyeing the skeleton key.

"The key brings me good luck. It's gotten me out of a lot of tight spots."

Big Al shook his head. "Say, Lucky, have you seen the posters around the city?"

"No, what do they say?" Lucky asked.

"They warn people that for every Nazi soldier who is killed by a member of the resistance, ten innocent Italian citizens will be shot."

"That's certainly enough to silence people," Lucky replied.

The two men continued to observe the German soldiers who were patrolling around St. Peter's Square.

"I don't get it," Lucky said. "Isn't Vatican City its own independent nation?"

"It is," Big Al replied. "There was a treaty made early in the war. Pope Pius XII wanted to remain safe from military attack under any circumstance and have the power of a sovereign nation."

"Then how can Hitler just take the city over?"

"Hitler broke the pact. Before the Nazis took over the city, the pope and I burned a lot of documents."

"Did the pope ever think about fleeing?" Lucky asked.

"Never. Pope Pius XII will not leave Vatican City and abandon his duties. When the Germans came to occupy Italy, the pope increased his personal army from one hundred men to a whopping four thousand. He was determined to stop the Nazis from getting anywhere near him."

"So, the pope is now a prisoner in the Vatican?" Lucky said.

"Essentially, yes, he is," Big Al replied. "Just as Pope Leo XIII considered himself to be a prisoner in the Vatican during the reign of Napoleon Bonaparte, and just as his successor, Pius IX, considered himself to be too, after the Pontifical States were taken away from him."

***

Later in the month, the Germans launched a second bombing attack on Vatican City. One employee of the Vatican died.

In response, a group of rebels, including Lucky and his Mafia pals, decided to take out as many Nazi soldiers as possible. The rebels dropped a bomb in the middle of the city while hundreds of Nazi soldiers gathered to run their drills.

Forty-two German soldiers died, and sixty were injured. Ten Italian civilians who were nearby when the bomb went off also died.

Lastra was outraged by the counterattack.

"I will kill fifty Italian civilians for every one German killed," Lastra announced.

He suddenly remembered the public poster, which he wrote himself, so he reduced the number back down to ten Italian civilians for every one German killed, as it was originally.

Lastra, though, could only capture three of the people who were actually responsible for the bombing, so he purposely targeted Jewish people for punishment, even though they were not involved in the plot.

In the end, seventy-five Jewish people were included with the 335 Italians chosen to die.

Lastra also made sure to include some women and children in that mix. The German soldiers ordered them to march to the Saint Callixtus catacombs, where the victims were pushed into a mass grave.

Many of the people were still alive as the Nazis dumped dirt over their bodies. The event came to be known as "The Ardeatine Massacre."

***

A short time later, Masons gathered secretly in the basement of an abandoned building in Rome. Eighteen-year-old Carlo Martinelli sat quietly as a nonmember at the meeting.

He listened intently as leaders of the secretive organization attempted to recruit new members.

Participation in the Masonic Grand Orient of Italy was on the rise again now that Mussolini was no longer the leader of Italy.

"Who here knows our recruiting slogan?" asked the Mason who was leading the meeting, known as the grand master.

Martinelli's hand shot up.

"Yes, you there," said the grand master.

"All you have to do is ask," Martinelli replied.

"Bravo! You are correct," said the grand master. "Members must ask to join. They cannot be otherwise approached. The question is, why are you here?"

"I want to be part of a fraternity of brothers," said one man.

"Excellent," replied the grand master. "There are many benefits to that, especially for businessmen."

A man wearing wire-rimmed glasses in the back of the room raised his hand. "May I ask a few questions?"

"What sort of questions?"

The man took a notebook out from his coat pocket. He looked over a long list of questions that he'd prepared in advance of the meeting.

"First, why is the relationship between Masons and the Church so complex?" the man asked.

The grand master took a step back and gave the man a sideways look.

"Masonry is not a religion, though our members are encouraged to believe in a Supreme Being, or 'Grand Architect of the Universe,'" the grand master replied.

"That leads me to my second question. If Masonry is not a religion, as you say, then why have so many clergymen gotten involved in your organization since the end of the nineteenth century?"

The grand master said nothing. He just stared at the questioner.

"In the twentieth century, there has reportedly been a large number of senior clergymen who are Masons," the questioner continued.

The grand master shook his head but still said nothing.

"Pope Leo XIII condemned Masonry as 'a deceitful and crafty enemy.' Why do you think he said that?" asked the man.

The grand master walked to the back of the room and stood in front of the questioner.

"Sir, are you here today to join us or to denigrate us?"

The man continued with his line of questioning.

"It's not just the Vatican that condemns Masonry. So do many Lutherans, Evangelicals, Pentecostals, Baptists, and Orthodox followers of the Holy Synod of Greece.

"Even the Mormons condemn Masonry. Why do you think that is?"

"Who are you?" the grand master asked.

"I am a reporter for *la Repubblica*, the newspaper published in Rome."

"Get out!" said the grand master. "This is a meeting, not an interview, and you're not welcome here."

"Yes, okay, I understand," countered the reporter. "However, please answer this question: Why does the Vatican say the Church and Masonry can never be reconciled?

"Is it because Masonry treats all religions as inferior to its Gnostic wisdom?"

The grand master cut the reporter off.

"I told you, we are not a religion."

"My final question: What is 'the Craft'?"

"Get out! Guards, show this man to the door."

When the reporter was gone, Martinelli raised his hand again.

"Yes," said the grand master with trepidation in his tone.

"Why did you let that man bother you so much?" Martinelli asked.

"Because he was mischaracterizing the intentions of Masonry."

"In my opinion, Masonry should encourage its members to be active in other religions, so as to change how those religions operate."

"Not a bad idea," replied the grand master.

"Who cares if the Church and other religions have an issue with Masonry?" Martinelli continued.

"That's their problem. If a Mason wants to become a priest, why stop him? Is it the job of Masonry to prevent a person from also being active in other religions?

"Why not indoctrinate those religions with your philosophy?"

"Well, I suppose you have a point."

"We agree, then? If a Mason wants to be a priest, he should be encouraged. If he wants to be a Presbyterian minister, encourage him. If he wants to be the pope, encourage him.

"What is the harm to Masonry?"

The grand master put his hand on Martinelli's shoulder.

"Son, our motto is that members only have to ask to join us. Are you asking today?"

***

The following week, Martinelli entered a Catholic seminary, the Society of Jesus, to study for the priesthood. He joined fifteen other young men in training at the religious order based in Rome.

"You are studying to be Jesuits!" a priest roared at them on a hot evening.

He leaned in and poked his finger into the chest of one of the seminarians.

"How do you not know the name of the Superior General of the Society of Jesus?"

The seminarian blushed.

"That would be like not knowing the name of the pope," the priest continued.

Carlo Martinelli raised his hand.

"Sir, I know the name of the Superior General," he boasted.

The priest stepped toward the young Martinelli.

"Tell me."

"His name is Jean-Baptiste Janssens, and he is the twenty-seventh leader of the Jesuit order."

The priest fixed his gaze on Martinelli, and the corners of his mouth raised.

"Bravo, Mr. Martinelli. I am impressed. However, I would expect nothing less from you. Your reputation precedes you."

The priest dramatically spun around and turned his back to Martinelli. He walked a few steps, then swirled back around again, his robe spinning spectacularly.

"Kudos to men like Mr. Martinelli here, who forgo wealth in order to pursue the richness of a Jesuit life instead."

The priest bowed to Martinelli. Then he continued with his animated lecture.

"Jean-Baptiste Janssens is indeed our Jesuit leader. He is to be addressed as 'Father General.' However, you will hear some refer to him as the 'Black Pope.' Why?"

Carlo Martinelli raised his hand again.

"Because his outfit is black, in contrast to the white garb of the pope."

The priest clapped. "Bravo!"

He walked to his desk and picked up a book with a melodramatic flair.

"Gentlemen, I am going to shake your faith! How many of you have heard of the writings of Father Pierre Teilhard de Chardin?"

No one raised their hand.

"Father Pierre is a Jesuit, a scientist, a religious man, and a progressive in every sense of the word," the priest continued.

"He has taken it upon himself to reconcile Darwinian evolution and Catholic theology."

Martinelli's mouth dropped.

"This revolutionary has resolved the differences between religious truth as proposed by the Church and scientific 'fact' as proposed by Darwinian evolution," said the teacher.

"But instead of hearing it from me, why not let Father Pierre explain?"

Father Pierre stepped out of the shadows. "Hello, gentlemen. How are you doing this fine evening?"

Carlo Martinelli looked closely at the Jesuit priest. He was young. His face was unshaven with mostly peach fuzz rather than a masculine beard.

The priest's hair was long and uncombed.

"If one thing defines us as Jesuits, it's that we are very innovative and tied to reality."

Martinelli sat a little taller in his seat, more attentive.

"What increasingly dominates my interest is the effort to establish within myself and define around me a new religion—call it a better Christianity, if you like—where the personal God ceases to be the great monolithic proprietor of the past to become the Soul of the World, as called for by the stage we have reached, both religiously and culturally."

Martinelli's thoughts raced back to Masonry and its understanding of God as an abstract "Great Architect of the Universe."

Is that the same thing as the "Soul of the World?" he wondered.

"I have a vision of great hope—the hope that faith in Christ and a scientific approach to the world can be brought together," said Father Pierre.

"I look at science and Christian faith as being connected, not separate."

A seminarian raised his hand.

"Father, are you not taking the Divine element out of religion and becoming preoccupied with the human?"

"My vision abolishes the places where souls are supposed to go after death: hell, purgatory, heaven," Father Pierre replied.

"The idea is that souls dominated by evil and unrepentant cease to exist upon death; there is no punishment but the annihilation of that soul, while those that have been redeemed from evil will be taken up into beatitude of living in the presence of the Cosmic Christ—the Creator of the Universe."

Martinelli's heart was pounding, and a huge smile came across his face. With his eyes wide, Martinelli raised his hand.

"Yes, go ahead," said Father Pierre.

"If I understand correctly, what you are saying is that unrepentant souls are annihilated and will not take part in the banquet with the Cosmic Christ.

"With the death of the body, their journey is finished."

"Correct. The Church must not simply seek to affirm its primacy and authority but rather, join with other religions in presenting to the world the Universal Christ, Christ in human-cosmic dimension, as animator of evolution."

Young Carlo Martinelli nodded his head in agreement. *A one-world religion. A new world order!*

Chapter 14

MAFIA CASINOS

Italy, 1947

That evening, Lucky joined Big Al and his family for dinner, which he did quite often. He told them that he and the American Mafia had recently gathered in Cuba for the Havana Conference.

"Since I can longer go to the United States, my goal is to create an empire in Cuba," Lucky revealed. "That's why we met there."

The Havana Conference kicked off an era in which the Mob funneled dirty money into Cuba to build casinos and hotels, which in turn generated the funds used to facilitate the corrupt political system led by Cuban President Fulgencio Batista.

At the conference, delegations representing crime families throughout the United States attended at the Hotel Nacional. Decisions made in Havana resonated throughout US crime families during the ensuing decades.

Lucky was still in charge of New York's Genovese crime family, running it from Italy. To welcome him back from exile and acknowledge his continued authority within the Mob, all the conference invitees brought Lucky cash envelopes that totaled more than $200,000.

They were given to him at dinner the conference's first night. Singer Frank Sinatra provided the entertainment.

Lucky also received a suitcase containing $2 million, his share of the US rackets he still controlled.

"What did you guys discuss at the conference?" Big Al asked.

"We discussed important Mob policies, rules, and business interests," Lucky replied.

"The most pressing items were the Mob-controlled Havana casino interests and leadership and authority within the New York Mafia."

Lucky then turned to look directly at Big Al. "We also talked about the West Coast operations of the new Flamingo Hotel."

Big Al squirmed in his seat. The last time he'd thought about the Flamingo was a month ago, when his sister in New York, Margie, called in a panic, reporting that their two younger brothers, Diego and Filippo, hadn't been seen in weeks.

"You remember the Flamingo Hotel, don't you, Al?" teased Lucky.

The diplomat's face flushed. "I thought my brothers were dead."

"What happened, Lucky?" Giuseppe asked.

"Unbeknownst to your papa, I'd asked Diego and Filippo to quietly go to Las Vegas to help Bugsy Siegel with our new Mafia-owned casino."

"Why did you send them?" Giuseppe asked.

"The Flamingo opened December twenty-sixth of last year at a total cost of six million dollars," Lucky noted.

"But in the first week, it lost three hundred thousand dollars. I asked Diego and Filippo to straighten things out. They're smart when it comes to business."

"Why didn't the grand opening go well?" Rosemary probed.

"Bad weather kept many of the expected Hollywood guests from arriving," Lucky explained.

"Plus, the hotel was not finished, so gamblers had no rooms at the hotel. They took their winnings and gambled elsewhere."

"Ouch," said Big Al.

Lucky shook his head and sighed. "We had to shut the Flamingo down and regroup. Diego and Filippo fixed things, and then we did a grand reopening on March first under a new name—The Fabulous Flamingo."

"Have things gotten better?" Rosemary continued.

"Yes, The Fabulous Flamingo reopened to a profit of two hundred fifty thousand dollars. The hotel still needed to be finished, but this time, the results proved far better."

But Lucky hadn't shared the full story with them. That could be found in the *Las Vegas Review Journal*, which reported that Bugsy Siegel had been stealing money from the casino early on.

"Bugsy Siegel, owner of the new Fabulous Flamingo Hotel, murdered," read the headline in the newspaper.

Rome, 1950

Now seventy-nine years old, Big Al decided it was time to retire. He'd been serving as the US president's special envoy to the Vatican for ten years, but with World War II long since over, the Italian immigrant was ready to go back to New York.

Pope Pius XII paid the entire family a visit just days before they were to leave. Pope Pius XII removed his red shoulder cape—called a "papal mozzetta"—and took a seat at the dining room table. He fidgeted and tapped his foot time after time on the floor.

"All packed up and ready to go?" the pope inquired.

"Yes, we are," Big Al replied.

"I have received some troubling information," the pontiff continued.

"What information?" asked Big Al.

"Our enemies have a plan to capture the Church."

"Who are these enemies?"

"Masons."

"And why are they against the Church?" Big Al probed.

"Masons belong to a secret brotherhood that wants radical Church reforms," the pope replied.

"Masonry puts all religions on equal footing and makes no distinction between Catholicism and Protestantism, or between Christianity and Islam, or any monotheistic religion, for that matter.

"What I'm saying is that all monotheistic religions are of equal value under Masonry. Ultimately, they want a one-world religion."

"And you are concerned that these Masons really have figured out a way to capture the Catholic Church?" Big Al queried.

"Yes, but I just don't know how they plan to do it."

Big Al stood from the table. He ran a hand through his thick, gray hair.

"Holy Father, my family and I are leaving. I don't know how to help you with this problem."

The pope put a hand on Big Al's shoulder.

"Remember when you brought back the Third Secret of Fatima from Spain?" Pope Pius XII asked.

"Yes."

"Sister Lúcia told us not to open it at that time, so I asked you to hide it in your villa. You locked it away in your safe. I think now is a good time to read it. Maybe it will shed some light on what our enemies are planning."

"Good idea," Big Al agreed.

"Go get it."

Big Al rushed out of the room. A few moments later he returned with an envelope in his hand.

"Let's read it together," the pope directed. When they were done, both men were left visibly shaking.

***

That evening, Lucky treated Big Al and his family to a goodbye dinner. They went to his favorite restaurant, La Campana, which opened in 1518 and offered traditional Roman cuisine, including *coda alla vaccinara*, artichoke *alla giudia*, roast lamb, *coratella*, and *cacio e pepe*.

As was his custom, Lucky requested a seat next to the big dining room window so he could see who came into the restaurant, an old mobster trick.

However, he did not notice the shadowy figure that had arrived before them and was already seated in a darkened corner.

"I wish I was going back to New York with you," Lucky said. "But the US government won't let me."

"There's nothing wrong with Rome, Lucky," Rosemary reassured him. "Besides, I hear you're seeing a young Italian dancer who performs at some of the better nightclubs around Rome."

Lucky's face turned red.

"Lucky Longo, are you blushing?" Rosemary teased.

"Forget about it. It's just a little hot in here."

"How are the casinos in Las Vegas doing?" asked Big Al, throwing a lifeline to his embarrassed friend.

"Very well," Lucky said. "Since the early 1940s, Mafia families from New York, Cleveland, Kansas City, Milwaukee, and Chicago have had interests in Las Vegas casinos."

Lucky went on to explain that in order to build casinos in Las Vegas, the Mafia got loans from the Teamsters Union pension fund, a union they effectively controlled and used legitimate front men to build casinos.

When money came into the casinos' counting room, hired men skimmed cash. Then, they delivered the stolen money to their respective bosses.

The money went unrecorded, but the estimated amount was in the hundreds of millions of dollars.

Lucky sprinkled Romano cheese on his spaghetti and meatballs and took a swig of wine.

From the corner of his eye, he thought he saw someone lurking in the shadows.

"How is Pope Pius XII taking the news that his envoy is leaving?" Lucky asked.

"Not so well," Big Al replied.

"Today, he told us about an organization called Freemasonry and how it is a threat to Christianity. He is really troubled by it."

"Oh, I know all about Freemasonry," Lucky replied.

"You do? How?" Rosemary asked.

"My grandfather told me about it. At the turn of the nineteenth century, during the French Revolution, my grandfather was living in Sicily, where an Italian sect of Masons known as the Carbonari, or 'charcoal burners,' emerged.

"My grandfather was a charcoal burner. That is how he made his living."

"How were the Carbonari involved with Masonry?" Giuseppe asked.

"The Carbonari was an offshoot of Freemasonry, and its members were part of a secret society advocating liberal and patriotic ideas.

"They possessed an overt political agenda. In the 1800s, they were a strong force of revolutionaries that fought for Italian unification."

Lucky looked over to where he had seen someone in the shadows earlier, but the person was no longer there.

"Like Masonry and other secret societies of the age, the Carbonari had an initiation ceremony, complex symbols, and a hierarchical organization," Lucky said.

"Their members were recruited mainly from the nobility, officeholders, and small landowners.

"After 1815, the lodges spread rapidly among those dissatisfied with the post-Napoleonic settlement, especially among the middle classes, which were favored under French rule.

"Although there were Carbonari lodges throughout Italy, their main centers were in central Italy—which at the time were designated as the Pontifical States—and in the south, where your family is from, Al."

"Around Naples?"

"Yes," Lucky replied. "The bottom line is this: Freemasons have been successful for a long time at influencing events and society as a whole.

"But people don't trust Masons because everything they do is shrouded in secrecy."

After they ate dessert, Lucky paid the bill.

"I'll meet you outside," he said. "I need to use the restroom before we head back."

"Sure, no problem." Big Al pushed his chair back and got to his feet. "We'll wait for you outside."

Big Al, Rosemary, and Giuseppe stood on the street corner and waited for Lucky. There were no streetlights, so it was very dark.

Suddenly, Big Al felt an arm grab him from behind.

"Don't move," a harsh voice instructed.

Rosemary screamed.

The man pointed a gun at her. "Scream again and he dies," said the attacker, who then repositioned the gun next to Big Al's head.

"What do you want?" Big Al kept his voice steady and calm.

"My sources within the Vatican tell me that you and the pope read the Third Secret of Fatima today. I want to know what it says."

"Honestly, I don't really understand what it said."

"Nonsense," replied the attacker. "You just don't want to tell me."

"Well, that's true. Even if I understood it, I wouldn't tell you. Who are you, anyway?"

The shadowy man swung around and faced Big Al.

"You don't remember me?"

Big Al's eyes flew wide open.

"You!"

"So, you do remember me!" declared Licio Lastra.

"How could I forget? You're the man who attacked Sister Lúcia at her convent while dressed like an exterminator."

"I could have had the Third Secret of Fatima way back then if you hadn't gotten in the way!" Lastra complained.

"Now talk or I will shoot you right here on this curb, and then I'll go shoot the nun—right after I get her to tell me the secret."

But before Big Al could say another word, he heard an awful sound. *Whack!*

Lastra crumpled to the ground.

"I knew that rat was up to no good when I saw him creeping around in the restaurant," said Lucky, who'd hit Lastra over the head with the butt of his revolver.

"I told you I would knock Lastra out if I ever saw him. Now, let's get out of here."

"What about him?" asked Big Al.

"Don't worry about him. My men will have a 'talk' with him when he comes around."

***

One month later, with Big Al and his family back in New York, communist North Korea invaded South Korea.

Chapter 15

LIKE FATHER,
LIKE SON

New York, 1952

Big trouble was brewing in the world. The United States tested the first hydrogen bomb at the Marshall Islands in the Pacific Ocean. Fascist-led Argentina was also testing a bomb, as was the United Kingdom and Soviet Union.

The Korean War had been underway for two years, pitting the United States and its United Nations allies against the communist powers under the influence of the Soviet Union and the People's Republic of China.

From her convent, Sister Lúcia grew increasingly concerned about the conflict in Korea.

In one particular meeting that was widely published in English and Spanish publications, Sister Lúcia emphasized that whole nations risked "disappearing from the world" as a result of the pope ignoring her requests to bless the Soviet Union.

Her warning unsettled people, so Pope Pius XII mentioned the Soviet Union in a blessing later that year. However, he did not perform the ceremony with all the bishops of the world, which Sister Lúcia said was a requirement the Madonna had been very clear about.

The nun openly criticized the blessing and called it a failure.

On behalf of the pope, the Vatican's press office countered her criticism by saying Pope Pius XII had recently blessed the Soviet Union by a letter.

"A letter won't do!" Sister Lúcia argued through the media.

These back-and-forth exchanges in the press between Sister Lúcia and the Vatican continued to alarm people all over the world.

Public pressure mounted for the pope to release the Third Secret of Fatima. He responded by saying it wasn't time.

New York, 1953

Big Al's youngest son, Giuseppe, was twenty-one years old and restless. He'd lived in Italy with his father and mother during World War II and was fascinated by world affairs.

These days, he was particularly interested in what was going on with the Soviet Union.

Joseph Stalin, the country's leader, was engaging in an anti-Semitic campaign. He accused a group of predominantly Jewish doctors from Moscow of a conspiracy to assassinate Soviet leaders.

This was accompanied by publications of anti-Semitic character in the media, which talked about the threats of Zionism (protection of Israel, a Jewish nation) and condemned people with Jewish names.

Many doctors, both Jews and non-Jews, were promptly dismissed from their jobs, arrested, and tortured to produce admissions.

Later, the Soviets said there was a lack of evidence and the case was dropped. Soon after that, the entire thing was declared to have been fabricated.

Big Al could see that his youngest son was drawn to such world events and that he was having trouble adjusting to life in New York. Giuseppe had no interest in the family businesses, which were prospering better than ever.

The restaurant did not provide enough mental stimulation to him, nor did the fish store or the boats.

As a boy Giuseppe had loved going out on the boats with his older brothers, but they were now Mafia members and were not fun to be around.

Giuseppe was a lot like Big Al in that he liked political strategy. He likened it to a chess game, only the moves made by politicians were not a game. They had very real consequences.

While growing up in Italy, Giuseppe watched as Pope Pius and Big Al stopped Hitler, one of history's most formidable madmen. They were cunning and brave. Giuseppe wanted to be just like them. He longed for it.

Giuseppe did not find enjoyment in the activities that other young men his age engaged in, such as going to a New York Yankees baseball game in the Bronx or a boxing match at Madison Square Garden.

Perhaps because he had been exposed to so much of life's horrors at such an early age, he found banality in life's simple pleasures.

Giuseppe saw a bigger picture than most people his age. He was drawn to solving the world's problems.

Giuseppe was not motivated by money.

He also did not share his brothers' lust for the mean streets of New York.

At night, as Giuseppe washed dishes at the family restaurant, his brothers would go out and rough up anyone who they thought needed it, particularly longshoremen.

Fighting was part of their Mafia activities, but Giuseppe did not condone it. That was how his older brothers operated in East Harlem, however.

By his way of thinking, the Tedescos were rich, so why not share the wealth, even with longshoremen?

Furthermore, Giuseppe had a kind personality, and he did not want anyone to get hurt if it could be avoided.

He liked to make people feel good. He felt bad when they were in any kind of pain.

Big Al increasingly took notice of his youngest son's way of thinking.

He also worried that because of Giuseppe's honest nature, he might tell the truth if the police ever interrogated him about his brothers' Mafia activities.

Giuseppe needed to go away from New York.

Despite his advanced age, Big Al was still politically connected. He called upon new Republican President Dwight D. Eisenhower for a favor.

He asked President Eisenhower to appoint Giuseppe as the US Ambassador to Italy.

"Mr. President, my son Giuseppe learned a lot while I was a special US envoy to the Vatican. I think he could be a real asset to you and the country."

"What do you have in mind?" President Eisenhower responded.

"Why not appoint Giuseppe to be the US ambassador to Italy? He already has a relationship with Pope Pius XII, and he knows the politics of the country, having spent most of his young life in Italy."

Eisenhower agreed. After everything Big Al had done for his country in the past, particularly for the Republican Party, the president did not think twice about appointing Giuseppe.

Besides, ever since Big Al had returned to New York, the country suffered from a lack of intelligence in Vatican affairs.

The prior president, Harry S. Truman, complained that when Big Al retired in 1950 the country had lost its best spy.

"I don't know what is happening in Europe without him in Rome," Truman complained.

"I don't know what's happening inside the Vatican, and you can't have that when the pope is one of the most powerful people in the world."

Truman was right—Big Al had known everything that was going on when he had been an envoy in Rome, particularly during World War II.

For his part, Giuseppe was excited to return to Italy. Despite being so young, he was more than qualified for the job. He was astute politically beyond his years.

***

On the day Giuseppe left for his new job in Rome, Big Al took his son aside.

"I have been hiding the Third Secret of Fatima in New York, here with us," Big Al said.

"I want you to take it with you. Protect it from the Church's enemies."

Perspiration ran down Giuseppe's forehead. His shoulders felt heavy.

"Maybe I should read it," the young man suggested.

"No, don't," Big Al warned.

"As long as you possess the Third Secret of Fatima, you are also in great danger. Should you be caught with it, your only chance of survival will be to plead ignorance."

Vatican City, 1958

Pope Pius XII passed away in October and was replaced by Pope John XXIII, who had big plans for rejuvenating the Church. He summoned Giuseppe to his study.

"My predecessor left a note for me," said Pope John XXIII. "He said you are hiding the Third Secret of Fatima."

Giuseppe clasped his hands together. "I've locked the secret away in a safe, just as my papa did."

"What does the Third Secret of Fatima say?" Pope John XXIII asked.

"I don't know," Giuseppe replied.

The new pope threw his head back in surprise.

"You mean to tell me that you haven't read it, Giuseppe?"

"That's correct. My papa warned me against reading it. He said my life would be in danger if I knew what it says."

The pope's mouth dropped.

What can it possibly say? the new pope wondered.

"When I summoned you here, I asked that you bring the Third Secret of Fatima with you," the pope said. "Do you have it?"

"Yes, Holy Father," answered Giuseppe, and he handed it over.

The pope carefully took the one-page letter out of its envelope and read it. His entire body froze. He quickly handed the Third Secret of Fatima back to Giuseppe.

"This can't be right," Pope John XXIII muttered.

"I can assure you, it is the real thing," Giuseppe responded. "My papa personally retrieved it from Sister Lúcia. He and I have guarded it ever since."

"This secret should never have been written down," the pope declared. "If people knew what it says, they would lose their faith."

"What do you want me to do with it?" Giuseppe asked.

"I don't know. Just get rid of it."

Troubled, Giuseppe returned to his villa. He was worried that spies inside the Vatican would now know that he was hiding the secret.

I need to find another place for it, and fast, he thought.

After thinking it over, Giuseppe went and hid the Third Secret of Fatima somewhere other than his villa safe.

***

A few days later, he was awakened from his sleep by a creak in the floorboards in the upstairs office directly above his bedroom.

Giuseppe quietly slipped his feet into his night shoes and pulled on his robe. The twenty-six-year-old American diplomat was in excellent physical shape.

In fact, he was so strong that he feared little, especially an intruder.

He did not search for a weapon because he was confident that his hands would do the trick.

He softly opened his bedroom door. There was a quiet rustling of papers in the upstairs office.

Then he heard the dial turn on the safe.

In a moment of bravery and pride, the young American ambassador called out to the intruder.

"My name is Giuseppe, the son of Big Al Tedesco. Soon you will wish you'd never crossed me or the honor of my family name."

Giuseppe broke into a full-on sprint. He charged up the stairs, taking two steps at a time.

He was fast and agile.

The office door was closed. Giuseppe reached it at full stride.

He grabbed the doorknob and turned it at full steam.
Bam!

Giuseppe was knocked backward.

Someone had locked the door from the inside.

His adrenaline was pumping, however, and the diplomat stepped back and did a roundhouse kick.

The door exploded from its frame.

When he entered the room, Giuseppe saw the window was wide open. The curtains blew in an easy breeze.

The intruder was gone. The safe was unopened, but other documents were scattered all over the floor.

Giuseppe collapsed to the ground in a seated position, completely exhausted.

Whoever it was, they did not get the Third Secret of Fatima because it is not here, he thought with relief.

***

Days later, Sister Lúcia told the media that the Madonna intended for the Third Secret of Fatima to be released to the public no later than 1960.

Pope John XXIII countered with a statement saying it was likely the Third Secret of Fatima would never be divulged.

"The Vatican doesn't want to assume the responsibility of guaranteeing the truth of the words that the three (Fatima) shepherd children attributed to the Madonna," the pope said.

Vatican City, 1962

Giuseppe sat in the very back pew of St. Peter's Basilica as hundreds of elaborately robed leaders strode in. He sucked in a deep breath and then anxiously blew it out.

Leading the senior clergymen was the eighty-one-year-old Pope John XXIII, who had surprisingly convened the Second Vatican Council, also known as Vatican II.

The pope shocked the world when he created Vatican II, which called thousands of bishops and other religious leaders to the Vatican to forge radical changes within the Church during a four-year period.

Jaime Nunez joined Giuseppe in the back of St. Peter's Basilica.

"Pope John XXIII says it is time to open the windows and let in some fresh air," said the young priest from Mexico, who was on a special one-year assignment in Rome to help the Vatican with preparations for the event.

"Yeah, well, get ready for change at gale force," Giuseppe replied.

Also, in attendance was Carlo Martinelli, now a young priest with radical views.

He was a huge supporter of new operating principles for the Church.

This is the day I have dreamed of, Martinelli thought.

***

Three days after the launch of Vatican II, Big Al watched on television as a thirteen-day political and military standoff began between the Soviet Union and the United States over the installation of nuclear-armed Soviet missiles in Cuba, just ninety miles from US shores.

In a TV address on October 22, 1962, President John F. Kennedy notified Americans about the presence of nuclear missiles in Cuba.

He explained his decision to enact a naval blockade around Cuba, and he made it clear the US was prepared to use military force, if necessary, to neutralize this perceived threat to national security.

Many people feared the world was on the brink of nuclear war. Sister Lúcia saw the conflict as a continuation of the Soviet Union spreading its errors about the world, and she once again called upon the pope to do a blessing of the Soviet Union.

Her request fell on deaf ears.

Rome, 1963

Just four and half years after he was selected as pope by the College of Cardinals, John XXIII died.

Cardinal Giovanni Montini took over as Pope Paul VI, and as if to remove all doubts instantly and fully, the new pope announced that the Second Vatican Council would go on—despite the fact that it had ushered in an era of profound and sometimes disconcerting change for the Church.

Sister Lúcia had hoped the change of popes would bring about a blessing of the Soviet Union, but it didn't.

Instead, Pope Paul VI abolished certain Church rules, thereby permitting anyone in the Church to publish on the subject of Marian (Madonna) apparitions without obtaining an official license by the Church to print a religious book.

Anyone, that is, except Sister Lúcia.

She alone, out of seven hundred million Catholics worldwide, was forbidden to speak or write on the subject of the Madonna. Bound by her vow of obedience as a nun, the one person who in 1917 had actually received secrets from the Madonna was not allowed to share her experience.

Why, though? she wondered.

Frustrated, Sister Lúcia traveled to see Giuseppe in Rome. He was surprised to find her waiting outside his villa.

"Giuseppe, I must talk with you. It's of utmost importance," Sister Lúcia said.

"What is it?" he asked. Giuseppe could tell by the way she moved that something was deeply troubling her.

"Where is the Third Secret of Fatima?" she asked.

"I hid it."

"You did?" she asked. "Why?"

"Because my father told me to protect it," he replied.

"Big Al is a wonderful man," said Sister Lúcia. "How is he?"

Giuseppe's eyes filled with tears.

"He is not well. In fact, he is quite sick."

Tears streamed down Sister Lúcia's cheeks.

"My mother called me just yesterday and asked me to come home to help care for Papa," Giuseppe continued.

"I have resigned my position. My fiancée and I will be leaving Rome later this week for New York."

"I'm so sorry to hear this terrible news," said Sister Lúcia. "Big Al did the world an incredible service during World War II."

"Thank you," Giuseppe said. "Say, do you want to see where I've hidden the Third Secret?"

The nun swung her arms in the air. "Of course I do!"

Several hours later they were walking up the spiral staircase that led to the Vatican Secret Archive.

"Is it okay that we do this?" Sister Lúcia asked.

"Oh, yes, I have a key," Giuseppe replied. "Pope Pius XII gave it to my papa, who gave it to me when I became a diplomat. I am allowed to do research here."

Giuseppe unlocked a door that opened to a second-floor flat with rows of library tables.

When they stepped inside, he thought he saw a figure move in the shadows.

"What kind of research would you do here?" Sister Lúcia asked.

"Mostly, my research was on the subject of Masonry. When I was eighteen years old, Pope Pius XII told my parents and me about the Masonic plan to reform the Church. I researched the organization because it is very secretive."

"I see," said Sister Lúcia. "And did you learn anything about their plans?"

"Yes, I did."

Giuseppe walked over to a file cabinet and pulled out a document titled *The Permanent Instruction of the Alta Vendita*, known as the *Alta Vendita* for short.

"What's that?" asked Sister Lúcia.

"The *Alta Vendita* was originally published in 1859 by the highest lodge of the Italian Carbonari as their blueprint to make revolutionary changes to the Church."

"I've never heard of the Carbonari, but I know all about Masonry," said Sister Lúcia.

"You do?"

"Oh, yes," she replied. "Masons staged a number of protests in Fatima after I saw the Madonna."

Giuseppe turned the pages of the *Alta Vendita* until he got to the middle of the document.

"Ah, here we are," he said. "This is where I hid it."

"You hid the Third Secret of Fatima in the Masonic blueprint to overhaul the Church?"

"Yes! Pretty clever, don't you think?" Giuseppe remarked.

"I figured it would be the last place anyone would look. I hid it right under their nose!"

Just then there was a loud crash. They heard footsteps running away from the room.

Giuseppe quickly closed the file cabinet.

He tucked the Third Secret of Fatima inside his coat pocket and grabbed Sister Lúcia by the hand.

"Come on, Sister, let's get out of here."

Later that night, Sister Lúcia told Giuseppe exactly what to do with the Third Secret of Fatima once and for all.

***

Nine months after that night at the archive, Giuseppe's son, Giovanni, was born in New York.

Big Al didn't get to meet his grandson, though. The immigrant passed away peacefully in his sleep that same day.

PART II:
THE REPORTER

The Doomsday Glacier

On January 31, 2020, scientists announced that they had detected unusually warm water underneath one of Antarctica's fastest-melting glaciers, Thwaites. The waters at the ground line, where the glacier meets the sea, were more than two degrees above the normal freezing temperature, according to scientists.

A nightmare scenario of crumbling ice and rapidly rising seas could spell disaster for a warming planet. Thwaites earned its "doomsday" nickname because it already accounts for 4 percent of world sea-level rise each year—a huge figure for a single glacier—and satellite data shows that it is melting increasingly rapidly.

Glaciologists have described Thwaites as the "most important" glacier in the world. If the Thwaites glacier were to completely melt, it would drain a mass of water that's about the size of Great Britain, and its collapse would raise global sea levels by almost three feet—potentially inundating coastal population centers.

"Masonry ought forever to be abolished. It is wrong—essentially wrong—a seed of evil which can never produce any good."

—US President John Quincy Adams, objecting to the Freemasons' oath of secrecy, in particular to keeping undefined secrets, and to the penalties for breaking the oath

Chapter 1

HOLY GRAIL

Rome, 2022

Although a man of the cloth, Carlo Martinelli was not a Church traditionalist. In fact, he was quite the opposite. Carlo, now a cardinal, leaned so far to the left of center, he could appropriately be considered an anarchist.

Much of how he thought was related to the way he had been brought up. Martinelli came from a poor agricultural family. He was the oldest of nine children.

His father had raised sheep, pigs, and cows. He also had grapes, but the vineyard business didn't catch on until well after young Carlo had left home.

The Martinelli's butchered their animals for food. Their dairy products were from their sheep and cows.

Carlo's father taught him how to hunt, and they lived off the land. His mother homeschooled him.

Every morning, young Carlo got up early and fed the animals and chopped wood during the winter. In the summer months, he plowed the land by hand for his mother's garden and his father's crops.

After his morning chores, the boy studied. He did chores again from midafternoon until sundown. When he turned eighteen, Carlo Martinelli left home at the first opportunity.

He had hated living on a farm, so he joined a local Jesuit seminary—not because he wanted to serve God, but because it offered him a chance to escape.

He became a priest in his late twenties, after being a seminarian. The Vatican assigned him to a diocese in the working-class Tiburtina area on the outskirts of Rome, known as a shantytown with elevated criminal activity.

The people of Martinelli's congregation lived in shacks made of concrete, wood, and corrugated metal.

Like him, the extremely poor residents of this shantytown had not chosen the life they had been born into. While Martinelli was fortunate to escape, they never would.

Martinelli came to believe that the Church's centuries-old rituals were not fair. They discriminated against the poor, requiring them to have more faith than people who were not so unfortunate.

"When you are not hungry at night when you go to bed, it's easy to have faith in God and be thankful," he preached one Sunday during a fire-and-brimstone sermon.

"But when you are hungry or suffering in some type of way, it requires more faith.

"How is that fair? How is that equitable?

"The Church teaches that it is a sin to steal, but what if stealing is the difference between life and death—like it is for many of the residents of Tiburtina?

"How can God judge you against a rich kid who steals?"

The men in Tiburtina worked as manual day laborers for hardly any money. Most turned to drugs and alcohol to cope.

The women were prostitutes, maids, and destitute wives whom their drunken husbands frequently beat. There were lots of backroom abortions, sickness, and starvation.

How can a God be so cruel? he wondered.

The plight of his parishioners underscored Martinelli's belief that life was not fair, nor was God.

Martinelli was hell-bent on reforming the Church in order to make it more equitable for everyone.

He threw his support in the 1960s behind the sweeping Church reforms of the Second Vatican Council. But in his view, they did not go nearly far enough.

Things took a turn for the worse, in his opinion, when Pope John Paul II ascended to the papacy in 1978 and rolled back many of the reforms that had been made during Vatican II as part of his "Restoration Policy."

That infuriated Carlo Martinelli.

He determined that in order to make the kind of meaningful reforms he wanted, there had to be a physical takeover of the Vatican and the papacy.

He likened the approach to a military coup of a bad government. With that goal in mind, Cardinal Martinelli made finding the Third Secret his Holy Grail.

That prophecy has to be a foretelling of the future and the people who will rule, he reasoned.

Why else would Big Al and his son Giuseppe have kept it from the public all these years?

I must get my hands on it!

But over the years, the Third Secret had proven quite elusive.

There was the time just before Vatican II when his friend, Cardinal Montini, who later became Pope Paul VI, visited Pope Pius XII on his deathbed in 1958.

Cardinal Montini thought for certain Pope Pius XII was going to divulge the Third Secret of Fatima to him. After all, Pope Pius XII had read the secret with Big Al during World War II and knew what it said.

"Holy Father, have you summoned me to your deathbed to tell me about the Third Secret of Fatima?" asked Cardinal Montini.

Pope Pius XII looked up at Cardinal Montini and laughed.

"Better luck next time," the pope said with his dying breath.

Then, there was that time in 2005, when Sister Lúcia had summoned Carlo to her deathbed. He was surprised by her invitation because he didn't think she knew him.

When he arrived at the nun's convent in Portugal, Cardinal Martinelli did not expect to find her deaf and blind.

How am I supposed to talk with her? he wondered.

He complained to a young nun who was sitting by Sister Lúcia's bed.

"Why was I invited here if Sister Lúcia cannot hear or see me?" he asked.

"Are you an envoy for the pope?" replied the young nun.

"Why, yes," he lied.

"Well, in that case, please give the following message to the pope. Sister Lúcia was able to talk up until two days ago.

"Her last words were, 'Tell the pope the Third Secret of Fatima does not die with me. In time, another person will reveal the secret, as well as a second one.'"

Cardinal Martinelli nearly fell over.

Who is this person? he wondered back in 2005.

There was more.

"Sister Lúcia asked me to tell you where the Third Secret of Fatima is hidden," said the young nun.

The cardinal rushed back to Rome. During his trip back, Sister Lúcia died. He didn't care.

Who has time for a funeral?

Instead, Cardinal Martinelli went directly upstairs to the place where the young nun said the Third Secret of Fatima was hidden, in the Vatican Secret Archive!

Sure enough, when he got to the Archive, Cardinal Martinelli found a sealed envelope tucked inside the *Alta Vendita.*

A very clever hiding place, he thought.

Cardinal Martinelli took a moment to calm his trembling hands. He did not want to accidentally rip the old, one-page letter inside the envelope.

Very gently he opened it and eased the letter out. With great expectation and excitement, he unfolded the parchment paper.

> It seems you are on a treasure hunt! The Third Secret of Fatima is not here any longer—we moved it someplace else, long

ago. I would say "see you in Heaven," but in your case, I doubt it very much.

Sincerely,
Sister Lúcia

Cardinal Martinelli blinked his eyes. Tricked! Even to this day, he fumed about that incident.

Fed up, Cardinal Martinelli decided to put muscle behind his effort to find the Third Secret.

He secretly started a clandestine combat unit within the Knights of Malta in 2005.

The Knights of Malta is one of the few orders created in the Middle Ages still active as a religious order of the Church.

In 1798, Napoleon's army dislodged the Knights from their home in Malta, and the order settled in Rome in the mid-nineteenth century.

The Knights hadn't had any military function since leaving Malta in 1798, but that changed when Martinelli started the splinter group.

They will be like my Knights of the Round Table, he decided.

On this particular day, Cardinal Martinelli called for a special meeting of the small yet powerful combat unit of modern-day Knights—secret soldiers whose goal was to find the Third Secret and one day, in a coup, overtake the Vatican.

The Knights came to the special meeting called by Carlo Martinelli by way of secret underground tunnels that had been dug beneath Rome during the Crusades.

They sat at a long wooden table in the basement of an abandoned building. Cardinal Martinelli was at the head of the table, wearing a black robe and a tall purple hat.

"This meeting of the combat forces of the Knights of Malta will now come to order," he said, rising from his chair.

"My brothers and sisters, we are gathered to discuss the Third Secret of Fatima, which, as you all know, is our Holy Grail. For decades we have searched for it, but the secret has eluded us."

The Prince of Naples, a member of the Italian royal family, raised his hand.

"A question already?" asked Cardinal Martinelli, bothered by the early interruption.

"My sources tell me that two former American diplomats, a man they called Big Al and his son, Giuseppe, destroyed the Third Secret of Fatima," said the prince.

"Your sources are wrong!" Cardinal Martinelli shot back. "Both men made a pact to protect the secret at all costs."

"So then, they must have hidden it," said the Dean of the College of Cardinals, Dominic Solano. "But where?"

Cardinal Martinelli's face flushed.

"Well, if I knew the answer to that, Dominic, we wouldn't be looking for it, would we?"

The dean lowered his head. His eyes also fell in a downward gaze, and he crossed his arms defensively across his chest.

"Any more irritating questions?" Cardinal Martinelli challenged.

The room was dead silent.

"Good. Hearing none, let's move on."

Cardinal Martinelli walked to the center of the room and stood next to a big fire that was burning in a barrel.

"For a long time, we've been thinking the Third Secret of Fatima has been lost to us," he said.

The Knights nodded in agreement.

"But there is a new lead."

"What is it?" asked the prince.

"In 1973, the Madonna appeared to a nun in Akita, Japan, named Sister Agnes Sasagawa. She was just a kid back then. I recently received news that during her encounter, the nun may have been told the Third Secret of Fatima."

Loud gasps came from the participants.

"Quiet down, everyone," said Cardinal Martinelli.

"As we speak, I have dispatched two of our soldiers to Japan. Hopefully, soon, we will know what the Third Secret is all about."

The Knights cheered at the good news.

Chapter 2

"THE MESSENGER"

Japan, 2022

John Tate, a reporter for the *Sacramento Union*, sat rigid in the back seat of a taxi. In the darkness, his hand felt for the door handle.

Torrential rain fell outside as the taxi rolled up to a stoplight. Tate's heart was pounding. Although the taxi driver was oblivious to what was going down, Tate knew. Ten minutes ago, he'd noticed the car that was following them.

Tate turned to take a quick look out the back window to see where the vehicle was now, but it was out of view. Then he looked side to side, first left. Nothing. Then right.

Bang!

The rear window on the passenger's side shattered as a gunshot rang out. Instinctively, Tate's hand squeezed the door handle, and he bolted out of the cab, running at full speed in the downpour toward Ameyoko Shopping Street, an area that sits under the rail line between JR Ueno and Okachimachi Stations.

More than four hundred stores lined the busy market street, selling seafood, clothing, dried food, sweets, and a range of other items.

The two Knights gave chase.

As usual for a weekend, Ameyoko was crowded with both foreigners and Japanese residents.

Tate tried his best to avoid colliding with people, but the same couldn't be said for his pursuers. They aggressively knocked people down and pushed them out of the way.

"Move it!" they yelled.

Normally, the polite Japanese locals would notice foreigners running down the street but not pay them too much attention.

However, the two soldiers in trench coats were causing such a commotion that they couldn't be overlooked.

As they ran, the bad guys raised their guns in the air for everyone to see, as if to say "move or else."

I've got to hide, Tate thought.

He ducked into a gambling facility called a "pachinko parlor," featuring a type of pinball machine that is widespread in Japan. The sound of balls bouncing from pin to pin and bells ringing like video slot machines was deafening.

Tate rushed to the back of the building and into a break room for employees.

They will be on me soon.

He quickly scanned the room for a place to hide. His eyes landed on the small supply closet. The door was wide open. He squeezed himself inside and locked the door.

Seconds later, Tate heard the two men come crashing into the break room, frantically calling out to each other in Italian. He heard several chairs and a table being kicked over.

Then, the handle of the supply room door jiggled. Tate held his breath.

Upon realizing the door was locked, the person on the other side of the door let out a frustrated howl. Tate flinched.

The doorjamb buckled as the thug pulled hard on the door.

"C'mon, let's keep moving," the other guy said. The two soldiers left the room.

Tate stayed where he was for what seemed like an eternity, but it was really only twenty minutes. Then he slowly opened the door and looked around.

The thugs were gone.

I've been in Japan less than an hour and already trouble has found me, Tate thought.

I need to do a better job of lying low.

He walked to the nearby Hotel Coco Grand Ueno Shinobazu, careful to stay in the shadows.

Every now and then he would stop and look around for several moments just to be sure he wasn't being followed.

Once, as he crouched behind a restaurant dumpster, he saw a star fall from the sky.

Can this night get any stranger? Tate wondered.

When he arrived at his hotel, the reporter checked in under an assumed name. Then he went straight to his room and called his managing editor, Ed Rollings.

"Hi, Chief, it's John."

"Tate, where in the dickens have you been?" replied Rollings. "You were supposed to call me once your plane landed. That was over an hour ago."

"I intended to, Chief, but once I got in my taxi I noticed two men following me."

"Tate, you're just being paranoid."

"Does the taxi window getting shot out count as being paranoid?" Tate asked.

"Huh?" Rollings replied. "The window of your taxicab got shot out?"

"Yes."

"Tate, why is it that trouble always seems to find you?"

"I don't know, Chief. Good question. But I am safe now. I checked into a hotel under an alias."

"An alias? What is going on over there?" Rollings barked.

"Like I said, two guys chased me. They were speaking Italian."

Rollings's heart sank. He'd never wanted to send his ace reporter to Japan in the first place.

A week ago, Tate had received an anonymous letter from someone calling him- or herself "The Messenger."

The tipster said they had an important secret that needed to be shared with the world.

At first, the reporter dismissed the tip as a prank. But then, he started to get text messages that explained why the source wasn't going to the pope with their information.

"The Church has been captured by corrupt forces," said the anonymous writer.

"I cannot trust anyone with the information that I have, including the pope."

Tate was the editor of the religion section on Sundays for the *Sacramento Union*.

He'd made a name for himself lately and won awards for his series of podcasts in which he interviewed some of the biggest names out there.

He figured that was probably why The Messenger reached out to him.

In one of the texts, The Messenger revealed that the information they had was related to the appearances of the Madonna in Akita, Japan, nearly fifty years ago.

Tate and the *Sacramento Union's* librarian, Liz LeClair, did some research and found out that three secrets had been given to a young girl back then who was now a nun.

Two of the secrets had been disclosed, but not the third.

In one text message, The Messenger said it was imperative that Tate go to Japan right away to retrieve the Third Secret of Akita before it fell into the wrong hands.

"The fate of Christianity depends on it, Mr. Tate," the latest text said.

After a lot of discussion, the newspaper's managing editor, Rollings, agreed to send his ace reporter.

Now, he was wishing he'd listened to his original instinct.

"Tate, you know I never wanted you to go," the managing editor shouted into the phone. "Now you're telling me people are shooting at you? Come home. This is out of your league."

But Tate wouldn't hear of it, especially now that someone had taken a shot at him. He was ready to fight.

Tate first noticed a man in a trench coat following him when he got off the airplane in Tokyo.

The man shadowed Tate to the luggage area, and then he followed him out to the street.

When Tate got in a taxi, the man also got into a waiting car, which trailed several lengths behind the taxi.

"Listen, Chief, it's been a long day," Tate said to Rollings. "I'm going to get some sleep and wait for The Messenger to contact me."

When their call ended, Tate got in bed.

But his mind was busy, so he took out a cigarette and slowly pulled long puffs from it while watching the rain fall outside.

The heavy, dark night was pierced by neon lights from the downtown businesses, creating an eerie illumination through the hotel window.

Tate leaned over the side of his bed and reached for the iPad in his travel bag. He connected with the hotel's Internet service and got online.

He noticed that Liz, the *Sacramento Union*'s librarian, had sent him an email, so he opened it:

> Hi John. I hope you are being careful over there. It was another hot day here! Sacramento was 120 degrees. The wildfires are not letting up. They are so bad that ash is falling like snow. This morning, I had to brush a thick collection of ash off of my car just so I could see out the windshield.

Tate lit another cigarette and thought about the condition of the world.

Wildfires, earthquakes, famines, and plagues were occurring more frequently.

Floods and droughts were also happening everywhere, as was an increase in violence, racial conflicts, and terrorist attacks.

Then there was the coronavirus disease in 2019 (COVID-19), which was declared a global pandemic by the World Health Organization.

Tate thought about the shooting star he'd seen earlier that evening while being chased. He had never seen one before, although he'd read stories about astronomers reporting an increase in falling stars, new stars appearing, and regular sightings of meteor crashes.

He turned on the television, mostly because he found the sound of it to be comforting. He liked the white noise.

Maybe it was because he lived alone, but the reporter always had his TV on at home, whether he was watching or not.

Tonight, it was no different. The sound was soothing, even though he did not know the Japanese language.

Tate flipped through the TV channels, landing on an American news station, CNN, which was reporting in English that the Department of Homeland Security's cyber arm revealed that Russian hackers were suspected of a massive, ongoing intrusion campaign into government agencies, private companies, and critical infrastructure entities using a variety of unidentified tactics and not just a single compromised software program.

Tate lit another cigarette, sucked it in with a deep drag, held it for twenty seconds, and then slowly exhaled. He crushed it out after five minutes more, and then rested his head on the pillow.

Several hours later, the buzzing of his cell phone awakened Tate. He'd drifted off to sleep, still in his clothes. The buzzing sound was a new text that had come in.

Tate leaned over and retrieved his phone from the nightstand. The text was from The Messenger.

"Meet me at the Ueno Zoo at noon. Go to where the giant pandas are. I'll find you there."

Swell, that means I have to go near Ameyoko again, Tate thought.

After the chase last night, he dreaded going back.

Even though it was midmorning, it was dark outside. That wasn't unusual for Japan in June, since their rainy season started around that time.

Tate looked over at the television, which he had never shut off the night before. The weatherman was outside in torrential rain, plus it was flooding in Tokyo.

Tate pulled on his trench coat and lit a cigarette.

He walked over to his suitcase and took out a small handgun hidden in a secret compartment, then tucked it inside his coat.

"Time to meet The Messenger," he said to no one in the room.

Once outside, Tate struggled against the powerful wind and rain. He decided to flag down a taxi rather than attempt to walk ten minutes in the storm.

"To the zoo," he told the driver, who looked confused that anyone would be going to see caged animals in such bad weather.

When he arrived, Tate looked around the empty area—there was absolutely no one there.

He paid the six hundred yen to enter, about five dollars and fifty cents, and made his way to the panda exhibit.

He constantly looked over his shoulder to see if anyone was following him, but it seemed like he was the only one dumb enough to be out in the storm.

The weather was so bad, even the animals took cover. They were inside their shelters and nowhere to be found. The place was totally deserted.

The gardens surrounding the exhibits had been obliterated by the wind.

A Sumatran tiger let out a growl as Tate walked past its cage, reminding him that there really were animals there, even though he couldn't see them.

He arrived at the new giant panda enclosure that had opened in September 2020, home to the fifteen-year-old couple Shin Shin and Ri Ri.

The exhibit mimicked the mammals' natural habitat in southwestern China's Sichuan Province.

Tate looked around for The Messenger, but he saw no one through the blinding wind.

He glanced down at a sign that said the newest panda, Xiang Xiang, born in June 2017 to Shin Shin and Ri Ri, was not housed at the new "Panda no Mori" (Panda's Forest) enclosure but rather was in her original panda facility separate from her parents.

Tate leaned in close to the glass exhibit and strained for a better look, hoping to see Shin Shin or Ri Ri in the bamboo habitat.

Nothing.

Clearly, they had been smart enough to get out of the rain.

Suddenly, Tate felt a strong tug on his sleeve from behind. He quickly turned around, reaching at the same time for the gun inside his coat pocket.

He raised the weapon and took aim, but then lowered it upon seeing who was standing in front of him.

"Don't shoot," said a diminutive nun.

"Who are you?"

"I'm The Messenger."

Tate blinked several times. "You are the person who has been contacting me?"

The woman nodded. She was very old.

The nun wore a white-collared button-up top with a light-blue vest and blue head covering. Her full-length blue skirt fell to her ankles, showing off the white tennis shoes on her tiny feet.

"Why did you want to meet at the zoo?" Tate asked. "In the middle of a torrential storm."

"I felt we would be safe here, in a public place, when no one wants to be out."

"Well, you're right about that, Sister. No one wants to be out in this weather, not even the animals."

Just then, the nearby monkeys whooped and screeched loudly.

Tate saw two men in trench coats running toward him and the nun. They were the same two thugs who had chased him the night before.

His heart pounded.

There is nowhere to hide, he thought.

And we surely can't outrun them.

The nun is probably ninety years old.

Tate tightened his grip on the pistol in his left hand. The nun's eyes were wide as saucers, and the muscles in her face were taut.

They gave each other an uncertain look.

"Over here!" came a hushed voice from inside the exhibit space. "Psst! Hey. Over here."

Tate looked over at a large area behind a bamboo jungle gym that resembled a cave.

He saw an animal keeper holding open a door with one hand while motioning them over with his other hand.

"I'm not going in," the nun said. "There are wild animals in there."

"Listen, Sister, you have two choices," Tate replied. "Stay here and let those thugs coming our way put a bullet in you, or go into the cage."

"Well, when you put it that way."

Without a second thought, she moved surprisingly fast toward the open door. Tate was right behind her.

When they reached the door, the animal keeper pushed them inside the exhibit area and closed what turned out to be a double door.

"The secondary door provides additional security in case of animal escape," the animal keeper said knowingly.

"You don't say," said Tate, pretending to be interested.

"Follow me," the animal keeper instructed. He led them to an off-exhibit area used to separate the pandas for feeding and sleeping.

"It really smells in here," said the nun.

"We also use this holding area for obtaining individual samples of urine or feces to assess the animals' health," the animal keeper said assuredly.

He then locked a gate behind Tate and the nun.

"The ability to transfer animals easily with a minimum amount of stress is of paramount importance," he went on, as if it were a teaching moment.

"But for right now, this off-exhibit area is a great place to hide both of you."

"Swell," Tate complained.

"Now sit tight," said the animal keeper. "I'll be right back."

"Where are you going?" asked the nun.

"There's a series of cameras outside the exhibit. I am going to head over to the workstation to see where those guys are on the TV monitor."

Once he was gone, the nun turned to Tate and reached out to shake his hand.

"We haven't properly met; my name is Sister Agnes Sasagawa."

"Happy to meet you, Sister," Tate said, shaking her hand.

"But how about we save the conversation for later? Right now, I just want to focus on us getting out of here alive."

They hunkered down and remained quiet. A half hour later, the animal keeper returned.

"They're gone," he declared. "You should have seen the confused look on their faces. I think they thought you vanished into thin air."

"Thank you for hiding us," the reporter said. "I have to admit, I never thought I would hide in an animal cage."

"Like I said, we use this as a holding area," the man explained. "Zoo animals don't stay in their exhibit area all the time. We shift animals into their exhibits in the morning and off exhibit every night.

"Some animals remain in holding areas to take a break from public viewing."

Tate turned away from the animal keeper and rolled his eyes.

The last thing I need right now is a Zoology 101 lesson, he thought.

"Can you get us out of here?" he asked out loud.

"Sure, let's go," he said. "I will take you somewhere safe, where the two of you can talk without being bothered."

The animal keeper led them to a 2022 black Dodge Mustang with tinted windows.

"I'm in the wrong profession if animal keepers can afford one of these," Tate cracked.

"Sorry, Mr. Tate, but everyone knows that being a print journalist these days means taking a vow of poverty," the man shot back. "Aren't newspapers becoming a thing of the past?"

Tate rolled his eyes again, this time so the man could see.

Ten minutes later, the black muscle car pulled up in front of a Japanese restaurant.

"My family owns this place," he said. "You will be safe here."

The animal keeper got out and opened the back doors for Tate and Sister Agnes, who had known the young man ever since childhood. She had once been his Sunday school teacher, which is why Sister Agnes had asked him to keep an eye out for them at the zoo.

A young woman came out of the building and directed them to follow her.

"Quickly," she called out as she led them inside.

They walked into the kitchen, where a boy no older than twelve slid open a hidden door on the floor under a commercial dishwasher.

There was a flight of stairs leading down to a basement.

"My grandparents built this place during World War II as a place to hide," the woman said. "Go on, you two. Someone will be back in an hour to get you."

Tate was in awe of the basement. As a kid, he liked hanging out in his grandparents' basement in South Dakota. Everyone had them in the Midwest, in case of tornadoes.

Like his grandparents', this one had been fixed up nicely. There was a kitchen, a big-screen television, several pinball machines, a bathroom with a shower, and a guest room for overnight stays.

"Do you know who I am, Mr. Tate?"

"Um, didn't you say you're a nun?" he replied.

"When I was a young girl, the Madonna appeared to me in the remote area of Yuzawadai, which is an outskirt of Akita, Japan. Our Lady of Akita gave me several messages."

Tate, who had been slumping in his chair out of exhaustion, straightened up.

Flashbacks of Sunday school crossed his mind, when the nuns would discipline him for slouching.

"I have heard of you," the reporter said. "Our librarian and I did some research before I came. What things did the Madonna tell you?"

"I was given three messages, just like Sister Lúcia and her two cousins in Fatima. In the first message, I was asked to pray the rosary and pray for the sins of others."

Tate nodded his head.

"In the second message, the Madonna said the following:

'Many men in this world afflict the Lord. I desire souls to console Him to soften the anger of the Heavenly Father. I wish, with my Son, for souls who will repair by their suffering and their poverty for the sinners and ingrates.'"

Tate scratched his head.

"Forgive me, Sister Agnes, but couldn't you have just told this to me over the phone rather than ask that I fly all the way here?"

The nun stared at Tate, who quickly pulled his hands off the table, another reflexive move.

As a kid, such a wisecrack would have gotten his knuckles rapped by a nun with a ruler.

"I have written the Third Secret down for you. Until now, it has not been shared with the world. Because it is so important, I needed for you to personally come here and get it. Too risky otherwise."

"What do I do with it?" Tate asked.

"When you feel the time is right, you need to publish it."

Tate swallowed hard.

The nun stood up and handed Tate an envelope.

"The message is inside," she said.

"Carry it safely back to the United States. You are now 'The Messenger.' Good luck, Mr. Tate. May the Lord be with you."

At that exact moment, there was a knock on the hidden door. The boy on the other side pulled the door back and leaned down.

"Time to go!" the boy called down.

"Where to?" Tate asked.

The animal keeper leaned inside.

"I am taking you to the airport, Mr. Tate. As for you, Sister Agnes, you are going back to the convent. A driver will take you there."

Chapter 3

THE VERY OLD MAN

Vatican City, 2022

The Vatican had released the Third Secret of Fatima in 2000—supposedly.

The 1917 prophecy was said to be about the twentieth century persecution of Christians, culminating in the failed assassination attempt of Pope John Paul II in 1981.

A lot of people, including Cardinal Martinelli and his secret band of followers within the Knights of Malta, doubted the Vatican's announcement.

The very old man who was eating outside of an Italian café across from St. Peter's Square certainly didn't believe it.

What complete rubbish. If only people knew where the Third Secret of Fatima really is, thought Giuseppe, who was now ninety years old.

With shaking hands, he carefully lifted a cup of espresso to his lips. Giuseppe was old and frail; it was a wonder his clothes didn't slide right off his body.

He put down the cup and nibbled on cannoli. The former US ambassador watched tourists go in and out of the Vatican.

The Third Secret of Fatima had always been a big part of his life.

In 1941, Lúcia revealed two of the three secrets in her memoir, but, for unknown reasons, she withheld the last one. Two years later, Giuseppe's father, Big Al, retrieved the Third Secret from her when Lúcia became deathly ill.

His mind drifted back again to 1943, when he was just a boy and Sister Lúcia wrote down the Third Secret of Fatima. Soon after that, Mussolini's soldiers, the Blackshirts, turned up at the pope's residence.

They demanded Pope Pius XII hand the secret over to them.

How do they even know I have it? Pope Pius XII had wondered. He eventually concluded that there must be spies inside the Vatican.

The second time the Blackshirts came to the Vatican for the Third Secret, the pope decided to play a trick on the soldiers. He gave them a forgery when they returned that said:

> The conversion of the Soviet Union to Christianity will one day be achieved, and my Immaculate Heart will then be triumphant. Unfortunately, that day is not now. A lion has arisen in Central Europe who will destroy the Soviet Union and the Church. Both will be wiped away. Only after then will a new kind of flower bloom.

Hitler was thrilled when he received the secret. He was convinced that he was the "lion" who would destroy the Soviet Union. He also believed his Nazi party was the "new kind of flower" that would bloom throughout the world.

"Sir, would you like the check?" asked the waiter at the café, interrupting the old man's thoughts.

"Yes, please."

Giuseppe looked at his watch.

The time had arrived for him to meet his longtime friend Carmine Luizzi, otherwise known as Pope Anthony.

He got up from the table, paid the bill, and ambled to the pope's residence.

Giuseppe hadn't noticed a man at the café spying on him from a few tables away.

***

At the pope's official residence, the Apostolic Palace, Pope Anthony was waiting for his guest to arrive. He nervously fiddled with his skullcap, then paced back and forth for several minutes.

These days, he had a lot on his mind.

At the top of the list was the conduct of his clergy. More and more, cardinals, bishops, and priests were speaking out without his approval.

"Shooting from the hip" would be a better description of it. They were also piling up sexual misconduct charges.

The pope had been working long hours these days.

In addition to problems with his clergy, he was busy removing cardinals who were not loyal to him and adding new ones who would be.

The process was time-consuming but necessary, and it was the reason for the visitor who was now knocking at his door.

"Giuseppe, how are you?" Pope Anthony said as he opened the big wooden door for his longtime friend.

"Do you want the truth? Or do you want the white lie I like to tell people, Carmine?"

Giuseppe always called the pope by his birth name when they were alone together. The pope actually preferred to be addressed that way by his friends.

"Give me the answer that won't require you to go to confession tomorrow," Pope Anthony replied.

"Ah, you want the truth. Okay. I am so old, Carmine, I think I am going to die soon."

"That's a depressing answer," the pope responded. "I think I want to hear the white lie instead."

The very old man giggled at the idea of lying to the pope.

"I tell them that by the time you're my age, you know everything there is to know. You just can't remember it."

The two men burst out in a hearty laugh. They patted each other on the back like long-lost friends, even though they visited each other all the time.

The pope led them to his study, where they sat in elegant wingback chairs. A butler served them freshly squeezed lemonade.

"Giuseppe, you know I am only six years younger than you. Age is just a number. What is it that they say? Ah, yes, a man's eighties are the new sixties in today's world."

"No one says that, Carmine."

They both laughed again.

"Giuseppe, do you realize we have known each other since the 1950s?"

"Yes, it has been a very long time," Giuseppe replied.

"You were a US ambassador in Italy when we first met. Do you recall?"

"I do recall," Giuseppe replied. "At the time you were a priest in Rome."

The pope's face suddenly tightened. His lighthearted mood changed.

"In all the time we have known each other, have I ever asked you for a favor, Giuseppe?"

"Never."

"Today, I must ask one of you."

"What kind of favor, Carmine?"

"Giuseppe, have you heard the story of the small Dutch boy who saved his community from flooding by placing his finger in a hole in the dike?"

Giuseppe's eyebrows raised.

"Indeed, I have heard that story. It's a cute one, Carmine."

"These days, I am like that boy in the story," Pope Anthony clarified.

"But, unfortunately, I do not have enough fingers to plug all the holes. The dike is about to break."

Giuseppe blew out a heavy sigh and shook his head. He knew what his friend was getting at. The pope's enemies were circling like vultures.

"I know times are bad for you, Carmine, but surely things are not that bad?"

The pope explained. "Did you read the article in the *Sacramento Union* newspaper recently about the priest who was excommunicated by his local bishop for claiming I am not the real pope?

"Father Jeremy Weathersby claimed my predecessor, Pope Emeritus Benedict XVI, was the true pope."

"How can that be? Pope Benedict retired in 2013," Giuseppe countered.

Pope Anthony stood up, walked over to his desk, and pulled out a newspaper article, which he read out loud:

> "'I continue to regard Benedict as retaining the Office of Peter, as mysterious as that might be,' said Father Weathersby. 'Therefore, I do not regard the current man in white as being the Supreme Pontiff of the Church.'"

The two longtime friends looked at each other. Giuseppe tried to read between the lines of the story.

"Wasn't Father Weathersby suspected of misconduct and improper relationships with at least two adult women?" Giuseppe asked.

"I seem to recall something about him confessing his love to at least one of the women in a video message that circulated online."

The pope shrugged his shoulders and continued reading from the newspaper article.

> "According to Father Weathersby, a schism—or divide—is crippling the inner workings of the Church. During the early stages of the coronavirus, when

the Vatican ordered Masses not to be celebrated, he continued to do so in private homes, which he said were offered 'in union' with Pope Benedict, not with me. Father Weathersby says that many who have joined him held, as did he, that Benedict was the one true pope."

Giuseppe waved his hand in the air, as if brushing off the remarks.

"Clearly, he was a priest operating outside the lines and deserved to be excommunicated."

"Is that all you think, Giuseppe?"

"What do you mean?" asked the old man.

"That article makes it clear that my enemies are from within the Church," Pope Anthony answered. "My own clergy wants me out."

Giuseppe's face fell.

"What are you talking about, Carmine?"

"My critics are cardinals, bishops, archbishops, priests, nuns, and brothers—and they want me to step down."

"You are just being paranoid," Giuseppe claimed.

"No, I am not. My critics are hoping that if they can cause enough doubt about me, then maybe the public will want a new pope.

"The constant drip-drip-drip of negative stories is being manufactured as part of a much bigger plan to discredit me."

Just then, the butler entered the room with a tray of antipasto that consisted of olives, anchovies, cheeses, and meats. He served them and then poured iced tea.

When the butler was gone, Giuseppe pushed back.

"The world today is a complicated place," Giuseppe argued. "Much of the problems are due to the fact that Russia was never blessed by the pope in a special ceremony with all the bishops of the world as the Madonna asked when she appeared in Fatima in 1917."

"Oh, here we go again," Pope Anthony moaned.

"If you look at the facts, Carmine, Russia is still spreading errors throughout the world because the blessing has never been done."

"What facts?" the pope asked.

"Russia has not changed from the old days of the Soviet Union. Look around, Carmine. Russia has renewed its military and diplomatic force and is supporting brutal regimes in Syria and Iran.

"Russia is giving aid to communist governments around the world, such as China and North Korea.

"Russia has built up conventional weapons and is modernizing its nuclear weapons.

"Russia has used military power to disembowel the Ukraine.

"Russia, the historic home of the Orthodoxy religion, has become increasingly inhospitable to smaller, disfavored faiths.

"Are you aware that it is a crime to be a member of the Jehovah's Christian Witnesses faith in Russia? Prison terms are imposed for such activities as leading or participating in prayer meetings.

"In 2019, Human Rights Watch noted the 'escalating persecution' of this particular group of Christians, with at least three hundred and thirteen people undergoing criminal charges, put on trial, or convicted of criminal 'extremism' for engaging in Jehovah's Christian Witnesses' activities.

"Unfortunately, this mistreatment continued throughout 2020 and 2021.

"Russian police increased the number of raids on private homes, restricted travel, confiscated church property, and imprisoned those who practiced the faith.

"Between five and ten thousand Jehovah's Christian Witnesses left the country to avoid religious persecution. I cannot adequately convey the brutality of such Russian enforcement practices."

Giuseppe looked at his friend to see if he had successfully made his point. Unsure as to whether or not he had, the very old man continued.

"Russia tampered in US elections in 2016 and 2020.

"The United States and Russia seem to be on the verge of another cold war.

"And did you see the December 2020 report that claims Alexei Navalny, a prominent opponent of Russian President Vladimir Putin, was poisoned by Putin's regime?"

"Yes, I heard it on the news," the pope replied.

Kremlin agents followed the Russian opposition leader for years and were nearby just before an attack with a deadly nerve agent almost killed him in August 2020, according to the research group Bellingcat.

"The German government said that Navalny was poisoned with a deadly nerve agent implicated in other attacks on Russians who have crossed the current regime," Giuseppe explained.

"So, you are saying everything bad in the world today is Russia's fault?" the pope asked in a disbelieving voice.

"Sister Lúcia said the Madonna wanted Russia blessed because it had turned its back on Christianity and, as a result, was making dangerous mistakes. Yes, those mistakes continue to this day!"

"I fail to see the point in this discussion," Pope Anthony said with a huge sigh.

"Giuseppe, I can't ignore the fact that my clergy is like a house divided, and it is devouring the Church from within. That's not Russia's doing."

The two friends stared off in different directions and pressed their lips together.

"Oh, heck, let's just eat," the pope declared.

They ate in awkward silence for several minutes.

After a while, Giuseppe broke the tension.

"How can I help you? I can see that you are obviously troubled. Tell me the reason why you summoned me here. I doubt it was to talk about your popularity."

"As a matter of fact, it is," said Pope Anthony. "I need your help with my clergy."

Giuseppe's eyes flew wide open.

"Really? How can I help with that? I have been retired for a long time now. I hardly know any of the clergy anymore. What can this tired old man do to help you?"

Pope Anthony knew differently.

Yes, Giuseppe was old.

Yes, he had been away from Vatican politics for a long time now, but his mind was still sharp, and Giuseppe knew things.

Plus, he had done certain things that Pope Anthony knew were still being kept hidden.

Pope Anthony patted his friend on the knee in a gesture of appreciation.

"Giuseppe, the College of Cardinals may hold a symbolic vote on whether or not it still has confidence in me."

Giuseppe let out a loud gasp. "What!"

"There is talk of it," Pope Anthony explained.

"As you know, there's no impeachment procedure for a pope. But the rumor is that the College of Cardinals may call for a symbolic vote as a way to put pressure on me to resign."

"That has never been done before," Giuseppe noted. "Are things really that bad?"

"Yes, they are," said Pope Anthony. "That's what I've been trying to tell you. A large number of cardinals with a vote in the College of Cardinals are disenchanted with me."

Giuseppe interlocked his fingers and rested them behind his head. He considered what his longtime friend had said.

"You are a great pope," Giuseppe remarked. "Who cares what these dissident cardinals think?"

"I care, especially if they follow through on a symbolic vote. Whatever the outcome is, the clergy will be even more divided if they hold a vote.

"Father Weathersby is right, there is a schism, and it is growing."

"Please, tell me what I can do," Giuseppe pleaded.

The pope studied his friend. "Your son, Giovanni, is the archbishop at the Archdiocese of San Francisco. I am going to promote him to the rank of cardinal."

A numbness came over the former American ambassador to Italy. His skin tingled all over.

"Really?"

"Yes. There are currently five cardinals in the United States with a vote in the College of Cardinals. I am going to make him the sixth voting cardinal.

"However, in return, I must have Giovanni's support. That's the deal."

Giuseppe stood and embraced his friend.

He was so proud.

As the very old man departed, he was determined that Giovanni would come through for his longtime friend.

Chapter 4

MONKEY IN A TREE

California, 2022

For as far back as he could remember, trouble had a way of finding John Tate. In fact, it nearly took him out of this world even before he arrived in it in 1971.

His parents were Peace Corps volunteers living in sub-Saharan Africa when his mother went into early labor.

There were complications, which didn't bode well for her baby since the country accounts for about two-thirds of all maternal deaths.

Tate's mother had obstructed labor, so he was not getting enough oxygen in his mother's uterus. His parents lived miles from any health center, and only a midwife was on hand.

No one thought the baby would survive. But at the last minute, as if by a miracle, the village midwife was able to successfully redirect the baby's position, ensuring his safe trip down the birth canal.

Then there was the time in 1981, when Tate and his parents took a month-long summer vacation overseas that ended in disaster. He was just ten years old.

A defrocked monk who demanded the pope release the Third Secret of Fatima hijacked their plane. Tate and his family survived the ordeal, but it left an emotional scar.

After the hijacking, *The New York Times* described the 1917 Fatima event in the following way:

> Fatima is a town in central Portugal, a famous shrine, and site of pilgrimages due to reported appearances of the Madonna to three children there in 1917.
>
> The children said the Madonna visited them six times and told them three secrets, two of which were communicated to the pope in 1941 and the third in 1943.
>
> The first two secrets have been revealed, but the third has not.
>
> The first secret described a vision of Hell. The second called for the conversion of Russia from atheism to Christianity.
>
> The third was a secret message to be disclosed by the Vatican in 1960, but it was not.
>
> There has been speculation among some believers that the Third Secret of Fatima is a detailed prophecy of another global war or of the end of the world.

Today, the fifty-one-year-old Tate was a news reporter. He embraced the chaos that seemed to be in his DNA.

Trouble gravitated to him, like it had recently in Japan, or how it had ten years ago in Redding, California, when he was watching an air show as a spectator. A pilot was doing spectacular zigzag maneuvers intermingled with 180-degree nosedives and 180-degree rises when the plane lost power and came crashing to earth.

The plane hit so hard that pieces of metal flew five hundred yards, the length of five football fields. Fragments of crushed metal flew into the audience like miniature Frisbees.

While everyone else ran away from the crash, Tate ran toward it, clicking away on his cell phone camera. He went directly into the hot spot. He always embraced the trouble other people wanted no part of.

Eighteen people were killed. Another seventy-five were sent to local hospitals with injuries.

The very next week, another plane crashed at an air show in Reno. That's when Tate decided to write an investigative series on the safety of all air shows held in the country.

As was his nature, he became obsessed with the subject matter. Tate worked day and night on the seven-piece series.

The main piece in his series was a lengthy probe into how the federal government was ignoring its own Federal Aviation Administration safety rules in order to placate the public's insatiable appetite for air shows, which Tate likened to "high-wire circus acts."

During a five-year period, there had been more than fifteen total pilot deaths at air shows across the country, an average of three a year.

The other stories in his series were about local communities ignoring safety risks in order to reap profits (air shows pumped millions of dollars into local economies); families grieving over the loss of loved ones because of air show crashes; the military's inflated spending on the US Navy Blue Angels, the Army Golden Knights, and the Air Force Thunderbirds, which are flight demonstration squadrons; and, the total number of deaths since the Navy Blue Angels began participating in air shows (twenty-six pilots and one crew member).

Hearings were subsequently held on Capitol Hill in Washington, DC, to determine what to do about the problem. By then there was blood in the water.

Air shows were ultimately banned altogether in the United States by an act of Congress. They became a thing of the past. Flight demonstrations were no longer allowed in the US.

Tate won a Pulitzer Prize, one the highest awards a journalist can receive. But it came at a heavy price.

Unable to unwind after the frenzied pace of investigating and writing, Tate started drinking.

At first, he drank just a couple of beers at night to numb his emotions and calm his head so that he could sleep. Over time, however, he was up to drinking a twelve-pack of beer every night. His marriage collapsed.

Tate was drinking so much that he was passing out at night rather than sleeping. The blackouts were bad.

Most nights he couldn't remember what he had done while he was drinking.

One morning, Tate woke up fourteen miles away from his home in a sketchy city park known for crime. He had no idea how he got there. Two drug addicts were sitting about fifteen yards away from him, smoking crack.

He failed to show up for work that day, again. He was missing lots of work. Tate's life was in shambles.

His city desk editor at the *Redding Record Searchlight*, who happened to be Ed Rollings, was tired of Tate's absences, so he complained to the publisher, who fired the unreliable reporter.

Rollings hoped Tate would take the next bus out of town and leave the area quietly, but he didn't. Instead, he bounced around from one Northern California newspaper to the next.

At first, the newspapers were thrilled to hire him, incredulous at their good fortune to get a Pulitzer Prize-winning reporter. They all soon learned about his drinking problem, however, and let him go.

The breaking point came after the *Mount Shasta Herald*, a weekly newspaper, fired him. He'd only been on the job for a month. Tate should have been able to keep up because there was no daily deadline pressure to file a story, but he was constantly falling behind due to all of his absences.

His life completely unraveled at that point.

Unemployed and unable to control his drinking, Tate's mother came to his rescue. Mary Jo Tate could not bear to see her only son fail. She put him into an alcohol recovery program.

The doctors recommended either a sixty- or nine-ty-day program, but his mom insisted on more. She paid for a deluxe 120-day recovery program at the Paso Robles Alcohol and Drug Treatment Center near her home in Morro Bay, California.

When the program ended, she paid to get him into a sober-living program for another three months.

During the time he was there, his mother died. Her unexpected death from a blood clot sobered him up, fast. Tate's safety net was gone, and he was scared.

There is no room for error in my life, he determined.

If I fall now, there is no one to catch me.

He got serious about his sobriety. He joined Alcoholics Anonymous, got a sponsor, and made a sincere commit-ment to stop drinking.

He relied on his newfound spirituality, a personal "Higher Power," to climb out of the hole he'd dug for himself.

Tate moved into a cabin in Lake Tahoe that his mom had left to him in her will, and he landed a job as a reporter at the *Tahoe City Gazette*.

To get the job, he lied. Tate told the publisher that after leaving the *Redding Record Searchlight*, he was a con-sultant to several newspapers and then took time off to care for his ailing mother.

He didn't mention his extended stay in rehab or the number of times he'd been fired. The lie bothered him because Tate had been raised a Catholic.

He felt guilty whenever he lied, even if the lie meant putting his life back on track, which it did in this instance.

Tate battled back anyhow.

He engaged in spirituality and mindfulness, using it to mentally escape from life's noise. He went on hikes, read, did yoga, and took scenic pictures.

Tate learned to slow down his hectic life and to be at peace living in the moment. In many ways, he was living his best life. He now noticed the little things that he had been too busy to see and appreciate.

Rollings, Tate's city desk editor in Redding, came back into the reporter's life after the success he'd found at the *Tahoe City Gazette*.

Rollings had felt personally responsible when Tate was fired in Redding. He believed he hadn't handled him well during their time together.

A former Navy officer in the Gulf War, Rollings had seen soldiers suffering from post-traumatic stress disorder, and he should have recognized the signs of PTSD in Tate.

"Instead, I yelled at him repeatedly," Rollings confided to his wife one day. "What Tate needed was my help, but I didn't give it to him."

Rollings was determined to correct his past mistake.

He kept tabs on Tate at the *Tahoe City Gazette*, just as he had at every one of Tate's stops along the way after the *Redding Record Searchlight*.

When Rollings was hired by the *Sacramento Union* as its new managing editor, he decided to give Tate another chance.

Rollings brought the reporter in with him, with certain conditions, one of which was to attend an AA meeting every day. And on this afternoon, Tate was sitting in the back of the room as a noon meeting of AA got underway.

"Take to your seats, everyone. We are going to get started," said the moderator, whose name was Beth.

The long line of people at the coffeepot looked confused and slightly panicked. They didn't know what to do.

Stay in line for their coffee or sit down?

The absence of alcohol had increased their reliance on caffeine and cigarettes.

"Please, go to your seats," Beth instructed. "That includes all of you who are in line for coffee. You can go back once we are underway."

The people who attended the meeting, like any you'd find at AA anywhere, fell into three categories: (1) those who wanted to be there and genuinely desired to turn their lives around, (2) those who didn't want to be there but were required to attend because they had gotten a DUI or broken some other law, and (3) those who were neither happy nor upset about being there; they were just there.

"Okay, let's get started," Beth said after going over the rules and announcements. "For those of you who don't know me already, my name is Beth, and I am an alcoholic."

"Hi, Beth!" came the chorus of replies from the audience.

"How is everyone doing today?" she asked.

The first group, made up of people who wanted to be there, answered enthusiastically. Everyone else remained silent.

"The topic this afternoon is our belief in a Higher Power," Beth continued.

A young man in the middle row groaned.

"You there," Beth said to the man. "What are your thoughts about a Higher Power?"

The man's head dropped in dramatic fashion, as if it had suddenly become detached from his neck.

"Ah, do I have to?" he complained. "My counselor said I have to come here but that I don't have to talk."

"Why are you even here if you don't want to talk?" someone shouted out. "You're wasting our time."

"Forget you, pal. I was ordered by the court to be here," the young man shot back.

Beth walked down the aisle toward him.

"You are correct. Participation is not mandatory; however, I think you'll get a lot more out of being here if you join in."

"I'll speak," said a middle-aged woman sitting toward the back of the room. Her hair was unkempt, and her shirt needed ironing.

"Great, please do!" Beth said.

"My name is Jackie, and I am an alcoholic."

"Hi, Jackie!" the audience called out.

"This is Day Six of sobriety for me."

Loud applause.

"Anyway, this is a difficult topic for me. I don't believe in God. I wouldn't say that I am an atheist. That would mean I've actively decided about the afterlife and the role of a Supreme Being and all that, which I haven't."

Jackie tilted her head toward Beth.

"I would say I have neither faith nor disbelief in God," she continued. "That makes me agnostic. How's that going to work in AA?"

Beth strolled to the front of the room with her hands interlocked out in front of her, as if in prayer.

"What we're really talking about here is Step Three of the AA Big Book, which reads as follows: 'Made a decision to turn our will and our lives over to the care of God as we understand Him.'"

Beth looked out at the audience. Blank faces stared back at her.

An older, diminutive woman clutching a rosary in her hand stood up.

"My name is Rosie Garcia, and I am an alcoholic."

"Hi, Rosie!"

"Jesus is the one and only true God. Anything else is blasphemy." The woman sat back down.

A man shot to his feet.

"Hi, I'm Ben, and I am an alcoholic."

"Hi, Ben!" came the chorus of replies.

"Define God," he said, challenging Rosie, his tone confrontational.

Heads in the audience nodded in agreement.

Beth intervened. "Rosie has found her Higher Power. Have you, Ben?"

The man stepped back, startled that the tables had been turned on him.

"Well, I guess I don't understand the darned topic," he said in a raised voice. "Unlike the young lady who said she is agnostic, I definitely have made up my mind. There is no God!"

Rosie shot the man a dirty look.

"Ben, in Alcoholics Anonymous we are talking about spirituality, not religion," Beth answered. "I would encourage you to embrace the God of your own understanding. This would be your Higher Power."

"Beth, I am not following you," Ben said. "If you are talking about worshiping a deity like Buddha or Jim Jones, that self-anointed Supreme Being who killed everyone with Kool-Aid at Jonestown, forget it!"

Beth walked over to Ben, put her hand on his shoulder, and gently guided him back down to his seat. Then she softly explained:

"Folks, your Higher Power can simply be your dream of what you want to be. As long it inspires you to live better and you feel you can trust it, it's acceptable.

"Then, and only then, can you turn over your will and life to the care of a Higher Power. Does that make sense?"

Beth looked around the room, which had gone totally silent.

"You there," she said, calling on Tate.

Tate groaned. He didn't feel comfortable in crowds, and spilling his guts to strangers wasn't his thing. Immediately, his skin felt like it had gotten twenty degrees warmer under his shirt.

Perspiration built on his forehead, and the room started spinning a little.

"What's your Higher Power?" Beth asked.

Tate stood up. His knees buckled a little. There were so many eyes on him that it was suffocating.

"The universe," he replied, "with all its stars and planets, and heaven and earth."

The other attendees politely applauded.

When Beth turned to call on someone else to speak, Tate tried to nonchalantly wipe the perspiration from his forehead. There was no hiding the sweat stains that had built in his armpit areas during his short time in the spotlight, however.

"I get it now," Ben said, once again springing to his feet.

"To answer your question, then, my Higher Power would be the younger version of me, the guy who was confident and self-assured back in his midtwenties, before I became a drunk!" he declared.

"Great, Ben!" Beth replied, walking back toward him. "That works."

***

After the meeting, Tate returned to the office. An envelope was waiting for him on his desk. It was addressed to him but had no return address.

Another anonymous letter? he wondered.

He ended up in Japan the last time he got one.

Tate poked his head out of his cubicle and looked around to see if anyone was playing a joke on him, but there was no one around. Therefore, he opened it.

The letter was written in elegant, very distinctive writing—unlike the one from Japan, which had been sloppy.

The anonymous writer took aim at the Knights of Malta and the pope.

> Pope Anthony has taken control of the Knights of Malta, one of the most ancient religious orders in the world.
>
> The pope recently forced the resignation of the current grand master, a conser-

vative, who had been approved by Pope Benedict in 2008.

Pope Anthony has installed his own person as the acting leader.

He has also named Bishop Gustavo Zanchetta—who has been accused of sexual wrongdoings—as his special delegate to the Knights of Malta.

This has given the pope all necessary powers to exert total control over the sovereign organization.

Tate blinked several times. Then, he scratched his head. *I've never even heard of the Knights of Malta,* he thought.

Tate picked up the interoffice phone and called Liz in the library.

"Hi, Liz. John here."

"Hello, John!" she replied, a bit too enthusiastically, as if she were a tad lonely down in the basement, where her office was located.

"Glad you're back. How'd things go in Japan?"

Tate sucked in a deep breath and blew it out. He'd forgotten all about the secret Sister Agnes had given to him. The reporter had been so busy lately, he hadn't figured out yet what to do with it.

"It was an interesting trip," Tate said. "Say, I need your help. Can you get me anything you can find on the Knights of Malta?"

An hour later, Liz was standing in Tate's cubicle with an iPad in one hand and a bunch of papers in the other.

"The Knights of Malta is a religious order of the Church," she said. "In 1113, the order was placed under the authority of the pope. Today it has about thirteen thousand members worldwide.

"In 1953, the Vatican recognized the sovereignty of the Knights of Malta, giving the order diplomatic immunity."

Tate nodded his head.

"According to dossiers, memos, and documents that I found during my research, in 2017 Pope Anthony asked Grand Master Matthew Fettering to resign, which was odd because grand masters usually stay in the position for life," Liz explained.

Tate pushed back in his chair and stared up at the ceiling.

"Who is the grand master of the order now?" he asked.

"Giacomo Russo. He was handpicked by Pope Anthony."

"Did Pope Anthony say why he replaced Fettering?" Tate probed.

"No, it was all kept hush-hush," replied Liz, who pulled up a chair and sat down.

She showed Tate a 2017 blog post written by several cardinals who didn't support the pope's decision to push out Fettering.

"The cardinals called upon Fettering to withdraw his resignation and to fight against Pope Anthony," Liz explained.

"And did Fettering fight?"

"No," Liz answered.

"You know, John, the timing of Fettering's resignation seems weird."

"How so?" he replied.

"Well, in 2013 Pope Benedict XVI resigned," Liz explained.

"His resignation was unexpected and unheard of in modern times. Popes don't quit."

"What's your point?"

"Fettering and Pope Benedict departed right around the same time," Liz said. "They were both conservatives."

"Is Pope Anthony a conservative?" the reporter asked.

"Not at all." Liz laughed.

Tate interlocked his fingers, then pulled back on them, making a loud cracking sound.

"You shouldn't pop your knuckles like that, John," Liz scolded. "You will get arthritis in them one day."

Tate drew his head back.

"Okay, Mom." He chuckled.

"Just saying."

Tate liked Liz. She had style.

Liz reminded him of the lead character in *The Girl with the Dragon Tattoo* novels, Lisbeth Salander, who was terrific at conducting research. Liz was also young and hip like Lisbeth Salander and was fantastic at research.

"Liz, what else can you tell me about Pope Anthony?"

"I can tell you that he's under attack," Liz said.

"By whom?"

"By the media, over his handling of clergy sex abuse," Liz continued. "In addition, he's under attack from his own clergy."

"How so?"

"Here's an article by Cardinal Gerhard Schmidt of Germany, who has been one of Pope Anthony's biggest critics," Liz said, handing the story to Tate, who quickly read the first few paragraphs, then let out a low whistle.

"According to this, Cardinal Schmidt wrote a five-page 'Manifesto of Faith' in 2019, in which he warned against 'the fraud of the anti-Christ,' which was a thinly veiled shot at Pope Anthony," the reporter summarized.

Liz nodded, then continued to explain the rest.

"Pope Benedict appointed Cardinal Schmidt as the Vatican's Chief of Doctrine in 2012," she noted.

"He basically interpreted Church teachings. Schmidt was said to have had the ear of Pope Benedict. They were close.

"However, the same wasn't true when Pope Anthony took over. In fact, the current pope removed Cardinal Schmidt from his Vatican position."

"Why?" Tate asked.

"The cardinal and pope had a falling out after Pope Anthony offered an opening to letting divorced and civilly remarried Catholics receive Communion."

"Being a divorced, former Catholic, I know how that one goes," Tate said.

"Church teaching holds that unless divorced Catholics receive an annulment, or a Church decree that their first marriage was invalid, they are committing adultery and cannot receive Communion unless they abstain from sex."

"Ouch," Liz added. "Abstain forever, that's harsh."

"I take it there were quite a few cardinals who agreed with Cardinal Schmidt, and they don't want divorced and civilly remarried Catholics to receive Communion?" Tate asked.

"Correct. Four conservative cardinals later attacked the pope's position as vague and confusing. They publicly requested that Pope Anthony clarify himself."

Tate gazed shortly out the window, as if looking for answers.

"Liz, are there other negative stories about the pope?"

"There are rumors that he wasn't properly elected in 2013 after Pope Benedict XVI resigned," she said.

"Wait, what?"

"Yes, it's true," she continued. "The media has written plenty about it. Just the other day, in fact, several reporters asked Pope Anthony after a Mass in Rome if his supporters canvassed behind the scenes for his election back in 2013."

"What's wrong with canvassing?" Tate asked.

"It's against Church rules," Liz said.

"Really?"

"Yup, and according to opposing cardinals, the penalty on the books should apply."

"What's the penalty?" Tate asked.

"His election would be invalidated."

Tate got up from his chair and walked around his desk to where Liz was sitting. He took a seat next to her in an empty chair.

"This is really fascinating, Liz! It reminds me of something Mark Twain once said."

"What did he say?" she asked.

"Twain said, 'The Church is always trying to get other people to reform; it might not be a bad idea to reform itself a little, by way of example.'"

They both laughed.

Just then, the *Sacramento Union*'s front desk phone operator, Gladys, called out across the newsroom floor to Tate.

"John, there's a caller on the main line who wants to talk to you! He says it is important."

Tate picked up the phone. Bishop Jaime Nunez of the Diocese of Sacramento was on the other end of the line. The diocese operated all the Catholic churches in the area.

The reporter's stomach fell.

The last time he saw Bishop Nunez was a year ago at Sacramento Valley High School, under bizarre circumstances.

"Mr. Tate, how are you feeling?"

"To be honest with you, my mind keeps going back to that day."

"That's understandable," the bishop replied. "The mind sometimes takes a little longer than the body to rebound."

Tate thought back to the incident that happened at Sacramento Valley High School.

Students had just returned to on-campus learning after having been engaged in distance learning (homeschool) during the early days of COVID-19.

Tate had been there for an interview with the principal. He'd just wrapped up the interview and walked out of the principal's office, which opened to an interior hallway, when he heard a loud pop, pop, pop.

Screaming students rushed out of their classrooms and into the interior hallway. They were sitting ducks for the shooter. Tate froze as it all went down.

His brain seemed to malfunction at the sight of injured students and blood.

The reporter just stood there as the shooter approached him. His feet were frozen in place.

Tate was taught to never get directly involved in a story. But now, he was smack dab in the middle of the action, with nowhere to go.

Then, Tate fainted.

When the reporter woke up, he was in the school parking lot surrounded by medical personnel. He had an intravenous tube connected to a vein in his arm.

A person with a white collar stood over him, Bible in hand.

"Who are you?" Tate asked, looking up at the holy man.

"My name is Jaime Nunez. I am the bishop of the Diocese of Sacramento."

"Am I injured? Was I shot?"

"No, but you are in shock. You fainted."

Tate rolled his eyes in obvious embarrassment.

Swell, the biggest news story of the year happens right in front of me, and I fainted, he thought.

"Would you like a blessing?" Bishop Nunez asked.

"No, but thanks anyway."

The bishop's mouth fell open.

"Why don't you want me to pray for you?"

"Sorry, Bishop, I don't mean to sound ungrateful. I'm thankful that you're here. I am a Christian, but not a Catholic anymore."

"Why not?" the bishop asked.

"I'm not a fan of the clergy abuse," Tate replied. "Besides, I'm sure there are others here who have real injuries and could use your help."

Tate pressed his lips together, stood up, and removed the IV drip from his arm. He let out an exasperated sigh and walked off toward his car.

"The best thing I can do right now is get out of everyone's way," the reporter grumbled.

After the shooting, Tate developed a terrible case of writer's block. He had a hard time concentrating.

His managing editor saw that Tate was struggling, but unlike what happened in Redding, this time Rollings was there for his star reporter.

"Look, pal, go easy on yourself," Rollings said one afternoon. "You never know how the mind is going to react in a crisis situation.

"I was an officer in the Gulf War and saw some guys pull through when I didn't think they would and others fail when I thought for sure they would make it."

"I just stood there, Chief," Tate remarked.

"Maybe, just maybe, you froze because you were out of your normal element as a reporter," Rollings said. "What is it I always tell you?"

"When the elephants are fighting down below, the monkeys are up in the trees," Tate answered.

"That's right," Rollings agreed. "When the shooting went down, you weren't up in the trees. You were on ground level, in the center of it all."

"That's true, Chief. But why didn't I do what any other man would have done, huh?"

"And what's that?"

"Punch that kid!" Tate replied.

The managing editor shook his head and dug his fingers into his temples. For several moments he thought about what to say next.

"You're being too hard on yourself," he finally said.

Tate rolled his eyes.

"During Desert Storm I got jumped by two bad guys," Rollings continued. "I didn't fight back. For days in my hospital bed, I wondered why I hadn't pulled a knife or done anything to defend myself. And you know what?"

"What?"

"I eventually came to terms with how I reacted," Rollings said.

"How so?" Tate asked.

"I lived because I didn't fight back. Here I am today, still alive, and glad that I am. Don't second-guess it."

"It's hard not to."

"Look," Rollings said, his voice softening. "Are you keeping up with your AA meetings?"

"Yes."

"Good. Staying off the booze?"

"Still sober."

"Excellent! You are doing great! Stay strong, John."

Tate's muscles tightened, and he bit his lip. "Am I going to get fired?"

"John, don't be concerned about your job. This is something different than what happened before in Redding. I've got your back. You've done everything I've asked you to do. You remember what that was?"

"How could I forget, Chief?"

"I told you to stay sober. Go to AA meetings every day, and don't miss work. As long as you do those three things—and you have—I'll protect you, even if all you do is stare out the window."

Tate stood taller.

Soon after their conversation, he started writing again. Rollings's support had made all the difference. In the process, the managing editor had learned how better to handle Tate.

"Hello? Hello? John? Are you still there, John?"

Bishop Nunez shouted into the phone.

The reporter leaned forward. He'd drifted, but the bishop's shouting brought him back.

"Um, yes, sorry," Tate apologized.

"Where'd you go there, John?"

"I got distracted," he replied. "Say, Bishop, is that the only reason for your call today, to see how I am doing?"

"Yes, that's it. Why?"

"Well, it isn't every day that a former parishioner gets a phone call from the local bishop," Tate answered. "I'm sure you are very busy."

"Never too busy to check on my flock, whether they come to church or not."

Tate felt his cheeks flush. He squirmed in his chair. Beads of sweat ran down his back, even though the temperature in the office was cool. His ex-wife used to call what he was feeling "Catholic guilt"—the sense of having done something wrong even when he hadn't.

"You sure there isn't something else you want to talk about, John?"

"There is something else, yes," the reporter replied.

"What is it?"

"I received an anonymous letter today," Tate shared. "The writer talked about the pope and the Knights of Malta. I was wondering, did you send that letter?"

Bishop Nunez was quiet on the other end of the line.

"The writer was critical of Pope Anthony's recent decision to take control of the Knights of Malta," Tate continued.

There still was no answer.

"I find it odd that I received an anonymous letter today, and then, out of the blue, you just happened to call me. Is it a coincidence, or are you behind the letter?"

"Someone else wrote it," Bishop Nunez finally said.

"Hmm, I still find it an odd coincidence."

"The Lord works in mysterious ways," the bishop joked, attempting to lighten the conversation.

"Bishop Nunez, a nun from Japan recently told me that the Church has been captured by corrupt forces. Do you know what she meant?"

"What I love about the Bible, John, are the parables. Instead of directly answering a question, Jesus often told a simple story, or a parable. I'd like to answer your question with a parable."

Tate rolled his eyes and checked his watch. He didn't have time for a sermon.

"During the papacy of Pope Paul VI, a nun from Portugal named Sister Lúcia received a letter from the leader of a Masonic group in Rome.

"In the letter, the Mason praised Pope Paul VI for his extremely progressive agenda for the Church.

"The Masonic leader said it was the first time in the history of Masonry that 'the dying head of the greatest Western religion' was not in a state of hostility with Masonry."

Tate let out a low whistle.

"The dying head? Is that a reference to the pope?" Tate asked.

"Yes, it was," Bishop Nunez replied.

"You asked me if the Church has been captured by corrupt forces. I would answer your question by instructing you to start your research with Masonry.

"Have a nice day, John."

Without another word, the bishop hung up.

Chapter 5

THE ANGRY BOY GROWS UP

California, 2022

Several weeks after his meeting with the pope, Giuseppe boarded a plane from Rome to San Francisco to see his son, Giovanni, who had yet to learn of his promotion.

The old man took an early flight out of Leonardo da Vinci International Airport.

Giuseppe hated to travel, particularly when it involved flying. His body was weary with age, and the flight he was now on was taking a bitter toll.

His body ached.

The trip was fourteen hours, and the airplane was jam-packed with people. Giuseppe was squeezed in between two very large passengers who pressed against him from both sides.

He did not notice the stalker watching him from four rows back.

Because he was uncomfortable, the old man did not sleep on the plane. He nibbled on cheese and crackers that he had packed in a knapsack and started to reminisce about the past, something he did quite often as he got older and older.

Giuseppe thought back to 1953 when he'd received an urgent phone call from US President Dwight Eisenhower.

"Giuseppe, Ike here."

"Mr. President, how may I help you?"

"Have you heard the news?" the president asked. "Joseph Stalin is dead."

Giuseppe had indeed heard the news on the radio earlier. The unexpected death of the communist leader of the Soviet Union for the past twenty-nine years left the world's second superpower with a pending regime change.

Depending on which news report you listened to, the totalitarian died of either cerebral hemorrhage, a stroke, a massive heart attack, or of poisoning at the hands of the Americans.

European radio reports all credited Stalin as the man who helped save his nation from Nazi domination during the war, but American journalists labeled him as the mass murderer of the century, having overseen the deaths of between eight and twenty million people.

"This is a problem," the president said.

"How so?" Giuseppe replied.

"This is an opportunity to shift world politics, and our enemies know it," said Eisenhower. "We have to be on high alert."

"Mr. President, are you going to use this as an opportunity for a showdown with the Soviet Union?" the

American ambassador asked. "That could force an end to the Cold War. Or at a minimum, will you seek an easing of hostilities?"

"No, Giuseppe, I am not interested in a showdown," said President Eisenhower. "I have only been in office for two months. There are other things more important that I want to accomplish at home than to go after the Soviet Union during its period of high vulnerability."

"Then, it's peace you seek?" Giuseppe asked with a hopeful tone.

"Yes, this is a chance for peace," said the president. "But there could be problem."

"What?"

"The Knights of Malta are becoming too powerful in international politics, with very little to no accountability," said the president.

"Despite having no fixed territory besides its head-quarters building in Rome, the order is considered a sovereign entity under international law.

"Because of this unique political status, the Knights of Malta wields a lot of political clout."

"Does the Knights of Malta have official relations with the United States?" Giuseppe asked.

"No," answered the president. "Therefore, we have no way of knowing what political agenda it is pushing and with whom."

"That's scary," the American diplomat said.

"With the death of Stalin, we don't know if the Knights of Malta will seek to somehow influence the government in the Soviet Union and have a hand in the selection of its next leader," President Eisenhower noted.

"How can I help?" Giuseppe asked.

"The leader of the Knights of Malta is elected for life in a secret conclave and must be approved by the pope. I need for you to get Pope Pius XII to clamp down on the order."

Giuseppe agreed. He immediately went to see Pope Pius XII and explained the urgent situation.

"I share President Eisenhower's concern about the growing influence of the Knights of Malta," said Pope Pius XII.

"That is why, two years ago, I tried to reel them in. I challenged their claim to independence, and I ruled that because the Knights of Malta lacked land, it only had functional sovereignty.

"My point was that the State of Vatican City, with one hundred ten acres, enjoyed true sovereignty, thus we outranked them."

"Was it your intention to put the Knights of Malta under the Vatican's watchdog office that is in charge of the other religious orders?" Giuseppe asked.

"Absolutely," said Pope Pius XII.

"And how did that go over?"

"Not so well," answered the pope. "The aristocrats who were used to running their own show pushed back. When Grand Master Don Ludovico Chigi-Albani died in 1951, there was a power play that backfired against me."

"What happened?" Giuseppe asked.

"The Knights of Malta selected a new temporary head, Count Antonio Hercolani, and announced it to the outside world—before informing me.

"I found myself confronted with a fait accompli. As a result of the power play, I agreed to grant sovereignty to the Knights of Malta in exchange for their promise to revise their constitution in order to curb their practices that led to criticism of the Church."

Giuseppe didn't know what to tell President Eisenhower.

He left his meeting with Pope Pius XII uncertain as to what his next move should be.

The pope had obviously tried once before to clamp down on the Knights of Malta, but it blew up in his face.

Then a bold idea came to Giuseppe.

He decided to write a letter directly to the Knights' grand master, Count Antonio Hercolani. Giuseppe requested a one-on-one meeting.

A week later, a reply came back, short and concise: "Tell us where the Third Secret of Fatima is, and we will grant your meeting." Giuseppe crumpled up the piece of paper and threw it in the trash.

Nine years later, in 1962, the Knights of Malta were still a problem. Giuseppe was unsettled by how much Pope John XXIII was using the order to work with the Soviet Union.

The prior year, Pope John XXIII had approved a new constitution for the Knights of Malta and installed Friar Angelo de Mojana di Cologna as grand master, replacing Count Antonio Hercolani.

Under Friar de Mojana, the Knights of Malta became one of the largest organizations of the Church.

The number of Knights increased from three thousand to more than ten thousand, and the number of national associations increased from twenty-eight to thirty-nine.

The Knights of Malta was regarded with the kind of high social prestige linked to ruling kings.

At the same time, Pope John XXIII began a policy of dialogue with Soviet leaders. He was also reaching out to the Eastern Orthodox Catholic churches—roughly half of which were in the communist Soviet Union—in an attempt to unite them under the Vatican, which troubled Giuseppe.

Furthermore, the pope's Second Vatican Council did not condemn communism and did not even mention it, which also bothered Giuseppe.

Given Pope John XXIII's active involvement with the Knights of Malta, Giuseppe was highly concerned that the pope could be cutting back-room deals with the Soviet Union that might not be in the best interest of the rest of the world, particularly America.

So, one day, out of an abundance of caution, Giuseppe asked for a meeting with President John F. Kennedy.

"Mr. President, Pope John XXIII is going out of his way to befriend the Soviet Union, and I don't trust it. He's heavily engaged with the Knights of Malta, which has diplomatic immunity and is very powerful."

"Don't we want the pope to help us with the Soviet Union?" replied President Kennedy, a Catholic himself. "Isn't that a good thing?"

"Not like this," Giuseppe responded. "Your predecessor, President Eisenhower, believed the Knights of Malta were becoming too powerful in international politics, with very little to no accountability.

"I am worried that some type of secret accord has been reached between Pope John XXIII and the Soviet Union."

***

Suddenly, turbulence jarred Giuseppe back into the present moment. "Sir, please return your seat to its upright position," the flight attendant cautioned.

An hour remained before landing, so Giuseppe decided to practice in his head what he would say to Giovanni. The two men hadn't spoken in quite some time. Their relationship was not a good one.

From a very early age, Giovanni was an angry kid in overbearing need of attention.

For example, when he was about twenty months old, he clashed with a boy at a New York park. Giovanni's mother soothed him—problem solved.

An hour later, however, Giovanni, who was already potty-trained, walked over to where the boy was playing, pulled down his pants, and peed on the other kid.

"He knew exactly what he was doing," his mother complained to Giuseppe that evening. "Giovanni waited until an opportune moment to exact his revenge."

When Giovanni got a little older, he would pinch, trip, or push other children and smile if they cried.

He would break into his mother's purse, remove her wallet, and rip up all the bills.

Once, when Giovanni was five, his mother scolded him for being mean to another child after Mass. Giovanni walked upstairs to his parents' bathroom and flushed his mother's eyeglasses down the toilet.

"His behavior isn't impulsive," his mother reported to a therapist. "It is very thoughtful, premeditated."

They admitted Giovanni to a psychiatric hospital three times before sending him away to a boarding school in Switzerland.

One psychologist at the boarding school assured Giuseppe that his son would grow out of it; the problem was merely delayed empathy.

Giovanni was impulsive, another said, and medication would fix the issue.

Yet another suggested that he had reactive attachment disorder, which intensive therapy would fix.

One day, the headmaster of Giovanni's boarding school reported to Giuseppe that he caught his son wrapping his hands around another child's throat.

The headmaster separated them, and once they were in his office, he pulled Giovanni aside.

"What were you doing?" the headmaster asked.

"I was trying to choke him," Giovanni said.

"You realize that would have killed him? He would not have been able to breathe. He would have died."

"I know."

"What about the rest of us?"

"I want to kill all of you."

Giovanni later showed the headmaster his sketches, and the boarding school headmaster watched in horror as the boy demonstrated how to strangle or suffocate his stuffed animals.

Four months later, the headmaster kicked Giovanni out of the boarding school when he tried to strangle another child.

His father enrolled him in a different boarding school in Switzerland, a cycle that repeated every couple of years.

Giovanni's mother divorced Giuseppe soon after the child was sent away to boarding school. She returned to Italy and stopped seeing Giovanni altogether.

***

When the airplane landed in San Francisco, a chauffeur met Giuseppe at the gate. He wore a tuxedo and a black hat.

"Mr. Tedesco, my name is Constantine. I will drive you to North Beach, also known as Little Italy.

"Unfortunately, while I know you came all this way, Giovanni will not be able to spend much time with you, other than at dinner tonight. His schedule is full.

"I am sure you understand. He is a busy man, and he did not know far enough in advance that you were coming."

Giuseppe's heart sank. His own son did not want to spend time with him.

"After dinner, I will take you to the Westin St. Francis Hotel in Union Square," continued the chauffeur.

They drove to Joe DiMaggio's Restaurant at the Fisherman's Wharf. The place was named in honor of the legendary New York Yankees baseball player.

Giuseppe sat alone in a darkly lit corner of the restaurant and waited for over an hour for Giovanni, who was late.

The waitress served him French bread, which he dipped in olive oil.

The stalker sat a few tables away, just out of sight but well within earshot. He wanted to make sure he could hear every word of their conversation.

Finally, Giovanni strolled in through the front door. His energy was so palpable, it seemed like everyone in the restaurant could feel his arrival in their bones.

The archbishop clasped his arms behind his body, lifted his head, and pushed his chest out. The archbishop stood tall.

Dressed in a black robe with a burgundy sash tied across his svelte waist, Giovanni was dashing. On his head, he wore a burgundy zucchetto.

Giovanni had boyish good looks. Even in his late fifties, his face was smooth and without wrinkles. He had olive skin that glowed and a full head of jet-black hair.

Giovanni's shoulders were strong, built like a boxer's. His large hands were soft, however, not like his grandfather's, Big Al, whose hands had been rough from years of ocean fishing.

The greeter at the front door took Giovanni to his table.

"Dad, I am so sorry to have made you wait," Giovanni lied.

Giuseppe attempted to stand, but he got up too fast, and his legs buckled. The old man nearly fell over.

"Don't get up, Dad, please."

Unable to sit still, Giuseppe stood with all his strength. "Giovanni, I have flown halfway across the world to see you, the least I can do is properly greet my boy."

Giuseppe paid Giovanni a kiss on the cheek. His son did not return the show of affection, however.

For an appetizer, they ordered clams on a half shell, and they ate seafood linguine for the main course.

Having dinner together in the restaurant reminded Giuseppe of a time long ago, when his entire family would eat together at his father's restaurant after closing time.

He missed those days.

After dinner, Giuseppe and Giovanni sipped espresso and ate *bombolone*, another type of Italian doughnut, soft and sweet, either empty or filled with crème pâtissière, chocolate, Nutella, or jam, and topped with icing sugar.

Then, Giovanni ran a hand through his thick hair as the conversation turned serious.

"Dad, why have you come all this way on a moment's notice?" the son wanted to know.

"What is it that brings you here in your frail condition that couldn't be discussed over the phone?"

Giuseppe gathered the thoughts that he had practiced on the airplane.

"Son, I recently met with my old friend Carmine Luizzi, whom you know as Pope Anthony. At his request, I promised to do him a personal favor."

"What sort of favor?"

"More than likely, Son, the College of Cardinals will take a symbolic vote soon on whether or not it still has confidence in Pope Anthony."

"Yes, I have heard the rumblings."

"He needs your support, Giovanni."

A puzzled look came across the son's face.

"I'm not a cardinal, Dad, which means I have no vote in the College of Cardinals."

"That will soon change," the old man replied.

"How so?" asked Giovanni.

"Son, Pope Anthony is shoring up his support. He is removing cardinals who don't support him and adding new ones who will."

Giovanni twisted his mouth and looked at his dad with suspicion.

"What does that mean?" he asked.

"Pope Anthony will soon make you the country's newest voting cardinal!"

The old man paused to let Giovanni embrace the good news, but his son just sat there, expressionless.

"Giovanni, there are currently one hundred twenty-four voting cardinals in the College of Cardinals. Realistically, a vote today could deadlock, sixty-two to sixty-two.

The pope needs one more person on his side to break a potential tie vote. You are going to be that person."

Giovanni's heart raced. He had always wanted to become a cardinal—a position one step away from being the pope, but he was careful not to let his excitement show in front of his father.

The archbishop knew it would hurt Giuseppe if he showed no emotion.

"I am so proud of you!" Giuseppe declared.

Giovanni defiantly straightened his shoulders.

"Giovanni, how do you feel about the news?" Giuseppe pressed. "I really cannot read you right now."

But the son continued to just sit there. He took a big gulp of wine and stared off into space.

"Don't you realize the magnitude of this? The pope is going to make you a cardinal! In exchange, he wants your support, and it's imperative that he gets it."

Giovanni took another large gulp of his wine.

"Pope Anthony needs someone like you on his side, with political savvy."

"Political savvy?" Giovanni burst out.

"You mean he wants someone like you and Grandpa Al, who will lie."

Giuseppe tilted his head. "What are you talking about?"

"You and Pope Anthony want me to be the latest member of our family to hide the Third Secret of Fatima!"

Giuseppe almost fell off his chair.

"You and Grandpa Al have not been honest about the whereabouts of the secret. You both have taken turns hiding it. That's not political savvy. It's called lying."

Giuseppe stared deep into his son's eyes. He saw hatred in them, and it scared the old man.

"Why are you talking about the Third Secret of Fatima?" Giuseppe replied. "This is about you being promoted."

But Giovanni dismissed his father.

"I never understood why you and Grandpa Al thought you had the right to hide the Third Secret of Fatima from the world," Giovanni continued.

The stalker sitting a few tables away listened intently as Giovanni pressed Giuseppe.

"Tell me where the secret is!" Giovanni demanded.

"The Third Secret of Fatima was revealed by the Vatican in 2000," Giuseppe countered, hoping his bluff would quiet his son down.

"Do not con me, Dad. We both know that was a lie. Pope John XXIII instructed you to get rid of the prophecy in 1958. But you didn't destroy it. You hid it. Where?"

The stalker leaned in even closer to hear the old man's answer.

Giuseppe did not take the bait.

"Your entire life you have been angry, Giovanni. Why?"

"Because I was disposed of like a piece of trash," replied Giovanni, who then blew a raspberry at his dad.

The noise sounded like flatulence.

Giuseppe rose from his chair with all his might.

"The pope intends to promote you, Giovanni, and this is how you react?"

Giovanni also rose from his chair. He was trembling with anger, but no words came out, so Giuseppe continued.

"I came here tonight to give you good news. I thought for certain you'd receive it with delight, but I see that I was wrong."

"Yes, you were," Giovanni said through clenched teeth.

"You are not a grateful person," the old man admonished. "You have no grace. You make a mockery of that holy outfit that you have on."

Giovanni snickered.

"I guess my work on Earth is not yet done," Giuseppe continued. "I am going to stick around on Earth a little longer, just to make sure you do the right thing and support Pope Anthony."

"Lucky me," Giovanni retorted.

"And when I finally die, I will haunt you for the rest of your days if you let me down!"

Then the old man turned and shuffled out of the restaurant.

The stalker sitting a few tables away got up and secretly followed Giuseppe before ducking into an alley to call his client.

"Giovanni pressed him hard," the stalker reported to Cardinal Martinelli. "No, the old man didn't say where the Third Secret of Fatima is hidden. Yes, I will continue to follow him."

***

Several hours after his dinner with Giuseppe at Joe DiMaggio's Restaurant, Giovanni received a phone call from Pope Anthony, who confirmed that he was to be promoted.

But there was a problem: Sister Peggy Paige.

Two decades earlier, Sister Peggy arrived at the Archdiocese of San Francisco after graduating from the University of San Francisco, a Catholic university.

From the day they met, Giovanni was attracted to her. Theirs was a long-running, consensual affair that they hid out of necessity.

Today, even at forty-three, Sister Peggy was lovely. She had beautiful facial features absent any kind of blemishes.

Her blue eyes were more magnificent than the most pristine ocean, and her blonde hair was prettier than an angel's wings.

The bloom had definitely not come off her rose.

Giovanni and Peggy were a sight to behold. Both were gorgeous, physically fit, and driven.

They enjoyed the companionship of being with each other in an otherwise lonely religious world that expected abstinence and celibacy.

Their being together sometimes had its disadvantages, though. Both had quirky personalities that could detonate if they weren't careful.

So, when Pope Anthony called about the promotion, Giovanni came clean and asked for the pontiff's help in hiding his lover. Pope Anthony agreed.

The next day, the pope personally called Bishop Nunez at the Diocese of Sacramento and instructed him to find a place for Sister Peggy within his operation.

Giovanni wasn't sure how she'd take the news because Sister Peggy was unpredictable.

But then again, everything she did defied the norm, clear down to how she dressed.

Whereas most modern-day nuns chose to wear pants and a blouse, Sister Peggy still wore a habit—a brown, ankle-length dress cinched at the waist by a white cord (a long rope with three knots tied into it, representing the three vows of poverty, chastity, and obedience).

On her head she wore a white "bonnet," a sort of close-fitting cap, and over that, a waist-length veil. She had sandals on her feet.

As if that weren't different enough, technically, she wasn't even a nun. She was a religious sister.

A nun is mostly sheltered inside a convent day in and day out, to pray and work as part of a "contemplative life," like Sister Lúcia of Fatima had been all of her adult life.

In contrast, a religious sister lives an "active" life and is out and about in the community and brings the Gospel to others where they are. They take simple vows to live a life of poverty, celibacy, and obedience.

Sister Peggy had a degree in psychology, and her job for the Church was to help parishioners who were struggling in their marriages—a contradiction itself, given she had never been married.

On the day Giovanni called to discuss the transfer, he held his breath. True to form, she exploded.

"I don't want to go!" Sister Peggy erupted.

"It's only for a short time," Giovanni lied. "Just long enough for things to blow over."

"What would I even be doing in Sacramento?" Sister Peggy inquired.

"You love to cook," Giovanni pointed out. "Why not be the lead cook at St. James Retreat Center in rural Sacramento County? It's beautiful out there, right along the Sacramento River."

Sister Peggy liked to cook; Giovanni was right about that. She grew up in an orphanage where most things were off limits, including the kitchen.

So, when she left the orphanage at eighteen and entered a convent, she asked the nuns there to teach her how to cook.

"Okay, Giovanni, I will do it," Sister Peggy reluctantly agreed. "But it's only for a little while, you promise?"

"Promise," Giovanni lied again.

"Remember, Cardinal Tedesco, I have the goods on you," she said, only half joking.

"I will not forget you," said the cardinal, liking the sound of his new title.

Out of sight, out of mind, Giovanni thought.

Later that day, she arrived at St. James Retreat Center just in time to cook dinner for a group of Church faithful who had come for a weekend of prayer and rest.

The faithful went home after dinner, so the center was very quiet, which made an already sad Sister Peggy feel even emptier.

"Oh where, oh where has my Giovanni gone? Oh where, oh where can he be?" she sang to herself over and over.

Sister Peggy sat down in the empty dining hall and looked outside. A deer walked past.

"Why, hello there. If you are here for dinner, the kitchen is closed." She giggled.

From the corner of her eye, she saw an old piano. Sister Peggy had taught herself to play when she was in the orphanage.

Children had been allowed to use the piano, and it was her one joy during that depressing time of her life. Playing it was her way of escaping the overbearing nuns.

Sister Peggy walked over to the piano, sat down, and played a couple of Christmas songs because it was the holidays.

First, she sang "Rudolph the Red-Nosed Reindeer," and then "Frosty the Snowman." When she finished, she closed the top of the piano and rested her heavy head on it.

Sister Peggy hadn't felt this lonely since she was twelve years old. That's when the station wagon she had been in with her family on scenic Highway 1 in Monterey, California, flipped after her dad swerved to avoid hitting an animal that had darted across the road.

Glass flew everywhere.

The sound of crushing metal pierced the night. Peggy was sitting in the back seat with her two sisters when the accident happened.

She managed to crawl out of a window just before the station wagon burst into flames, killing her entire family. She was never the same after that.

"Peggy is a nice girl, but she can be detached from reality," said the note in her official mental health file at the orphanage.

Sister Peggy stood up from the piano, her body droopy, and decided to take a tour of the center.

She dragged her feet as she went. Midway through, she realized the place wasn't all that bad. In fact, if the circumstances were different, she'd probably like it a lot.

There were spectacular walking trails along the river, designed to encourage personal reflection.

The center had sixty guest rooms, conference rooms, a banquet hall, a pool, and the most comfortable queen-sized beds you would find anywhere in Sacramento County.

Things it didn't have were room service or in-room television. After all, the purpose wasn't to watch CNN.

Sister Peggy was upset that Giovanni hadn't texted or called her since she'd left San Francisco early that morning. Then again, he was probably busy with his new job.

I will give him a pass this time, she decided.

But he'd better not forget about me.
I was serious about that.

***

The next day at the office, Rollings was watching CNN in the newsroom. He jumped back when it was announced that the pope planned to hold a "Discussion on Clergy Conduct" in nearby San Francisco.

"Pope Anthony is convening priests, bishops, and cardinals from across the country tomorrow, and I want you there, Tate!" barked Rollings.

The reporter groaned. He really didn't want to go.

"Chief, for the record, I just want to say this is just a public relations ploy by the pope to cover up his problems. It's like putting lipstick on a pig."

"Noted, Tate. Have a good trip tomorrow. The discussion is being held outside, in Golden Gate Park. Dress warm and don't be late. The event starts early, and traffic is bad in the mornings."

***

Tate did not sleep well that night, which always happened whenever he had to get up early and travel somewhere. He always worried, first about falling asleep, and then about oversleeping.

That night he took a melatonin and set two alarms, but he still tossed and turned.

At four a.m., unable to fall asleep, Tate gave up. He got dressed and started out on the drive from Sacramento to San Francisco.

There was no traffic that early in the morning, so he arrived in the city by six a.m., which was way too soon. The discussion wasn't scheduled to start until eight a.m.

He parked his car, lit a cigarette, and turned on the radio.

"This is going to be a swell day." He moaned his frustration.

On the radio, two hosts were talking about the "Discussion on Clergy Conduct" on an AM station.

"Have you heard about the event today organized by the pope?" said a cantankerous announcer with far too much energy for Tate that early in the morning.

"Yes, I heard," replied a pleasant female co-host. "Five US cardinals will be discussing clergy conduct and problems within the Church."

"How do you think that discussion among the cardinals will go?" the man asked.

"Should be interesting," the lady said. "After all, it wasn't long ago that one of their very own—Cardinal McCarrick of Washington—was defrocked by the Vatican for sex abuse."

The two radio announcers snickered loudly.

At eight a.m., Tate walked to a roped-off area within the park and found his seat in a spot designated for the media only.

When the discussion got underway, the news came at him fast.

First, it was announced that Pope Anthony had selected Giovanni as the country's newest voting cardinal.

Then, with Giovanni joining them, the five other US cardinals took to the stage and openly aired their dirty laundry. The pope was their target.

And just like that, Tate felt like a monkey in a tree as the elephants were fighting below him.

"Our complaints against the pope include his efforts to expand relations with China, which is an atheist country, his efforts to include other faiths in the Catholic religion, and his position on the family, which accepts gays," one of the cardinals complained.

"Pope Anthony should be more faithful to the centuries-old teachings of doctrine," another quipped.

"His idea of reform is really an attempt to tear down the Church," said yet another.

Cardinal Supan from the Archdiocese of Chicago came to the pope's defense.

"Pope Anthony is a moderate. He is not the radical reformer you are making him out to be!"

"A group of us have drafted a twenty-page letter accusing him of heresy," shot back Cardinal Thomas O'Reilly of the Archdiocese of Boston.

"He's a heretical pope," shouted a cardinal.

The moderator, a priest, grabbed the microphone. He could see the session was spiraling out of control.

"Thank you," he said in frustration.

Before the moderator could get the session back on track, however, Cardinal O'Reilly continued with his diatribe.

"The pope recently said same-sex couples should be allowed to marry," he asserted. "That is blasphemy!"

The moderator knew he had to do something right away, so he cut the discussion short and opened it up to media questions, which went fine until the final minutes.

"Hi. My name is Regina Purcell, and I am from *Tagblatt*, a daily newspaper in Switzerland.

"Can one of you please tell me why the Vatican continues to conceal the Third Secret of Fatima?

"Everyone knows that what was announced in 2000 was a hoax. It has been well over one hundred years since the message was given to Sister Lúcia and her cousins at Fatima.

"Can we please have the truth, finally?"

There was dead silence.

"I am sorry, but your question has nothing to do with our topic," the moderator interrupted.

The reporter continued on anyway.

"And while we are at it, can you please tell us the real reason why Pope Benedict XVI retired? He continued afterwards to wear the white clothing of a pope, lived on the Vatican grounds, and acted like the pope.

"Pope Benedict said his retirement was due to his health, but anyone who followed his schedule, like I do, knows he was just as active in retirement as he was when he was pope.

"He traveled to Austria not long after he retired and gave a flawless speech without any notes.

"This all begs the question: Did Pope Benedict retire, or was he forced out? Maybe he was blackmailed?"

There was a loud gasp from reporters sitting in the area that was designated for media.

"No, no, no. We are not going there!" insisted the moderator.

But the reporter did not stop there.

"Is the resignation of Pope Benedict XVI connected in some way to the Third Secret of Fatima, Father Romano?" the reporter shouted at the moderator.

"You, of all people, should know the answer."

Tate's ears perked up.

What is the reporter implying? Tate wondered.

"A different, last question, please," the moderator ordered.

"Yes, allow me. My name is Vito Romo. I am a reporter with the Italian newspaper *la Città di Salerno*.

"Father Romano, you may not know me, but I know who you are."

The priest squinted at the reporter and studied him hard.

This moderator gig is not going as easily as Bishop Nunez said it would.

"I am sorry, sir, but I do not recognize you," the moderator said. "Your question should be directed to the cardinals, however, not to me."

"Why would I want to waste my time asking a question of them when I have the opportunity to speak directly to you, the boy who saw the Madonna in the woods of Cava de' Tirreni near my hometown of Salerno, Italy, in 1975?"

Again, the audience fell completely quiet.

The moderator froze.

"It happened many decades ago, Father Romano," the Italian reporter continued.

"You are that person who saw the apparition, are you not? Tell us, what secrets did the Madonna share with you that you have not told anyone all these years?"

In the press area, Tate literally dropped his pen. His mouth also dropped.

Chapter 6

THE
WHISTLEBLOWER

California, 2022

Pietro shouldn't have been surprised by how the event at Golden Gate Park was unfolding. Things had been strange for the past several days.

The day before the discussion, Pietro—also known as Father Romano—had gotten up early and went for a five-mile jog along the Sacramento River. The weather was cold out, so he made sure to dress accordingly.

In non-Church clothes, Pietro didn't look like a priest. He was physically fit and youthful looking, with a heavy, dark beard that was well manicured. He resembled a G.I. Joe action figure.

No one else was on the jogging trail at six a.m., his favorite time of the day.

Nature seemed to be alive at that hour.

The air was crisp. There were few people around.

He thought about that day in 1975, when he encountered the Madonna.

The story, which wasn't something he liked to think about, went like this:

> Eight-year-old Pietro and his older sister, Tina, were playing a game of hide-and-seek in the woods behind their house when he saw a brilliant blue light emanating from beyond a canopy of trees.
>
> Being a naturally curious boy, Pietro made his way over to the light.
>
> As he ventured into a clearing beyond the trees, Pietro saw what looked like a ghost—a figure glowing so bright that he had to shield his eyes with his hands.
>
> On closer look, it was a beautiful lady wearing a brilliant white dress.
>
> The apparition was levitating just above the ground and holding a baby in her arms. A rosary hung from Her neck.
>
> The Madonna wore a crown of magnificent jewels on her head. Under the crown she also wore a bright-white veil.
>
> A blue sash with beautiful jewels was tied around her waist.
>
> Pietro rubbed his eyes. He couldn't believe what he was seeing. Then he dropped to his knees.
>
> His local priest at that time, Father Dominic Solano, who liked to tell stories,

had once told a tale about the Madonna appearing in Fatima to three children.

Never in a million years did Pietro think he would see the Madonna too.

Scared to death, he started to cry.

"Do not be afraid, my child," the Madonna said in a gentle voice.

She proceeded to tell him the future. He shook when hearing it.

"My precious little child, you are favored by my Son," the Madonna said. "You will do good works during your lifetime.

"What I have just shared with you must remain a secret until such a time when the world should know. When the time is right, you will know it."

Pietro remained transfixed.

"When that time comes, write down what I have told you. Tell it to the world."

The boy nodded his head.

"Remember, Pietro, I will be with you always."

And then, the Madonna disappeared. He never saw the apparition again.

"Pietro, you must tell Mama and Papa what happened," Tina pressed.

"We have to tell Father Solano too. But first, tell me what the Madonna said!"

"I can't," he replied. "She told me not to share what I heard. The time isn't right."

Disappointed, Tina tried to figure out if there was anything she could tell her family and friends now, so that she would look important.

After all, Tina liked feeling important. She had been in the general area when the Madonna appeared.

"Well, is there anything we can say?" Tina pressed.

"Yes. The Madonna told me to tell Father Solano that the Soviet Union must receive a special blessing from the pope with all the bishops of the world. If not, Russia will 'continue spreading her errors throughout the planet.'"

Tina rolled her eyes.

How boring, she thought.

"Are you sure there isn't anything else we can say right now, Pietro?"

But the boy did what he had been told to do, remain quiet. He did not divulge the secrets now.

Nonetheless, Tina made sure the villagers knew what happened just as soon as they got back.

She told anyone and everyone who would listen that the Madonna had shown up during her game of hide-and-seek with Pietro.

No one believed the story.

The villagers thought they were crazy.

Pietro was labeled a nutcase, a liar, a bad seed, and called other derogatory names.

His parents took him to the doctor.

School officials had him undergo psychological tests.

Even Father Solano thought the boy was nuts.

The priest stopped coming to the Romano house for weekly dinner. He said he didn't want parishioners to get the wrong impression about him. Father Solano did not fraternize with liars, after all.

Pietro was now the black sheep of the village, and his entire family wasn't too far behind him.

"The apple doesn't fall far from the tree," the villagers said.

A short time after the incident, Pietro's life came completely apart. One morning before school, Pietro and his sister visited their dad's bakery, as they often did.

This time, however, was different. They found him dead on the floor. "Bob the Baker," as he was known by everyone, lay in a pool of his own blood.

Not a single customer was around. A note was on the floor beside their father's limp body.

"This is what happens to thieves and the parents of little liars," the note said.

Later that day, the police revealed that Bob was shot and killed by the Camorra, the Naples Mafia family.

"He never said anything about the Camorra," his wife, Madonna, told the police. "How was he involved?"

"He was a numbers runner in the Mafia's Italian lottery and was stealing profits," an investigator told Pietro's mother.

The Italian lottery is a numbers racket, a form of illegal gambling played mostly in poor and working-class neighborhoods, where the bettor attempts to pick three digits to match those randomly drawn the following day.

"Gamblers placed their bets with Bob at the bakery," the investigator continued.

"Your husband then carried the betting slips and money between his shop and the Mafia headquarters, called a numbers bank.

"The bakery was a convenient place to run betting out of because it drew a lot of customers. The Camorra made it worth his while to participate."

The investigator went on to explain that bettors mostly stopped going to the bakery after Pietro's supposed vision of the Madonna.

That was the beginning of the Romano family falling on very hard times.

Because customers stopped going to the bakery, money got tight. When no help came from the Mafia, the elder Romano got upset.

Bob had always been loyal to the Mafia. Never once had he stolen money.

The baker always made sure the money and the betting slips reconciled.

But when the Mafia turned its back on him in his time of need, he started skimming (stealing) money.

Bob hoped no one would notice, but they had. In normal situations, the Mafia would have merely warned the elder Romano to stop; after all, he had never stolen money before.

But this wasn't a normal situation. The Mafia believed Bob's kids made up the story about seeing the Madonna, something it couldn't tolerate.

The Camorra regarded it as blasphemy.

Before his father was killed, Pietro's life was wonderful.

The Romano house was always full of extended family and friends. Sunday dinner was Pietro's favorite thing.

The tiny dining room in their modest Mediterranean-style house would be crammed with people—cousins, aunts, uncles, and grandparents.

The women spent all day preparing pasta, sausages, meatballs, braciole, fish, and antipasto.

The local fishermen would bring clams, cod, and crab. Bob the Baker made bread and desserts, including cannoli, gelato, tiramisu, zeppoles, panforte, *pandoro*, and *panna cotta*.

Espresso brewed throughout the day in a moka pot on the stove.

Father Solano was a regular guest at the dinner table. The village priest dazzled everyone with his after-dinner stories about life in Italy during the Italian renaissance from the late 1950s to early 1960s. The economic boom was so strong that the media dubbed it "The Miracle."

"What is the best car?" Father Solano would call out.

"Fiat!" Pietro and Tina would roar back.

"And where are they made?" he would ask.

"In Turin!"

"Who makes the best scooters?"

"Vespa!"

"And where are they made?"

"In Genoa!"

"Who makes the best tires?"

"Pirelli!"

"And where are they made?"

"Milan!"

"Who makes the best luxury car ever?"

"Alfa Romeo!"

"And where is it made?"

"Milan, Milan, Milan!"

Pietro felt a huge sense of pride in having been born in Italy. That feeling multiplied around Christmas, when they not only celebrated the arrival of Santa Claus, but also the coming of La Befana, an old woman in Italian folklore who delivers gifts to children throughout Italy in early January.

La Befana comes on the evening of the Epiphany, which, in Italy, is celebrated twelve days after Christmas and is the time when Christians remember the traveling Wise Men who arrived to visit Jesus.

"There is nothing better!" Tina would cry out after La Befana visited with gifts.

The Romano's were a deeply religious family, like everyone else in their village. In their house, every room had a crucifix.

The pope's picture hung in the kitchen. There were religious statues in the dining room and a small altar in the living room, where they prayed the rosary each day.

They attended Mass, not just on Sundays, but every morning during the week as well.

Also, there was no shortage of the name "Madonna" among the women in the village, a nod of respect to the mother of Jesus.

But things changed drastically after Bob was murdered. Pietro's extended family stayed away.

A Mafia hit will do that. No one wanted to be on the wrong side of the Camorra.

The funeral was especially depressing. No one came. Not even Father Solano. Pietro's mom had to get a priest from Salerno, some fifteen minutes away, to perform the burial ceremony.

Mrs. Romano was completely cut off from family and friends.

She had never worked a day in her life, but now she found herself with no source of income, so she took a job as a waitress at a café in Salerno.

At thirty-five, Madonna Romano was gorgeous, like a model.

Not too long after her husband's burial, she caught the eye of a visiting American businessman, and just months later they married and moved to New York with Pietro and Tina.

Pietro looked at his watch and checked his speed. He needed to pick up the pace of his run, or else he would be late for the trip with Bishop Nunez to San Francisco.

An hour later, with suitcase in hand, Pietro unlocked the car, walked over to the passenger side, and opened the door for his superior, Bishop Nunez.

Once they got on the road, the bishop's normally jovial mood turned serious. He wrung his hands.

"Pietro, we need to talk."

"What about?"

"Change is coming," said Bishop Nunez.

"What kind of change?"

"Tomorrow at the Discussion on Clergy Conduct it will be announced that Pope Anthony has named a new person to the College of Cardinals. He is from California."

"Is it you?" Pietro asked.

"No, it is the archbishop from San Francisco, Giovanni Tedesco."

"Wait a minute, the pope is selecting someone from California and it is not you?" Pietro asked. "That's not fair! You are the most senior clergyman in California."

"Life is not fair," Bishop Nunez replied. "Besides, the pope knows my health hasn't been so good these last few years."

Pietro's shoulders slumped, and his face tightened.

"How well do you know Giovanni Tedesco?" Pietro asked.

Bishop Nunez knew Giovanni all too well. They had a difficult past; the most recent interaction came just days ago, when the pope asked him to hide Giovanni's lover, Sister Peggy Paige.

"That's a story for a later time, Pietro. Let's just relax now and take in the beautiful scenery along the way."

***

Later that evening, as Bishop Nunez and Pietro reclined in chairs on the hotel's balcony that overlooked the city of San Francisco, the bishop decided to share more of his story about Giovanni.

"In 1961, I was a young priest in Mexico," he began. "My superior assigned me to go to Rome to help Pope John XXIII organize the Second Vatican Council.

"During that time, I developed a close friendship with Giovanni's dad, Giuseppe."

"You knew his dad?" Pietro asked.

"Oh yes, and he is still alive," replied Bishop Nunez. "A very nice man.

"Anyway, many years later I received a letter from Giuseppe. He said Giovanni had been sent away to a boarding school in Switzerland. Giuseppe shared with me that his son was a strange kid."

"Strange how?"

"According to Giuseppe, Giovanni did not smile, ignored adults, did not play well with other children, and was downright mean. He said Giovanni was too much for him and his wife to handle. They were at their wit's end, so Giovanni was sent away."

"Wow!" Pietro replied. "That's pretty extreme."

"Giuseppe said that Giovanni was like a child possessed," the bishop continued. "He also worried about Giovanni being raised around the Mafia."

"The Mafia? Who was in the Mafia?" Pietro asked.

"Giuseppe's four much-older brothers, which would be Giovanni's uncles," said the bishop. "Their violent ways seemed to appeal to the boy's dark nature."

"How so?" Pietro asked.

"On summer breaks, when Giovanni returned home to New York from boarding school, he liked to be with his uncles, particularly when they conducted Mafia business. He shadowed them everywhere, and they seemed to like that.

"Turns out, Giuseppe was right. His brothers were grooming Giovanni for that kind of life, and the boy welcomed it.

"In fact, upon graduating from high school, Giovanni went to work full time with his uncles on Mafia rackets, which included extortion, corruption of public officials, gambling, infiltration of legitimate businesses, labor racketeering, loan sharking, tax fraud schemes, and stock manipulation schemes."

Pietro was wide-eyed.

A cold fog rolled in. Bishop Nunez shivered.

"Well, I must turn in," the bishop said.

"Goodnight, Bishop Nunez," Pietro called out as his mentor went inside the hotel.

Back at his room, Bishop Nunez opened a bottle of Cabernet Sauvignon from the nearby Napa Valley. He slowly drank the fine wine.

He had not shared with Pietro that his head ached, and his stomach was crashing like waves in the nearby the sea.

The trip, while short, had been too hard on the bishop, who was quite old and in poor health.

Bishop Nunez suffered from severe gout that caused intense pain, swelling, and stiffness in his joints.

Some days it was a real chore for him to get out of bed. Many days he just didn't.

More and more, Bishop Nunez couldn't remember things in crisp detail, either.

Several years earlier, Pietro had taken over the day-to-day responsibility of running the diocese.

On this evening, like most anymore, Bishop Nunez needed wine to help him to sleep.

***

The next day, which was the morning of the event, Bishop Nunez didn't answer the hotel phone when Pietro called. Five minutes later Pietro tried again, but there was still no answer.

Maybe the bishop is having another rough morning with his health? Pietro thought.

He decided to let Bishop Nunez rest for a little while longer. He went downstairs to the restaurant for breakfast. Once he got there, Pietro ordered an omelet. He read the *San Francisco Chronicle* while he waited for his food.

A headline caught his eye: "The pope is confusing, is weak on enforcing doctrine, and sows discord among believers, according to the faculty at the University of San Francisco, a Catholic institution."

Pietro let out a heavy sigh. Just then, a sad-looking Hispanic lady approached his table and asked him if she could have a few moments of his time.

"Sure, how may I help you?" Pietro replied.

"Father, my sister Lucinda is a newly ordained nun," the woman began.

"She works right here at the Archdiocese of San Francisco. All of her life she wanted to be a nun. But now that she is one, she may quit."

Pietro did a double take.

"Why would your sister want to quit if she has only been at the job for a very short while?" he asked.

"Because of the archbishop, Giovanni Tedesco," the woman said. "My sister wants to quit because of him."

Pietro froze. This was the same man Bishop Nunez mentioned to him yesterday in the car, the one who was going to be the country's newest cardinal.

"There was a scandal not long ago within the archdiocese," the lady continued. "Did you happen to read about it in the *San Francisco Chronicle*, Father?"

"No, I didn't."

"Anyone among the clergy, and that includes nuns like my sister, who call Giovanni to account for sexual harassment are brought in before archdiocesan lawyers and threatened with sanctions," the woman explained.

"Panels go around questioning those who 'leak' information."

"Your sister was a whistleblower?" Pietro asked.

"Yes! She reported to her superiors some things that were going on that were not okay.

"The archdiocesan lawyers tried to silence her, so she retained her own counsel, which seemed to scare them away.

"Others were not so fortunate. They were sent away for 'evaluations' and not returned for a long time."

Pietro was at a loss for words. He genuinely did not know what to say, so he blessed the lady and left the restaurant, no longer hungry.

Sitting just a few tables away, another person was thunderstruck. Giuseppe had heard the entire conversation. Tears ran down his face.

Pietro took the hotel elevator up to the thirty-first floor, where the luxury suites were. The priest knocked on the door of Bishop Nunez's room, but there was no answer.

After ten minutes, Pietro called the front desk for help. When the bellboy arrived with a key, they entered the room together.

Bishop Nunez was on the ground. He was conscious, but he looked terrible.

"Pietro, you have to go on in my place today as the moderator. It's no big deal. You will handle it just fine."

A short time later, Pietro arrived at Golden Gate Park. The stalker who was following Giuseppe took notice of him.

Well, well, well. Pietro Romano, he thought.

We should have silenced you for good in 1975 when we took care of your dad, Bob the Baker.

Then the stalker saw Giuseppe arrive.

It's a wonder you are still alive, old man, the stalker thought.

I guess there really are such things as miracles.

The stalker was the leader of the Camorra, one of the oldest and largest criminal organizations in Italy, dating to the seventeenth century.

These days, the stalker was engaged in large-scale rackets, such as stealing from the Vatican Bank and fixing construction-project awards in Rome.

In 2012, he'd blackmailed Pope Benedict XVI's butler into stealing papal documents, which he then leaked to the media in order to damage the pope and the Church.

"Come on, let's get this show on the road," the stalker grumbled.

In his opinion, someone of his stature and prominence was too important for the type of work he was doing today. There were other people below him to do it.

But this is what his client, Cardinal Martinelli, wanted. He was told the assignment was too important to pass off to someone else.

In his view, though, there were much bigger issues to deal with back home in Rome.

Suddenly, the stalker's attention shifted back to Golden Gate Park. He noticed a lovely blonde-haired woman dressed like a nun walking up to the roped-off area.

"Well, hello," he said, letting out a sharp whistle. "Look at those long legs!"

A short while later, he observed Pietro take to the stage.

"Folks, let me begin with a few announcements," Pietro began. "Obviously, I am not Bishop Nunez. He is much better-looking than me."

That got a few laughs.

"For over a decade, I have had the pleasure of working with Bishop Nunez. I, however, regret to inform you that he is not feeling well.

"He sends his apologies for not being here. You are stuck with me as the moderator for the discussion with our cardinals."

There was mumbling in the audience. Pietro waited for the buzz to die down before he continued.

He introduced Giovanni as the newest cardinal, which caused a huge commotion.

Frenzied reporters from all over the world were tweeting, blogging, and otherwise losing their minds.

An hour later, word spread among the press that Bishop Nunez wasn't just ill, he'd suffered a massive stroke and was in intensive care four miles away at St. Madonna's Medical Center.

That was newsworthy because Bishop Nunez was highly regarded for providing the homeless population in Sacramento with work and homeownership opportunities.

His programs were said to be ahead of their time, and they were a national model for other cities and organizations.

In the media area, Tate was scribbling like mad in his notebook. He definitely hadn't expected this kind of whirlwind action when Rollings assigned him to cover the event.

When the discussion with the cardinals was over, Tate watched as Giovanni stormed off the stage and left the park. He exited into a waiting black car.

"That was a disaster," Giovanni complained to the stalker. "Pietro stole my thunder. The reporters asked questions of him rather than me."

"Why was he even up on that stage?" asked the stalker.

"Bishop Nunez had a stroke," Giovanni replied. "Pietro filled in as the moderator. A reporter from *la Città di Salerno* asked him about his encounter with the Madonna as a kid."

The stalker shook his head in disgust. "We sent him very clear message years ago not to talk about that."

Just then, there was a knock on the heavily tinted back-seat window, where Giovanni was seated.

He rolled it down to see Sister Peggy standing there. She leaned in and tried to give Giovanni a kiss.

"What are you doing here, Peggy?" Giovanni asked, pushing her away with both hands.

"I came to see you, my love," she replied, somewhat confused by his unenthusiastic greeting of her. "Oh, Giovanni, I am so proud of you!"

"I told you to stay out of sight. Now go away. Someone might see you here."

Across the street in a parked taxi, someone had indeed noticed. Giuseppe watched as the lady dressed like a nun attempted to kiss his son.

At that same moment, Pietro walked past the taxi.

"Follow that priest," Giuseppe told the taxi driver.

As they drove off, someone else was watching—Tate. He had followed Giovanni when he stormed away. Tate had also seen Sister Peggy lean in for an attempted kiss.

Are they having an affair? Tate wondered.

***

The next day, back in Sacramento, Tate's suspicions were raised again when he received another anonymous letter.

This time the secret source claimed Giovanni and a religious sister named Peggy Paige were in a long-running, secret relationship.

According to the anonymous source, theirs was also a volatile love affair that had boiled over a few years back, when the local police were called to the Archdiocese of San Francisco for a domestic dispute.

Tate let out a loud whistle, heard throughout the news-room. Rollings came running over.

"What have you got, Tate?"

"A juicy one, Chief. Our anonymous writer now claims that a religious sister, Peggy Paige, is involved in a relationship with the country's newest cardinal, Giovanni.

The writer also says Sister Peggy was recently transferred from the Archdiocese of San Francisco to St. James Retreat Center in Sacramento County in order to hide her."

Rollings let out his own whistle. "Well, you don't say?"

"The anonymous writer also goes on to say that it is uncommon for a religious sister to be transferred to another diocese in a different county," Tate continued.

"Who would have agreed to transfer her?" Rollings asked.

"You are not going to believe it, Chief, but according to our source it was Bishop Jaime Nunez with the involvement of Pope Anthony."

"What!" Rollings barked. "Why would big people like them be involved in some low-level personnel move?"

"I don't know," Tate replied. "Maybe Bishop Nunez and Pope Anthony are trying to protect the Church from some sort of embarrassment?"

The reporter studied the letter for additional clues. "Should I write the story up, Chief?"

"Tate, this is not the *National Enquirer*," Rollings bellowed. "We don't print gossip stories around here, particularly those involving clergy. You need to be careful. Do some research and get more facts."

Tate dug in. He placed several phone calls to Giovanni at the Archdiocese of San Francisco, which went unreturned.

Next, Tate turned to the other half of the equation—Sister Peggy Paige. Liz's research turned up an old police report. A few years back, an unnamed archdiocese employee had reported an assault on a female employee.

San Francisco Police Department
INCIDENT REPORT
Report Type: Supplemental 334565432
NARRATIVE
On October 15, 2015, at approximately 1206 hrs., an aggravated assault occurred at the Archdiocese of San Francisco. The victim, a female, was uncooperative and refused to identify the person who committed the assault.

The victim was taken to Saint Madonna's Medical Center for treatment. An employee who works with the victim had called the police department after noticing significant bruises to the woman's face and torso. The reporting employee also asked to remain anonymous.
CONFIDENTIAL

Had Giovanni been the abuser? Tate wondered.

Was Sister Peggy the victim?

What Tate did next was brilliant. He placed a small ad in the *San Francisco Chronicle* and asked anyone to step forward who may have been sexually harassed or sexually assaulted by a high-level clergyman from the archdiocese in the past twenty years.

The tip could be anonymous, and definitely no names would be revealed.

In no time at all, Tate received messages from women pointing the finger at Giovanni.

And just like that, Tate was off and running, just as he'd been so many years ago with the air show investigation.

***

The next day, Tate went to see Sister Peggy, who was still missing Giovanni terribly. She thought her heart would explode on the day Tate visited her.

With her cooking duties over for the day and the guests departed, Sister Peggy had hung up her apron and was moping around.

She walked into the empty dining hall, sat down at the piano, and played Beethoven's *Moonlight Sonata*. Next, she played *The Well-Tempered Clavier* by J. S. Bach, then back to Beethoven again for the *Emperor Concerto*.

When the medley was over, Sister Peggy stood up and did a curtsy. From the back of the room a person clapped. Tate then let out a good-natured, "Hooray!"

Sister Peggy turned around, blushing. She was surprised that someone else was in the room. She flashed a huge smile.

"Why, thank you. Thank you very much," she said with a giggle.

Tate walked to the front of the room and stood across from Sister Peggy.

"I am John Tate, a reporter with the *Sacramento Union*."

"Well, how do you do, Mr. Tate?" she said playfully.

"I do just fine," he played back.

"Surely you didn't come to hear me play the piano?"

Tate chuckled. "No, I came to talk to you about Giovanni."

The woman bit her lip and looked at the reporter with questioning eyes.

"What exactly do you want to know?"

"I want to know why you didn't press charges against him when he hit you in 2015. The police were called."

Sister Peggy's face flushed. She took a step back for a moment and then leaned in real close to Tate.

"My private life is just that, private," she whispered with a wink.

"Okay, I understand this must be hard," Tate replied. "How about a different question then? Why were you transferred to Sacramento?"

"Because I needed a change."

"You were transferred because you've been having an affair with Giovanni."

She blushed and broke off eye contact with the reporter.

"With all due respect, and I mean that sincerely, it is none of your business, Mr. Tate. I have broken no laws, and I am an adult."

"I have been doing some digging," he continued. "You are not the only woman Giovanni has hurt."

"I don't know what you are talking about, Mr. Tate," Sister Peggy retorted.

She nervously adjusted her headpiece, a cornette that consisted of a white cloth that was starched and bent upwards. Then she broke out in a strange tap dance.

Tate recoiled. He shook his confused head. The reporter could see Sister Peggy was not totally right in the head.

He could also tell that he was not going to get anywhere with her.

"Here's my business card," the reporter said. "Call the office if you decide to talk. You can ask for either me or my boss, Ed Rollings."

***

That afternoon, Tate headed back to San Francisco, this time on the Amtrak train. During the trip, Liz called him.

"I found something," she exclaimed.

"What?" Tate asked.

"Remember when I was telling you that Pope Anthony is accused of having been improperly elected?" she asked.

"Yes, I do," Tate replied. "You said his supporters canvassed behind the scenes, which isn't allowed."

"According to a report I've found, a group called the St. Gallen Mafia, also referred to as the St. Gallen Group, did the canvassing."

"Since you're talking in the past tense, does that mean the group is now defunct?" Tate asked.

"Hard to say, John. The group was secretive. They may still be around, but operating underground."

Just then the train pulled into its station.

Tate hung up, departed the train, and took a taxi to the archdiocese office, where he waited for Giovanni to return from lunch.

When the new cardinal finally showed up two hours later, his normally dour mood became even darker when Tate introduced himself.

"You say you're a reporter?" Giovanni asked with disdain. "How may I help you?"

"Giovanni, I mean, Cardinal Tedesco, I would like to ask you a question."

"I really don't have much time," Giovanni remarked. "If it's an interview you want, why don't you go back out and see my receptionist? She can make you an appointment for a time when I have more flexibility in my schedule."

"I tried that, for several days, but no one returned my calls," Tate noted. "Therefore, I came here to see you. I am afraid this can't wait any longer."

Giovanni sat down and pushed back in his chair. He shot his visitor a grimacing look.

"Is that so? Well, Mr. Tate, even Jesus had to wait. In fact, he waited six hours before he died. Surely your matter is not more pressing?"

Tate was momentarily speechless.

What a strange analogy, he thought.

"Well, sir, I've always had trouble understanding time in the Bible," the reporter said.

"How so, Mr. Tate?"

"Let me give you an example. Noah was said to have died three hundred fifty years after the flood, at the age of nine hundred fifty. Those numbers seem exaggerated to me. Don't you think so? I've never met anyone that old."

Giovanni gave the reporter a sideways look. He wanted Tate gone as soon as possible.

"Go on, ask your question."

"Why was Sister Peggy Paige transferred from this office in San Francisco to St. James Retreat Center in rural Sacramento County?"

"That is your burning question?" Giovanni fired back. "That's why you came all the way here from Sacramento? You want to know about a cook?"

"A religious sister," Tate corrected. "And, yes, I want to know the reason why."

"Mr. Tate, personnel matters are confidential. You've asked your question. Goodbye."

Giovanni stood up and walked out of his office. He got into the car waiting out front.

"You look like you've seen a ghost," said the stalker, who was again behind the wheel.

"A reporter from Sacramento just came to see me," Giovanni fumed. "He has somehow connected the dots between Sister Peggy and me."

"How did he do that?"

"Someone is feeding him information," groused Giovanni.

"Do you think it's Sister Peggy?" the stalker asked.

"No, she may be peculiar, but Peggy is loyal to me."

"Do you think it's Bishop Nunez?" the stalker continued to question.

Giovanni thought about it for a few seconds but then dismissed the idea.

"No, the stroke has left him too weak to put up any kind of fight."

"Well, then, the big mouth has to be Pietro Romano," the stalker asserted.

"I think you are right," Giovanni agreed. "He pretends to be so special, so holier than everyone else, but in reality, Pietro Romano is nothing more than a big phony."

"What do you want to do about it?" the stalker queried.

"Let's drive to Sacramento and pay a visit to the blabbermouth," Giovanni said.

***

They found Pietro at a local Catholic high school, where he had been pressed into emergency service as interim principal after the regular principal was hospitalized with COVID-19.

Pietro was so busy that he almost didn't notice when Giovanni burst into the lobby.

"You have a visitor, Father Romano," the receptionist called out.

Giovanni's mood, as usual, was dark.

"Cardinal, what brings you here?" Pietro asked.

"I came to talk with you about your recent trip to Medjugorje."

Pietro's head snapped back. *Huh?*

Medjugorje is a controversial topic within the Church.

Located in Bosnia on the border with Croatia, Medjugorje has been a destination annually for millions of people due to claims by six locals of monthly visits by the Madonna, since 1981.

Referred to as "seers," the six locals stand by their claim even though Pope Anthony has said he is doubtful they are true.

Unlike Fatima and Akita, the Vatican hasn't recognized the Madonna's appearances at Medjugorje as genuine.

"You recently returned from a fact-finding trip to Medjugorje, did you not?" Giovanni snarled.

"I did, yes."

"As I understand it, your mission there was to determine if the reported apparitions of the Mother of Jesus are really happening," Giovanni continued.

"Yes," the priest agreed. "You are correct."

"What makes you such an expert on Marian apparitions, hmm?" Giovanni mocked.

Pietro folded his arms across his chest. He didn't answer the question. He knew Giovanni was goading him.

"Pope Anthony tells me that you wrote a report for him about your findings," Giovanni continued on. "He says your report concludes that the apparitions are real."

"In my report, I suggest the apparitions probably occurred in the beginning, but that over time they probably are being faked," Pietro explained.

"And you've come to this conclusion because you have experience with such apparitions?" Giovanni said in an effort to draw out Pietro's own experience.

The bearded priest did not reply. He just kept his arms folded across his chest and his eyes locked on Giovanni's.

"Let me try asking it in another way," Giovanni continued.

"You claimed to have seen the Madonna as a child. Now you want the pope to believe the so-called 'seers' from Medjugorje have also seen the Madonna?

"Of course, if it were true, that would lend more credence to your own bogus claim, right, Father? Strength in numbers, I suppose."

Pietro did not blink.

"I was sent by the pope. I did not ask to go."

Giovanni's eyes narrowed.

"Are you being insubordinate with me, Pietro?"

"No, sir, I mean no disrespect," he answered.

"Are you aware that the so-called 'spiritual director' for the six 'seers' was recently excommunicated from the Church?" Giovanni growled.

"It is all a hoax, every last bit of it."

Pietro felt steam building under his white collar.

"I stand by my report."

"Uh-huh, I see," Giovanni hissed. "Let's talk about this alleged vision of your own. Are we to believe it really happened?"

"Yes."

Giovanni snapped his fingers.

"Then how come you never reported it to the Vatican? Or at the very least, Pietro, why didn't you report it when you entered seminary school?"

"At the time it happened, in 1975, I told my parish priest in Italy, Father Dominic Solano."

"And?"

"He did not believe me," Pietro replied. "No one believed me, except for my sister."

"That should tell you something," said Giovanni with a smirk.

"It tells me people were scared," Pietro fired back.

"Scared of what?" Giovanni challenged.

"The Mafia. The Camorra killed my dad in order to silence me."

"The Camorra killed Bob the Baker because he was dumb enough to steal from them."

Pietro's blood was really boiling now.

"That's a lie!" Pietro shot back. "That is what the Mafia told the police. My dad was killed to silence me."

Giovanni laughed.

"Did it ever occur to you, Pietro, that your parish priest probably did not believe you because you were lying? Just like the six liars from Medjugorje!"

Pietro stared deeply into Giovanni's eyes. He did not like what he saw. There was evil in them.

"The Madonna told me not to speak about my encounter with Her until the time was right," Pietro clarified.

"When the time is right, I will write down the things She told me."

Giovanni stared with wide eyes and raised eyebrows. He couldn't believe what he'd just heard.

Pietro Romano just admitted that the Madonna gave him secrets.

I wonder what they are.

Giovanni collected himself and pressed on. He decided to keep on goading Pietro because it seemed to be working. The priest was losing his cool.

"If I am to understand, the Madonna chose you to impart secrets to because you're better than the rest of us," Giovanni pushed.

Pietro narrowed his eyes. He really wanted to slap Giovanni upside the head.

"Perhaps, Pietro, you kept quiet because you didn't want to be rejected from the priesthood on the grounds of insanity?"

Pietro bit his tongue. He didn't want to completely lose his cool. If he did, he might slip up and tell Giovanni everything.

I need a distraction, he thought.

Pietro focused on Matthew 4:1–11, the Bible passage in which Jesus was led by the Spirit into the desert to be tempted by the Devil, during which time he fasted for forty days and forty nights and afterward was hungry.

The tempter approached and said to Jesus, "If you are the Son of God, command that these stones become loaves of bread."

"Pietro!" Giovanni shouted.

The priest came back to their conversation.

"I asked you, do you believe the Church would have permitted you to become a priest if it knew your supposed story about seeing the Madonna?" Giovanni barked.

"I do," he replied.

"I don't," Giovanni disagreed. "There's no doubt the Church would have deemed you mentally unstable and rejected you on the grounds of insanity."

Pietro burst out in a laugh.

"I already told you that I informed Father Solano, my village priest, when the encounter occurred. I'm certain my claim made its way to the right people in the Vatican, maybe all the way to Pope Paul VI."

Giovanni sneered. It was an eerie sound.

Then he decided to take a different approach. His voice lowered and became nicer.

"Pietro, after the event at Golden Gate Park in San Francisco, I decided to contact the Italian reporter from *la Città di Salerno* newspaper, the one who asked you about what you saw."

Pietro nodded to show that he remembered the reporter.

"The reporter believes you did, in fact, see the Madonna," conceded Giovanni, letting the statement hang out there for several moments, to sink in.

"That's right, the reporter believes you," Giovanni said in a sweet voice.

"He also believes you were told about the Third Secret of Fatima."

"I was," Pietro eagerly replied, then instantly regretted it.

Darn it, Pietro.

You played right into his hands.

"Well, well, well," Giovanni said with a sly smile. "Now we are getting somewhere. Tell me about it."

"No."

Giovanni's face turned red.

"This is insubordination!" Giovanni declared.

But Pietro was determined not to share anything else.

"Pietro, the Vatican released the Third Secret of Fatima in 2000. Surely you are not claiming that what the Vatican released was a lie?"

Pietro looked down at the floor. Then his eyes drifted back up and met those of the person standing in front of him.

This was certainly no holy man.

"Well, tell me, Father!" Giovanni shouted.

"When the time comes, I have a duty to tell the world what I know," Pietro proclaimed.

"Until then, not you or anyone else will force me to talk."

Giovanni pulled his head back.

"You are a liar! First, Pietro, you dignify the false sightings in Medjugorje. Next, you want the world to believe that you, too, were the recipient of a divine visitation by the Madonna.

"Lastly, you assert that the Vatican lied about the Third Secret of Fatima in 2000!"

"You forgot one other thing," Pietro responded.

"What did I forget?"

"I believe you are a bad person!" Pietro exclaimed.

"This is nonsense. Pietro, you are nonsense! Let's get something straight. I don't want to hear any more about your special connection with the Madonna.

"I also don't want to hear about the Third Secret of Fatima, not even a peep.

"You, Father Romano, are delusional. A disgrace!"

With that, Giovanni stormed out of the principal's office.

In a yellow taxi hidden behind some cars just down the street, Giuseppe watched as his son barged out the front door.

He waited until the car Giovanni got into was gone. Then, he went inside the school.

Pietro was sitting behind the principal's desk when Giuseppe entered. The priest's head was buried in his hands.

"Hello. I am Giuseppe. May I have a moment of your time?"

The priest looked at the old man with curiosity.

What is it with surprise visitors today?

"Yes, yes, come in, please," Pietro said. "How may I help you?"

"We have a mutual friend," Giuseppe began.

"Who?"

"Jaime Nunez," the old man replied.

"A long time ago, I became friends with him in Rome. We worked on preparations for Vatican II together."

"Wow! You have known Bishop Nunez for a long time."

"Indeed," Giuseppe replied.

"Throughout the years, we have shared our most intimate secrets with each other. For example, I would tell him about the challenges I was having with my son, Giovanni."

Pietro felt thunderstruck.

This is Giovanni's dad.

"Sir, your son just left my office," Pietro replied.

"Are you here looking for him? I am confused."

"No, I came to see you," the old man said.

Pietro blinked several times. Then he scratched his head.

"When I was a boy, my papa retrieved the Third Secret of Fatima from Sister Lúcia," Giuseppe continued.

"The nun who encountered the Madonna in 1917 in Fatima?" Pietro asked.

"Exactly," Giuseppe replied.

"Bad people, including Hitler, wanted to steal the secret. My papa, who was a US envoy in Italy, hid it for years.

"When I became a US ambassador in Italy after him in the 1950s, he gave the secret to me and told me to protect it.

"I eventually hid it in a place where it remains to this day."

Pietro's mind was working hard to process everything he was hearing.

"Do you know what the secret says too?" Pietro asked.

"No, I never read it," the old man replied. "But *you* know what it says, don't you?"

Pietro looked deeply into Giuseppe's eyes. His gaze cut straight to the visitor's soul. The priest could see the old man was trustworthy.

"Yes, I know what it says," Pietro admitted.

"That is the reason why I came to see you," said the frail man.

"Why?" Pietro asked.

"To tell you that you are in great danger, Pietro."

Chapter 7

EMERGENCY MEETING

Vatican City, 2022

Giovanni called his mentor, Cardinal Martinelli, who listened carefully as his protégé summarized his conversation with Pietro.

Back when Pietro's claim was first reported to him, Martinelli wasn't sure how much truth there was to it. But now, he knew it was true.

"Pietro said that when the time is right, he will share his secrets with the world," Giovanni reported.

This is not good, Cardinal Martinelli thought.

"What would you like us to do?" Giovanni asked over the car's speaker phone.

"I can take care of it the way it should have been handled back in the first place," the stalker volunteered.

Cardinal Martinelli considered the situation for several moments.

"Don't do anything yet," the cardinal said. "Things went sideways in Japan, and we don't need a repeat of that."

The cardinal tapped his fingers on the desk in front of him.

"I have an idea, but it requires some further thought."

When the call ended, Cardinal Martinelli sat for a while longer, deep in thought, his chin buried in his left hand.

Well, well, well.

Pietro knows the future.

He was told the Third Secret of Fatima.

Cardinal Martinelli and Giovanni had known each other for a long time. They met by accident, literally, in Switzerland in 1974, when Giovanni was eleven years old.

The boy had ventured into town one afternoon on his bike to get an ice cream and was struck by a car. The driver got out of his vehicle and was demonstrably concerned, which was something few people had ever shown to Giovanni.

"*Scusami, scusami,*" said the driver in a scarlet outfit, his face flushing red.

"Are you hurt?" the cardinal asked.

"No, sir. My bike is a little bent, though."

Giovanni pointed at the Schwinn bike he'd gotten in a trade with a classmate for a rookie year Willie Mays baseball card.

"Don't worry, I will buy you a new bike," the cardinal said. "My name is Carlo Martinelli.

"Where are you headed? I will take you there."

"To the diner, sir," Giovanni replied. "I was going for a banana split."

"Perfect, let's go," said Cardinal Martinelli. "Banana splits on me!"

The cardinal's kindness felt weird to Giovanni. He wasn't used to anyone caring about him.

The bike accident in Switzerland was the start of what turned out to be a lifelong relationship between Giovanni and Cardinal Martinelli, who became like a surrogate father to Giovanni.

For decades after that incident in Switzerland, Cardinal Martinelli groomed Giovanni to become the pope one day.

But now, an unsettling thought occurred to him.

What if Pietro got in the way of his plans for Giovanni?

If people discovered that Pietro had been visited by the Madonna and that She entrusted him with secrets, they might regard him as more special than Giovanni.

Actually, that wasn't a hard case to make anyway.

Pietro Romano represented all that was good in the world. He had a strict conscience and stood by his principles.

Pietro fought for justice, and he believed in mankind.

In contrast, Giovanni believed in none of those things. His apprentice was unscrupulous.

Furthermore, any baptized Catholic male can technically become a pope. One did not have to be a cardinal to be considered for the papacy, although that was usually how it worked.

That would qualify Pietro.

Cardinal Martinelli picked up the phone on his desk and called for an emergency meeting of the secret combat unit within the Knights of Malta, right away.

***

When the Knights convened later that day, Cardinal Martinelli shared the troubling news with them.

"Our brother Giovanni has learned that someone alive definitely knows about the Third Secret of Fatima!"

There were loud gasps throughout the room.

"What about the Japanese nun?" asked the Prince of Naples.

"We don't know for sure what Sister Agnes knows because the Knights I sent to Japan were foiled by an American reporter named John Tate," Cardinal Martinelli replied.

"But we do know with certainty that a priest named Pietro Romano was given the Third Secret as a boy when he was living in Cava de' Tirreni, Italy."

"I know him," exclaimed Cardinal Solano, the Dean of the College of Cardinals.

"Pietro was a young boy when he reported the encounter to me. I was his village priest at the time. I didn't believe him, but I reported it to you when it happened, Cardinal Martinelli, because you were my superior."

"I remember it well," said Cardinal Martinelli. "The Camorra put its best hit man on the job, a guy named Frank Tallerico Sr., and we tried to shut the kid up."

The room fell silent.

"So, what will be done?" someone asked.

"We need to make a move on Pope Anthony," Cardinal Martinelli declared.

He stood up from the table.

"Cardinal Solano, will you please join me in the other room for a quick chat?" the cardinal asked.

The two men conferred away from the rest of the group.

"Dominic, please convene the College of Cardinals," directed Cardinal Martinelli. "Time for a vote."

He put on his red cassock and scarlet zucchetto, and then made his way to see Pope Anthony, who was waiting for his visitor in his study.

"Cardinal Martinelli, how are you? Please, come in."

The pope's butler took Cardinal Martinelli's red jacket and hung it up.

The two men sat in the wingback chairs and waited while the butler poured them iced tea.

"What brings you here today?" Pope Anthony asked.

"I want you to hear it from me first," Cardinal Martinelli replied. "There will definitely be a vote by the College of Cardinals as to whether or not the body still has confidence in you."

"I knew it was coming," Pope Anthony remarked. "I've been planning for this day."

"How do you feel about it?" Cardinal Martinelli asked.

"I am feeling rather confident," the pope replied. "I've added a lot of people to the College of Cardinals who will support me, like Giovanni.

"This is nothing more than sour grapes. Certain people didn't want me elected in 2013, and they have been coming at me ever since."

Pope Anthony saw by the look on Cardinal Martinelli's face that he didn't agree, which made the pontiff uncomfortable.

"Cardinal Martinelli, what is it? You seem troubled."

"Carmine, you have been the pope for more than seven years now, and yet, in all that time, not much has happened, at least, not in the way we had hoped."

The color drained from Pope Anthony's face.

"Cardinal Martinelli, how can you say that? I have put action behind my words."

"Talk is cheap, Carmine."

The remark felt like a punch to the gut.

"I have made it possible for divorcees to receive Communion, and I have supported gay marriage," said Pope Anthony.

"I have also asked my clergy to show mercy to all sinners. By the way, I am paying a price for that one."

"Paying a price how?" asked Cardinal Martinelli.

"Have you seen the posters of me scowling? They are all over the city."

He was right. The residents of Rome awoke several days ago to posters all over the city with the words "Ah, Pope Anthony, you have intervened in congregations, removed priests, seized the Knights of Malta…but where is your mercy?"

The reference to mercy was a referral to his "Year of Mercy," a yearlong campaign during which time clergy were instructed to "reach out to all sinners in a spirit of radical forgiveness."

Cardinal Martinelli rocked back and forth in his chair and thought about what to say next.

"I will not be directing my followers one way or the other on how to vote," Cardinal Martinelli lied. "I will tell them that each person must vote as their own conscience dictates."

"Cardinal Martinelli, you are willing to take such a risk? What if the majority of cardinals vote that they no longer have confidence in me?

"There would undoubtedly be pressure on me to step down, and then you will lose too, because we are friends."

"There is no risk, Carmine. Another person waits in the wings who believes in our cause, clear down to his very soul.

"Should you lose, he will carry our mantle. He has the conviction you never possessed."

With that, the cardinal stood up and walked out.

Pope Anthony felt a wave of panic and anxiety.

Who has Cardinal Martinelli lined up to replace me? he wondered.

The pope got on the telephone and called his friend Giuseppe.

***

The former American ambassador had heard about the pending vote and took a red-eye flight back to Rome from California, anticipating that his longtime friend would need emotional support.

At the moment, he was dining at his favorite café across from St. Peter's Square when a loud beeping noise erupted.

The alarm on Giuseppe's wristwatch had gone off. He needed to leave the café in five minutes.

The old man turned off the alarm, finished drinking his espresso, and scanned the newspaper, *la Repubblica.* The headline read, "Pope Anthony Blocks Recruitment in Tussle for Control of Knights of Malta."

The story was about how a subgroup within the Knights of Malta was fighting for total control of the entire organization. In response, the pope increased his involvement in the order's affairs.

According to the news report, Pope Anthony had forced the resignation of the previous grand master and ordered the Knights of Malta to stop admitting any new members until certain reforms were made.

Giuseppe put down the newspaper and gathered his coat.

He then slowly walked to the pope's residence. The old man decided not to tell Pope Anthony that he didn't know how Giovanni would vote.

***

While he waited for his visitor to arrive, Pope Anthony went to his study to look over the day's newspapers.

He took notice of an opinion piece in *The New York Times* entitled, "When Priest Weds Nun."

The story read:

> It made news around the world when my parents married fifty years ago this summer. My mother was a teaching sister for a decade, but she had left her order the previous summer; my father had been a priest for eight years.
>
> On the day of the wedding, he was on a leave of absence from his nearby parish and, according to canon law, was auto-

matically excommunicated for marrying without first receiving dispensation from the obligations of his ordination.

As he told reporters waiting outside, he knew that his decision broke the rules of the Church, but he had done so for its benefit.

For him, to marry publicly as a priest was an act of protest meant to nudge Rome toward reconsideration of clerical celibacy and the Church's view of sexuality generally—a reconsideration he had come to regard as inevitable after the reforms of the Second Vatican Council earlier in the 1960s.

For my mother, though she shared these sentiments, their wedding day was more about becoming a bride than a modern-day Martin Luther.

Pope Anthony shook his head and stared thoughtfully at the big stained-glass window in his study that was elaborately etched with a picture of the last supper. He read on:

After decades of growth, the ranks of Catholic clergy in the United States began to decline around the time of my parents' wedding.

Between 1969 and today, the number of priests has fallen nearly 40 percent;

the number of nuns is down roughly three-quarters.

Those who left did so for all kinds of reasons: ambition for secular careers, a longing to start families, just a yearning for another way of life.

Yet entwined with those practical desires was the fact that many among my parents' generation of priests and nuns recognized the Church's fault lines—its tendency toward secrecy, its culture of obedience, its history of abetting abuse— long before outsiders learned the extent of the problem.

As adolescents, both of my parents endured unwanted physical contact from priests who were supposed to be their spiritual mentors, the very men who guided them into religious life.

My mother's memories of the convent also include being required to use a medieval self-flagellation device she and the other sisters called "the discipline."

My father's classmates in seminary included several of the most notorious of Boston's pedophile clergy. Is it any wonder they began to ask to what else their faith might aspire?

Catholic sisters around the world are also now being seen in a new light. Scandals like the abuse suffered by nuns at the hands of priests and bishops recently acknowledged by the pope, have allowed figures too often caricatured as parochial school despots or cardboard saints to be more fully understood.

Yet, it is clear that in the twenty-first century the issue of sexuality and its implications for religious service, long simmering beneath the surface, is in the open as never before.

Pope Anthony hung his head. There were tears in his eyes, and his lips trembled. The pontiff walked back to the foyer to wait for his guest.

He fiddled with his skullcap some more and looked in the mirror. Tired eyes looked back at him. They were puffy and had dark circles under them.

When Giuseppe finally arrived, the pope greeted his guest warmly at the door.

"Giuseppe, how are you?"

The two men hugged and went inside to the pope's study. Just a short time ago, they had met in this very same spot and the pope told him Giovanni was going to become a cardinal.

So much has happened since then, the old man thought.

"Thank you for coming," the pope said.

"Always my pleasure, Carmine. I heard about the vote. How are you feeling about it?"

"Nervous. On paper, I have the numbers to win. You never know what can happen, though. But that is not the reason why I asked you here."

"What is the reason then?" Giuseppe asked.

"In 2000, the Vatican disclosed what it said was the Third Secret of Fatima," said Pope Anthony.

"But how can that be? Didn't Pope John XXIII ask you to get rid of it?"

Giuseppe froze. He crinkled his nose and creased his brow. The old man hadn't seen this question coming.

"Why are you asking me about the Third Secret of Fatima tonight, especially with everything else going on?"

Pope Anthony got up from his wingback chair and, with steepled fingers, walked back and forth. His head was down.

"Did you ever read the Third Secret of Fatima, Giuseppe?" he asked.

"No."

"But your father, Big Al, he surely read the secret after he retrieved it in 1943 from Sister Lúcia when she was very ill? Did he tell you about it?"

Giuseppe ignored the question.

The pope sat back down in his chair. He had throbbing veins in his neck and a jutting chin. His jaw was clenched.

"I have always known you to be an honest man, Giuseppe. I will take your word for it that you never read the Third Secret of Fatima.

"I suppose if Big Al had told you about it, you would tell me."

Pope Anthony looked at his friend, who refused to make eye contact with him.

Then the pope swallowed hard several times and played with his zucchetto. He got up again, paced around the room with a hunched posture, and then sat back down.

Suddenly, he leaned forward, so close to Giuseppe that the former US ambassador could smell the garlic on the pope's breath.

"If there is a vote of no confidence in me, then I will be forced to resign," said Pope Anthony, pointing his finger at Giuseppe.

"I need to know what the Third Secret of Fatima says! Don't you understand, it could be about my future?"

Giuseppe threw back his shoulders.

"I really don't know what it says," the old man replied with his chin up.

The pope's head dropped. In that moment, he looked beaten.

"Ah, well, I guess it doesn't matter anyway," the pope said dejectedly. "Sister Lúcia was the last person to know what the Third Secret of Fatima says. She took the secret to the grave with her."

Giuseppe knew otherwise, but he wasn't going to volunteer that information because Pope Anthony was acting very strange.

"Carmine, try not to focus on what we don't know," Giuseppe responded. "Instead, concentrate on what we do know."

A puzzled look crossed the pope's face.

"And what might that be, Giuseppe?"

"Ever since 1917, Sister Lúcia maintained that Russia needed to be blessed," Giuseppe explained. "That has not been done. As a result, Russia continues to spread her errors throughout the world."

"Not this again." The pope groaned. "I told you already, the blessing happened."

"No, it has not," Giuseppe argued. "The ceremonies that were done were never done by a pope in unison with all the bishops of the world."

"Pope Pius XII did it by a papal letter," Pope Anthony countered.

"Didn't count," Giuseppe refuted. "Sister Lúcia repeatedly explained that various ceremonies all failed to meet the specific requirements of the Madonna's request."

Pope Anthony let out a dramatic sigh.

"Russia is now embracing Christianity," the pope shot back.

"That's just a smoke screen," Giuseppe argued. "The country hasn't been converted."

"That is your opinion, Giuseppe, not fact."

"Russian president Vladimir Putin is a former KGB officer who was devoted to defending the atheist Soviet Union," Giuseppe said. "That's a fact."

"What is your point?"

"Putin is using Orthodox Christianity today for ideological attacks that used to be made in the name of communism."

"Oh brother." Pope Anthony groaned.

"There is no line between Church and State in Russia," Giuseppe continued.

"Again, that is your opinion, not fact," the pope said.

"You want facts? Seventy-one percent of all Russians identify as Orthodox Christian; that's according to *World Atlas*. It's like a US citizen identifying as either a Republican or a Democrat.

"Being an Orthodox Christian in Russia is like being a member of a political party. Putin has masterfully made the

Russian Orthodox religion the central ideological pillar of his new Russian government. Putin uses it to disseminate propaganda."

"You're saying Putin has replaced the Communist Party with the Russian Orthodox religion?" the pope asked.

"Yes," Giuseppe asserted.

"Well, none of this matters now," the pope stated. "Like I said, I'm probably on my way out the door."

"Carmine, no matter how the vote turns out, please be kind to yourself. You tried your best."

The pope's shoulders dropped. His lips trembled.

"It was a difficult path for me to become the pope in the first place. I needed help getting here.

"Unfortunately, I turned to the wrong people for assistance. Do you understand what I am saying, Giuseppe?"

"Not really."

"Because I couldn't do it on my own, I asked certain people for help," Pope Anthony elaborated. "But they had their own agenda for the Church."

"What kind of agenda?" Giuseppe asked.

"They want to dramatically reform the Church," said Pope Anthony.

"I don't understand." Giuseppe stared at his friend.

"The people I am talking about are not Church traditionalists," the pope explained. "They want major reforms."

"Carmine, surely you rejected them?" Giuseppe asked.

"I tried after I became the pope. I attempted to put some distance between them and myself, but they blackmailed me. They said they would tell the world I am gay."

Giuseppe looked at his friend with pity.

"You definitely got yourself into a fine mess," the former diplomat observed.

"That I did," Pope Anthony agreed.

Giuseppe got up from his chair and patted his friend on the back.

"Good night, my friend," he called out.

Chapter 8

MESSAGE ON THE WHITEBOARD

California, 2022

The next day, Rollings watched as Pope Anthony was interviewed live on CNN. The pope was backpedaling, saying
the world needed to understand that sex abuse wasn't just a
problem among his clergy.

"Have you heard about pedophilia within the Boy
Scouts of America?" Pope Anthony asked. "This is a human
problem."

Rollings pumped his fist at the television.

"He's deflecting! Don't go throwing others under the
bus with you!"

As Rollings yelled, a vein popped out of his forehead.
His face was flushed.

"Remember your blood pressure, Ed," shouted Gladys
at the front desk.

Rollings loosened his tie. Even though it wasn't hot
out, he was sweating under his signature outfit: a short-

sleeved white dress shirt with a pocket protector (to guard against leaky ink from the pens he collected during the day), and brown slacks from Walmart.

"Where's Tate?" Rollings called out.

He looked anxiously at his wristwatch. His head swiveled as he looked for his reporter.

Rollings then picked up a competitor's newspaper. Liz stacked them in the newsroom each day.

The managing editor was obsessed. He looked at them often to see what the competition was covering.

The New York Times had a story about the resignation of Father Hermann Geissler, the Vatican's head of moral doctrine, who was accused of making advances toward a German nun during confession.

He called out again for Tate. "Someone find John!"

"He's in the library with Liz," a cub reporter shouted.

Just as Rollings was about to completely lose it, Tate came scrambling in.

"There's a story today about an incident involving a priest and nun," Rollings stated.

"Which reminded me to check in with you. Where do things stand with Giovanni and Sister Peggy? How's your investigation going into that?"

Tate explained how he'd placed an ad in the *San Francisco Chronicle* and had received a big response.

Rollings dropped his head and did a little circle dance.

"Write it up!" exclaimed the managing editor.

***

That evening, the following story was posted online:

The Sacramento Union

Local Clergyman Accused of Misconduct
By John Tate

Sacramento—Giovanni Tedesco, the country's newest cardinal, has a history of abuse against women, the *Sacramento Union* has learned.

Scores of women came forward anonymously with claims against Giovanni after the *Sacramento Union* placed an ad in a San Francisco newspaper asking for their stories.

The allegations against him brings more trouble to a Church already embroiled in controversy.

Just yesterday, the Vatican's head of moral doctrine was fired from that position by Pope Anthony after a nun accused him of making advances toward her during confession.

Among the accusations against Giovanni is an account by a new nun at the Archdiocese of San Francisco, who said she was retaliated against after reporting the clergyman to her superiors.

The nun said people who call Giovanni into account are brought in before archdiocesan lawyers and threatened with canonical sanctions.

She said there are panels that go around questioning priests and nuns who leak information.

The nun alleges that clergy at the Archdiocese of San Francisco have been sent away for evaluations and not returned for a long time after reporting their claims.

At five p.m., Tate, Liz, and Rollings celebrated his breaking news story by drinking cheap beer in the newsroom. As they whooped it up, the receptionist, Gladys, wandered over from the front desk with a letter in her hand.

"This came for you today, John," she said. "I forgot to give it to you earlier."

The anonymous tipster had struck again.

"I wonder what it's about this time!" Liz exclaimed.

"Well, open it, Tate!" Rollings roared.

Inside was a letter of resignation.

"Who resigned?" Liz asked.

"Bishop Jaime Nunez," Tate replied.

"Who is it addressed to?" Rollings asked.

"Pope Anthony," Tate said. "It's dated several weeks ago, before his stroke."

Tate read the hand-written resignation letter to them:

Dear Holy Father,

I was recently informed by the Vatican's secretary of state that I was being passed over for a promotion. He told me Giovanni would be named the country's newest cardinal.

We both know this is part of a much bigger plan by you to increase your support in the College of Cardinals, just in case you are subjected to a vote of confidence/no confidence.

You have been "stacking the deck," as the expression goes, appointing cardinals who will support you and getting rid of those who don't. Instead of promoting people based on their qualifications, you are looking out for your own interests above the Church's.

What you are doing is wrong. As a result, I intend to resign my position and retire from the Church.

Sincerely,
Bishop Jaime Nunez

"Can I please see that letter?" Liz asked.
Tate handed it to her. She studied it carefully.
"The writing, it is different!" she exclaimed.

"Different than what?" Rollings asked.

"From the other anonymous letters John received," she replied.

"How can you tell?" Tate asked.

"Check for yourself," she answered. "The other letters were written elegantly and in distinctive writing. This one is, to be blunt, much sloppier."

Tate pulled out the other letters from the top drawer of his desk and laid them next to the one he'd just received.

"You are right!" he declared.

"That means someone other than Bishop Nunez wrote the other letters that weren't about his resignation." Rollings was clearly intrigued.

All three lowered their heads, deep in thought.

"Okay, okay," Rollings said, breaking the silence. "Let's go back to what this resignation letter tells us."

"Which is what?" Tate asked.

"Pope Anthony has been planning for a vote by the College of Cardinals," Rollings said.

Tate and Liz nodded in agreement.

"In preparation for such a vote, he has been naming new cardinals who will support him."

Again, Tate and Liz agreed.

"That's probably the reason why he selected Giovanni to be a cardinal, in exchange for his vote," Rollings continued.

"With the addition of Giovanni, there are now one hundred twenty-five voting cardinals," Liz said. "Which means the vote cannot end in a tie. Giovanni, being the newest voting cardinal, would vote last and break a potential tie."

"Chief, we have got one heck of a story here!" Tate declared. "Can I write it up? We can use the resignation letter as our source."

"Not so fast," the managing editor replied. "While it is very likely that Bishop Nunez wrote the resignation letter, we have to be sure. You need to confirm its authenticity."

"You think the letter is a fake?" Liz asked.

"Probably not," said the managing editor. "But we are in the business of reporting facts, not speculation. We can't just write a story using unconfirmed sources."

"How does John confirm the authenticity of the retirement letter?" Liz asked. "Bishop Nunez is in the hospital, and he probably can't speak due to his stroke."

"That's a good point," Tate concurred. "And furthermore, the Vatican's press office probably won't talk about the resignation letter because it is a personnel matter."

The managing editor got up from his chair, walked forward a few paces, and then turned back to his ace reporter.

"John, go see Bishop Nunez tomorrow," he instructed. "I hear he's been transferred to Mercy Medical Center in Sacramento. See if there's a way to confirm whether or not the bishop wrote that resignation letter.

"Now get out of here, you two. Chase this story down!"

Tate hurried off to his car. He decided to pay a visit to Pietro at the diocesan high school where he was still filling in as the interim principal.

The school bell had just rung when he arrived, signaling the end of the lunch hour.

Pietro was in the cafeteria assisting the cook when he was told that a visitor was waiting for him in the main office. He removed his apron, washed his hands, and walked to his office.

"Hi, I am Father Pietro Romano," he said once he arrived.

"Hello, I am John Tate from the *Sacramento Union*. May I talk with you?"

Pietro shook the reporter's hand and inspected him from head to toe. Tate gave off an intense vibe, but he appeared to be a good-natured soul.

"Sure, Mr. Tate. Would you like some coffee?"

"No, I had better not," the reporter replied. "I've already had four cups and five cigarettes today."

Pietro looked at his watch and did a double take.

"You really ought to watch that, Mr. Tate. It's barely after lunch. Remember, we are what we put into our bodies."

A slack expression came across Tate's face.

Is this guy Mister Rogers? wondered Tate as he thought about the wholesome, cardigan-wearing Presbyterian minister and television host.

They went into an office normally used by the regular principal. Pietro was now temporarily occupying the space.

Tate, however, stopped dead in his tracks at the door and shifted from foot to foot.

"Everything okay, Mr. Tate?"

"Um, this is the first time I've been on a high school campus since the shooting at Sacramento Valley High School," the reporter replied. "Bad memories."

"Oh, I see," Pietro said. "You were there?"

"Yes."

"I am so sorry," the priest said kindly. "That had to be a very traumatic experience for you."

The reporter lowered his gaze. "Yes, it was."

"Well, just one minute, Mr. Tate. I have something that might cheer you up. Every day I post a special message on the whiteboard behind my desk."

Pietro took an erasable marker out from the desk and walked over to the board.

"I haven't gotten to today's message yet," he continued. "Where has the time gone? Half the day is over already. Anyway, I am going to write a message just for you. Let's see if it doesn't make you feel better!"

Again, Tate was taken aback by Pietro's warm and caring approach.

"You're going to write a message, for me?"

"Indeed, I am, Mr. Tate. I am a big believer in writing something every day on that whiteboard. Something inspirational. Hopefully what I write will lift you up!"

In his best writing, Pietro wrote the following message:

Wherever you go, no matter what the weather, always bring your own sunshine.

"There!" Pietro said, smiling.

"Are you always so chipper, Pietro?" Tate asked.

"I try to be because it is up to us to bring our own sunshine," the priest replied, tapping the marker on the whiteboard as he said it.

Tate almost expected the *Mister Rogers' Neighborhood* theme song to play next. He fiercely shook his head back and forth, trying to clear the tune from his brain.

"Yes, well, okay," the reporter said. "Thank you for that. Say, Father, I was in San Francisco for the discussion with the US cardinals. I saw you there. There is something I'd like to follow up on."

Pietro cringed. He was certain the reporter wanted to ask him about his encounter with the Madonna.

"Can you tell me about Bishop Nunez's resignation?" Tate asked.

Pietro's face went blank. He wasn't expecting that question.

"Prior to his stroke, Bishop Nunez submitted his resignation to Pope Anthony. Why?" the reporter continued.

Pietro continued to just stare at his visitor openmouthed.

"I have a copy of the resignation letter right here," said Tate, pulling the document out of his coat pocket. "Do you want to see it, Father?"

"Sure, I would be interested in taking a look at it," Pietro answered.

The bearded priest quickly read the letter.

"Can you verify this is authentic?" Tate asked of the resignation letter.

"That is his writing," Pietro replied.

That's good enough for me, the reporter thought.

Tate handed Pietro his business card. "Call me if you want to talk some more."

***

The next day, the anonymous tipster struck again. This time Tate received an envelope with several news articles inside.

444

There was a story about Bishop Gustavo Zanchetta, described as Pope Anthony's protégé, who had recently been promoted as the pope's special delegate to the Knights of Malta—even after the bishop's secretary found lewd pictures on his phone.

There was another story about Cardinal Theodore McCarrick of Washington, who was removed from public ministry in 2018 for sexually abusing a teenager when he had been a priest in New York. The story alleged that Pope Anthony was aware of the behavior by McCarrick but did nothing about it.

After reading both articles, Tate let out a whistle, loud enough for his managing editor to come running over.

"What's up, Tate?" Rollings asked.

Tate briefed his managing editor, who sat heavily in a chair.

"I am glad you are sitting down, Chief. Here's another one," Tate said.

The managing editor groaned. Tate held up a newspaper article from Chile.

"Listen to this headline: 'Chile's Clergy Guilty of an Avalanche of Abuse Cover-Up Cases.'"

Rollings grabbed his stomach. His face turned pale.

Tate pulled the last item out of the envelope, an obituary from the Italian newspaper, *la Città di Salerno*.

"Why is an obituary included in here with articles about clergy?" Tate said to Rollings.

la Città DI SALERNO

OBITUARY
ROBERT ROMANO, Died October 1, 1975

Funeral services will be held next Tuesday for Robert "Bob" Romano, 40, of Cava de' Tirreni. He was the owner of Il Panificio, a popular establishment where villagers ate and socialized over desserts and coffee.

Romano, the village baker, was found dead by gunshot last week. Local police say he was killed inside his business for stealing money.

He is survived by his wife, Madonna, 32; daughter, Tina, 10; and son, Pietro, 8, who earned a reputation as an exaggerator when he claimed to be visited by an apparition of the Madonna.

Dominic Solano of the local Church parish deemed the boy's claim to be unfounded, so understandably, most in the village were not pleased.

The police say the boy's claim might have also had something to do with the elder Romano's death.

There are to be no flowers or gifts.

Tate scratched his head. Rollings frowned.

"This is an obituary about the death of Pietro's dad," the reporter noted.

"Our Pietro?" queried Rollings. "The priest from Sacramento?"

"The obit says he claimed to have been visited by the Mother of Jesus, and that could have been a reason why his father was killed," Tate summarized.

The reporter picked up his desk phone and dialed Liz in the library.

"Hello, Liz. Can you please get me everything you can on an Italian family named Romano? The dad was a baker in Cava de' Tirreni in Italy. He was killed in 1975.

"I really want to know what you can find out about them when they lived in Italy."

An hour later Liz was standing at Tate's desk, looking a bit astonished.

"What's up, Liz, you find anything?" he asked.

The librarian looked down at the papers in her hand, then back up at Tate.

"In the mainstream media and on regular Internet services, I only found an obituary for Robert Romano, which mentions Pietro and Tina," Liz said.

Tate held up the obituary that he'd received in the mail and waved it in the air.

"Got that already," he declared.

"Yes, well, there's more," Liz continued.

"Let's hear it," he requested.

"I found a police report from 1980," she said. "Well, it's more like notes from an interrogation."

"The interrogation of whom?"

"A guy named Frank Tallerico Sr. from Salerno, Italy," Liz said. "He was a Mafia member who was arrested for killing a well-known businessman in Sorrento.

"During the interrogation he talked about another hit, this one on Robert Romano, whom he repeatedly referred to as 'Bob the Baker.'"

"What Mob was responsible for the hit?"

"The Camorra," Liz replied.

"What else does the police report say?" Tate quizzed.

"Tallerico received a life sentence," Liz explained. "He admitted to killing the businessman from Sorrento because he was caught red-handed at the scene of the crime.

"There was no way Tallerico was going to beat the rap."

"Go on."

"Knowing he was headed to jail, the mobster bragged about other hits, like the one on Bob the Baker," Liz continued.

"I suppose he figured that if he was going to be locked up for the rest of his life, why not go away looking like the tough guy?

"He told the police that he hoped a book would be written about his life."

"Swell guy," Tate said.

"Tallerico listed dozens of murders that he carried out as a member of the Camorra," Liz resumed. "He said the hit on Bob the Baker brought him the most satisfaction, however."

"Why so?" Tate asked.

"He didn't like that Pietro had claimed to have seen the Madonna," Liz clarified. "Apparently, Tallerico was a

Catholic, and he thought it was blasphemy for the boy to claim that."

"Oh, brother," Tate replied. "A hit man who has no trouble killing people, but he gets a conscience when it comes to talking about the Mother of Jesus?"

"Apparently so, John. Anyway, here's the rest of the story. Bob the Baker owned a little shop in his village not too far from Salerno. However, the shop wasn't how he made his money."

"How did he earn money, then?" Tate questioned.

"Bob was a numbers runner for the Camorra, meaning he had a hand in the underground, illegal Italian lottery. He was stealing from his lottery sales."

"Not a good idea to cross the Mafia," Tate noted.

Just then Rollings came barging into Tate's cubicle and interrupted them. He had a book in his hand entitled *In God's Name*, written by David Yallop.

The managing editor handed the book to Tate, who noticed that a personal message had been written to Rollings on the inside.

"Chief, I never knew you were interested in religion," Tate said.

"In 1978, I was a reporter for the *Los Angeles Times*," Rollings answered. "My editor assigned me to read this book and write a review about it."

"You wrote a book review, Ed?" asked Liz, surprised by that.

"Hey, I haven't always been an editor," he replied. "There was a time, very long ago, when I was a reporter. And yes, I did write book reviews."

"Ed, tell us more," Liz pleaded.

"The book was a bestseller," he continued. "It's about the death of Pope John Paul I."

"Death? How'd he die?" Tate asked.

"That's a mystery. Pope John Paul I's papacy was the shortest in history. He was selected to replace Pope Paul VI, and then he died just thirty-three days later."

Tate put his hands over his mouth.

"Surely the cardinals would not have selected a pope they knew to be sick," Tate reasoned.

"He wasn't sick, and he didn't have any known health issues," Rollings replied.

"Then what happened?" Liz asked.

"Many questions were raised at the time of Pope John Paul I's death," Rollings answered.

"Yallop questioned the Vatican's account of the events surrounding John Paul I's death. He pointed to the Vatican's inaccurate statements about who found the body, when, where, and whether an autopsy was carried out."

"Was an autopsy done?" Tate asked.

"No."

Tate examined the book.

"Says here, the pope was murdered and had been in danger ever since he was elected," Tate said.

"Yallop believed the pope was aware of corruption within the Vatican Bank and that he was killed to stop him from uncovering it," Rollings explained.

Tate gave a low grunt. "That's interesting because the Vatican's banking practices are still a problem," the reporter said.

"Pope Benedict XVI fired the head of the bank in 2012 amidst allegations of money laundering."

Liz took out her iPad and entered a Google search word.

"Here's a news story from 2019 that says Pope Anthony commissioned an external audit of the Vatican Bank, a first," Liz said.

"According to the article, during the bank's eighty-plus-year history, it has been plagued by its rumored associations with organized crime and alleged criminal violations of laws, such as embezzlement and money laundering to Mafia murder conspiracies."

"Yallop claimed that when Pope John Paul I's dead body was found, there were notes in his hand that contained the names of bank members involved in Masonry," Rollings pointed out.

"Yallop interviewed a witness, Sister Margherita Marin, who found Pope John Paul I dead in his bed. The nun told Yallop that the pope also held a sheet of paper that contained a quotation from a Gospel passage."

"What was the passage about?" Liz asked.

"It was about gluttons and drunkards," Rollings answered.

Tate drilled down.

"Chief, who were these gluttons and drunkards?"

"According to the nun, they were priests, bishops, archbishops, and cardinals."

Tate's heart skipped. Liz had goosebumps.

"Chief, do you really think it's possible that Masons had something to do with the death of Pope John Paul I?"

"I don't know, but keep digging," the managing editor directed. "We are getting close to some answers."

Rollings then leaned in and addressed Tate in a hushed voice. "Have you talked to anyone yet about the bishop's resignation letter?"

"I have," the reporter responded. "I went and saw Pietro. He confirmed it's the bishop's writing on the letter. That means the source has been verified."

"But Pietro didn't actually see him write the letter?" Rollings questioned.

"No, he didn't."

"Tate, go pay the bishop a visit. If he is able to talk, ask him about the letter."

Tate left immediately and raced over to the hospital. When he arrived, the nurse at the front desk directed him to the bishop's room.

Bishop Nunez was in worse shape than Tate could have imagined. An oxygen tube was connected to his nose, and he was receiving intravenous fluids in both arms.

The bishop's eyes were closed, exposing deep bags under them. The sockets of his eyes were hollowed, and his face was ashen.

The nurse said Bishop Nunez was blind in both eyes from the stroke and that the entire left side of his body was temporarily paralyzed. Bishop Nunez could talk, but it wasn't easy.

Tate trembled at the sight. The last time he'd seen such suffering was during the school shooting incident.

"Bishop, it's John Tate from the *Sacramento Union*, can you hear me?"

"Yes."

"I would like to ask you a couple of questions."

"Anything."

"Did you write that resignation letter?"

"Yes, I did."

Bishop Nunez explained that because he knew a lot about the country's newest cardinal, most of which wasn't good, he couldn't support the pope's selection.

"I learned through my friendship with Giovanni's dad, Giuseppe, that his son is psychopathic," said the bishop. "I couldn't in good conscious agree to his promotion. So, I resigned."

Tate scribbled furiously in his notebook.

"Bishop, one other thing. Why did you agree to transfer Sister Peggy Paige?" Tate asked.

"Giovanni and Sister Peggy have been having a consensual relationship, but Giovanni wanted to stop it, particularly since he'd become a cardinal. Giovanni asked for help in turning his life around."

"And you believed that, Bishop?"

"Giovanni wants to be the pope so bad one day, I wouldn't be surprised if he's made a deal with the Devil himself for it to happen," said Bishop Nunez.

"If there's any chance I can help him change and become a good person before then, it's a chance I'm willing to take."

Tate closed his notebook and turned to leave.

"John, before you go, may I have a glass of water?"

In the corner of the room was a small dresser with a pitcher of water and a glass. Tate walked over to it. As he poured the water, the reporter noticed a letter addressed to him, so he read it:

Dear Mr. Tate,

Are you familiar with the prediction made by Saint Malachy in the twelfth century?

He predicted there would be only one more pope after Benedict XVI, after which comes the end of the world.

The prediction in full is this:

"In the final persecution of the Church, there will reign Peter the Roman, who will feed his flock amid many tribulations, after which the seven-hilled city will be destroyed and the dreadful Judge will judge the people. The end."

Mr. Tate, if Saint Malachy is right, there will only be one more validly elected pope after Benedict, and then the seven-hilled city will be destroyed.

Here's a wrinkle for you to consider. Some say Pope Anthony was never validly elected.

If this is true, then there will be one more pope after him before the dreadful Judge will judge the people. Who will it be?

Sincerely,
Bishop Jaime Nunez

Tate's mouth fell wide open, and his body went limp. He accidentally dropped the pitcher of water, which splattered everywhere. A nurse came running in.

"Is everything okay in here?" she asked. "Oh my, look at all this water on the floor. Be careful, everyone; we don't want anyone to slip."

She grabbed a towel from the bathroom and wiped up the mess, then gave Tate a nasty look and walked out.

"Excuse me, Bishop, but did you intentionally leave that letter there for me to read?"

Bishop Nunez tilted his head. "Letter, what letter?"

"The letter that was right next to the pitcher of water. I read it because it was addressed to me and signed by you," Tate said.

The bishop's face reddened.

"I am blind, Mr. Tate, so clearly I did not write that letter. I am unable."

The bishop has a point there, Tate thought.

Still, something seemed off. At that moment, the door swung open, and in walked Pietro.

Just then Tate remembered where he had seen the distinctive writing before: on the whiteboard at school.

Tate froze in his tracks.

"It's you, Pietro! You're the anonymous sender."

Pietro didn't know what to say.

"It is okay, Pietro, tell him," encouraged the bishop.

"You're right," Pietro replied. "I'm the one who has been anonymously sending things to you."

Tate covered his mouth with his hands.

"Um, excuse me," he said as he ducked out of the room and went into the hallway.

The reporter fumbled for his cell phone and then called his managing editor.

"Chief, meet me at the office right away."

Rollings was at home eating dinner when he got the call. He got so excited that he drove to the office still in his pajamas and slippers.

Soon after Rollings arrived, Tate walked through the office door with Pietro right behind him. The men went directly to the managing editor's office.

Like a hunting dog that had just found its prey, Tate was fidgety. On the other hand, Pietro was calm and resolute, definitely sure of whatever it was he had to say.

"What's this all about?" Rollings asked. "I don't normally walk away from my wife's Tuesday-night meatloaf."

"Pietro is our anonymous tipster," Tate answered.

Rollings looked the priest up and down. "Explain yourself."

Pietro got straight to the point.

"Gentlemen, unethical things have been going on within the Church. I would like the *Sacramento Union*'s help to reveal it."

"Does this have anything to do with Giovanni's promotion and Bishop Nunez's retirement?" Tate replied.

"Yes, but it goes much deeper than that," Pietro continued. "It also has to do with corruption, abuse of power, and blackmail."

"How high does the problem go?" Rollings asked.

"Straight to the top."

Tate let out a whistle. He opened up his notebook and listened as Pietro told his story.

Rollings paced the newsroom floor like a caged animal. When the interview was over, Tate felt wrung out.

"Pietro, one more thing," the reporter said.

"What is it?"

"Can you tell us about the time you saw the Madonna?"

After all these years, Pietro felt like talking about it.

Just like the Madonna had said, I would know when the time was right, Pietro thought.

He told the two men his story.

When it was over, Tate stood up from his desk.

"Let me walk you out, Pietro," he said. "Ed has called a taxi to take you back to the diocese."

"Good night, Pietro," Rollings called out. "I am going to stay here and write up my notes. I like to do that when I've finished an interview, while the conversation is fresh in my mind."

Pietro walked out the door with Tate and into a dimly lit parking lot.

Then, gunshots rang out.

Chapter 9

THE VOTE

Vatican City, 2022

The College of Cardinals—including its newest member, Giovanni—wearing their red outfits, gathered inside the Sistine Chapel. They looked like something out of a movie.

Outside the chapel, the media crammed into St. Peter's Square to cover the vote.

"Hello, this is Stan Wright from CBS News. Today the College of Cardinals is meeting to possibly decide the fate of Pope Anthony. This is an unprecedented vote as to whether the pope still has the confidence of his cardinals."

The BBC covered the story this way: "The College of Cardinals encompasses one hundred twenty-five voting cardinals. Among the most important role of the College of Cardinals is to select a new pope. This is the first time ever that it decides whether a sitting pope should consider resigning."

The New York Times blogged the following: "It is hard to dismiss the change Pope Anthony has made to the College of Cardinals. He has loaded the voting body with cardinals who support him, possibly to get out in front of today's vote."

Finally, Cardinal Solano called the session to order, and the doors to the chapel closed to the outside world.

Inside, the elderly dean pounded his gavel. He was anxious to get the voting underway.

Numerous speeches were given by the most-senior cardinals. Then, the dean gave voting instructions.

"Each cardinal is to come forward when his name is called, turn and face his colleagues, and then publicly declare his vote, either confidence or no confidence," said Cardinal Solano.

The voting got underway. Because he was the newest cardinal with the least seniority, Giovanni would vote last. He saw that as a good thing.

With any luck I will cast the deciding vote, he thought.

The dean cast the first vote. "No confidence!"

Cardinal Berlone, the Vatican's secretary of state, went next. "Complete confidence!"

"No confidence!" bellowed Cardinal Martinelli, which drew a loud gasp from the audience.

Well now, that tips the scales, doesn't it? Giovanni thought.

Four cardinals from the United States voted "no confidence," while Cardinal Supan voted a spirited "confidence!"

The votes went back and forth.

When it came down to the final vote, the tally was deadlocked 62–62.

Moments later, the doors to the Sistine Chapel swung open. Cardinal Solano walked out and declared the outcome.

The Sacramento Union

College of Cardinals Votes "No Confidence" in Pope Anthony; Reporter and Priest Shot
By Ed Rollings

Vatican City—In the past twenty-four hours, members of the College of Cardinals voted "no confidence" in Pope Anthony, and a *Sacramento Union* reporter and a local priest were shot.

The significance of the vote is unclear because it was only symbolic and is not binding.

The vote was tight, 63–62, with the country's newest cardinal, Giovanni Tedesco of San Francisco, casting the final and deciding vote.

Just hours before the vote, *Sacramento Union* reporter John Tate and Father Pietro Romano of the Diocese of Sacramento were shot outside the newspaper's downtown office by an unknown assailant. They had just finished an interview about problems within the Church.

Tate and Father Romano have been hospitalized. Their conditions are unknown at this time.

Earlier, Tate had also interviewed Bishop Jaime Nunez, who recently suffered a stroke and is also in a Sacramento hospital.

Father Pietro Romano and Bishop Jaime Nunez reported to the *Sacramento Union* that Giovanni's recent promotion to the rank of cardinal was approved by Pope Anthony in order to pad his number of supporters in the College of Cardinals ahead of the voting.

Given the promotion, Giovanni's vote of "no confidence" comes as a huge surprise.

The voting was conducted in private and was supposed to be kept secret.

However, Cardinal Solano, the dean of the College of Cardinals, addressed the media after the vote and informed the press that Giovanni cast the deciding vote.

The Vatican's press office will neither confirm nor deny the final vote count nor how each cardinal voted.

There is no word yet on whether Pope Anthony will step down.

The stalker finished reading the article in the *Sacramento Union* and violently pounded his fist on a table. Pietro had given an interview! Cardinal Martinelli would not be happy.

That was not supposed to happen, the stalker thought.

The bad man drove to the local hospital.

Pietro must pay!

"Give me the room number for Pietro Romano," he said to the person at the nursing station.

"I am sorry, sir, but he checked out."

The stalker stomped his foot. His face turned bright red.

"He checked out already?"

"Yes, sir, about an hour ago. His injury was not severe."

Dang that poor parking lot lighting, the stalker thought.

His gunshots had been off because he couldn't see his targets well enough.

Someone must die today.

"What about the reporter, Tate?"

"He also left," the nurse replied.

The stalker lowered his head and slapped his hands together.

Then he asked about one more person. "Where can I find Bishop Nunez?"

"He's in room 314."

***

At St. James Retreat Center, Sister Peggy could hardly believe what she'd just read. That nice reporter who'd come to see her, Mr. Tate, had been shot, as was a local priest!

Equally distressing was that scores of women had come forward against the man she loved.

And why had Giovanni voted against Pope Anthony?

Ever since her transfer, Giovanni had dropped completely out of Sister Peggy's life. No texts. No phone calls. No nothing.

Sister Peggy was now having serious doubts about him. Maybe he was no different than the nuns and that priest in the orphanage who had been so awful to her.

She thought back to the day of the car crash. One moment her family had been in the car, laughing, and the next they were gone.

The orphanage after that was horrible. Most of the kids had been turned away by their parents, unwanted.

The orphans were spanked, yelled at, and harshly treated—and that included young Peggy, even though she was a good and compliant girl.

The priest who ran the orphanage was especially vile. Peggy never examined what he did to her, until now. And he did it over and over again.

The priest told her she was special, and that what he did made her closer to God because of who he was.

Eventually, the offending priest was promoted, and he moved away. But the trauma never left.

To cope, Peggy learned to detach herself from her feelings. But today, as she objectively looked at herself, she could see that her behavior was not normal.

Emotions rushed at her all at once, as if the floodgates had finally been opened.

Sister Peggy wished that someone was with her now. A family member, a friend, anyone.

Now that she thought about it, though, there really hadn't been anyone close to her since the car accident.

She was all alone in this world and had been for a long, long time.

Sister Peggy fell to the floor and curled up to her knees. Tears streamed down her face.

I miss my family.

If she was being completely honest, maybe she'd only been drawn to Giovanni because she was mad at God. He took her family away and, maybe, she only got together with Giovanni because she knew that God wouldn't approve of it—her way of getting back at Him.

Speaking of God, did he really love her? She was wondering about that now too.

Why had God killed her entire family? And then, He allowed that pedophile priest to abuse her at the orphanage.

Why?

Maybe she had only been attracted to Giovanni because, like her, he'd been raised by people other than his own family. They both felt rejected in that regard.

But that wasn't true love.

Tears streamed down Sister Peggy's face.

Her sobs grew until she was wailing. After a while, though, all cried out, she shot to her feet. She flipped over tables in the dining room in a nasty rage.

Giovanni is no better than that priest who abused me!

He has destroyed lives too.

Sister Peggy took the cell phone from her pocket and made two phone calls.

First, she called the Sacramento County Sheriff's Office. Next, she found the business card that Tate had given her and called Ed Rollings at the *Sacramento Union.*

Hell hath no fury like a woman scorned, thought Rollings after his conversation with Sister Peggy.

With his ace reporter, Tate, injured, Rollings wrote and filed the following story himself:

The Sacramento Union

District Attorney Files Charges against Cardinal Giovanni Tedesco
By Ed Rollings

Sacramento—Charges were filed today by the Sacramento County District Attorney against Giovanni Tedesco, the country's newest cardinal, for allegedly assaulting a religious sister in 2015.

District Attorney Susan Glass said charges were filed after Sister Peggy Paige of St. James Retreat Center in rural Sacramento County reported the assault.

Giovanni runs the Archdiocese of San Francisco, which is where Sister Peggy used to work.

"Assault is unacceptable in any form, but particularly when it's committed by our most trusted professionals, who in this case is a clergyman," said District Attorney Glass.

"It doesn't matter that the incident happened more than five years ago. What matters is that the victim found her voice and did the right thing.

"What she did took courage."

Sacramento County Sheriff R. Charles Brewer said law enforcement in San Francisco attempted to serve a warrant today for Giovanni's arrest, but he could not be located.

"Last we heard, Giovanni was in Rome taking part in the historic vote by the College of Cardinals," Sheriff Brewer reported.

"Our sources informed us that he'd boarded a plane to San Francisco after the voting. We had officers waiting for him at the San Francisco airport, but he gave us the slip.

"Unfortunately, it was not a direct flight, and it seems Giovanni was tipped off that we were waiting for him. He escaped during a changeover in flights, probably in Denver."

The *Sacramento Union* recently reported that scores of anonymous women pointed the finger at Giovanni after the newspaper ran an ad asking them to come forward if they had been abused by him.

According to a 2015 police report, an unnamed female employee was assaulted at the Archdiocese of San Francisco.

Earlier today, Sister Peggy Paige confirmed that she was that victim. She said Giovanni had been her assailant.

She also admitted to having had a long-running, consensual relationship with him.

Prior to his recent promotion to the rank of cardinal, Giovanni transferred Sister Peggy from San Francisco.

"He wanted to hide me," said Sister Peggy, who claims Pope Anthony had a hand in facilitating the move.

Phone records obtained through the Freedom of Information Act show a series of phone calls were made from the pope's residence in Vatican City to the Diocese of Sacramento just days prior to Sister Peggy's transfer.

Bishop Jaime Nunez, who runs the diocese, has admitted to receiving a request from Pope Anthony to take her in.

Phone records also show that a series of phone calls were made between the Diocese of Sacramento and the Archdiocese of San Francisco, which would indicate that Bishop Nunez and Giovanni discussed the transfer.

Giovanni declined to be interviewed when the *Sacramento Union* recently sought him out.

Bishop Nunez recently suffered a stroke. He remains hospitalized. However, he was able to confirm Sister Peggy's account of the assault.

The Vatican's press office declined comment.

###

Chapter 10

RETURN TO
THE ARCHIVE

Rome, 2022

After he was released from the hospital, Tate drove around Sacramento all night. The reporter had no destination in mind. He just needed to think.

The sniper's bullet did not permanently damage his shoulder. The shot went clean through.

Now, he was determined more than ever to bring down whomever had done this. Tate took a pack of cigarettes from the glove box and lit a cigarette.

Endless thoughts swirled around in his head. He was obsessed. Tate knew this feeling—it was the same way he felt all those years ago when the air show crash happened in Redding.

He drove for hours until the sun came up over the horizon. Tate figured there was no sense going home now. He might as well go to the office.

When he arrived, the reporter was surprised to find Rollings and Liz already there.

"Couldn't sleep either, huh, Tate?" Rollings asked.

"No, too much on my mind," he replied. "I have a ton of questions."

"You do realize that the answers aren't here, don't you?" Rollings asked. "The answers are in Italy.

"I want you and Liz to go there tomorrow. She can help you with research. Plus, I think it'd be safer if you traveled with a partner."

Tate bit his lip. Sweat poured out across his forehead.

"Go tomorrow?" he asked.

"You got a problem with that?" Rollings asked, noticing his reporter's hesitance.

"No. Well, yes," Tate replied.

"Which one is it?" the managing editor asked.

The reporter's eyes darted back and forth.

"It's just that I hate to fly, ever since the hijacking."

"That's another reason why it'll be good that Liz goes with you," Rollings remarked.

Tate nodded in agreement.

"Maybe we should leave today?" he asked.

"No, go tomorrow. If Pope Anthony makes an announcement today about his future, I don't want you stuck on an airplane. Let's give this story a day to play out, then go."

***

The next day, Tate and Liz caught a very early flight out of Sacramento International Airport. Before they departed, Pietro called Giuseppe and told him the pair were coming.

The old man promised to have a driver pick them up at Leonardo da Vinci International Airport and then taken to a hotel near Giuseppe's villa in Rome. He also promised that they would get an interview with the pope.

They hadn't even cleared the Midwestern states before Tate was dying for a cigarette. He was thinking about the hijacking. Tate had been traveling with his parents aboard an Aer Lingus flight to London from Dublin. He'd been reading about the Hardy Boys—Frank and Joe—and drinking hot chocolate when things got bumpy.

The pilot switched on the "fasten seat belt" sign.

"Ladies and gentlemen, please stay in your seats. We are experiencing turbulence."

Suddenly, a passenger cried out, "He has a bomb!"

Screams pierced the sky. All of the 102 people on board panicked, except for the lanky ex-monk in his midfifties with an overgrown and unkempt beard who was standing in the center aisle.

"See this?" the man said calmly in a loud voice.

He brandished a lighter and a gas-soaked firebomb.

Back in Dublin, before takeoff, the hijacker had simply walked onto the green-and-white Aer Lingus Boeing 737 plane with the bomb under his jacket.

"If my demands are not met, we will all die today."

People trembled in their seats. A young mother tried to calm her baby, who was crying loudly.

The hijacker walked slowly toward the cockpit, which did not have a locked door.

"Pilot, what is your name?" asked the hijacker.

"Eddie Foyle."

"Okay, Mr. Foyle, do what I say and you will not be hurt. Please alert traffic control at Heathrow Airport that we are going to be circling above them until my demands are met."

The pilot nervously fumbled with his headphones while his co-pilot checked the fuel levels.

For the next hour, the plane circled above Heathrow, and the hijacker listed his demands. Traffic control at Heathrow Airport would not agree to bargain with the man, however.

Fuel was getting low.

The hijacker demanded refueling of the aircraft at Heathrow and a flight to Tehran, but Iran said it would not allow the jet to land.

"Everyone is going to die if we continue this—we will run out of fuel," the pilot warned.

"Then take us to Charles de Gaulle Airport in France," the hijacker ordered.

"But, sir, I am not certain we have enough fuel," the pilot argued.

"Go anyway!"

An hour into their flight to Paris, the plane ran out of fuel and was forced to make an emergency landing at Le Touquet, a small seaside town in Northern France near the English Channel.

"The Third Secret of Fatima must be revealed to the world," the hijacker demanded. "Also, I want my manifesto published."

French authorities refused to give in to his demands.

Inside the plane, Tate's parents and other passengers pleaded with the former monk to give up. They were tired, scared, and hungry.

Four hours after the emergency landing, Tate and his mother were freed, along with other women and children.

After another four hours, French anti-terrorist police stormed the plane and forced the former monk to surrender.

When Tate's father rejoined them at the airport, they all huddled together and cried.

"John, hey, John! Are you doing okay, John?" Liz shouted.

A large amount of sweat had built up on Tate's forehead. He looked dazed.

"Thinking about the hijacking?" Liz asked.

"Yeah, is it that obvious?"

She pointed to his sweat-soaked shirt. "Maybe just a little."

Tate rolled his eyes.

"I'm really glad Ed sent you along," he said. "I guess the chubby little guy really does know what he's doing."

They laughed together.

"Laurence James Downey," Tate said.

"Excuse me, what?" Liz asked.

"That was the hijacker's name," said the reporter. "Downey served five years in a French prison for his crime. He did an interview with the *Irish Echo* in the 1990s and said he was sorry for the trauma he caused, but I don't think I will ever get over it."

"Did Downey say why he did what he did?" Liz asked.

"Since the age of eight, Downey said he believed he had a sense of destiny," Tate explained.

"During the five years he was a monk in Rome, he became obsessed with the Third Secret of Fatima. Downey was convinced he was the instrument to force the Vatican to disclose the secret."

"His stunt didn't work," Liz noted.

"No, it didn't, but he sure gave us a scare. I remember he had a bomb in one hand and a briefcase in the other."

"A briefcase? What was in it?" Liz wanted to know.

"Downey said he was carrying a copy of the Third Secret of Fatima," Tate replied.

"Really? Did he say where he got it?" Liz asked.

"He never revealed his source."

***

When they arrived at Leonardo da Vinci International Airport, Giuseppe's driver was waiting for them. He took them to the Hotel Vaticano, located across the street from the Vatican's museum entrance.

Tired from their trip, Tate and Liz went to their rooms and took a short nap before dinner. Afterward, the driver took them to Giuseppe's villa.

The former diplomat was waiting at the door when they arrived. He grinned broadly and clasped his hands together. As he led them inside, Giuseppe almost seemed to be skipping.

They went outside on a balcony, where a table with hors d'oeuvres awaited.

"I am so glad you are here!" Giuseppe said.

"You are?" Tate asked. "Honestly, most people are not excited to meet journalists."

"Any friends of Pietro's are friends of mine," the old man replied. "Besides, I have read your stories, and I admire your work."

The librarian and reporter flinched.

"Excuse me, sir, but the stories I've written about Giovanni have not been flattering," Tate pointed out.

"Please, call me Giuseppe. The truth is not always easy. However, it must be told. My son committed grave offenses, for which he must answer."

"Do you have any idea where Giovanni is?" Liz asked.

"No, but if I were to guess, I would say he is in Switzerland," Giuseppe predicted. "He knows that country well, having grown up there."

Tate took a notebook out from his coat pocket. "Do you mind?"

"Not at all. I would prefer that you take notes," Giuseppe replied. "A lot has happened, and things can get confusing. I find it best to write things down, particularly at my age. Helps to keep everything straight."

"When will we be meeting with Pope Anthony?" Tate asked.

"Tonight," said the old man. "He has invited us to dinner at his residence."

"How is he feeling about everything?" Liz asked.

"I have not talked to him since the vote," replied Giuseppe. "He called and left me a telephone message the day after it happened. He sounded okay, but he said he needed some space, so I am giving it to him. I made arrangements with his butler for our visit."

"I see," said Tate.

"Giuseppe, I know how the two of you became acquainted, because I talked with Bishop Nunez. You met in the 1950s when he was a young priest in Rome and you were an American diplomat."

"That is correct."

"And you are still friends, even to this day?"

"We are still friends, yes."

"Giuseppe, is the friendship clouding your judgment?" Tate pressed.

"What do you mean?"

"I just don't understand why you stand by Pope Anthony. He has done so many questionable things," Tate noted.

The old man lowered his head.

"From my perspective, he has been a true leader at a time when the right and the left within the Church are divided," Giuseppe explained.

"He's tried to lead from the center. Besides, he has been kind to my son, Giovanni, promoting him and all. What is there not to like about Carmine Luizzi?"

"Is that how you refer to him?" Tate said with a chuckle.

"Privately, yes. I call him by his birth name. It keeps our relationship genuine."

Tate resumed his questioning.

"Bishop Jaime Nunez shared with me that Giovanni has always been a difficult person."

The old man nodded his head in agreement.

"According to the bishop, the relationship between you and Giovanni has never been easy," Tate remarked. "Is that true?"

Giuseppe felt a lump build in his throat.

"It is true, John. Giovanni has been both my greatest joy and my greatest sorrow."

Tate could see tears well up in Giuseppe's eyes. He decided to change the subject.

"Is Pope Anthony being blackmailed?" Tate asked.

Giuseppe bit his lip.

"Pope Anthony recently shared with me that he needed help getting elected," Giuseppe said. "He turned to people who have a different agenda for the Church than he does."

"What kind of people?" Liz asked.

"Progressives."

"Are these progressives blackmailing him?" Tate asked.

"Yes," Giuseppe replied. "Once he became the pope, Carmine tried to put distance between himself and them, but they blackmailed him for being gay.

"He has tried to manage the situation as well as possible, but obviously, his papacy has been compromised."

"Did he tell you *exactly* who these people are who have been blackmailing him?" Tate pushed.

"No, but that's a question you can ask him tonight."

"We can be that candid with him?" Tate asked.

"Yes, he is expecting your tough questions," said Giuseppe.

Tate closed his notebook. He was about to put it away when another question came to him.

"To your knowledge, Giuseppe, have any other popes been blackmailed?" the reporter asked.

"That's hard to answer," the old man replied. "There is a rumor in Vatican City, one that has never gone away."

"Which is?" Liz asked.

"Pope Paul VI was blackmailed too."

"Really? How so?" Liz questioned.

"Rumor has it that Pope Paul VI was also gay. There are news accounts that his lover was an Italian actor named Paolo Carlini, a stage, television, and film actor who appeared in forty-five films between 1940 and 1979."

"And he was being blackmailed because he was gay?" Tate queried.

"According to the rumor, yes," said Giuseppe.

"If this rumor is true, then is it possible that whoever was blackmailing him had a hand in the radical reforms made during the Second Vatican Council?" Tate asked.

"Quite possible," Giuseppe acknowledged. "Pope Paul VI was in charge for many years during Vatican II."

Tate held his pen against his temple and tapped it there several times.

"Giuseppe, you were at the opening day ceremony of Vatican II," said the reporter.

"I have heard you were among those who opposed the sweeping reforms that were being made, along with the two future popes, John Paul II and Pope Benedict XVI."

Giuseppe nodded.

"Why did you oppose the radical reforms of Vatican II?" Tate asked.

"Two reasons," Giuseppe answered. "First, Vatican II sought to include other churches and nations into Catholicism, and it acknowledged that other faiths had a common belief in a common Creator," Giuseppe said.

"Worldwide Christian unity, also called 'Cooperation' was injected into Catholicism during Vatican II."

"And you were opposed to that?" Tate asked.

"I'm all for being inclusive, don't get me wrong," Giuseppe replied.

"But the problem was that we suspected Masons were involved in the process, and the blending of religions into a 'one-world religion' has always been their goal."

Tate and the librarian gasped.

"So, if I am following along correctly, during Vatican II the Church injected worldwide Christian unity into Catholicism—otherwise known as 'Cooperation'—as a direct result of the presence of certain participants at the Second Vatican Council who were Masons," Tate summarized.

"Well done. You are correct," Giuseppe said.

"These delegates were far from being observers, which was my second complaint. Many of them were Masons, who acted as consultants and served on an advisory board to the Second Vatican Council."

***

They arrived for dinner at the pope's residence promptly at six p.m. The butler took them to the dining room and showed them to the table. Pope Anthony joined them several minutes later.

"Forgive me for being late," he apologized. "I was receiving a briefing."

The butler brought them each a glass of cold mineral water. Shortly thereafter, he served them rack of lamb with a red wine sauce, potatoes, carrots, and green peas.

For dessert, they ate tiramisu. The conversation during dinner was light, but it turned serious after they retreated to the pope's study.

"John, you have a natural talent for writing," the pope said. "Your coverage of the event in San Francisco was quite entertaining."

Tate's cheeks flushed. "I apologize if you found any of my stories inappropriate or offensive."

"On the contrary, I think you captured what happened quite nicely."

"You weren't bothered by how the cardinals were talking about you?" asked the reporter.

"Oh, I didn't say that," the pope replied. "I only meant that I think you covered it all very well."

"I see," Tate replied. "I have a few questions."

The pope twisted the papal ring on his finger. "I am sure you do."

"Why have you taken control of the Knights of Malta? You ousted the grand master and installed your own person.

"Why are you exerting total control over what is supposed to be a sovereign order?"

"I took control, yes, but there is a perfectly good explanation."

"Which is?" Tate queried.

"A small, yet influential, splinter group within the Knights of Malta is growing too powerful," the pope said.

"This splinter group is now trying to take over the larger body, but what concerns me are reports that they have been trading goods on the black market.

"I needed to step in and find out what is going on."

Tate scribbled madly in his notebook in a version of shorthand that only he could decipher.

"Another question," Tate said. "Are you being blackmailed?"

"Yes."

"By whom?"

"Masons," Pope Anthony answered.

"How are they blackmailing you?" Tate asked.

"They have threatened to tell the world that I am gay."

"Didn't the same thing happen to Pope Paul VI?" Liz asked.

"That is the rumor," said Pope Anthony. "Supposedly, the first blackmail against him happened as soon as he became pope. He reportedly got a Black Hand letter."

"What's that?" Tate asked.

"It's an extortion letter typically associated with the Italian Mafia," Giuseppe explained.

"Pope Paul VI was allegedly pressured by Masons, who were also Mafia members, to do away with the Church's condemnation of those who ask to be cremated after death, which he did."

Liz scratched her neck. "Isn't homosexuality frowned upon by the Church?"

"In truth, there are a lot of gays within the Church," said Pope Anthony. "A recent book by a French journalist claims that four in five Vatican priests are gay, and I don't doubt it. But how is that a surprise?

"There is an abundance of gay bathhouses right here in Rome that cater to priests and other clergy."

"Is homosexuality the reason for all of the clergy abuse?" Tate asked.

481

"No, just because someone is gay doesn't mean they are a predator," the pope replied. "But there are cardinals who believe otherwise.

"For example, in 2019, two prominent Church cardinals urged an end of what they called 'the plague of the homosexual agenda,' telling bishops to break their complicity over cases of abuse.

"In an open letter to me, Cardinals Raymond Burke and Walter Brandmüller said the cases of clergy sex abuse involve gay priests who have 'gone away from the Gospel.'"

"Okay, but let's talk, then, about your handling of clergy abuse," Tate challenged.

The pope shifted in his chair. "What would you like to know?"

"You knew about some of the behaviors that were going on within your clergy, yet you looked away," Tate said.

"In the case of Bishop Gustavo Zanchetta, who was charged with sexual and financial misconduct, you intervened. You even gave him a promotion and refuge within the walls of the Vatican. Why?"

"This is not a new issue for the Church," the pope explained. "As far back as 1629, there existed a record of priests who were accused of abusing children at a Catholic school that provided free education to boys in Rome.

"According to letters and documents in the Vatican Secret Archive, there were 'impure' friendships with 'schoolboys' and 'many accusations of impurity and ill-renown.'

"Historically, the Church has handled the problem by promoting the violators.

"This is a policy known as *promoveatur ut amoveatur*, or 'promotion for avoidance.' The priestly violators at the school for boys in Rome were promoted and moved to new schools once they were discovered."

Tate squinted his eyes at the pope.

"Is that why Giovanni was promoted and Sister Peggy was moved—promotion for avoidance?" the reporter asked.

"Yes," admitted the pope, whose face turned bright red.

"Let's go back to the issue of being blackmailed. Are you telling me that your handling of clergy misconduct has nothing to do with you being blackmailed?"

"Not at all," replied the pope. "You must understand, during my papacy my greatest challenge has been trying to differentiate between sexuality issues and abuse. The two are very different."

"Explain, please," Tate said.

"Well, for instance, Giovanni and Sister Peggy have been having a consensual relationship," the pope explained.

Giuseppe squirmed in his chair.

"Giovanni and Peggy are only human," Pope Anthony continued. "They are lonely. Human companionship is a natural emotion. They are both young and attractive. People want to be loved—all of us."

"Is this the reason why you recently said that priests in remote parts of the Amazon should be allowed to marry?" Tate asked.

"For companionship, yes."

Tate leaned forward. The pope could tell that the reporter's big question was coming—a question the entire world wanted to know.

"What are you going to do now?" Tate asked.

The pope pressed his lips together and shook his head.

"I am going to step down. I have made mistakes, and I must pay for them."

"Can't you just apologize?" Liz asked. "Why not say you are sorry and stay on? Tell the world you were being blackmailed."

"I allowed myself to be blackmailed because of my own ego. I wanted to be the pope so badly that I made mistakes that have hurt a lot of people.

"But with your help, John and Liz, the corrupt people will be exposed and the Church and its faithful will be allowed to heal."

The room became very quiet.

"I will not go immediately," the pope continued. "I will take a couple of months to transition out. I want to help the next pope get his sea legs under him."

"Whom do you think that person will be?" Tate asked.

"I know the person I will be recommending, but I am not prepared to share that information with you tonight."

"Why not?" Tate asked.

"Because there are some technicalities that I still need to look into. I was doing that before you arrived.

"In the meantime, Giuseppe has shared with me that you will be doing some research of your own tomorrow, at the Vatican Secret Archive. I am betting that you will discover many answers there to the questions that you may still have."

The guests looked at each other and smiled.

"Carmine, will you canvass behind the scenes for the person you recommend to replace you?" Liz asked.

"You mean like how the St. Gallen Mafia canvassed for me? No, that's against the rules."

"If it's against the rules, why did you allow them to canvass for you?" she pushed back.

"I just wanted to win. Like I said, I made mistakes. Now it's time for me to pay for my sins.

"Stepping down is the right thing for me to do. It will show that I'm just a man in need of forgiveness."

Tate snapped his fingers. "I almost forgot. There's one more thing."

"Fire away, John," the pope said.

"I recently went to Japan and was given a secret by a nun who saw the Madonna in Akita in 1973. May I write about it?"

"Can I see the secret, please?" the pope asked.

Tate froze. He remembered the warning by Sister Agnes in one of her texts that the Church's problems went directly to the top.

The reporter reached into his coat pocket and pulled the secret out.

"Sure. Have a look."

Pope Anthony reviewed it quickly.

"This is the last of the three secrets of Akita, and it has never been told," he said. "Yes, please write about it. I don't mind at all."

"As they say, 'the truth shall set you free.' So please, set me and the Church free, John Tate."

***

The next evening, Giuseppe took Tate and Liz to the Vatican Secret Archive. They walked up a spiral staircase that led to a second-floor flat with row after row of library tables.

The librarian, Liz, looked like a kid in a candy store.

"I've never seen so many books and documents in one place before!" she said.

"You name it, it's all here," Giuseppe stated.

"Everything from handwritten letters by historic people, such as Mary, Queen of Scots, and Abraham Lincoln, to papal decrees such as the one excommunicating Martin Luther, a German monk who began the Protestant Reformation in the sixteenth century.

"Luther was one of the most influential and controversial figures in the history of Christianity. He called into question some of the basic tenets of Roman Catholicism, and his followers split from the Church to begin the Protestant tradition."

Liz was several feet away from Giuseppe, looking at other documents.

"This is an interesting document over here," she called out. "It's from 1918, written by German Masons to German Emperor Wilhelm II."

"What does it say?" Tate asked.

"The German Masons warned that the Grand Orient, the largest of several Masonic organizations in France, planned to force all sovereign monarchs in Europe to step down," Liz replied.

"That happened, as a matter of fact," Giuseppe remarked. "The sovereign monarchs of Europe relinquished their thrones, right, power, claims, and responsibilities."

"That's not all of it," Liz continued. "The German Masons went on to warn that they intended to destroy the Church."

Tate gave a low whistle.

Liz went over to another file cabinet and took out a more recent news article from the *National Catholic Register.* A former Masonic officer in France who had converted to Catholicism was interviewed.

"It is absolutely no conspiracy theory to say that Masonry holds strong political power over society even today," the former Mason was quoted as saying.

Liz searched deeper in the file cabinet, landing on a 2018 article in England's *The Times* newspaper. The headline read, "Italy Clamps Down on Masons After Mafia Links Exposed."

The librarian read the article out loud:

> "Italian politicians will be forced to declare whether they are Freemasons under laws being drawn up after revelations that mafia bosses are joining lodges to strike deals with elected officials.
>
> "The legislation is being proposed after police raids on the four largest Freemasonry orders in Italy discovered one hundred ninety-three mob-linked masons on the orders' secret membership lists in Sicily and Calabria, southern Italy.
>
> "The findings were published last month by the Italian parliament's anti-mafia commission, which alleged that mob-

sters used secret lodge meetings to do business with politicians and entrepreneurs.

"Laws proposed by the commission would ban magistrates from joining the Masons and compel public officials to say if they are members.

"Rosy Bindi, the commission president, said she also hoped to compel Masons to compile proper membership lists.

"'About twenty-five percent of the names that were found on their lists were just initials or in code,' she said. 'There was no transparency and we believe societies should keep proper records.'

"Stefano Bisi, grand master of the Grande Oriente d'Italia, Italy's largest Order with twenty-three thousand members, condemned the proposed new laws.

"'The proposed new laws are inspired by the ban on the Masonic Orders put in place by the fascist dictator Benito Mussolini in 1925.

"'These new proposals are a throwback to the fascist ban and are a wider threat to democracy as a whole,' he said."

Tate gave a whistle.

"Freemasonry isn't just some kind of myth from the past," he said. "The organization is still active even today."

A few minutes later, Liz spoke up again.

"Um, John, I think I may have found something."

"What?"

Liz pulled out an obituary about the death of Licio Lastra, written on December 16, 2015. She read the headline to them: "'Italy's Shadowy Masonic Leader and Underworld Figure Dies Aged Ninety-Six.'"

"That's a creepy headline," Tate said. "Who writes that for an obituary? Aren't they usually warm and fuzzy?"

"According to this, Lastra was the leader of a Masonic organization called Propaganda Due, or P2, which was implicated in a number of Italian scandals, including the execution of Italian Prime Minister Aldo Moro in 1978 and the bombing of a Bologna train station in 1980."

Liz looked up at the two men.

"According to this, Lastra was buried in St. Gallen, Switzerland, and a prominent Church cardinal, Carlo Martinelli, gave the eulogy."

"Why would a Church leader give the final words for an 'Underworld Figure' like Lastra?" Tate quizzed. "It doesn't make any sense."

Liz read some more from the lengthy obituary:

> "P2 was a Masonic lodge under the Grand Orient of Italy, founded in 1877. Its Masonic charter was withdrawn in 1976, and it transformed into a clandestine, pseudo-Masonic, ultra-right organization operating in contravention of Article 18 of the Constitution of Italy that banned secret associations.

"In the 1980s, Lastra used the Vatican-linked Banco Ambrosiano to recycle funds, some of which were moved out of Italy via the Vatican's bank.

"The bank's chairman was found hanging beneath London's Blackfriars Bridge after the collapse of the bank in 1982—exactly one year after law enforcement thought P2 disbanded.

"No one was ever charged in the death of 'God's banker,' but it was the work of Lastra and the Masonic lodge.

"P2 was later shown to also have been involved in a major 1990s political corruption scandal known as Tangentopoli, or Bribesville.

"In some accounts, as many as five thousand public figures fell under suspicion. At one point, more than half of the members of the Italian Parliament were under indictment, while more than four hundred city and town councils were dissolved because of corruption charges.

"The estimated value of bribes paid annually in the 1980s by Italian and foreign companies bidding for large government contracts reached four billion in US dollars.

"P2 was described as a shadow government of Italy.

"Documents found hidden in the suitcase of Lastra's daughter in 1982 outlined goals for political and economic domination.

"Lastra's plans revolved around defeating the influential communist party and destroying Italy's then powerful trade union movement.

"His plans also included taking over the Vatican and installing a pope of the group's choosing, someone who would move the Church toward a more radical agenda."

Liz continued reading:

"In 1981, Lastra is said to have recruited a former Trappist monk to hijack a plane on May second.

"The monk had been excommunicated from the Church in the 1950s by Pope Pius XII for speaking out against the Vatican and its silence about the Third Secret of Fatima.

"Lastra convinced the former monk to retaliate by hijacking Aer Lingus Flight 164 going from Dublin to London.

"The hijacker demanded that Pope John Paul II reveal the Third Secret of Fatima, but the attempt failed after a long standoff with authorities following an emergency landing.

"When that effort failed, Lastra is believed to have hired a hit man eleven days later—on May thirteenth—to shoot Pope John Paul II in St. Peter's Square.

"The assailant was a Turk named Mehmet Ali Ağca, who also happened to be a Mason like Lastra.

"Ağca fired several shots and wounded the pope, but he was grabbed by spectators and Vatican security. Pope John Paul II survived.

"The pope later claimed the Madonna guided the bullets away from his vital organs, and that the assassination attempt ended the twentieth-century persecution of Christians.

"Later that year, in 1981, the police seized a list of nine hundred sixty-two notable and powerful people from all walks of society who belonged to P2.

"The list of Freemasons included bankers, secret service chiefs, former premier Silvio Berlusconi and Victor Emmanuel, who was the son of Italy's last king.

"Lastra went on the run to Switzerland and escaped jail, where he was sentenced in absentia to serve eighteen years."

Tate paced back and forth, tapping his index finger to his lips. While he did, Liz typed away on her iPad.

"Hey, John, check this out," Liz said.

She walked over to him and showed him an online picture.

"See this?" she asked. "This picture was taken at a high school track meet. Recognize that fifteen-year-old boy with a gold medal around his neck?"

"No, who is it?" Tate asked.

"That's Giovanni," she replied.

"And who is the man standing next to him?"

"That's Lastra."

Tate's eyes opened wide. "Where was the picture taken?"

"In Switzerland, where Giovanni attended boarding school."

"Interesting," Tate said. "That means Lastra, the head of a Masonic organization, knew Giovanni."

Tate sat down in a chair and scratched his head.

"Let's do some research on Masonry, Liz."

She typed a search word into Google on her iPad.

"Since the Church first prohibited membership in Masonic organizations and other secret societies in 1738, scores of popes have made pronouncements about the incompatibility of Catholic doctrines and Masonry," Liz revealed.

"Why is it incompatible?" Tate asked.

"Masons claim that God's grace is not needed," she said. "In contrast, Catholicism and plenty of other religions teach that God's grace is obtained through the merits of Jesus Christ and is what makes men holy and sanctified."

Tate sank his chin deep between his thumb and forefinger.

"What are you thinking, John?" Liz asked.

"Going back to the picture, the one with Lastra and Giovanni that was taken in St. Gallen, Switzerland," he stated.

"Uh-huh," Liz replied.

"Remember a while back, when you told me about the St. Gallen Mafia, which was canvassing behind the scenes for their papal candidate?"

"Yes."

"I asked you who was in charge of the St. Gallen Mafia, remember?"

"I do recall that, yes," Liz replied.

"Given that Cardinal Martinelli is listed as the speaker at Lastra's funeral, which was held in St. Gallen, do you think it's possible he was the leader?"

"It's possible," she answered.

"Can you do another quick search for me?" Tate asked.

"Sure."

"The obituary mentions nine hundred sixty-two notable and powerful people who belonged to P2 back in 1981," the reporter said. "Can you pull up that list?"

Liz nodded.

"Found it!" she declared several minutes later. The librarian covered her mouth with her hands.

"You are not going to believe whose name is on the list," she exclaimed.

"Who?" Tate asked.

"Cardinal Martinelli."

"He's a Mason!" Tate cried out.

"I bet Cardinal Martinelli, Lastra, and Giovanni first met in Switzerland," Liz guessed.

"That would explain why Cardinal Martinelli is grooming Giovanni to be the pope," Giuseppe said sadly. "They want my son to move the Church in a more radical direction."

Tate turned to Giuseppe.

"Giuseppe, where would I find the Prophecy of the Popes?"

"Probably in this section over here," the old man said, and he led them both to the other end of the room. "Ah, yes, here we go."

Tate took a few minutes to read the prophecy.

"Interesting," he said. "The Vatican has written a summary of the prophecy."

"What does it say?" Liz asked.

"The Vatican's summary says Saint Malachy had a twelfth-century vision, in which he predicted the next one hundred twelve popes, in order. It also says his prediction has been spot on."

"Yeah, well, not so fast," Liz interrupted. "The Vatican has also written a disclaimer that says it believes the document was a forgery created by Cardinal Girolamo Simoncelli, who died in 1605."

"Why would he create a forgery?" Tate asked.

"According to the Vatican's notes, Simoncelli possibly forged the prophecy in order to support his bid for the papacy in 1590," Liz replied.

"Well, forgive me, but I'm not trusting what the Vatican says about the Prophecy of Popes," Tate countered. "So just to be sure, let's walk through it."

Tate took out the letter from the hospital.

"The prophecy says the seven-hilled city will be destroyed," Tate began. "What is the seven-hilled city?"

"Rome," Giuseppe answered.

"Okay, so Rome is going to be destroyed," Tate summarized. "Bad news there."

"Who is this 'Peter the Roman' who will feed his flock during many tribulations?" Tate asked.

"Many scholars believe that a person named 'Peter' will be the last pope before the End Time cited in the Book of Revelations," Giuseppe continued to explain.

"Well, that certainly rules out Carmine Luizzi—or Pope Anthony—as the last pope," Tate said.

"Probably because he wasn't validly elected," Liz added. "So, there will be one more pope before the end of the world."

Tate nodded in agreement.

Suddenly, Giuseppe looked as if he'd been hit by lightning.

"Wait a minute," he said. "Do any of you know the Italian word for *Peter*?"

"Pietro?" Liz guessed.

"Correct. And do either of you know what the Italian word *Romano* means?"

"No," they both said.

"Rome," Giuseppe continued.

"Peter the Roman!" Liz cried.

"The last pope will be Pietro Romano!" Tate shouted.

A loud clapping erupted from the back of the room.

Lights switched on.

Standing there were Cardinal Martinelli, Giovanni, and the stalker.

"Well, well, well. The Three Stooges finally figured it out," Cardinal Martinelli said.

The stalker pointed his gun at them.

"I take it you are Cardinal Martinelli?" Tate said.

"What gave it away? My red cassock?" the cardinal hissed.

"No, the foul stench," Tate replied, which drew a slight chuckle from an otherwise terrified Liz, who was trying her hardest not to make eye contact with the perpetrators.

"Giovanni, I know you," Tate continued. "We had that lovely meeting in your office in San Francisco. But you with the gun, I don't know who you are."

"Let's just say I am the guy who is going to help you meet your Maker," the stalker said.

"Cute," Tate mocked. "I am assuming you are with P2?"

"I'm a Mason, yes," he replied. "But you should know, I'm the leader of the Camorra!"

"Ah, well, we just found out that Cardinal Martinelli is also a member of P2," Tate said.

"You figured it out, with the help of good old Giuseppe over there," croaked Cardinal Martinelli.

"Is it you, Cardinal Martinelli, who has been blackmailing Pope Anthony?" Tate asked.

"Carmine, Carmine, Carmine," Cardinal Martinelli sang out. "Let me tell you about him.

"I first met Carmine in the 1960s at a Vatican City party hosted by the Vatican's gay clergy. He was a closeted homosexual back then, as he still is today.

"A deeply ambitious guy, but Carmine lacked the charisma to go far in Vatican politics.

"He badly wanted to ascend up the ranks, so I helped him. The problem was that Carmine had ideas that neither attracted the left nor those that interested the right.

"He was truly boring. That actually was in my favor, though. I was able to take what was an especially blank canvas in the man's personality and paint a new picture of who he really was.

"I helped the bland priest move his way up the ranks to become a cardinal. I painted him as a moderate, someone who was not too far to the left and not too far to the right.

"Carmine was presented as the man in the middle. In 2005, he nearly beat Cardinal Ratzinger, who took the papal name Pope Benedict XVI.

"For the next eight years, we canvassed behind the scenes for Carmine Luizzi, and when Pope Benedict resigned in 2013, he was positioned to win as pope, and he did."

"You were the leader of the St. Gallen Mafia?" Liz asked.

"The cowardly lion speaks!" Cardinal Martinelli said, mocking Liz.

Her eyes shot wide open at the insult.

"Cardinal Geoffrey Daniels and I formed the St. Gallen Mafia, an informal collection of high-ranking, like-minded reformist clerics in the Church.

"We are a circle of friends who meet annually in St. Gallen, Switzerland, to freely exchange ideas about Church issues.

"Our meetings are held in secrecy, and members observe one simple rule: everything can be said, no notes are taken, and discretion is observed.

"The problem is that after we got Carmine elected in 2013, he stayed in the middle, which is not what we wanted.

"He claimed that he needed to govern the Vatican from the center because of a divide that exists within the clergy, but we knew he was using that as an excuse.

"Carmine stayed in the middle because it was safe there. He has always been risk averse. Being in the center is safe."

"You haven't answered my question," Tate pressed. "Are you blackmailing him?"

"I sent him a Black Hand letter, yes," said Cardinal Martinelli. "An old extortion trick."

"You held his sexuality over him?" Liz snapped. "That's unconscionable."

"Why blackmail him?" Tate asked.

"Carmine asked for my help in ascending up the ranks of the Church's hierarchy," said Cardinal Martinelli.

"He knew he couldn't do it without me," the cardinal continued. "I built support for him. I blackmailed anyone and everyone along the way—including Pope Benedict XVI."

"You blackmailed Pope Benedict?" Liz asked with a hint of doubt.

"That's right," sneered Cardinal Martinelli, who then pointed at Giuseppe.

"Ask Giuseppe all about it. His brothers stole from the Vatican Bank, which Pope Benedict knew all about, along with their construction rackets."

"I had nothing to do with them or their corruption," Giuseppe shouted. "Don't drag me into your cesspool of lies, Carlo!"

The cardinal let out an eerie laugh.

"Relax, Giuseppe. We don't want to put too much pressure on your old heart."

"Leave him alone!" Liz warned.

Cardinal Martinelli sized her up and down. "I may have misread you. Maybe you have more moxie than I originally gave you credit for."

The corrupt cardinal turned back to Tate.

"In 2012, at the direction of Licio Lastra, Pope Benedict XVI's butler stole sensitive papal documents that revealed money laundering involving the Vatican Bank, P2, the Mafia, and Giuseppe's four older brothers," Cardinal Martinelli explained.

"When Pope Benedict XVI was presented with the evidence, he offered to resign rather than risk the world believing he knew about the corruption. The Vatican's press office spun the pope's resignation as a retirement."

"You were the mastermind behind all that?" Tate asked.

"Me and Licio Lastra," said Cardinal Martinelli proudly.

"When did you first get involved with Lastra?" Tate asked.

"In the early 1970s, Licio was a member of my church parish in Tiburtina. I was drawn to his strong will and determination."

"Licio Lastra was a torturer for Hitler during World War II," Giuseppe shot back.

Cardinal Martinelli's eyes looked Giuseppe slowly up and down. Then he smirked.

"Licio believed people must make their own breaks in life," Cardinal Martinelli explained.

"If that meant breaking some man-made rules along the way to change one's fate, then Licio was all for it. After all, they were man's rules, not God's."

"There's something I don't understand," Tate interjected. "In the recent vote by the College of Cardinals, why didn't you protect Pope Anthony?

"If he was your boy and you got him elected, why did you let him get run over by the bus?"

"I was committed to keeping Pope Anthony in power at all costs. But like I said, the man didn't hold up his end of the deal.

"Carmine backed away from our support once he got into power. Then, the pope came under attack from every direction over how his clergy was behaving. Bickering. Sex abuse. Et cetera.

"Masons have been using the scandals against him to damage his public image, and it has been working. Holding a discussion in San Francisco was a huge mistake.

"You saw what the US cardinals did. They aired their dirty laundry against the pope for the entire world to see.

"The event backfired on him. After that, he was a sitting duck."

Giuseppe stepped forward. "Giovanni, stop this nonsense. It's not too late, Son."

"Quiet, Dad," Giovanni yelled. "You have made a mess of everything with your meddling."

"How so?" Giuseppe asked.

"You and Grandpa Al just had to protect the Third Secret of Fatima all these years, didn't you?" Giovanni continued.

"Your big egos wouldn't let you simply do what you were told. Oh, no."

"I have no idea what you are talking about, Giovanni," the old man said.

"Why couldn't you both have just forgotten about the Third Secret of Fatima?" Giovanni shouted.

"Speaking of the secret, I want it," Cardinal Martinelli remembered. "Who has it?"

"Not so fast," came a voice from behind in the spiral staircase.

Cardinal Martinelli spun around to see Pope Anthony step up on the second-floor landing, flanked by a dozen Swiss Guards, all of whom were carrying SIG Sauer 9mm pistols and H&K submachine guns.

"Hey, I thought Swiss Guards didn't carry guns," the stalker protested, realizing he was outgunned.

"They do today," said Pope Anthony. "Drop your weapon!"

The stalker did as he was told.

"I knew better than to trust you, Carmine," hissed Cardinal Martinelli. "You have always been a two-faced weasel."

"Arrest them," the pope said. "Get them all out of my sight!"

"How did you know they would be here?" Tate asked Pope Anthony.

"We have been aware for quite some time that Giuseppe was being stalked," the pope said. "We have had a tail on the stalker. Imagine our surprise when he was spotted in his car tonight, picking up Cardinal Martinelli and Giovanni."

"Your timing was perfect," said Liz as she hugged the Holy Father.

The next day, with the pope's blessing, Tate wrote up and filed the following story about his encounter with the nun in Japan:

The Sacramento Union

A Message for the People
By John Tate

Sacramento—Recently, the *Sacramento Union* was summoned to Japan by a nun who saw the Madonna in 1973. She shared the third and final secret of Akita that she had been given back then. Until now, it has not been told to anyone.

The following is the message that was given to Sister Agnes Sasagawa of the Handmaids of the Eucharist Convent:

"My dear daughter, listen well to what I have to say to you. As I told you, if men do not repent and better themselves, the Father will inflict a terrible punishment on all humanity.

"It will be a punishment greater than the deluge, such as one we will never have seen before.

"Fire will fall from the sky and will wipe out a great part of humanity, the good as well as the bad, sparing neither priests nor faithful.

"The survivors will find themselves so desolate that they will envy the dead.

"Each day recite the prayer of the Rosary. With the Rosary pray for the pope, bishops, and the priests.

"The work of the Devil will infiltrate even into the Church in such a way that one will see cardinals opposing cardinals, and bishops against other bishops.

"The priests who venerate me will be scorned and opposed by their confreres.

"Churches and altars will be sacked; the Church will be full of those who accept compromises, and the demon will press many priests and consecrated souls to leave the service of the Lord.

"The demon will be especially implacable against souls consecrated to God.

"The thought of the loss of so many souls is the cause of my sadness. If sins increase in number and gravity, there will be no longer pardon for them.

"Today is the last time that I will speak to you in a living voice."

###

PART III:
THE COUP

Genocide of Christians

Today, Beijing has reportedly imprisoned hundreds of thousands of Uighur Muslims in concentration camps.

According to a 2019 review in *Newsweek* magazine, the persecution of Christians across the world is fast becoming genocide, and the faith will soon disappear, even in locations where its presence dates back to antiquity.

The review found that eradicating Christians and other minorities through violence was the explicit objective of extremist groups in Syria, Iraq, Egypt, northeast Nigeria, and the Philippines.

These groups are not only murdering Christians for their faith but also whitewashing all evidence of their existence by destroying churches and removing religious symbols such as crosses. Clergy are also being targeted for kidnapping and killing.

"They are already judged; their ends, their means, their doctrines, and their action, are all known with indisputable certainty. Possessed by the Great Deceiver, whose instrument they are, they burn like him with a deadly implacable hatred of the Church, and they endeavor by every means to overthrow and fetter it."

—Pope Leo XIII on Masonic Sects, 1884

Chapter 1

NEW BEGINNING

California, February 2023

Before his departure from office, Pope Anthony worked hard to heal the Church and build bridges. Surprisingly, his popularity grew.

A contrite and apologetic Pope Anthony earned the forgiveness of the public, especially after revealing that he had been blackmailed by Masons.

Cardinal Martinelli and Giovanni stood trial for their crimes and were sent to prison.

John Tate won his second Pulitzer Prize, for the stories he wrote about Church corruption.

The College of Cardinals selected a new pope—Pietro Romano—whom Pope Emeritus Anthony recommended for the job. The outgoing pope shared with the voting cardinals that Pietro had been visited by the Madonna as a boy, "which makes him special."

The College of Cardinals said the Church needed a fresh start, which is why it broke from tradition and selected someone who wasn't a cardinal. Pietro's selection as the pope came after the quickest vote ever—just one day—eclipsing the previous record in 1939 when Pope Pius XII was elected in two days on the third ballot. Pietro was elected on the first ballot.

News quickly leaked from the College of Cardinals that the new pope intended to hold a Vatican III "to heal the fracturing within the Church."

Pietro took the papal name Pope Pius XIII.

Back in Sacramento, Tate settled back into his usual routine. On this particular evening, he was more than happy to be at an AA meeting because no one was chasing after him.

In the front of the room, Beth, the AA moderator, called the meeting to order.

"The topic tonight is hope or faith. Please share with the group how you find either hope or faith in a life without the distraction of alcohol."

"Can it be both hope and faith?" asked a lonely looking elderly lady in the front row, who was probably only there because she had no other place to be.

"Yes," Beth replied. "It can be both."

Beth pointed to Tate, who groaned.

"Tell us how you find hope or faith during your day," said Beth.

"Hi. My name is John, and I am an alcoholic."

"Hi, John," the crowd bellowed.

"That's a hard one," he began. "Who here knows about the shooting spree that happened at Sacramento Valley High School?"

Everyone in the room raised their hand.

"I was there when it happened," Tate continued.

It felt like the oxygen had been sucked out of the room as all eyes bored into him.

"I looked straight into the eyes of the shooter," Tate continued. "There was pure evil in them."

Ben shot to his feet.

"My nephew was injured in that shooting," he said. "I'm telling you, there's too much violence in the world today. A kid can't even go to school without worrying about another Columbine-type shooting."

"That's true," Tate replied. "The shooter in Sacramento wore a camouflage coat, and he had a belt of bullets across his waist. When I first saw him, he was at the other end of the hallway, walking straight at me.

"Several long guns hung from his shoulders. He was also carrying a camouflage backpack that had even more ammunition in it.

"The shooter was taller than me but skinny. When he saw me, I thought I would be shot on the spot, but instead, the shooter continued walking past me.

"He said something about it being my lucky day, but I didn't feel lucky.

"The media later reported that the kid was a twenty-year-old dropout who invaded his old high school because he wanted to get even with some kids who harassed him when he was a student there. He wounded ten students and held sixty hostages into the night."

Beth looked puzzled. "What does this have to do with our topic, John?"

"Despite all of the violence in the world, which, like Ben says, seems to be getting worse, I still have both hope and faith in mankind."

The uncomfortable silence returned. Even the normally bubbly Beth was at a loss for words. A tear streamed down her face.

After what seemed like an eternity, though, she managed to find her voice again.

"John, thank you for sharing your story."

"Sure, Beth. I'd like to add one more thing. Every day, I look for little things that are like tiny miracles."

"What kind of miracles, John?" Beth asked.

"Well, for example, your smile and the kind way you talk is like a miracle in my view," he explained.

Beth's cheeks turned bright red.

The lonely lady in the front row chimed in.

"I saw a butterfly today circling outside my kitchen window. That's a small miracle! Nature is a gift. The butterfly made me feel good."

People clapped at her contribution. The sound reminded Tate that he was being watched, which made him want to shrink under his chair.

A nervous-looking man stood up.

"Tom, alcoholic."

"Hi, Tom!"

"I totally understand what's being said here," he said. "The rain this past winter was a small miracle after two years of drought."

More clapping.

A young lady raised her hand.

"Yes, you," Beth said.

"Debbie, two months sober. When I was driving here, I saw someone give food to a homeless person. That kind of selflessness seems like a miracle to me, especially in this day and age of people only looking out for themselves."

Beth nodded. Then she turned back to Tate.

"John, have you always been such an optimistic person?" she asked.

"No, Beth. My life spiraled out of control for a long time. I'm sure we've all experienced that, and it is the reason why we are here. But look around. I see a bunch of fighters.

"Every one of us is fighting. We all have been knocked down but have gotten back up. Generally speaking, most people want a better life, and that gives me hope and faith for the future."

Chapter 2

THE BARONESS

Italy, March 2023

From the balcony of her expansive castle, Cassandra Capalbo looked out at the rolling hills lined with row after row of grapevines. Valentino Vineyards was by far the largest vineyard in southwestern Italy.

Cassandra's castle was old, built in 1141, and protected by walls nearly fifty-three feet tall. Imposing bastions and spring towers looked over the breathtaking views.

In 1835, the castle underwent renovation according to the Gothic tastes of the time.

She lived in Amalfi, a town set below steep cliffs in an area otherwise known for its ancient ruins and dramatic coastline.

Between the ninth and eleventh centuries, Amalfi was the seat of a powerful maritime republic.

Naples, the regional capital, was a nearby, bustling city with a striking natural setting between the iconic gray cone of Mount Vesuvius and the deep blue waters of the Golfo di Napoli.

Cassandra's great-grandfather, a military man, started the family's grape business in 1872, two years after Rome fell and the pope lost the Pontifical States.

For a long time, the farm struggled to make money, and it wasn't until Cassandra's grandfather Mario took over that it turned around in his later years.

He changed the destiny of Valentino Vineyards and the whole region by perfecting the "recipe" for the most famous wine ever: Chianti.

Cassandra was the only offspring remaining to keep the family business going. Her grandfather left everything to her after Cassandra's own father opted not to stay on the farm.

Due to her inheritance, she was rich beyond her wildest dreams at forty-five years old.

A shrewd businessperson and extremely determined, Cassandra was also very attractive.

She had long, wavy black hair that fell to the length of her shoulders, olive skin that seemed to glow, and a magnificent, athletic body.

Although many men courted her, Cassandra was not married, and she liked it that way. She had divorced long ago and didn't let anything get in the way of her work.

"Madam, your guest will be arriving shortly," her butler announced.

"Thank you, Orazio. I'm ready. We'll sit in the parlor. Please show Ms. Cuomo in when she arrives. I'll be waiting."

Fifteen minutes later, the butler showed journalist Marissa Cuomo to the parlor, where Cassandra, wearing an exquisite floral dress, sat in an oversize wicker chair that looked more like a throne.

She stood and extended a hand to her guest.

"Very pleased to meet you!" Cassandra declared as the reporter entered the room.

"Oh no, the honor is all mine," the young reporter replied. "I have wanted to meet you for a long time. Successful women are such an inspiration."

The butler motioned for the reporter to sit in a seat opposite Cassandra's opulent wicker chair.

"May I pour you both iced tea?" he asked.

"Thank you, yes, that would be great," the reporter replied.

Orazio poured them each a beverage and excused himself from the room.

"I have read your work," Cassandra said. "Writing about food, travel, and wine must be an enjoyable profession."

"Every day I pinch myself," the reporter replied. "My job with the magazine doesn't feel like work. It's more like play."

"Well, there's the old expression 'Do what you love and you'll never work another day in your life,'" Cassandra noted.

The reporter burst out in nervous laughter.

"I've never heard that one before," she said. "But it's true, for me at least. Like I said, I'm blessed."

The butler returned with an antipasto dish of cured lunch meats, olives, pepperoncini, mushrooms, anchovies, artichoke hearts, pickled meats, vegetables in olive oil, and various cheeses, such as provolone and mozzarella.

"What about you, Ms. Capalbo, do you feel blessed in the work you do?" the reporter asked.

"Please, call me Cassandra."

The reporter blushed.

"I'll try, but you're so accomplished, it doesn't seem right for me to be informal."

"We are friends here," Cassandra replied. "In answer to your question, yes, I feel fortunate, just like you."

The reporter took out a small notebook and pen from her oversize purse. She also pulled out a tape recorder.

"Do you mind if I record our conversation?"

"Not at all," Cassandra replied. "I'm flattered that you're writing about the one hundred fiftieth anniversary of our business. However, you must know, our story goes back further than 1872."

"Please share the full story!" exclaimed the reporter, barely able to contain her excitement.

"In 1860, barns and other structures were on fire," Cassandra began. "They burned night and day. The Carbonari, a secret society, torched everything south of Rome. They were protesting the foreign governments that ruled in Italy at the time. Mostly, it was the Austrian Empire that controlled Italy."

The reporter interrupted. "Um, excuse me, but can you tell me more about the Carbonari? Who were they?"

"The Carbonari were freedom fighters," Cassandra said. "They did not hesitate to use assassination and armed revolt to fight against the Austrian monarchy.

"Ultimately, the Carbonari wanted an Italian king and a constitutional monarchy to rule Italy, not foreigners."

The reporter waved her hand for Cassandra to continue. "Sorry I interrupted. Please, continue with your story."

"A brave general—my great-grandfather—had taken over the Carbonari in 1860. He helped to unify Italy, at least partially, a year later."

"How so?" the reporter asked.

"His secretive freedom fighters burned down structures and engaged in dramatic riots," Cassandra explained.

"Thanks to their efforts, the Italian Peninsula came under the control of King Victor Emmanuel II, an Italian from Sardinia, which, as you know, is a large Italian island in the Mediterranean Sea. Several problems still stood in the way of the full unification of Italy, though."

"What sort of problems?" the reporter asked.

"First, Venice continued to be under the control of Austria. However, that problem got resolved five years later when the German state of Prussia asked for Italy's support in the case of war against Austria, which quickly gave in.

"Once Austria learned that Prussia was readying for war, it transferred Venice back to Italy. Problem solved.

"After that, only the pope and his refusal to give up the Pontifical States remained in the way of full Italian unification.

"French troops were guarding the territory, but when they left to fight another battle back home, the Italian government—with assistance from my great-grandfather and the Carbonari—stormed the Pontifical States. They claimed the Vatican's territories in 1870 in a bloody battle, and Italy became a constitutional monarchy."

"Your great-grandfather was a hero!" the reporter exclaimed.

Cassandra puffed out her chest.

"Indeed, he was. Two years later, he started Valentino Vineyards, and here we are today."

The reporter turned off the tape recorder.

"What an amazing story! This is going to be a great piece for our magazine."

She put her notepad and tape recorder back in her oversize purse and shook Cassandra's hand.

"Thank you for your time, Cassandra. I know you are a busy woman. May I contact you if I have any follow-up questions?"

"Please do!" Cassandra replied.

When the reporter was gone, Cassandra sat down in an extravagant chaise lounge and swallowed hard. She'd left out an important detail when talking with the magazine reporter.

Cassandra hadn't told the reporter that long before the Fatima apparitions in 1917, after capturing the Pontifical States, her great-grandfather had gone in search of his own Holy Grail: the three secrets of Lourdes.

Hoping the three secrets of Lourdes were a foretelling of the future, he went to see thirty-five-year-old Sister Bernadette Soubirous on her deathbed in 1879. She'd reported eighteen encounters in 1858 with the Madonna, in a grotto just outside of Lourdes in southern France.

The Madonna had worn a white veil and blue girdle, and there was a golden rose on each of Her feet. In Her hands, the Madonna held a rosary of pearls.

During the seventh apparition, the Madonna entrusted Bernadette with three secrets, which Cassandra's great-grandfather, the general, desperately wanted to know because he believed they were a revelation of the future.

When the general arrived at Sister Bernadette's deathbed, anxious to know the future, the Mother Superior took him to the nun's room. Sister Bernadette weakly rolled her eyes toward them as they entered.

"Sister, my apologies for the intrusion," the general said. "I wouldn't have come if it weren't important."

The nun tightened her grip on the rosary beads in her hand.

"When you saw the Madonna, She shared with you three secrets," the general continued. "Is that true?"

Sister Bernadette nodded her head.

The general grinned and clasped his hands together. His heart pounded fast.

"Could you please share the secrets with me?" he asked.

The stout Mother Superior stepped forward. She'd been protectively standing guard in the doorway.

"Sir, what's your business here? Who sent you?"

"I am the leader of the Carbonari. We helped to unify Italy. To be perfectly honest, I want to know the secrets the Madonna shared with Sister Bernadette at Lourdes because I want to know the future."

The Mother Superior flinched.

"No one needs to know the future," she replied. "God asks us to have faith. If people knew the future, they wouldn't need faith."

The general's blood boiled.

"Faith won't stop an enemy's bullet," he retorted. "Knowing the future could keep our country safe."

The Mother Superior grabbed the general by the arm.

"You must go," she ordered. "Now!"

The general leaned his entire body close to the Mother Superior and lowered his face to hers.

"I'm not going until Sister Bernadette tells me the secrets that were given to her at Lourdes."

The Mother Superior took several steps back. His brazenness surprised her.

"The Madonna instructed Sister Bernadette to never reveal them!" the Mother Superior argued.

"The secrets of Lourdes cannot die with her!" the general protested. "Italy needs to know them; *I* need to know."

The general turned around to face Sister Bernadette, but she had taken her last breath.

***

Later that day, Cassandra went out to the vineyard and walked among the rows of grapes with the elderly farm supervisor. Every few feet they would stop, bend down, and check the vines for disease and pests.

"I'm seeing signs of bugs," she said.

"I will do a mixture of liquid dish washing soap with vegetable oil, shake it, and make an emulsion," the veteran supervisor said. "Then, I'll add water and spray it every ten days. That will kill the spiders, mites, and aphids."

"Sounds good," said Cassandra. "By the way, how are your grandchildren doing?"

"Very well, thank you, ma'am."

"And your wife?"

"She is doing excellent too. Olivia took a part-time job at the port in Praiano. She is working at the fish packing plant. Olivia likes to keep busy, but not too busy at her age."

They both chuckled.

"Praiano is not too far from here," Cassandra remarked.

"Only twenty-five minutes," the man replied. "My wife enjoys the bus ride to the port."

"I'm so pleased. It sounds like everything is going well for you and your family."

"No complaints," the supervisor said.

"I have quite a few," Cassandra uttered softly.

"With me?" The supervisor stiffened.

"What? Oh, sorry, no," said Cassandra. "What I meant to say is that I have complaints with our ever-changing Italian government."

The supervisor breathed a sigh of relief. "Me too. What has there been, something like sixty governments since the country's unification?"

"More than that," Cassandra replied.

"Our current parliament just can't seem to get its act together," the man groused. "I would prefer the old monarchy to what we have today. The king cared about his people back then."

"I completely agree," Cassandra said. "There was stability under the king and his constitutional monarchy from 1870 until 1922," Cassandra said.

"Then, Mussolini and his National Fascist Party came along and ruined it. Italy hasn't been the same since," she continued.

"People forget that the monarchy returned for a short while after Mussolini was deposed," the supervisor pointed out.

"Only briefly, for two years. Then, in 1945, the voters of Italy foolishly passed a referendum ending the monarchy."

"I wish we could bring it back," the man said.

"A lot of Italians do as well," Cassandra agreed.

They walked along, each staying quiet, for several minutes.

"Did you know my great-grandfather was a nobleman?" Cassandra said, breaking the silence.

"No, I wasn't aware of that."

"Italy had a feudal system in many regions of the country well into the twentieth century," she continued. "It wasn't until 1945—the same year we did away with the monarchy—that Italy stopped using nobility titles."

"Do you wish we'd return to the nobility system?" the man asked.

"Feudalism worked well with the monarchy," Cassandra replied. "Back then, land barons like my great-grandfather were invested in the welfare of their workers."

"Just like you!" the man replied. "You take good care of your workers and are always asking about our families. You are truly concerned about our welfare."

"Thank you," she replied. "Do you know that if nobility titles were still used today, I'd be a baroness? I like to conduct myself like one."

"The title suits you," said the supervisor.

"Feel free to call me by it if you like. I don't mind. Anyway, land barons like my great-grandfather took care of their workers and were responsible for them. If they didn't do that, the king held them accountable. He'd take their land away."

"Well, like I said, you definitely are invested in your workers, Baroness."

Cassandra smiled and put a hand on one of the seasoned supervisor's slightly hunched shoulders.

"I am seventy-seven years old," he continued. "Been with Valentino Vineyards for more than fifty years now. Your grandfather Mario hired me. He took good care of my family, just like you do. That's rare in this day and age."

***

That evening, Cassandra drank Chianti alone in her parlor and thought about the conversation she'd had earlier in the day with the supervisor.

Times had definitely changed, not just in Italy but everywhere. People were no longer held accountable for their actions, in her view.

She stood and walked out to the second-story balcony. The cold air bit her lungs and made her face tingle, but it also seemed to clear her mind a little.

A revelation came to her.

She darted back inside and made her way to the large library, which was filled with countless books.

Her mind raced.

Where is it? Ah, here it is.

On one of the shelves, Cassandra found a document entitled "Plan for Democratic Rebirth," which called for the rewriting of the Italian constitution, a consolidation of the media, and suppression of trade unions.

The document, written by Licio Lastra, the former leader of P2, called for Masons to overthrow the Italian government and assert their political and economic domination.

The "Plan for Democratic Rebirth" was discovered by police in a search of Lastra's villa after the arrest in the 1980s of a banker and P2 member named Michele Sindona, who had murdered a lawyer commissioned to liquidate his failing banks.

This will be my playbook, she thought.

As Cassandra stepped back from the shelf, another document caught her eye—a memoir written by Pope Leo XIII long ago. She picked it up and turned the pages.

In the memoir, Pope Leo claimed to have had a vision in 1884 after he celebrated a Mass. According to the memoir, the pope's vision went as follows:

> Pope Leo turned pale and collapsed as though dead. Those standing nearby rushed to his side. They found him alive but frightened.
>
> He recounted a vision of Satan approaching the throne of God, boasting that he could destroy the Church. The Lord reminded the Great Deceiver that his Church was imperishable.
>
> Satan then replied, "Grant me one hundred years, and give me more power of those who will serve me, and I will destroy it."
>
> The Lord granted Satan a century to test the Church.

Pope Leo says the Lord then revealed future events. The pope saw wars, immorality, genocide, and a lack of faith in Christianity (atheism and agnosticism) on a large scale.

Cassandra left the library and walked back to the balcony.

When did the one-hundred-year test start? she wondered.

Cassandra rested her chin between her thumb and pointer finger. *Was it in 1917, with the beginning of World War I and the visitations by the Madonna in Fatima?*

She recalled that 1917 is also the year when the Communist Revolution in Russia was unleashed.

She figured that if 1917 was the start of the one-hundred-year test, that would explain why people had become increasingly callous over the past century.

In that very moment, Cassandra was sure of her plan.

We need to go back to the way things were before 1917.

***

The next week, Cassandra put her plan into action. She stood off to the side with a clipboard in her hand as hundreds of people engaged in an anti-government protest rally against Prime Minister Alberto Regio and the parliament.

Protests were nothing new in Italy's dysfunctional history of government; however, on this particular day, no one knew who the demonstrators were.

The right-wing League, the far-right Brothers of Italy, and the center-right Go Italy parties all said they were not behind the protest.

"Who Were Those Protesters?" screamed the head-line later that day in *la Repubblica,* one of Rome's leading newspapers.

They will know soon enough, Cassandra thought.

***

An ocean away, Rollings watched the protest on TV as it was being carried out in the central streets of Rome.

"Tate, you seeing what's happening right now in Italy?" the managing editor called out.

"Does it have anything to do with Italy's economic collapse?" Tate hollered back from his cubicle.

Italy was suffering its worst recession since World War II. Even before COVID-19, the country's public-debt-to-gross-domestic-product ratio was 135 percent, the Eurozone's second-most indebted country after Greece.

Then, along came the pandemic, which turned Italy's already-bad debt situation even worse.

Tate walked over to the television and stood next to Rollings, who was mesmerized by CNN's coverage of the protest.

"What are they protesting, Chief?"

"They want the parliament to resign."

Tate's head snapped back. "Really?"

"Evidently, people in Italy are pretty upset with how the parliament is handling the economy," Rollings stated.

Tate picked up the phone in the newsroom and called Liz.

"Can you please pull up any breaking news you can find online about a big protest happening right now in Rome?" he asked.

A few minutes later, the librarian arrived with the breaking news story in *Corriere della Sera*. A picture accompanied the article.

"That's a lot of protesters!" said Tate as he studied the picture.

Rollings leaned in to get a look.

"Say, Liz, can you enlarge that picture on your iPad?" the managing editor asked.

She zoomed the view, increasing the image from 100 to 200 percent.

"Hold it!" Rollings instructed. "See that lady standing right there?"

"You mean the woman in a red business suit and stilettos?" Tate asked. "What about her?"

"What's that under her arm?" Rollings leaned in closer, trying to make it out.

"A clipboard," Liz answered.

"So? What's the big deal about that?" Tate asked, unimpressed.

"Casual bystanders don't usually carry clipboards," Rollings responded.

"You think maybe she is an organizer?" Tate asked.

"Maybe."

"Or, maybe she's just an average person who found herself caught in the middle of a protest," Tate countered.

"Could be that too," agreed the managing editor.

Tate turned to Liz. "Can you find out who that person is?"

"I may be able to do an image search online," Liz responded. "That will take some time, though."

"Thank you, Liz."

***

The following evening at her castle, Cassandra held a meeting of twenty-five influential people from Italy's Campania region, mostly landowners, but there were also business owners and prominent community leaders.

"Congratulations, Cassandra, yesterday's protest was a huge success," said Carla Pasquinelli, whose late grandfather, Supremo, had owned Pasquinelli's Seafood Restaurant in Salerno for decades.

"Yes, good job, Cassandra!" the group cheered.

"The media has no clue who was behind the protest." The mayor of Palermo giggled.

"Which is a good thing," Cassandra noted. "We're not ready yet to reveal our identity."

"What's our next step?" Carla Pasquinelli asked.

"We're all in agreement that Italy needs to go back to a constitutional monarchy," Cassandra replied. "So, our next step is to overthrow the parliament."

"Yes!" the members of the group agreed unanimously.

"My great-grandfather and the Carbonari fought for a unified Italy under the rule of a monarchy, not a parliament," Cassandra continued. "A monarchy is our heritage!"

"Hear, hear," said Lorenzo Pirelli I, manager of the port at Praiano. "We need to take back our past and erase the mistake of Mussolini and Fascism."

Pirelli turned his head to the side. "But I have a question. How will the monarchy work if we don't have nobility too? Don't we need to bring back the feudal system as well?"

"I have thought about that," Cassandra replied. "While we cannot bring back the feudal system, we can take a page from England's playbook."

"Which is what?" Pirelli asked.

"We can reinstitute nobility titles," explained Cassandra.

"You mean go back to the societal titles of baron/baroness, duke/duchess, and so on?" Pirelli asked.

"Yes."

"Oh, bravo!" Pirelli clapped his hands.

"Nobility titles would let everyone know who the most powerful people are after the king," Carla Pasquinelli said in agreement.

"Or the queen," Cassandra corrected.

"Queen?" Carla asked.

"Perhaps it is time for a queen to run things." Cassandra stared at the other woman intently.

"I love that idea!" Carla exclaimed. "Women are running the Mafia now, why not the country?"

"There are plenty of constitutional monarchies today that are governed by a queen," Pirelli interjected. "Denmark, New Zealand, Jamaica, and more."

Chapter 3

OUT OF JAIL

California, April 2023

Tate was visiting in Las Vegas for the weekend. He walked past a row of slot machines in the Flamingo Casino, stopped, turned his head to the left and then right, and continued walking.

He was certain someone was following him. When he came to the card tables, Tate took a seat.

This is my best play. I will sit here, he thought.

Outside, the rain fell hard, which in and of itself was strange because Las Vegas only gets approximately four inches of rain a year.

"Drink for you, sir?" asked the pretty server in a scanty outfit.

"Mineral water, please."

The dealer cut the cards and dealt them to the players. Tate's first card was a six. The next was a ten. Sixteen.

"Hold," he said and groaned.

The dealer turned over a seventeen. Bust.

"Sorry, sir," said the dealer, feigning disappointment.

Tate turned around and looked at the people on the gambling floor. No one seemed to be watching him now. He was certain someone had been earlier, though.

A man in a trench coat had been lurking behind a bank of slot machines and keeping a close eye on him.

Just then, Tate charged out of his seat and through the front door.

"Taxi," he hollered while on the run.

"Where to, Mister?" the driver asked.

"The airport."

Time to get out of Vegas, Tate thought as he caught the next plane to Sacramento.

***

On Monday, the reporter was back at the *Sacramento Union* in its downtown office building, built at the turn of the twentieth century in 1900.

"Tate, why did you go to Las Vegas this weekend?" his managing editor asked.

"I wanted to see some of the casinos that Giuseppe's family was involved with back in the day," Tate replied to Rollings.

Liz greeted Tate with a stack of papers in her arms.

"Here's a ton of information about the Empire State Building and other public works projects that Giuseppe's family helped to build," she said.

"I also included information about the Pontifical States that used to be under the control of the pope."

"Why do you want *that* information, Tate?" Rollings asked.

"Giuseppe's family is a real rags-to-riches story," Tate said. "His dad, Big Al, came to America from Italy with nothing. He became a somebody, as did Giuseppe."

"When you were in Sin City, did you research the old gangsters, like Bugsy Siegel and Lucky Longo?" Rollings asked.

"I did! They have a Mafia museum in Las Vegas, and I went there. Loved it. I also visited some of the casinos that the Mafia ran back in the 1940s."

"Which casinos?" Rollings asked.

"The Tropicana and the Stardust hotels were run by the Mafia, as was the Flamingo Casino, which mobster Bugsy Siegel opened in 1946."

"What else did you learn when you were down there?" Rollings probed.

"Maybe a bit too much," said Tate.

"What's that supposed to mean?" said Liz, furrowing her eyebrows.

"I would swear I was being watched."

"Watched? By whom?" the managing editor asked.

"I don't know. But there was a man in a trench coat following me."

"Tate, it was raining," Rollings pointed out. "When it rains, people wear coats. Don't you think you could be a little paranoid after everything that happened last year?"

"Ed is right." Liz looked sympathetic, but she obviously thought he had been overreacting.

Tate looked through the stack of information.

"Did you know that from 1870 to 1940, there wasn't a US envoy to the Vatican until Big Al?" Tate asked. "The position was vacant for seventy years."

Rollings shrugged. He seemed bored with the tidbit.

"Do you know *why* the position had been vacant for seventy years?" Tate continued.

"Why?" Liz played along.

"In 1870, the US envoy to the Vatican was assassinated!" Tate replied.

"Really?" Rollings perked up. "Okay, now maybe we are getting somewhere. This could be juicy."

"In 1870, the Carbonari, a secret society like the Masons, fought for the unification of Italy," Tate explained.

"The Carbonari wanted an Italian king to rule the country. They were dissatisfied with the patchwork of foreign rulers in Italy. The pope, however, opposed unification."

"Why wasn't he supportive?" Liz asked.

"Because it meant losing the Pontifical States. The pope controlled a huge territory that included Rome, Venice, and other places."

Rollings scrunched up his face as if he'd swallowed sour milk. "The pope controlled land?"

"The Pontifical States were a series of territories in central Italy under the direct sovereign rule of the pope, from the eighth century until 1870," Tate shared.

"Picture it this way: the Vatican was like the government, the Pontifical States were like the country, and the pope was the ruler over both."

"What happened?" Liz asked.

"In 1870, with the outbreak of the Franco-Prussian War, Napoleon called his French troops out of Italy," said Tate.

"Napoleon had been guarding the Pontifical States for the pope. With the French now gone, no one was there to protect the pope's land.

"Italian troops moved in. There was an attack on Rome. The US envoy was killed in the battle. After that, the position remained vacant for seventy years, until Big Al filled it."

Liz's jaw dropped. "That's a really interesting story."

"There's more. After the attack, Rome was annexed by the Kingdom of Italy. However, the Apostolic Palace, which is the pope's residence, was spared.

"The pope was granted a very small area, called Vatican City."

"I bet the pope wasn't too happy about losing practically all of his land," Liz said.

"Not at all," Tate replied. "The pope declared himself a prisoner in the Vatican. Pope Pius IX and his successor, Pope Leo XIII, refused to leave the Vatican, in order to avoid any appearance of accepting the authority wielded by the new Italian government.

"During this period, the popes also refused to appear at St. Peter's Square or at the balcony of the Vatican Basilica facing it because Italian troops occupied the square in front of the basilica.

"The popes granted blessings from a balcony facing a courtyard, or from inside the basilica. Papal coronations happened at the Sistine Chapel instead."

"Well, John, you are today's trivia winner!" Liz said jokingly. "Seriously, though, that was fascinating."

"Thank you, Liz!" Tate turned and chortled at Rollings.

"Okay, Tate. You won that one," the managing editor conceded.

"Was Big Al a mobster?" Liz asked.

"Oh, no," Tate said quickly. "Big Al knew people in the Mafia, but he was never a made Mafia member."

"What's a 'made member'?" Liz asked.

"A person who is fully initiated into the Mafia," Tate responded. "To become made, an associate first must be Italian or of Italian descent and sponsored by another made Mafia man. Big Al was never sponsored by a Mafia member."

one had to make his "bones"

"Was Giuseppe involved with the Mafia?" Liz asked.

"Oh no, not at all," Tate replied. "Giuseppe wanted nothing to do with the Mafia. He despised the Mob. In fact, a defining moment happened when Giuseppe was twenty years old."

"What happened?" Liz asked.

"One evening, Giuseppe was washing dishes at Big Al's Restaurant, like he did every night," Tate explained. "His much-older brothers—Alfred Jr., Alessandro, Maximo, and Francesco—saw the president of the International Dockworkers Association walk past their restaurant on the street outside. The brothers charged out the door after the union leader.

"From a restaurant window, Giuseppe saw his brothers push the union leader into an alley. The following day, the headline in *The New York Times* read: 'Top Union Official Hospitalized with Broken Jaw after Beating.'

"From that moment on, Giuseppe swore he would never be associated in any way with the Mafia."

"Well, it may be true that Giuseppe didn't like the Mafia, but we know from our investigation last year that his son, Giovanni, did," Rollings said.

"I'm just glad he and Cardinal Martinelli are both in jail," Liz said with a sigh of relief.

***

The next day, Rollings was going through the stack of newspapers that Liz had left in the newsroom when he let out a loud whistle.

"Tate, you are going to want to take a look at this," he shouted.

"What's up, Chief?" said Tate, jogging over from his cubicle.

"See the headline?" asked Rollings as he held up the *Corriere della Sera*, which is the largest daily newspaper in Milan, Italy.

Tate gasped as he read it: "'Cardinals Released from Jail!'"

"Can't be!" he declared, horrified.

Rollings called Liz on the interoffice phone and asked her to come up from her office in the basement to join them. When she arrived, Rollings read the entire story to them.

𝕮𝖔𝖗𝖗𝖎𝖊𝖗𝖊 𝖉𝖊𝖑𝖑𝖆 𝕾𝖊𝖗𝖆

Cardinals Released from Jail!

Rome—A judge released two clergymen today who were imprisoned last year for brandishing a gun on Vatican grounds.

Cardinals Carlo Martinelli and Giovanni Tedesco were set free after their attorney successfully argued that neither man had committed the violent act.

Their attorney contended that Mafia hit man Frank Tallerico Jr. of Milan was the person who brandished the gun, not the two clergymen.

Swiss Guards caught Tallerico Jr. red-handed in the Vatican Secret Archive last year holding members of the *Sacramento Union* and a former American diplomat at gunpoint.

The reporters from Sacramento had been in Italy last year investigating corruption within the Church.

Tallerico Jr. remains in jail. He has a long history of criminal activity, as did his father, Frank Tallerico Sr., who, in the 1970s, assassinated Pope Pius XIII's dad, a baker in Cava de' Tirreni named Bob Romano.

The judge also dismissed charges that the cardinals trafficked black market goods, such as drugs and stolen merchandise, on behalf of a secretive combat unit within the Knights of Malta. He ruled that there was insufficient evidence.

Representing the cardinals in court was attorney Raphael Lastra, the son of the late Licio Lastra, a former liaison officer between Benito Mussolini's Italian government and Nazi Germany.

Licio Lastra had also been the grand master of Propaganda Due (P2), a Masonic lodge that in the early 1980s was found to be actively planning to overthrow the Italian government.

Cardinal Dominic Solano, Dean of the College of Cardinals, told the *Corriere della Sera* today that he plans to speak with Pope Pius XIII about immediately reinstating both cardinals to their former positions within the Church.

###

Tate shook his head. "How can that be? They wanted to kill us!"

Liz hung her head. "I thought all this was over."

Rollings put one arm around Tate and the other around Liz.

"Chins up, you two!" he exclaimed. "After everything you went through last year, what more could happen?"

A lot more can happen, said a little voice inside Tate's head.

Chapter 4

MISSING

Vatican City, May 2023

At the Vatican, Cardinal Luca Berlone blinked several times at the letter he held in his hands. The Vatican's secretary of state read it several times:

> Dear Cardinal Berlone,
>
> In 1945, Italy abolished its constitutional monarchy. That was a mistake. Since then there have been more than sixty government changes.
>
> The current parliamentary government is an utter failure. Change must occur.
>
> The Church will be stronger if Pope Pius XIII joins our movement. We are calling on him to publicly condemn the parliament and ask for it to resign.

If the pope were to do this, we will return the Pontifical States to him, formerly known as the Republic of Saint Peter.

Just in case he balks, we have taken out a little insurance policy—we have one of your people.

If you go to the police, the prisoner will die.

Signed,

This is an extortion letter! Cardinal Berlone thought.

Just then, the phone rang. The cardinal's stomach lurched.

"Um, hello," he answered.

"Your Excellency, I believe we have problem," the caller said.

"Who is this?"

"This is Maximilian Müller, the prefect of the Papal household and personal secretary to Pope Emeritus Anthony."

"Ah, yes, Maximilian, how may I help you?" asked Cardinal Berlone.

"The retired pope is missing."

Cardinal Berlone put his hands over his mouth.

"What do you mean he is missing?"

"Pope Emeritus Anthony has not been seen or heard from in the past twenty-four hours," said the prefect.

"Are you certain?"

"Yes. The former pope keeps a strict schedule," the caller replied. "He gets up early and begins each morning with Mass in a small chapel inside the Vatican's Mater Ecclesiae Monastery, where he lives."

"And?"

"He didn't attend Mass this morning," reported the prefect. "Pope Emeritus Anthony also goes on daily afternoon walks in the Vatican garden, but he hasn't been seen."

"Maybe he had an unexpected trip?" Cardinal Berlone suggested hopefully.

"Even if that were so, I would have been told," replied the caller.

Cardinal Berlone's knees felt like rubber.

"Let's keep this just between us until further notice," the cardinal advised. "Whatever you do, don't call the police."

Cardinal Berlone slumped in his desk chair.

Are Cardinal Martinelli and Giovanni behind this? he wondered.

The two men had just gotten out of prison, and they certainly had a grudge against quite a few people, including Pope Emeritus Anthony.

A thought came to Cardinal Berlone. He reached across the desk and picked up the phone.

"Hello," came an old man's voice on the other end of the line.

"Is this Giuseppe Tedesco?"

"Why, yes, it is. May I ask who is calling?"

"This is the Vatican's secretary of state, Cardinal Berlone. We have a problem. I don't know who else to turn to."

When he hung up the phone, Giuseppe stared up at the ceiling for several moments. He could not believe what the Vatican's secretary of state had shared.

"The former pope is missing," the official had said.

"Sir, call the police right away!" the old man had ordered. "This must be reported."

"I can't do that," Cardinal Berlone answered.

"And why not?"

"I received a letter saying the prisoner will be killed if I go to the authorities."

"You got a letter?" Giuseppe asked.

"Yes, signed only with a black hand."

Giuseppe froze. He knew all too well what a Black Hand letter meant.

Growing up, Big Al had told Giuseppe stories about how, at the turn of the twentieth century, the Morello-Lupo Gang in New York would extort money from Italian families by sending letters signed with a black hand.

People who did not meet the extortion demands died. Often, their bodies were stuffed in a barrel.

"Cardinal Berlone, why are you contacting me?"

"Because this could be the work of your son, Giovanni, and Cardinal Martinelli."

Giuseppe's hands shook.

He could be right, the old man thought.

"They are out of jail, and I would not put it past them to want payback," Cardinal Berlone continued. "You may be on their hit list too, Giuseppe."

"How can I help?" the former American ambassador to Italy asked.

"Find your son," the cardinal advised.

That would be no easy task. Giovanni had lots of places to hide.

"Try Switzerland," Cardinal Berlone suggested. "Giovanni and Cardinal Martinelli have strong ties there. In fact, Cardinal Martinelli still maintains a second home in St. Gallen."

"I don't think they are in Switzerland. That's the first place the authorities would look," Giuseppe had replied.

The old man pulled on his coat. He needed to clear his mind, so he went for a walk.

Several minutes later, he found himself at his favorite Italian café across from St. Peter's Square. The waiter greeted him like the regular customer that he was.

"Would you like a table outside on the patio, Giuseppe?"

"Yes, please," he said, removing his fedora.

The waiter led Giuseppe to his customary spot and brought him espresso and cannoli, his favorites from the menu.

As he ate and watched the tourists go in and out of the Vatican, the very old man considered the situation.

An idea hit him.

Giuseppe called the waiter over and paid his bill.

I need to get home right away and make a phone call.

***

A half hour later, Gladys, the front-desk receptionist at the *Sacramento Union*, shouted across the newsroom to Tate.

"Long-distance phone call from Rome! I am transferring it."

Tate scratched his head.

I am not expecting a phone call from Italy, he thought.

His desk phone rang.

"Tate here."

"John, it is Giuseppe!"

"Giuseppe? This is unexpected. Is everything okay with you?"

"I am fine. Have you heard the news? Giovanni and Cardinal Martinelli were released from jail."

"I heard," Tate answered. "I can't believe it."

"The judge is a Mason," Giuseppe replied. "So, believe it."

"You know that for a fact?" Tate questioned.

"Yes, I do. His was among the nine hundred sixty-two notable names on the P2 member list found when the police searched Licio Lastra's house back in the 1980s," Giuseppe replied.

Tate let out a low whistle.

"John, there is another issue."

"What is it?"

"Pope Emeritus Anthony is missing."

"Are you serious?" asked a wide-eyed Tate.

"Very serious. The Vatican's secretary of state received an anonymous letter today from the people responsible for abducting him."

"Have you gone to the authorities?" Tate questioned.

"We can't," Giuseppe replied. "The abductors warned that Pope Emeritus Anthony will be killed if the police are notified."

Tate drummed his fingers on his desk.

"Do you think Giovanni and Cardinal Martinelli abducted the retired pope?" the reporter asked.

"Maybe. They do have an ax to grind."

"Have the abductors made any demands?" Tate inquired.

"They want Pietro, err, Pope Pius XIII, to denounce the Italian parliament and call for its complete elimination."

"Elimination? Abolish the government?" Tate asked.

"Yes, in favor of a return to the old constitutional monarchy before Mussolini," Giuseppe replied. "Long live the king."

"Apparently so," quipped Tate.

"There is something else, John."

"What is it?" asked the reporter, raising his eyebrows.

"I also received an anonymous letter today," Giuseppe revealed.

"You did?"

"Yes, it was under my door when I got back from the café."

"You say the letter was anonymous?" Tate asked.

"Correct, there was no signature. Just a black hand."

"A black hand? What does that mean?"

"For centuries, the black hand has been an Italian symbol of extortion. The letter says I have seventy-two hours to get Pope Pius XIII to denounce the parliament."

Tate let out a heavy sigh.

"Does this make sense to you, Giuseppe? I mean, changing governments doesn't seem like the kind of thing Giovanni or Cardinal Martinelli care about. They are focused on installing a Freemason as pope."

"You need to get over here," Giuseppe pleaded.

"What? I can't just up and fly to Italy."

"You came here last year," Giuseppe replied.

"That was different. Liz and I came because our readers have an interest in Giovanni and Pietro—both are local figures. I'm sure our readers don't feel the same kind of connection to Pope Emeritus Anthony, simply because he's not from around here."

"You are needed here again," Giuseppe persisted.

"To do what?"

"Investigate," the old man said. "I cannot go to the police. You are our best hope to get to the bottom of this."

"Are you familiar with how the newspaper industry is doing these days?" Tate replied. "Not so good. Our budgets are tight."

"Pope Emeritus Anthony could die. I might be killed too, John. Please. At the very least, will you do some digging from over there?"

Tate massaged his temples. His head ached something fierce.

"For you, Giuseppe, yes."

When they hung up, Tate called Liz on the interoffice phone.

"Hi, Liz, any luck identifying the person in the picture who was holding a clipboard at the recent protest in Rome?"

"The answer is 'yes,' and you owe me, John."

Tate clapped his hands.

"You figured out who it is?" he asked.

"I called my counterpart at *la Repubblica*, the newspaper in Rome. I asked the librarian if she had any idea who the woman is in the picture."

"And?"

"Turns out the person is quite well known," Liz said. "Her name is Cassandra Capalbo. She owns Valentino Vineyards on the Amalfi Coast. Her great-grandfather was a former general, and her grandfather Mario invented Chianti."

"Interesting. Did your colleague speculate as to why Cassandra Capalbo from the Amalfi Coast would be some one hundred seventy miles away in Rome at a protest, carrying a clipboard?"

"She owns a restaurant and winery in Rome," Liz said. "The librarian at *la Repubblica* thinks maybe Cassandra had a clipboard in her hands because she was doing inventory or a grocery list for her business there, or something along those lines."

"Well, that's a wrinkle," Tate murmured.

"You can't assume Cassandra was the organizer of the protest just because she was there and was carrying a clipboard," Liz cautioned. "It's plausible she was in Rome on business and that the clipboard was also for work. Maybe she simply got caught in the demonstration when it began and waited until it passed by.

"Or, perhaps, she simply decided to come on out and watch the protest."

"That's true," Tate conceded.

The reporter rhythmically tapped a pencil on his desk. Then he decided to go see Rollings in his office.

"What's up, Tate? You look troubled," the managing editor said.

"I just received a phone call from Giuseppe. He says Pope Emeritus Anthony is missing."

"Missing? What do you mean?"

"He hasn't been seen or heard from in twenty-four hours. Furthermore, both Giuseppe and the Vatican's secretary of state received extortion letters demanding Pietro renounce the Italian parliament."

Rollings rubbed his hands together, delighted at the news.

"The elephants are on the ground fighting, and the monkeys are in the trees," said the managing editor.

Chapter 5

THE ARGENTINE "MANHATTAN PROJECT"

Argentina, May 2023

Cardinal Martinelli and Giovanni went to Argentina, by ship. They figured going there would draw less attention than if they went to Switzerland, where everyone probably assumed they would go.

They boarded a twenty-one-day cruise from Civitavecchia, a medium-size town about fifty miles north-west of Rome. When they arrived at the Port of Buenos Aires, which is the main maritime port in Argentina, a driver was waiting for them.

As they got in the back seat of the car, the driver turned around and gawked at them.

"There must be a mistake," the driver said. "My instructions say to take you to Villa Thirty-One. That can't be; it's too dangerous for you guys to go there."

"Take us anyway," said Cardinal Martinelli. "There is a church there."

"Sir, I must protest," argued the driver. "While the port is very safe, you should be advised that Villa Thirty-One is not. It's a slum and a very rough neighborhood. There are a lot of criminals and outlaws there."

Cardinal Martinelli and Giovanni smirked.

"Drive!" demanded Cardinal Martinelli.

Within minutes, they arrived at their destination. A local priest was waiting out front of the church. The clergyman took Giovanni and Cardinal Martinelli inside and then down into a basement.

"This will be your quarters, gentlemen," the priest said. "As you can see, it is untouched since Licio Lastra last used it as his office and sleeping residence."

When World War II ended, Lastra had fled to Argentina with top Nazi officials. He helped establish "ratlines," which assisted the flight of high-ranking Nazi officials from Europe to South America.

Argentine Army General Juan Perón also secretly assisted Lastra in establishing these escape routes through ports in Spain and Italy. They smuggled thousands of former Nazi officers and party members out of Europe.

As many as nine thousand Nazi officers and collaborators from other countries escaped from Europe after the war to find sanctuary in South American countries. By far the largest number—as many as five thousand—relocated to Argentina.

The Vatican played a significant role in helping Nazis flee from Europe to Argentina, although this was often inadvertent.

Powerful Vatican priests aided people who they apparently thought were Church refugees, helping them to escape from oppressive postwar communist regimes, though many turned out to be some of Germany's worst war criminals.

However, some in the Vatican had full knowledge of these refugees' dark history. For example, Hitler sympathizer and Vatican Bishop Alois Hudal later admitted to providing known Nazi war criminals with Vatican passports so they could enter the ratlines and resettle in Argentina.

Perón, who was preparing to take charge as Argentina's president, liked the ideologies of Benito Mussolini and Adolf Hitler. He had served as a military attaché in Italy during the early years of World War II, which is how Lastra became acquainted with him.

Lastra settled down in Argentina as an industrialist whose principal activity was exporting oligarchist fortunes and Fascist money out of the new Republic of Italy.

Licio Lastra had also established Masonic lodges in Ecuador, Argentina, Uruguay, and Brazil. Later he moved to Switzerland, but he maintained operations in Argentina from the church basement until his death.

Cardinal Martinelli looked over the accommodations and found them to be acceptable.

"That will be all, thank you, Father," he instructed.

Cardinal Martinelli turned to Giovanni and gave him instructions. "Go down to the docks at the Port of Buenos Aires. When you get there, ask for a man named Guido Silvestri."

"Who is he?" Giovanni asked.

"He's the port manager," said Cardinal Martinelli. "Guido is with the local Mafia and is my hired man down here. When you meet him, give him the code word."

"What's the code word?"

"Masonry."

Giovanni nodded his head in agreement.

"Tell Guido to begin executing Operation Fasci Siciliani."

Giovanni walked heavily to a car waiting out front. As usual, he was angry.

Down at the docks, he moved like a one-man army. He looked completely out of place in his scarlet cassock, but that didn't bother him.

The dockworkers stared at him as he went by.

Once Giovanni reached the manager's office, he barreled inside and asked for Guido, as instructed. A short, hefty man in his midfifties met him at the door.

"What's the code word?" Guido asked.

"Masonry," Giovanni replied. "It's time to execute Operation Fasci Siciliani."

The port manager stepped back as if he'd been slapped.

"Really? You're not joking?"

"Yes, really," Giovanni admonished.

Guido crinkled his nose and twisted his mouth.

"Let's go to the back room and talk privately," the rotund man instructed.

Giovanni followed him into a messy room filled with plates of leftover food, empty soda cans, and fast-food containers.

"Sorry for the mess," Guido said. "I don't get many visitors."

"You could still clean up every now and then," Giovanni scolded. "Pigsties are for pigs. Are you a pig?"

Guido's face turned red. He bowed his head.

"What kind of rackets do you run here at the port?" Giovanni asked.

"A number of things," replied Guido, happy to change the subject.

"First off, we get shipments from the Mafia in Italy. I falsify the paperwork, certifying that the shipments are legal. The local Mob picks up the goods and delivers them."

"What kind of goods?"

"Black market stuff like weapons, narcotics, laundered money, stolen equipment, et cetera."

"What else?" Giovanni demanded.

"The ships that come in and out of this port pay us for 'the privilege' of operating here."

"I see," Giovanni said. "The Mafia extorts money from delivery ships. Anything else?"

"Well, you should know that there are no unions here," Guido noted proudly.

"That means we don't have to deal with strikes by the dockworkers or fishermen. There aren't any protests. No demonstrations.

"I hire everyone who works here, and they either accept what I give them or they don't. No hassles."

"Got it," Giovanni replied. "Tell me about Operation Fasci Siciliani. What's that all about?"

"It's our revolution," Guido explained. "We are Masons who want to overthrow the leadership of the Vatican, which governs the Church, and install our own pope.

"We also want to take down the Italian government in order to support the pope of our choosing.

"Our ultimate goal is a one-world religion and world domination.

"For years, our secret combat unit within the Knights of Malta has been stockpiling weapons and conducting combat training to eventually launch a coup on both the Vatican and the Italian parliament."

Giovanni stepped back. He knew Cardinal Martinelli was convinced that in order to make the kind of meaningful reforms he wanted for the Church, there needed to be a leadership change at the top ranks of the Church.

He just hadn't realized that meant a military coup.

"Cardinal Martinelli says it will be like a military takeover of a bad government," Guido continued to explain. "That's the reason for the secret combat unit within the Knights of Malta."

Giovanni could not hide his smile.

"When does the coup happen?" he asked.

"You just gave me the green light," said the plump port manager. "Let the revolution begin!"

Giovanni was giddy. He turned around and seemed to skip out of the office. He got in the back seat of the waiting black sedan and instructed the driver to take him to Villa Thirty-One and the Church.

I may get another shot at being the pope after all!

They rode in silence. Giovanni was a dangerous, antisocial person and had been all his life. Whereas people often admire certain psychopathic traits in small doses—the cool dispassion of a surgeon, the tunnel vision of an Olympic athlete, the ambitious narcissism of many a politician—

in Giovanni these attributes existed in extreme forms and were uncomfortable for others to be around.

The driver certainly felt that way now. Giuseppe, without even saying a single word, gave off a very uncomfortable vibe. The driver could not get rid of his passenger soon enough.

Back at Villa Thirty-One, Cardinal Martinelli was waiting for his protégé. When Giovanni returned, the mentor laid out his plan.

"There is a lot of work to do, Giovanni."

"How can I help?" the protégé said, taking a seat at a dilapidated wooden table.

"I need for you to go somewhere and wait for my signal," instructed Cardinal Martinelli.

"Go where?"

"The jungle."

"Cardinal Martinelli, I don't understand."

"In 1947, the Fascist leader of Argentina, Juan Perón, was interested in developing fusion power that would produce an unlimited power source," Cardinal Martinelli explained.

"He hired a physicist named Dr. Ronald Richter, who had worked on such a project in Nazi Germany under Hitler."

Giovanni nodded his head. "I'm following you."

"Perón gave the physicist a blank check to create the Huemul Project, which was essentially the Argentine version of the Manhattan Project.

"For four years, Dr. Richter worked secretly on the sixty-million-dollar project to build a nuclear reactor.

"Dr. Richter put up vast structures for his experiments, some with walls almost three feet thick. He used up to forty thousand freight-car loads of bricks, stone, and concrete."

"Where was this located?" Giovanni asked.

"Deep within the country, on Huemul Island," answered Cardinal Martinelli.

"In 1951, Perón announced to the world that successful thermonuclear experiments were carried out on Huemul Island in the atomic energy pilot plant.

"The United States and Soviet Union discredited the tests, however. They said Perón was lying."

"Why would they say that?" Giovanni asked.

"You have to understand the times. There was an arms race going on. After World War II, more than one hundred former Nazi rocket scientists were relocated to the West, principally to the United States.

"The Soviet Union countered the US by hiring scores of German scientists after the war.

"Each country wanted nuclear supremacy, and they certainly didn't want Argentina in that space."

"Was Perón lying?" Giovanni asked. "Did he really carry out successful thermonuclear tests?"

"Yes, he was lying, and no, he was not lying," Cardinal Martinelli replied.

"That's a clear answer. Clear as mud," Giovanni cracked.

"Originally, the nuclear reactor plant was to be built in the jungle on the Suquía River, about four hundred thirty-five miles northwest of Buenos Aires.

"However, Dr. Richter claimed a fire in 1949 destroyed some of the equipment."

"A fire?" Giovanni asked.

"Dr. Richter told everyone it was sabotage," Cardinal Martinelli elaborated. "He demanded a more protected location free from spies, which is why the project moved to Huemul Island.

"However, there never was a fire. Huemul Island was a distraction."

"A distraction from what?"

"While the world focused on the work at Huemul Island, Dr. Richter secretly built a laboratory in the jungle that is still there even to this day."

"Wait, did Dr. Richter and Juan Perón successfully create nuclear energy or not?" a confused Giovanni asked.

"Yes, but not on Huemul Island—that was a decoy. It was done in the jungle."

"And you say the world doesn't know about this lab in the jungle?" Giovanni asked.

"No one knows."

"How is that possible?" Giovanni asked. "Wouldn't satellites or even drones pick it up?"

"The laboratory was built underground," said Cardinal Martinelli. "Perón was run out of office before Dr. Richter could ever unveil it or his achievement."

Giovanni gave a crooked smile.

"People believed Dr. Richter worked alone on the project on Huemul Island," Cardinal Martinelli continued. "That part is also not true. He never was there.

"Dr. Richter teamed up with Nazi scientists to build the nuclear reactor in the jungle."

"Who controls the reactor now?" Giovanni asked.

"We do," said Cardinal Martinelli. "Freemasons. Licio Lastra and P2 obtained it when he was living down here after World War II."

"What's the plan, other than me going to the jungle?" Giovanni asked.

"If the pope doesn't step aside, then we'll go to war with the Vatican," said Cardinal Martinelli.

"If any country steps in and tries to stop us, we'll use nuclear weapons against them. This is a coup."

Giovanni grinned again. He was barely able to contain his excitement.

"In the meantime, you'll go to the plant in the jungle and wait, Giovanni. There are armed guards there. They will protect you. You are a valuable asset.

"Stay there until I tell you to go to Vatican City and take your rightful place on the throne of St. Peter as the new pope."

Chapter 6

THE POPE'S SISTER

California, June 2023

"There's a call for you, John," Gladys, the front-desk receptionist, shouted across the newsroom floor. "She says she's from New York."

New York?

"Put it through," he replied.

The woman on the other end of the line spoke deliberately, pausing after each word.

"You. Are. In. Danger," she said.

Tate bit his lower lip.

"Who is this?"

"You don't know me, but you know my younger brother," she said.

"Who is your brother?"

"Pietro."

"You are the pope's sister?" Tate asked.

"Yes. My name is Tina."

"And you live in New York?"

"Yes," she continued. "Pietro and I moved here from Italy with our mother and her new husband when we were young."

Tate opened his notebook.

"Why do you say I am in danger?" the reporter asked.

"We are both in danger."

"How so?"

"I am being followed, and I think you are too," Tina said.

Tate's mind flashed back to Las Vegas and the man who had been spying on him.

"A man in a trench coat?" he asked.

"That's the one," she replied. "I first noticed him a few days ago on the subway. He was pretending to be reading a newspaper."

"Go on," Tate told her.

"Yesterday, as I was walking home from noon Mass at All Saints Roman Catholic Church in East Harlem, I saw him following me once more."

"The man in the trench coat?" Tate clarified.

"Uh-huh," she answered. "Then, when I got home, there was an envelope under my front door. Inside of it was a letter, signed only with a black hand."

"What does the letter say?" the reporter inquired.

"Pope Emeritus Anthony will die unless Cardinal Berlone makes good on their demand."

Tate thought back to his conversation with Giuseppe.

We can't go to the police.

The abductors warned that Pope Emeritus Anthony will be killed if they're notified.

"John, I think you should talk to Cardinal Berlone," Tina said. "The kidnappers have been in contact with him. Obviously, he knows what's going on."

Tate pressed his cheek against his fist for several moments.

"Okay, I will talk with him, but first I need to come to New York."

"You want to come to New York? Why?" Tina asked.

"Because it is not safe to talk on the phone. They probably have your phone bugged. Hang up."

Tate rushed over to his managing editor's office.

"Chief, got a minute? I just got a strange call."

"From whom?"

"Tina Romano. Pietro's sister. She says I'm in danger."

Rollings froze. He stared at his ace reporter with wide eyes and raised eyebrows.

"What did she say, exactly?"

"Tina said she and Pope Emeritus Anthony would die if the Vatican doesn't make good on the demands made by the abductors," Tate replied. "She also said that I'm being followed, and so is she!"

The managing editor's eyes narrowed.

"So, you weren't imagining things down in Las Vegas."

"Nope."

"Do they still want Pietro to renounce the Italian parliament?" Rollings asked.

Tate nodded.

"Call the Vatican's secretary of state, Cardinal Berlone, right now, and tell him what just happened!" ordered Rollings.

"I don't think that's a good idea," Tate replied. "We don't know who is listening in. Our phones could be tapped."

Rollings paced the newsroom floor. His palms were clammy.

"Perhaps Giuseppe is right," the managing editor declared. "Time for you to go back to Italy."

Tate gave his boss a thumbs-up. "Agreed, Chief. I will do a layover in New York and go see Tina while I'm there."

"Take Liz with you," Rollings replied. "As we learned last year, it never hurts to have backup."

***

Tate and Liz departed that same evening. When they arrived in New York, the pair checked into a hotel in Manhattan and then took a short cab ride to Rao's restaurant in East Harlem, where Tina was waiting. She gave them a warm embrace.

"Pietro has told me good things about you both," she said. "You were so brave to do what you did last year."

"Pietro is the one who deserves the credit," Tate countered. "He was our anonymous tipster."

On the wall opposite from where they were seated, Tina pointed to a picture.

"See the guy in the fedora, standing next to the other three men?" she asked.

Tate got up and moved closer. There were lots of pictures on the wall of famous people who had eaten at the restaurant, such as Frank Sinatra, Sylvester Stallone, and even Pope John Paul II.

"You mean this picture?" asked Tate.

"That's the one," she answered. "That's Giuseppe's dad, Big Al! He used to love eating here. This place has been around since 1896."

"Who are the other three men in the picture?" Liz asked.

"The man in the silk suit is Lucky Longo," Tina said. "He was a Mafia kingpin.

"The guy with a crooked nose is Paul Vaccarelli, a former boxer who started out as a street-gang member but went on to become a big shot with the International Dockworkers Association and Tammany Hall, which was a political machine manipulated by the Mafia. The smaller guy is Luigi De Sio."

"Do you know when the picture was taken?" Tate asked.

"In 1935," said Tina. "The men attended a title fight earlier that evening between heavyweights James Braddock and Max Baer at the Madison Square Garden Bowl.

"Lucky Longo won a big bet on the fight, so he brought the men here for steaks afterwards."

"Lucky Longo is a handsome guy!" Liz said.

"He was an interesting man too," Tina told her. "Lucky started out as a member of Vaccarelli's Five Points street gang.

"Later on, he developed the modern-day model for Mafia families in the United States, called the 'Commission,' which still today regulates the five major Mafia crime families in America."

"How did Big Al get involved with Lucky Longo?" asked Tate.

"When Big Al left Italy for America, he was given the name of the former boxer in that picture, the one with the crooked nose, Paul Vaccarelli. Vaccarelli was the person who introduced him to Lucky Longo. The two became super good friends."

"How fascinating," Liz said.

"The story doesn't end there," Tina continued. "Shortly after that picture was taken, Lucky received a lengthy prison sentence because of his Mafia activities.

"However, during World War II the Department of the Navy worried about Italy and the Germans attacking America through its ports, so it cut a deal with Lucky."

"What kind of deal?" Tate asked.

"Lucky and the Mafia controlled the docks in New York and New Jersey through the International Dockworkers Association.

"During the war, he turned over the names of Italians whom the government should be worried about as Nazi sympathizers.

"As a result, he was released early from prison and deported back to Italy, where he and Big Al reconnected."

"Oh, that's right!" Tate realized. "Big Al was in Rome starting in 1940 working as a special envoy between the US president and the Vatican."

"The two men remained close even after Big Al returned to the United States in 1950," Tina explained.

"Then, when Giuseppe became an American Ambassador to Italy in 1953, Lucky kept a protective eye out for Big Al's youngest boy."

"That's really cute that Lucky Longo was protective of both Big Al and Giuseppe," Liz said, her eyes on the image of the man in question.

"When did Lucky die?" Tate asked.

"He died in 1963 of a heart attack at Naples International Airport," Tina said. "His body was permitted to be transported back to the United States for burial."

"Where is he buried?" Tate asked.

"He was quietly buried in the family's vault at St. John's Cemetery in Queens, New York," Tina said.

Tate furrowed his brows.

"What is it, John?" Liz asked.

"Oh, nothing." Tate shrugged.

"Spill it," Liz insisted.

"I'll tell you later." Tate gave her a look, clearly asking her to table the discussion for now.

***

After dinner and dessert, with their stomachs full, Tate suggested they all take a three-mile walk to Central Park "to burn off our meal."

"Sure, why not?" Liz said. "Besides, the weather is really nice."

As they set out, Tate asked Tina questions about her brother, Pietro, the new pope.

"Did he always want to be a clergyman?" the reporter wanted to know.

"Oh, yes," Tina replied. "Not only that, but Pietro loved the Sacramento area of California, where you both live. He always said he was going to be a priest in Sacramento one day."

"Really?" Liz replied. "How did a boy living in the Big Apple fall in love with a small city on the West Coast?"

"One summer, our family flew to Sacramento for a vacation in Lake Tahoe," Tina said.

"Pietro fell in love with the Sacramento River that cuts through the city. He also liked the Forty-Niner gold mining history. I liked it too.

"On that trip, this girl didn't care about diamonds. I was really hoping for gold!"

"Any idea why someone would abduct his predecessor, Pope Emeritus Anthony?" Tate asked.

"No idea," Tina said. "I do know Pope Emeritus Anthony has become a source of fascination for the public eye since his resignation last year. Have you seen the increasing number of papal television shows that have emerged from Netflix and HBO?"

Liz nodded. "There have been a lot of shows about him, that's true. I watch some of them myself."

"Many Vatican watchers and insiders say the mere fact of his abdication has made the modern papacy more vulnerable, emboldening voices of dissent," Tina continued.

"The possibility of blackmail or pressure relating to scandals within the Vatican bureaucracy has been a concern."

"Well, blackmail is in fact happening," Tate said. "We know that you, Giuseppe, and the Vatican's secretary of state have all received Black Hand letters."

In the shadows, Tate saw a figure move. The person walked parallel to them in the trees, keeping out of sight.

"Ah, ladies, bad habit. I am sorry, but I need a smoke break," the reporter said.

"Now? Really, John?" Liz complained.

"Yeah. Can we just stop here and take a moment?"

Tate saw the figure hide behind some trees, approximately forty yards out.

"Okay." Liz groaned in frustration and shot John an impatient look, but she stopped walking.

Tate lit his cigarette and looked out at the trees from the corner of his eye. He took a couple puffs of the cigarette.

Then, the reporter crouched over like a speed skater getting ready for the starter pistol to go off.

"What are you doing?" Liz asked.

"Um, everything okay, John?" Tina was looking at him like he had lost his mind.

Suddenly, Tate blasted off.

"What in the heck?" the women cried out together.

Tate sped toward the trees.

Before the man hiding behind them saw him coming, Tate was on him. He crashed hard into the follower, who crumpled to the ground. Tate wrapped him up tight, like a swaddled baby.

"Get on your feet," the reporter demanded.

The mystery man stood up, weak in the knees.

"You!" Tate said. "This is the person who was spying on me in Las Vegas."

The man nodded.

"You're the man from the subway," Tina chimed in as she and Liz rushed over.

"Talk!" Tate demanded.

"My name is Paul, and I'm a member of the Swiss Guard."

"Wait, what?" Tate exclaimed. "The same Swiss Guard that protects the pope?"

Paul nodded.

"Pope Pius XIII dispatched me to keep an eye on you."

"Pietro sent you?" Tina asked.

"Why?" Tate pressed.

"Pope Pius XIII received intelligence that Cardinal Martinelli and his protégé, Giovanni, are out of jail. They will likely make a move on both of you."

"He thinks we are in danger?" Tate asked.

"Yes."

"A simple phone call would have sufficed," Tina retorted. "Wait until I talk to Pietro!"

Paul continued. "Pope Pius XIII did not want to risk the chance of talking on the phone. The lines may be tapped."

"Tina and I have been under surveillance?" Tate questioned, as if he hadn't heard right the first time.

"Yes, and we've also been watching Giuseppe and Liz here."

"You've been watching me?" Liz said excitedly. Then, her head fell.

"I didn't even notice!" she grumbled. "So much for a woman's intuition."

"We knew you hadn't picked up on us," said the Swiss Guard, patting Liz on the shoulder. "However, John and Tina are another story. We were pretty sure they'd gotten wise to us."

Tate looked up at the night sky and tapped a forefinger to his head.

"Paul, I need a favor from your boss, Pope Pius XIII."

"What sort of favor?"

"Take a walk with us," Tate said. "I will explain along the way."

***

Tate and Liz met early the next morning for coffee in the hotel lobby.

"I have a hunch," Tate declared. "Do you have your iPad with you?"

"Right here," she said and pulled it out of her shoulder bag. "What are we researching?"

"Tina said there was a quiet burial in New York for Lucky Longo after his body was transported from Italy."

"Yeah, so?" Liz replied.

"Lucky was the founder of the modern-day Mafia in the United States," Tate pointed out.

"Do you really think the Mafia would bury someone of his stature quietly, without fanfare? That's just not how the Mafia operates," he reasoned.

Liz nodded her head in agreement, then typed away on her iPad for several minutes.

"Your hunch is right, John! According to *la Repubblica* newspaper, there was a huge funeral for Lucky in Milan. Hundreds of Mafia members from the United States attended."

Tate snapped his finger. "I knew it!"

"I don't get it," Liz said. "If the plan was to transport Lucky's body to New York for burial, why did members of the US Mafia travel all the way to Italy to pay their final respects? Why wouldn't they have just waited until the body arrived in New York for the burial?" she asked.

"Maybe the plan was never to bury him in New York," Tate answered.

Liz's eyes flew wide open. She tapped away again on her iPad.

"Hmm," she muttered.

"What?" Tate asked.

"Well, it seems that after he struck a deal with the US government and was deported back to Italy, Lucky Longo found love."

"Really?"

"I am reading from a tabloid newsletter online. It says in 1947, when he was fifty years old, Lucky met a twenty-six-year-old Italian dancer who was the featured performer at some of the better nightclubs around Rome immediately after World War II.

"In the spring of 1948, she moved in with Lucky. They eventually married and were very much in love. They even had a son together."

"A son? Wow. Lucky had a second life after returning to Italy," Tate said.

"But it wasn't a happy ending." Liz frowned.

"What do you mean?"

"Sadly, his wife died of breast cancer in 1958, when their son was two years old. Lucky died of a heart attack five years later."

Tate ran his hand through his thinning salt-and-pepper hair.

"I wonder what happened to their son."

"I don't know. The tabloid story doesn't say," Liz replied.

"Does it say where Lucky's wife is buried?" Tate inquired.

"Yes. At the Cimitero di Musocco in Milan."

"Milan? Where the Mafia turned out in large numbers for Lucky's funeral," Tate noted.

Just then, Paul the Swiss Guard arrived.

"Everything is arranged," Paul said to Tate.

"What's arranged?" Liz asked.

"The favor I've asked of Pietro," Tate responded.

"We need to go," Paul insisted. "The caretaker is waiting for us at St. John's Cemetery in Queens."

"That's where Lucky was supposed to have been buried, in a vault," Liz said, starting to suspect what John was up to.

When they arrived, the caretaker took them to the Longo family vault and opened it. Nothing was inside, except a letter and a small jewelry box.

"What on Earth!" Liz exclaimed.

The caretaker removed the letter and box and handed it to Paul, who slowly read it aloud:

> "Since you have come looking here, it means certain events are happening in the world. Big Al, who was my dear friend, planned for this day. He asked me to hide this box. Inside is a key that will get you out of tight spots. ~Lucky."

Chapter 7

DINNER SURPRISE

Italy, June 2023

The next day, Tate and Liz arrived at Leonardo da Vinci International Airport in Rome. Giuseppe's driver was waiting, and he drove them to the same hotel where they had stayed the year before.

"Signore Tedesco invites you to dinner at six p.m.," the driver said.

"Tell Giuseppe we are happy to join him," Liz enthusiastically replied.

Because the dinner wouldn't be for a few more hours and they had jet lag, Liz suggested they get some rest. After only a short while, though, they heard loud chanting coming from the street.

"Bring back the king! Bring back the monarchy!"

Tate pulled back the curtains in his room. He slid open a door to the balcony, which overlooked the Via Sacra, Latin for "Sacred Road."

Nearly a thousand demonstrators—way more than the last time—marched down the main road of ancient

Rome, which stretched from the top of the Capitoline Hill, through some of the most important religious sites of the Forum, to the Colosseum.

The protesters carried banners and the Italian flag. Television crews followed them, but Tate noticed none of the protesters stopped to give interviews.

He also noticed the attractive woman wearing a red business suit and stilettos who was at the back of the procession, carrying a clipboard.

"That's her!" he cried out. "The same woman in red as the last time."

Tate ran out the door and to the street in the direction of the woman.

"Hey, wait a minute," Tate called out to the stranger in English.

Cassandra saw the man charging at her and froze. She wasn't sure of his intentions.

What does this American want? she thought.

Undecided as to whether or not she should run, Cassandra made the snap decision to stand her ground.

"Is it me you're yelling at, sir?" she said in flawless English.

Tate stopped in front of her, out of breath. He doubled over and put up an index finger.

"I need just a moment," he said, gasping for air. "Too many cigarettes. My name is John Tate. Sorry to scare you."

He reached out to shake her hand, still hunched over.

"Cassandra Capalbo."

Tate stood up straight and clasped his hands behind his head.

"Are you the organizer of this protest?" he asked, still huffing and puffing.

"Why are you asking?"

"Oh, my bad," Tate said, and he withdrew an official press badge from his pocket. "I'm a reporter with the *Sacramento Union* newspaper."

"You're a reporter?" Cassandra asked. "And you came all the way from California to cover this protest?"

"Well, no, not really," he replied. "I was here last year for the selection of Pietro Romano as the new pope. I'm back to do a story on how the first year in office is going for Pope Pius XIII."

Cassandra tilted her head.

"What has that got to do with me?" she asked.

She has a good point, he thought.

Why did I chase her down if I am doing a story on the pope?

Tate exhaled and decided to go with the truth.

"You were recently pictured in the local newspaper during a similar protest. I happened to notice you."

Cassandra blushed and flirtatiously played with a lock of her hair, which she twisted behind her ear. "You did?"

Oh, my goodness, she thinks I am hitting on her, Tate thought.

"Um, what I meant is that I noticed you at both events and was wondering if you organized them?"

Cassandra flashed a wry smile.

"Obviously, you don't understand politics in Italy," she said.

Tate crinkled his forehead and eyebrows. He had no idea what she meant.

"Protests in Italy, especially against the government, are a common occurrence," she explained.

"Oh, uh, I see," Tate stammered. "But is it common for no one to take credit?"

Cassandra took a step back. She could see this reporter was no slouch. He was observant.

"At the last protest, no one spoke to the media," Tate continued. "I noticed the same thing happening again today. That's odd. Normally, protesters are eager to identify themselves."

Cassandra reached into her expensive Gucci handbag and took out a business card.

"How about we do this," she said, handing Tate the card.

"Why don't you and anyone else from your newspaper come to my home in Amalfi? Let's meet at Valentino Vineyards tomorrow at five p.m. for dinner."

"Sounds good," Tate replied.

"The high-speed train takes two and a half hours from Rome to Salerno. There are thirty-six trains back and forth each day. Pick one.

"I suggest coming early and taking a few sightseeing tours of the area. When we meet for dinner, I will tell you everything you want to know."

"Deal!" Tate replied.

Cassandra smiled. "See you then."

Tate took his time walking back to the hotel. He was not sure if he had just scored an interview or a date, although he was fairly certain his out-of-shape introduction ruled out the latter.

"Any luck?" Liz asked when Tate returned to the hotel.

"Of course," he replied. "I'm the king of chasing down stories."

Liz rolled her eyes.

"Let's go see Giuseppe," Tate suggested. "I'm hungry!"

When they arrived, the old man greeted them warmly at the door, dressed in a heavily starched Ralph Lauren solid sport oxford shirt, navy-blue slacks, and loafers.

"You're the snazziest dresser!" Liz declared.

Giuseppe put one arm around each of them and led them to the dining room.

A butler brought them antipasto, the first course in what would be a traditional five-course Italian meal that evening.

"Does Pietro, err, I mean Pope Pius XIII, intend to publicly condemn the parliament and ask the government to resign?" Tate asked.

"Not a chance," Giuseppe replied.

"We need to hurry up and find Pope Emeritus Anthony," Liz proclaimed. "There isn't a lot of time."

Giuseppe swallowed hard.

"He will turn up," he said in his most confident voice.

"What's with the protests?" Tate asked the old man. "We noticed the one recently, and then another one took place today. A whole lot more protesters took part in this one. They marched past our hotel."

"The parliament is in trouble," Giuseppe replied.

"People aren't happy with the economy. They want to go back to a constitutional monarchy.

"These protests are building momentum. Funny thing is, no one seems to know who the leader is behind the protests."

"I think I know," said Tate.

"You do?" Giuseppe replied. "Who?"

"A lady named Cassandra Capalbo. She owns Valentino Vineyards on the Amalfi Coast. She also owns a restaurant and winery in Rome. Liz and I are having dinner with her tomorrow night."

Giuseppe rubbed the nape of his neck, which he twisted nervously.

"What's wrong?" the reporter asked.

"Just be careful," the old man warned. "Protests are unpredictable."

"You sound like you've experienced a few," Tate said.

"I have," Giuseppe answered.

"Let me tell you a story about one in particular from when my papa was a teenager. There was a group of protesters called the Fasci Siciliani, which is short for Fasci Siciliani dei Lavoratori—or Sicilian Workers Leagues."

"Let's hear it," said Tate.

"The Fasci Siciliani were among the poorest and most exploited classes. One day, they presented a proposal for sharecropping and rental contracts to landowners and mineowners, who rejected it. Protests, strikes, and riots erupted."

"When was this?" Tate asked.

"Between 1889 and 1894. My papa, Big Al, was born in 1871, so he was eighteen when the protests started.

"Anyway, a reporter wrote about what happened. In fact, I still have the article."

The old man shuffled over to a desk drawer and took out a yellowing and worn newspaper story from *La Questione Sociale*, titled "Fasci Siciliani Leadership Loses

Control of its Protesters" by Cosmo Ricci. He showed it to Tate and Liz.

"The Fasci Siciliani channeled people's frustration and discontent into a movement based on the establishment of new rights," Giuseppe summarized. "They wanted land redistributed. However, in the autumn of 1893, the leadership of the Fasci Siciliani lost control of the movement, and the popular agitation got out of hand.

"With extreme force, including executions, the old order was restored by King Umberto I. His army and the police killed scores of protesters and wounded hundreds. The leadership of the Fasci Siciliani was jailed. Some one thousand persons were deported to the penal islands without trial. All working-class societies and cooperatives were dissolved, and the freedom of the press, meeting, and association were suspended.

"So you see, protests can start out with the best of intentions, but they can change and get out of hand. Be careful poking around government protests."

The butler brought out the second course of the meal, which was minestrone soup. He went around to each person and asked if he could scoop a spoonful of Parmesan cheese on top.

When the butler had left, Liz commented about the picture they'd seen on the wall at Rao's restaurant in New York.

"That Lucky Longo was a good-looking guy!" Liz exclaimed. "Tina says he watched out for you when you were a diplomat in Rome."

"He did!" Giuseppe declared. "Lucky had a heart of gold."

"His burial sure was odd," Tate chimed in.

"How so?" Giuseppe asked.

"He was never buried in New York as people were led to believe by media accounts," Tate explained. "We went to Lucky's vault. The caretaker let us in. There was no body."

"What?" Giuseppe asked.

"The only things in the vault were a box with a key in it and a note written by Lucky."

"Huh. What did the note say?" Giuseppe asked.

"It said the key would unlock many doors."

"That's vague," the old man said. "Is that all the note said?"

"Yeah, pretty much," Tate answered.

"Do you happen to have the key with you now?" Giuseppe asked.

"I do. Here it is."

Tate handed Giuseppe the key.

"A skeleton key," Giuseppe said, looking it over closely. "Very old."

The butler brought out the main course of spaghetti, meatballs, sausages, and a bitter vegetable called "rapini."

After that, they had salad and then dessert, which was a molded gelato made with layers of different colors and flavors containing candied fruits and nuts. The spumoni had three flavors, with a fruit/nut layer between them mixed with whipped cream.

"I have another treat after dessert," Giuseppe announced.

"What is it?" Liz asked, clasping her hands together.

"Pietro has agreed to let us visit the Vatican Secret Archive again, since our visit last year was cut short. We can go, if no one is still suffering ill effects from our previous visit?"

"I'm down with it!" Liz declared.

"Sure, but let's bring Paul with us this time," Tate said.

"Who is Paul?" Giuseppe asked.

"He is a Swiss Guard who has been spying on us," Tate replied. "If you haven't noticed already, the Swiss Guard has been following you too, Giuseppe."

"They have?" he asked.

"That's what I said," Liz grumbled. "I didn't know they were following me either."

Tate pushed his chair back from the dinner table and rested his hands on his stomach, which felt like it was going to explode.

"Pope Pius XIII has been having all of us followed," he explained. "Pietro is concerned for our safety since Cardinal Martinelli and Giovanni are out of jail."

"Sure would have been nice if he'd warned us," Giuseppe complained.

"He didn't want to risk the bad guys finding out, I suppose," Tate replied.

***

Later that evening, as they walked up the spiral staircase leading to the Vatican Secret Archive, Giuseppe took a key from his pocket that Pope Pius XII had given to him when he was an American ambassador in Rome in the 1950s and '60s.

The old man put the key in the lock and turned it. Pop.

The door opened.

"Still works," Giuseppe said, beaming. "I'm always worried they'll change the lock, but they never do."

They entered the room, which opened to row after row of library tables. Everything seemed quiet, unlike a year ago.

Liz walked off in the opposite direction from Tate. Unsure of which person to follow, Giuseppe moved into the middle of the room.

The Swiss Guard, Paul, stood by the door and kept watch.

After a few minutes, Tate gave a loud whistle.

"What is it?" Liz asked him.

"Here's a letter written in 1942 from Big Al to Pope Pius XII!" Tate exclaimed.

"Oh wow, read it," Liz said impatiently, eager to hear the contents.

> Dear Holy Father,
>
> As you know, Sister Lúcia is very sick with pleurisy. She has agreed to write down the Third Secret of Fatima, once she has the strength to do so. She refuses to dictate the secret to me, so I must wait.
>
> Every day, I sit around and hope for her to become well enough to begin writing. However, I'm not sure whether Sister Lúcia will survive. In the meantime, she and I talk a lot while she rests in bed.

According to Sister Lúcia, the Madonna has been making appearances on Earth for centuries, to show us the way to redemption. She is like a messenger sent by God to reconcile us to Him.

Sister Lúcia says that over the years, the Madonna has come to her many times at her convent. Our Lady has shared with Sister Lúcia three additional secrets that were originally revealed to Sister Bernadette in Lourdes in 1858 but never revealed to the public.

Sincerely,
Big Al

The color drained from Tate's face.

"What's the matter, John?" Liz asked.

The reporter's tongue was tied. He couldn't answer, so Liz walked over and took the document from his hand.

"These are the three secrets of Lourdes!" she declared. Liz read them out loud:

"'After the first and second world wars, Russia's errors will be spread into the twenty-first century,'" she read. "'This is the First Secret of Lourdes.

"'Through Masonic sects, Satan will infiltrate the Vatican from top to bottom. This is the Second Secret of Lourdes.

"'Christianity will be torn asunder. This is the final secret of Lourdes.'"

Tate thought back to the warning by Sister Agnes: "The Church has been captured by corrupt forces."

A hush fell over the room.

After what seemed like an eternity, Liz spoke up again.

"Giuseppe, I have a question for you."

"Sure, anything," the very old man replied.

"I've been dying to know. Did you ever meet Sister Lúcia?"

"Yes, I did!" Giuseppe responded. "Sister Lúcia came to see me in 1963. I was finishing up my time in Italy as an American ambassador.

"One evening we visited the Vatican Secret Archive. I wanted to show Sister Lúcia where I hid the Third Secret after Pope John XXIII told me to get rid of it."

Tate almost fell out of his chair. *The monkeys are in the trees again.*

"Wait a minute, you hid the Third Secret of Fatima, Giuseppe?" Tate asked.

"Yes."

"Where exactly did you hide it?" Liz asked.

"Inside of *The Permanent Instruction of the Alta Vendita*, which is the Masonic manifesto for capturing the Church."

Giuseppe led them over to a tall file cabinet.

"Ah, this is the one, right here," he said.

The old man opened the file cabinet and took out the manifesto. He handed the *Alta Vendita* over to Tate.

"But where's the Third Secret?" Tate asked. "It isn't in here now."

"While we were at the Vatican Secret Archive, Sister Lúcia and I heard footsteps. So I grabbed the Third Secret and we ran out.

"Later that night, Sister Lúcia told me a better, more permanent place to hide the Third Secret of Fatima."

Tate's eyes were wide as saucers.

"But what about the Vatican's announcement in 2000?" Liz queried. "How could it have disclosed the Third Secret if it's still hidden?"

"I don't know," Giuseppe said. "Good question."

"Will you take us to where the Third Secret is now?" Tate asked.

The old man fidgeted in his chair. "Um, I don't think I should."

Tate rubbed his temples.

Giuseppe could see the reporter was agitated.

"John, I know you have come a long way," Giuseppe said. "But I am not sure I should tell you where the secret is."

Liz could see the old man needed convincing, so she gave it her best try.

"From the research I've done," she interjected, "the Madonna wanted the Third Secret of Fatima shared with the world no later than 1960. If what the Vatican revealed in 2000 isn't the original, shouldn't you disclose it?"

"Sister Lúcia told me to hide it," Giuseppe repeated.

"But certainly not forever!" Liz shot back.

"Well, about that. I am uncertain as to how long it should be hidden," he admitted. "I've always wondered."

Chapter 8

THE DUNGEON

Italy, June 2023

Cassandra boarded a train at Naples Central Station. She was scheduled to meet in Rome with Cardinal Dominic Solano, Dean of the College of Cardinals.

As the train departed, she removed a list from her briefcase with the names of more than 962 people belonging to P2. No name on the list of Masons was more important than the very first one—Carla Pasquinelli.

Carla was the new P2 leader and the boss of one of Italy's roughest Mafia crime organizations, the Camorra. She represented a new breed of Mafia bosses, *le madrine*, or "the godmothers."

In recent years, there had become a proliferation of women running Mafia organizations in Italy. Some were just as ruthless as the men they replaced atop Italy's underworld.

The reason for the rise of women as heads of crime organizations in Italy was mostly about demographics: they took over as more and more men went to prison—just as the previous Camorra boss, Frank Tallerico Jr. had—or were otherwise dispatched.

At one time, Carla's grandfather, Supremo Pasquinelli, had been the leader of the Camorra in the Campania region of Italy. Back then, the Mafia was more like a mutual aid society.

Supremo Pasquinelli ran the Camorra like a family operation. To the residents of the Campania region of southern Italy, he was their father figure, particularly among poor people who had no one else to turn to in the feudal-class system dominated by land barons.

In the twenty-first century, however, Mafia organizations were less about taking care of families and more about profits. They were cutthroat.

Carla certainly ran the Camorra that way.

Whereas Supremo operated the Camorra like a father protecting his children, Carla would step on anyone and everyone to get what she wanted. She was ruthless.

Never a mother, Carla had zero maternal instincts. It was all business with her, and power.

Carla believed men like her grandfather, Supremo, tended to be complacent. She thought that was the case when southern Italians were suffering in the 1880s and 1890s.

They were in economic despair, but in her opinion, Supremo didn't help the peasants nearly enough when they needed it.

The landowners and coal miners ran roughshod over them, even though the lower class paid Supremo and the Camorra protection money to resolve such problems.

There was another reason why Carla Pasquinelli was so important to Cassandra's plan. Her connections were seemingly endless.

Carla could provide anything and move mountains. During the first protest in Rome, Carla turned out hundreds of protesters when Cassandra wasn't sure where she'd find anyone who would march for her yet-to-be-identified cause.

Carla Pasquinelli took over as grand master of the P2 Masonic organization in 2015, when Licio Lastra died. Law enforcement still hadn't figured out that she was in charge.

In fact, the police assumed that after the implications of P2 in numerous Italian crimes and mysteries, it disbanded in the 1990s, which was a false narrative that Carla didn't mind.

If people think we don't exist, then we can operate off of everyone's radar, Carla thought.

P2's crimes and mysteries in the latter half of the nineteenth century included a kickbacks scheme that involved the Mafia, including Giuseppe's four older brothers in New York, that ended up exposing vast corruption.

Public works projects routinely doubled in cost due to these kickbacks. Political parties received financing from bribes, from companies big and small. Prosecutors went after thousands of officials and businesspeople from all over Italy.

Before and during World War II, P2 was certainly not on anyone's radar because Mussolini had cracked down on Masonry and other secret societies like it, such as the Carbonari.

Then, however, came the 1980s, when the investigation into banker Michele Sindona on a murder charge revealed his membership in P2.

Sindona, who murdered a lawyer commissioned to liquidate his failing banks, received a life sentence in prison, where, ultimately, someone—believed to be contracted by P2—poisoned him to keep him from talking to the authorities.

In a subsequent search of the villa owned by P2 founder Licio Lastra, police found a document entitled "Plan for Democratic Rebirth," which called for the overthrow of the Italian government.

Today, with Lastra's "Plan for Democratic Rebirth" in her briefcase, Cassandra hoped to breathe new life into that past effort.

She looked out the window as the high-speed train hit full speed and bustled down the tracks.

Cassandra reviewed the rest of the P2 membership list. The names of so many valuable people were on it, including representatives of the parliament, prominent journalists, industrialists, military leaders, and the heads of all three Italian intelligence services.

When the train was just minutes from Rome, Cassandra took lipstick out of her purse and carefully applied it.

Finally, as the train pulled into the station at Roma Termini, the main railway station of Rome, Cassandra collected her things and hailed a cab.

Sixteen minutes later, she arrived in Vatican City to meet with Cardinal Solano at Giuseppe's favorite café across from St. Peter's Square.

"Cassandra, I enjoy your vino!" the cardinal said when she arrived. "To what do I owe the honor of your beautiful presence?"

She took a seat next to him at a table outside on the patio.

"Have you been following the protests in Rome against the government of Italy?" she asked.

"How can I not?" Cardinal Solano replied. "The streets have been packed with people. So many people turned out for the last one that I couldn't find a parking spot.

"You know, the funny thing about these protests is that no one seems to know who the leader is."

"I am," she replied.

"You are? How? Why?"

"There is a silent majority in Italy that wishes the monarchy to return," Cassandra answered. "Italy should never have gotten rid of it. That was a mistake, and one I intend to correct."

"How do you change it?" replied the cardinal. "Abolishing the monarchy happened so long ago."

"And the country has been paying a terrible price ever since," Cassandra retorted.

"Why do you believe it was a mistake?" asked the dean.

"Let me give you but one example," she replied.

"Under the king, Italy was seeking the colonization of Africa in the present-day countries of Libya, Ethiopia, Eritrea, and Somalia.

"The king, smartly, was looking for new trade markets because northern Italy was undergoing booming industrialization on par with leading countries like the United States."

"Oh, I recall," said Cardinal Solano, reflecting back to the days when he would ask Pietro and his sister which Italian cities made certain products.

"Had the king been given the time to colonize Africa, I believe that Italy would be a world superpower today," Cassandra noted. "But then Mussolini came along and ruined everything."

"We cannot go back in time, Cassandra."

"True, but we can do something about the future," she shot back.

They sat in silence for several moments as the cardinal looked over the menu. He ordered spaghetti and meatballs.

"Just coffee for me," Cassandra told the waiter.

"You're not eating?" asked Cardinal Solano.

"I have a busy schedule today," she replied.

Cardinal Solano shrugged his shoulders and then turned his attention to the pigeons in the plaza. There were a lot of them, and every now and then a child would chase after the birds. They would fly up in the air, soar around, and then return. The cycle repeated all day long.

"You know, I was thirteen years old when Mussolini left office," said Cardinal Solano. "It was 1945. In April, he and his mistress were shot by Italian partisans who'd captured the couple as they attempted to flee to Switzerland.

"Their bodies were left in a suburban square, the Piazzale Loreto, to be insulted and physically abused. They were then hung upside down from a metal girder above the service station on the square. The bodies were beaten, shot at, and hit with hammers."

"That's pretty morbid," Cassandra said.

The waiter returned and served them.

Cassandra, being polite, waited to continue the conversation until after the cardinal had settled into eating his meal, but that took longer than she'd expected.

First, he had to bless his food, and then he applied a healthy helping of Romano cheese followed by salt and pepper. Then Cardinal Solano cut his meatballs up into tiny, bite-sized pieces.

After that, he sliced up his spaghetti because he didn't want to go through the messy process of twirling the noodles with a fork and spoon.

"Would you agree that Italy's government has been unstable ever since Mussolini took office in 1922?" asked Cassandra, slightly perturbed at the amount of time the dean took to finally start eating.

"Honestly, I would say the country's downward spiral started in 1900, when King Umberto I was assassinated," said Cardinal Solano. "The majority of people loved the king. Italy never really recovered from that."

"Why was he assassinated?" Cassandra asked.

"King Umberto's assassin came from the same village as me, Cava de' Tirreni. That's also where I started out as a priest. The assassin had been an out-of-work fisherman whom I knew. He epitomized the angry sentiment of southern Italians."

Cardinal Solano finished his meal and pushed his plate back.

"Why are you coming to me today with this talk about overthrowing the parliament?" the cardinal asked.

"Because the pope carries a lot of weight," Cassandra replied. "We want his support. As the Dean of the College of Cardinals and an elder statesman inside the Vatican, you have influence. Will you speak with Pope Pius XIII?"

Cardinal Solano fidgeted.

"The pope and I aren't exactly close," he said. "Besides, I can tell you with certainty, Pope Pius XIII will not support any plan to overthrow the Italian government."

Cassandra leaned in close to Cardinal Solano.

"I have an offer," she said in a quiet voice.

"What kind of offer?" he asked.

"Do you want the Pontifical States back?"

***

Later that day, Tate and Liz took the train going to Amalfi for their dinner with Cassandra. Paul, the Swiss Guard, rode with them.

"What's the goal of this meeting?" Liz asked.

"I want to see if the protests are connected in any way with the Black Hand letters and Pope Emeritus Anthony's disappearance," Tate replied.

Liz took a magazine out from her shoulder bag.

"What's that?"

"An article written by Marissa Cuomo for a travel magazine about Cassandra and Valentino Vineyards."

"Anything interesting?" Tate asked.

"I only skimmed it last night after I purchased it," Liz replied. "Cassandra is a fascinating person. She lives in an actual castle!"

"A castle? Should I have worn my suit of armor to dinner instead of this monkey suit?" joked Tate, pulling at his three-piece suit.

"Don't be silly," Liz replied. "You look very handsome. Besides, we're not going to a meeting of the Knights of the Round Table."

The train pulled into the Salerno station. Liz put the magazine away while Paul leaned over and spoke quietly to them both.

"From here on, I'm going to be out of sight," said the Swiss Guard. "I don't want anyone to see us together. I've arranged for a taxi to take you the rest of the way to Valentino Vineyards."

"What if we need you?" Liz asked.

"I will still be close by, just out of sight."

Paul handed Tate a small gadget resembling a cigarette lighter.

"If something goes wrong, lift up the top and push down on the igniter," Paul instructed.

"I'm supposed to signal you with a flame?" Tate mused.

"There isn't any flame," the Swiss Guard responded. "When you open the lid and push down on the igniter, it will page me."

"Wow, I feel like James Bond," Tate said. "Cool gadget."

"Be careful," Paul warned. "We don't know what we are dealing with here."

They took a taxi to the castle, where Cassandra was waiting for them out front.

"Welcome to paradise!" she exclaimed with her arms outspread.

"This is amazing," Liz gushed. "Just look at this incredible view!"

Orazio, the butler, joined them outside with a bottle of Chianti and glasses.

"A toast!" Cassandra said. "To a beautiful future!"

"Hear, hear," Tate agreed.

"Let me give you a tour of Valentino Vineyards," Cassandra said. For the next twenty minutes, they walked the property.

"Here are white grapes, and over there are black Mission grapes," Cassandra pointed out.

"What kind are these?" Liz asked.

"Those are Concord grapes," Cassandra answered. "We grow them for the Church. Concord grapes make dark wine. The priests love it, and that's what is served at Communion."

In the not-too-far-off distance, a bell rang.

"That's Orazio ringing the dinner bell," Cassandra said. "We need to get back."

Once inside, they sat at a large wooden dining room table that seemed better suited for the Knights of the Round Table than their intimate gathering of just three people.

"I told you I should have worn my suit of armor," Tate whispered to Liz, who jabbed him with her elbow.

"So, John, you said you are doing a story on the first year in office of Pope Pius XIII?" Cassandra asked.

"Yes, I am."

"Have you met with him yet since your arrival?" the host continued.

"No, not yet. We just arrived two days ago."

"So, you haven't talked with him at all?" Cassandra probed.

"Nope."

Cassandra stared off in the distance for several moments.

"What have you been doing since your arrival, then?" she asked, coming back to her line of questioning.

"We met with a friend," Liz answered.

"Oh? Who?"

"His name is Giuseppe Tedesco," Liz said. "A long time ago, he was an American ambassador in Rome."

"Does Giuseppe know anything about the Third Secret of Fatima?" asked Cassandra.

Tate shrugged, but under the table, he kicked Liz as if to say "don't tell her anything."

Odd that she would be asking, Tate thought.

Cassandra continued quizzing her guests as Orazio removed the antipasto dish and brought out the second course, which was ravioli.

"Will you be meeting with Pope Emeritus Anthony?" Cassandra delved deeper.

Tate scratched his head.

First Cassandra asked about the current pope.

Now she is asking about the prior pope.

Why is she so focused on the Vatican?

I thought her focus was the protests and changing the government?

"I don't have any plans to talk to the retired pope," Tate answered.

"You don't?" asked Cassandra. "Why not?"

Because no one knows where he is, Tate wanted to say.

"Our readers are more interested in Pope Pius XIII, given that Pietro is from Sacramento," Tate expounded. "He is the one we want to interview."

Tate shot Liz a puzzled look when Cassandra wasn't looking. This time he threw up his hands.

Orazio brought out meatballs and sausages.

Tate decided to start asking questions of his own.

"At the protest the other day, I asked if you were the organizer," Tate said. "Are you?"

Cassandra stared back at Tate. He could not make out the intent behind her eyes. Her face was blank, and she did not blink.

"I'm a concerned citizen of Italy who is unhappy with the parliament," she replied, purposely evasive.

"Just a concerned citizen?" Tate pressed. "Not the organizer of the protests?"

"No," she lied.

"Then who has been organizing these protests?" Tate looked at her intently, sensing she wasn't being honest with him.

"I don't know," Cassandra lied again.

"You want me to believe that you attended both protests as a concerned citizen, but not as an organizer?" Tate pushed.

"Correct."

The reporter's eyes narrowed.

"Who were the people marching?" he pressed.

"I don't know."

Tate pushed his empty ravioli dish forward, which sent Orazio rushing over from his post by the back wall to collect it.

"Cassandra, you told me the other day that if I came here, you would tell me what I want to know. So far, however, you've told me nothing."

The host simply shrugged.

The room was quiet. Orazio returned with the next course, a beef tenderloin in tomato sauce, and broccoli.

Seeing that Tate and Cassandra were at an impasse, Liz got up and walked over to her shoulder bag. She took out the article that had been published in the travel magazine.

"This story about Valentino Vineyards is really interesting," said the librarian.

"Oh, is the article out already?" Cassandra asked. "I've not seen it yet."

"Here, you can have my copy," replied Liz, who reached across the table and gave it to Cassandra.

"Thank you!"

"Cassandra, the magazine article references a general who led the Carbonari in a fight for the unification of Italy," Liz said. "The general's name is not identified in the story. What was it?"

"His name was General Valentino," Cassandra said.

"Oh, like your orchard—Valentino Vineyards. Your family named your business after him, in his honor?"

"Yes, he started the grape business, and he named it," Cassandra said.

"So, your family name isn't Capalbo?" Tate asked.

"No, that is my married name. I never changed it back after my divorce."

Just then, the butler stepped forward and interrupted. "Would you like me to serve the dessert now, Baroness?"

Tate's mouth fell open. *Baroness?*

"Give us a few more minutes, Orazio," Cassandra said. "Our stomachs need time to settle."

"Should I bring out some anise?" the butler asked.

"That would be great," replied Cassandra, who turned to her guests. "Anise decreases bloating and settles the digestive tract."

The butler quickly returned with a platter carrying several green stalks that looked like celery.

"Try it!" Cassandra encouraged. She grabbed a stalk for herself.

"Now, getting back to General Valentino," Cassandra said. "The general and his supporters wanted an Italian king and a constitutional monarchy."

"Funny, that's what you want too," Tate pointed out. "By the way, Cassandra, was your family from nobility?"

"Excuse me?" she answered. "I don't understand."

"The butler just called you 'Baroness.'"

"Oh, that," Cassandra replied. "Yes, he did. My great-grandfather was a land baron."

"I thought Italy stopped using feudal titles long ago?" Tate asked.

"They did," Cassandra replied.

"So why did Orazio just now call you 'Baroness'?"

"Just a little inside joke between us."

Tate wasn't convinced it had been a joke.

"I have an idea," Cassandra said. "Let's take a tour of the castle before dessert. I've not shown it to you yet. How rude of me."

"Sounds like fun!" Liz exclaimed.

"Okay then, let's go," the hostess agreed. "We'll start downstairs and work our way up. There are five levels to the castle. I hope you're in better shape today, John, than you were the other day."

"I'll do my best," Tate replied.

Cassandra led them to a wooden door just off the kitchen pantry, and she opened it.

"Looks heavy," Liz said.

"Trust me, it is," Cassandra replied. "I will lead the way. Be careful. The staircase is narrow and old."

Halfway down the stairs, Tate thought he heard a sound.

"So, what is this?" Liz asked once they reached the bottom.

"A dungeon."

"Dungeon?" Liz repeated. "Like, where prisoners were kept in medieval times?"

"Yes," said Cassandra.

"Maybe you should have worn a suit of armor after all," Liz kidded with Tate.

Cassandra walked up to another huge wooden door, took a key from her pocket, and put it in the lock. Then she turned the key. The door opened.

When Cassandra turned back around, Tate noticed she was holding a gun.

"Both of you get in," she said.

"Is this a joke?" Liz asked.

"I doubt she's joking," replied Tate, stepping inside.

"Your turn!" Cassandra ordered Liz.

When they were both inside the dungeon, they saw a man lying in the dirt. Pope Emeritus Anthony groaned in pain. His face was battered.

Cassandra closed the door. From her side of the big wooden door, she opened a sliding panel that was hidden behind thick bars, allowing them all to see each other.

The prisoners saw that a man was now standing next to Cassandra.

"Cardinal Martinelli!" Tate cried.

"Well, well, well. We meet again," the cardinal said maliciously. "Sacramento's two finest reporters, back to dig up more dirt on the Church. Looks like your pal Pope Emeritus Anthony has found some dirt of his own—a face full of it. Tsk, tsk.

"Oh, would you look at that. His white robe has gotten dirty. How sad."

Cardinal Martinelli pointed at Pope Emeritus Anthony. "Speaking of him, have you heard the story about the Man in White? Well, there he is, lying on the ground."

"I'm afraid they didn't teach us that story in Sunday school," Tate retorted. "Perhaps you could share?"

The cardinal snickered. "Sister Lúcia once told about a vision she'd had of a bishop in white who passed through a big city half in ruins. A group of soldiers killed him with bullets and arrows.

"Pope John Paul II thought he was the Man in White after he was shot, which is why the Vatican said in 2000 that the Third Secret of Fatima was about his assassination attempt and the twentieth-century persecution of Christians, but the Vatican was wrong."

"You want us to believe that Pope Emeritus Anthony is the Man in White?" Tate replied.

"Sister Lúcia said the bishop was dressed in white like a pope, but he was not the pope," said Cardinal Martinelli. "You make your own assumptions."

"John, Pope Emeritus Anthony dresses like a pope but he is not the pope anymore because he stepped down," Liz whispered. "I think the story *is* about him."

"You're so smart," Cardinal Martinelli said sarcastically to Liz.

"Yes, our friend over there, Pope Emeritus Anthony, has continued to wear white, just like a pope, even though he resigned in disgrace. To me, it's blasphemy!"

Cardinal Martinelli pulled out a piece of paper from his scarlet robe and read it out loud:

> "What I have seen is terrifying! What is certain is that the man in white will leave Rome and, in leaving the Vatican, he will have to pass over the dead bodies of his priests!"

The crooked cardinal looked at Tate and Liz.

"That's an excerpt from Sister Lúcia's so-called vision," he said. "But there's more."

"Swell," Tate remarked.

> "Just before he died, Pope Pius X also had a similar vision. He claimed to have seen a future pope fleeing over the bodies of his brethren, before he is killed.

> The man in white will take refuge in some hiding place while other clergy are killed; but after a brief respite, he, too, will die a cruel death."

"If I'm to interpret these visions correctly," Tate replied, "you're telling us the man dressed in white—Pope Emeritus Anthony—is going to die."

"John Tate, you are brilliant!" the cardinal teased. "See, you didn't need to bring Liz all the way here. You are smart enough to figure things out on your own!"

Cardinal Martinelli clapped mockingly.

"Hooray for John!"

Tate stuck his hands in his pockets. His fingers found the lighter.

I will signal to Paul the Swiss Guard that we are in trouble, he thought.

Just then, the heavy wooden door swung open.

A woman stood in the doorway with a semiautomatic rifle in her hand. She pushed Paul inside the dungeon.

"Forgive me," said Cardinal Martinelli. "I forgot to introduce my dear friend Carla Pasquinelli. She found your friend the Swiss Guard snooping around the vineyard."

"Sorry, guys," Paul said dejectedly.

Carla closed the heavy door after pushing Paul inside the dungeon.

"So, Cardinal Martinelli, you're the one responsible for sending Black Hand letters to Giuseppe and Cardinal Berlone," Tate declared.

"And to the pope's sister," the cardinal replied. "Don't forget about Tina. We surely haven't."

"Who's *we*?" Tate asked.

"Masons," Cardinal Martinelli said.

"The Mafia," Carla added.

"The Carbonari," Cassandra put in.

"I thought the Carbonari faded away by the 1900s," Liz noted.

"Everyone thinks that," said Cassandra. "But that isn't true. My great-grandfather General Valentino Martinelli simply moved them underground like Masonry. The Carbonari are still around."

"What a minute, did you say your great-grandfather's last name was Martinelli?" Tate asked.

"Yes, General Valentino Martinelli was my great-grandfather," Cassandra replied.

Tate felt like a thunderbolt had hit him.

"What was your grandfather's name?" the reporter asked.

"Mario Martinelli, the man who discovered Chianti."

"And who is your father?" Tate pressed.

"You're looking at him," said Cardinal Martinelli.

"That can't be," Liz replied. "Priests don't marry and have children."

"Plenty of priests have fathered children," Cardinal Martinelli countered.

"But for the record, I was in Jesuit seminary school and dropped out for a few years before returning to finish. During that break I fathered Cassandra."

Liz thought back to the magazine story, which mentioned that Cassandra's grandfather had left everything to her.

"And the reason you inherited everything from your grandfather is because your dad, Carlo Martinelli, joined the priesthood?" Liz asked Cassandra.

"My father had a different calling," Cassandra quipped. "Isn't that how the magazine reported it, anyway?"

"What now?" Tate said. "Obviously, people will come looking for us."

"Like who?" Cardinal Martinelli sneered. "No one will be missing you."

"My boss, Ed Rollings, will get suspicious," the reporter said.

"People go missing in foreign countries all the time," Cardinal Martinelli noted.

"He'll never find you here in my daughter's dungeon. You'll all just be another unsolved mystery."

"The Swiss Guard will come looking for Paul," Liz said.

"The Swiss Guard is about to have their hands full," Cardinal Martinelli shot back.

"Are you going to abduct Pope Pius XIII, Cardinal Martinelli?" Tate asked.

"No, he is going to run away," the cardinal said. "After he does, Cardinal Solano will convene the College of Cardinals, and a new pope will be chosen."

"Let me guess, Giovanni is your choice?" Tate questioned.

"He is." Cardinal Martinelli cackled. "How'd you know?"

Liz turned to Cassandra. "And what about you? What is your next step?"

"Pope Pius XIII had his chance, but he did not call on the parliament to resign," Cassandra replied. "Time is up. Our people will march on Rome, just as Italians marched on the capital to install Mussolini. And like then, there will be a change in governments."

"Bringing back the king, eh?" Liz questioned.

"Who said anything about a king?" Cassandra replied. "We'll be installing a queen."

"Queen?" Tate asked.

"You don't think I am doing all this so someone else can wear the crown, do you, John?"

"Cassandra likes her titles," Liz bellowed. "Right, Baroness?"

"*Queen* sounds better than *baroness*," Cassandra chortled.

Just then, the heavy wooden door swung open again. This time, Giuseppe was pushed inside.

"All the rats in one place!" Cardinal Martinelli exclaimed. "You may have gotten away from me last year, but there's no getting away this time."

The door slammed shut, and the window slid shut too, locking them in.

Chapter 9

GOOD SAMARITAN

Vatican City, June 2023

Led by Cassandra, thousands upon thousands of protesters marched on Rome. She yelled into a bullhorn.

"Down with the parliament. Bring back the monarchy!"

The protesters walked in a single line, which made the size of the event appear even bigger.

Several military tanks paralleled the protesters, as did knights carrying guns.

In Vatican City, Cardinal Martinelli led his own coup. He was joined by several hundred people and military tanks. They moved quickly toward the Vatican.

"Holy Father, it's time to go," said Cardinal Berlone, the Vatican's secretary of state. "Staying is too dangerous."

Pope Pius XIII followed Swiss Guards to an ancient hidden passageway with a hollow wall, constructed in 1277.

The passageway ran from the papal apartments to the Castel Sant'Angelo, the tomb of the Roman emperor Hadrian, which looked like an impregnable castle with a moat around it.

In the Middle Ages, the tomb of Hadrian was made into a fortress.

"Popes have used this passageway to seek refuge before," the head Swiss Guard assured Pope Pius XIII. "This place likely saved the life of Pope Clement VII during the toppling of Rome in 1527. Let's hope it does the trick again."

Helicopters carrying television news crews circled above both the Vatican and the Palazzo Montecitorio, where the Chamber of Deputies met since 1871, shortly after the capital of the Kingdom of Italy moved to Rome.

On CNN and all the prime-time cable news shows, Italian Prime Minister Alberto Regio gave a live interview.

"The parliament resigns," the prime minister announced. "We don't want any Italian blood spilled.

"Effective immediately, Italy will go back to being a constitutional monarchy. Cassandra Capalbo, whose great-grandfather was a nobleman, will be the country's new queen."

Minutes later, Cardinal Solano came on the television. He said the College of Cardinals would soon vote again for a new pope, one who supported the return of the Pontifical States to the Vatican.

He said Pope Pius XIII had abandoned his post.

When the coup led by Cardinal Martinelli arrived at the Vatican's doors, Cardinal Martinelli demanded that Pope Pius XIII come out of hiding.

The heavily armed Swiss Guards dug in.

"We do not negotiate with terrorists," the head guard called out.

"Then I will unleash my nuclear weapons and level everything within a three-hundred-mile radius from here," said Cardinal Martinelli. "We will rebuild this place if we have to."

From a safe house not too far away from all of the action, a Good Samaritan watched the standoff on television.

Oh, no, you don't, he thought.

This has gone far enough!

***

Back at the castle, Liz and Giuseppe rushed over to Pope Emeritus Anthony, who slipped in and out of consciousness.

"I have a protein bar and bottle of water in my shoulder bag," Liz said. "Giuseppe, can you please bring them to me?"

The old man shuffled there and back while Tate and Paul looked over their confines.

"Do you see a way out?" Tate asked the Swiss Guard.

"None. This place is like a tomb," Paul replied.

Tate crossed his arms and shook his head.

"Does the head of the Swiss Guard know you are here?" the reporter asked.

"He knows I am with you, but not exactly where," Paul replied.

"I have a gadget in my pocket that tracks my whereabouts. However, there's no reception down here, so it'll take the team time to find us, if their hands aren't too full with the coup."

"Sounds like the Swiss Guard is going to be under attack," said Tate, who pushed his back against a wall and slowly let himself slide down into a sitting position.

"Don't give up," Paul said. "Eventually, they will come looking."

"But it may be too late," Tate murmured. "No one will find us down here in this dungeon."

Paul slid to the ground too.

"I knew the lady who abducted me," he said. "Carla Pasquinelli. She's a bad person."

"How bad?" Tate asked.

"She runs the Camorra," he said. "She was also going on outside about being the leader of P2."

"So that means she brings a lot of firepower to this overthrow attempt," Tate said.

"Well, she isn't without her own detractors," Paul replied.

"What does that mean?" Tate asked.

"The Swiss Guard monitors criminal activity in Italy. For years we have been hearing that there's strife between Carla's Camorra and someone else, a person who runs all the other Mafia organizations in Italy."

"What kind of strife?"

"Carla is very popular and dynamic, but we've heard this other person is bigger, and he opposes her," Paul said.

"She wants to be the top Mafia dog, but this other person is already in that space, and he isn't about to give it up."

"Who is it?" Tate asked.

"We don't know," said the Swiss Guard. "This person keeps a very low profile, but he has far greater clout than Carla or anyone else in the Mafia.

"For quite some time, Carla has wanted all of the Mafia organizations to come together under her and operate as one united organization. She believes one Mafia organization would be stronger than a patchwork of organizations throughout Italy."

"But this other person doesn't agree?" Tate asked.

"No. He already influences all the other Mafia organizations. Realistically, they are already under him. The Camorra is the only Mafia group that he doesn't control."

Several hours passed. The only daylight in the dungeon came through a keyhole in the big, wooden door.

The retired pope started to come around. He looked better than when they first found him, but he was still very weak.

"Did they hurt you?" Liz asked Pope Emeritus Anthony.

"They put me down here and barely kept me alive. I received little water and no food."

"How about you, Giuseppe, are you okay?" she asked.

"I am fine," the old man replied. "They did not hurt me much."

"Paul, if there is an attack on the Vatican, will Pietro be safe?" Tate asked.

"The Swiss Guard will move Pope Pius XIII to a safe hiding spot, if they haven't already done so."

"Can Cardinal Martinelli possibly pull his Vatican coup off?" Liz asked.

"With P2, the Camorra, and the secret combat unit of the Knights of Malta behind him, maybe," Paul said. "Who knows what kind of weaponry and firepower he has."

"This is a double move?" Tate asked. "One move is to remove the pope and replace him with a Mason, and the other is to topple the parliament and replace it with a queen?"

"Cassandra wants to be queen, and Cardinal Martinelli wants a true Mason as the pope, yes," said Paul.

Giuseppe struggled to his feet.

"Are you sure you are okay?" Liz asked him.

The old man nodded. He had a thought.

"John, that skeleton key you showed me earlier, do you have it with you now?" Giuseppe asked.

"Yes, why?"

"Are you familiar with how a skeleton key works?" the old man asked.

"No," Tate answered.

"A skeleton key is a type of master key in which the serrated edge has been removed in such a way that it can open numerous locks, most commonly the warded lock—meaning a jail cell door," Giuseppe said.

Tate looked at the door with sunlight shining through the lock.

"Are you saying the skeleton key might open this door?" the reporter asked.

"Quite possibly, yes," Giuseppe said. "Give it a try."

Tate stood and slowly walked over to the door. He inserted the key into the lock and turned. The heavy door opened.

"Well, what do you know? Thank you, Lucky Longo!" Tate said. "This key definitely got us out of a tight spot."

The prisoners quietly slipped out of the dungeon and tiptoed up the stairs leading to the kitchen pantry.

"What if they're still here?" Liz asked.

"Doubtful," Paul said. "I overheard Cardinal Martinelli talking with Cassandra and Carla about leaving immediately to implement their coup attempts. However, they may have left a couple of guards behind, so be careful."

Once they reached the top step, Tate cautiously opened the door to the kitchen pantry, poked his head out, and looked around.

"Don't you move another muscle," a waiting gunman instructed.

Caught already? Tate thought.

That was a short-lived escape.

The man with the gun was older, probably in his midsixties, but was in excellent shape. His muscular body had not an ounce of fat on it.

The man stood six feet tall, and his receding salt-and-pepper hair matched that of his beard and mustache.

Behind him, three men lay crumpled on the floor.

When the bearded man with a gun saw the retired pope, he lowered his weapon and got up from his crouched shooting position.

"Pope Emeritus Anthony? Is that you?" he asked.

"Yes."

The gunman wiped a hand across his sweaty forehead. "Whew!"

Tate and the others looked quizzically at each other.

"What's happening here?" the reporter asked.

"My name is Lucky Longo, but everyone calls me 'Junior.'"

Tate did a double take.

"Who did you say you are?" the reporter asked.

"Lucky Longo Jr., but please, call me 'Junior.' Everyone else does."

"You're the son of Lucky Longo, the mobster?" Tate asked.

"Don't call my dad a mobster," Junior snapped. "Show a little respect for the dead."

"I'm so confused." Liz rubbed her hand across her face.

"My father, Lucky Longo Sr., and my mother, an Italian dancer, had a son—me!

"Unfortunately, they both died when I was young, so the Mafia in Italy took me in and raised me."

I should write a story about him, Tate thought.

"How did you find us?" Tate asked.

"Through him." Junior pointed at Giuseppe.

"I don't get it," Tate said.

"My dad, Lucky Sr., was very protective of Big Al and Giuseppe. After the incident last year at the Vatican Secret Archive, I swore on my father's grave to keep an eye out for Giuseppe."

"Thank you, Junior," Giuseppe said, shaking his hand.

"I am doing this out of respect for my dad," Junior said. "He would have wanted me to protect you, Giuseppe."

"Those thugs who are lying on the floor, did you do that?" Tate asked.

"Yes. I was doing a sweep of the castle when I encountered them. Let's get out of here."

"What is your plan?" Tate asked.

"The Mafia is good at smuggling things," Junior said. "I'm going to smuggle all of you out of the country, except for Paul."

"How are you going to do that?" Liz asked.

"I'm going to put you onto one of our ships at the Port of Salerno. Then I'm going to ship you to America with some of my guards. The airlines are too risky. Carla has people at every airport in Italy. They protect her drug shipments."

"What about Pope Pius XIII?" Tate asked.

Junior looked at the Swiss Guard.

"Paul and I will sneak the pope out of the Vatican through underground tunnels."

"Then what?" Tate asked.

"I'll get the pope out of the country too," Junior said. "He's not safe in Italy right now. I'll get him to a safe house in America."

"And what about you?" Tate asked Junior.

"My Mafia associates and I will go to war with Carla… and Cardinal Martinelli."

"Junior, it's you who is at odds with Carla!" Tate exclaimed as it all became clear in his mind.

"Yes, I am," he replied. "My dad wielded huge influence over the American Mafia, and I have that same kind of influence over the Italian Mafia, probably more, since I grew up in it.

"I've known for a while that Carla wants to unseat me, so it's high time that she and I had it out."

Chapter 10

BIG AL'S GRAVE

Italy, July 2023

Tate took a cigarette from his coat pocket and lit it. He took a long drag and looked up to the sky.

"What are you thinking, John?" Liz asked.

Her colleague turned to Giuseppe.

"You said Sister Lúcia came to see you in 1963?" Tate asked the very old man.

"Yes."

"And during that visit, she told you where to hide the Third Secret of Fatima?"

"Correct."

"Giuseppe, I think it's time we retrieve the Third Secret," Tate declared. "Something so important needs to be shared with the world, especially now."

The old man tugged on the collar of his finely starched shirt, and paced back and forth.

"I think maybe you're right," he concluded. "Let's do it."

"Where's the secret hidden?" Tate asked.

"I buried it with my papa, Big Al."

"Wait, what? The Third Secret of Fatima is six feet under?" Tate asked.

"Yes, in my papa's coat pocket," Giuseppe revealed.

"Oh great, now we have to wait until we get back to the US to exhume his body," Tate groaned.

"He was buried in Rome," Giuseppe corrected.

"He was?" Liz asked.

"Papa wanted to be buried in the country where he was born."

"Is the cemetery nearby?" Tate asked.

"Yes, it is," replied Giuseppe. "And the good news is that I personally know the caretaker. I will call him now and ask that we exhume my papa's body right away."

***

A short time later, the limo driver pulled into the Commonwealth War Cemetery.

"The sign out front says this is a war cemetery built to commemorate the dead from both the First and Second World Wars," Liz said. "How is it that Big Al is buried here?"

"My papa is considered a hero by Italians for his role working with Pope Pius XII to liberate Italy during World War II," Giuseppe said.

The caretaker came over to the guests. Workers behind him had already been digging for about an hour.

"Only a few more minutes," said the caretaker. "Just as soon as I retrieve the Third Secret of Fatima from Big Al's coat pocket, I'll bring it to you, Giuseppe. That way you won't have to see the decayed body."

"Thank you," Giuseppe said with tears in his eyes. "You are so thoughtful."

Ten minutes later, the caretaker returned holding a single sheet of paper.

"Here you go, Giuseppe," he said. "I am giving this to you. We will return Big Al to the ground now."

"Thank you," the old man said. "Please, everyone, let us say a short prayer for my papa."

When they were done, Giuseppe read the Third Secret of Fatima out loud:

> "Satan will be granted one hundred years to test mankind. During this time period, an unholy council consisting of Freemasons will be held. The Church—and all of Christianity for that matter—will be drastically changed.
>
> "A division will grow out of this unholy council. People (the sheep) will search for the clergy (the shepherds) in vain. People will lose their faith.
>
> "During this time of unrest, a false savior will appear. He will be aided by a false prophet—a person who, like John the Baptist, proclaims the coming of the savior. The proclaimer and false savior will appear as holy men, but they are not.
>
> "As Matthew said in 7:15, 'Beware of false prophets, which come to you in

sheep's clothing, but inwardly they are ravening wolves.'"

Tate looked over at Liz.

"That's exactly how Pietro described the Third Secret of Fatima to me and Ed when he came to the office," he said.

"The Third Secret refers to an unholy council," Liz remarked. "That has to be the Second Vatican Council that began in 1962."

"Which is why the Madonna wanted the Third Secret of Fatima revealed in 1960—two years before the Second Vatican Council began," Tate replied.

"She was warning us," Liz concluded.

Tate took out his notebook.

"Mind if I ask a question, Giuseppe?"

"Not at all. Ask away."

"Do you know why the Vatican allowed Masons to participate in Vatican II?"

"Pope John XXIII knew there were dangerous, secret elements in the Church," Giuseppe explained.

"To bring them out in the open, he included Masons in the Second Vatican Council. The Council had no sooner opened when the secret elements took control."

"You're saying Pope John lost control of Vatican II?" Tate questioned.

"That is correct."

Lucky Longo Jr. stepped forward. "Sorry to break this up, but we really need to go. Time is of the essence."

Tate looked at the Mafia leader, who could see the reporter was confused as to what to do about their situation.

"John, I believe nothing in life is a coincidence," Junior said.

"What do you mean?" Tate asked.

"Do you think it was merely by chance that you were on that hijacked airplane? Do you also believe that it was simply a matter of coincidence that you are here today, reading the Third Secret?"

Tate scratched his head and then nodded that he understood Junior's point.

"You are a writer for a reason," the gangster continued. "Your job is to expose the truth. So, tell it. Write it down.

"Tell the world what's happened here. Use the power of the pen to fight Cardinal Martinelli, Giovanni, Cassandra Capalbo, Carla, and Freemasons.

"That's the only way to change the current situation, John. Maybe you can prevent World War III from breaking out."

***

A short time later, from a secret, undisclosed location, Pietro broadcasted the following message to the world:

"My brothers and sisters," the pope began. "These are difficult times. Blinded despite the light, more and more the followers of Christianity will give their hand to the Enemy—the Great Deceiver—and do Satan's bidding.

"During this tribulation, there will be much suffering. We have already seen a sharp increase in civilian violence.

"Mass shootings, terrorism, and wars are on the rise. The Doomsday Clock has moved closer to midnight than ever.

"The elements of nature have been unchained, as the melting of the Doomsday Glacier in Antarctica proves. Global climate change is real.

"Those who fearlessly defend the rights of Christianity are being persecuted. This discrimination—against Christians of all faiths—is fast becoming genocide.

"Soon, faith may disappear altogether, even in locations where its presence dates back to antiquity.

"But do not lose hope. When evil seems triumphant and when authority commits all manner of injustice, oppressing the weak, their ruin shall be near. They will fail and crash to the ground.

"When I was a boy, the Madonna visited me and shared several secrets, one of which I have never revealed. Here's what She told me:

> "'These evils can be avoided by you; the dangers can be evaded. The force of His merciful love always can change the plan of God's justice.
>
> 'When I predict chastisements to you—such as I did at Fatima—remember that everything, at any moment, may be changed by the power of kindness, good deeds, prayer, reparation, and penance. Do these things.
>
> 'The light of human kindness and love still shines in the world, and this makes God happy. Now is the time to turn up that flame.

'Take comfort in knowing that the future is not yet set.

'*And remember, wherever you go, no matter what the weather, always bring your own sunshine.*'"

The End

BIG AL'S RECIPES

LASAGNA

Total Time: 1 hour, 30 minutes
Prep: 15 minutes
Cook: 1 hour
Servings: 12

Ingredients:
6 cups Italian meat sauce
16 ounces dry lasagna noodles
2 (15-ounce) containers ricotta cheese
1 (8-ounce) package shredded mozzarella cheese, divided
½ cup grated Parmesan cheese, divided
2 eggs
1 tablespoon parsley flakes
2 teaspoons Italian seasoning
½ teaspoon salt
¼ teaspoon ground black pepper

Preparation:
Prepare Italian meat sauce.
Preheat oven to 350°F. Cook pasta as directed on package.
Drain and rinse with cold water. Lay flat on wax paper or
foil to keep pieces from sticking together. Set aside.

Mix ricotta cheese, 1 ½ cups of the mozzarella cheese, ¼ cup of the Parmesan cheese, eggs, parsley, Italian seasoning, salt, and pepper in large bowl.

Spread ½ cup of the sauce onto bottom of 13 x 9-inch baking dish. Top with ¼ of the lasagna noodles, overlapping edges. Spread ⅓ cheese mixture over noodles. Top with 1 ½ cups of the sauce. Repeat layers two more times, ending with a layer of pasta and 1 ½ cups sauce. Cover with foil.

Bake 40 minutes. Remove foil. Top with remaining ½ cup mozzarella and Parmesan cheeses. Bake 10 minutes longer or until center is heated through. Let stand 15 minutes before cutting. Serve with remaining sauce, if desired.

MEATBALLS

The key to succulent meatballs is to mix in the soaked and squeezed pieces of day-old Italian bread instead of using breadcrumbs. The chunks of bread make for a lighter, spongier texture.

Total Time: 2 hours, 15 minutes
Prep: 20 minutes
Cook: 60 minutes
Servings: 10–12 meatballs

Ingredients:
8 ounces ground pork
8 ounces ground beef
4 slices sandwich bread or home bread
½ cup milk
1 tablespoon oil
2 tablespoons grated Parmesan cheese
2 tablespoons parsley
1 egg
1 garlic clove
Dash of salt and pepper (to taste)

Preparation:
Begin by breaking the bread in small bits inside a bowl and then soak it with the milk.

Remove the leaves of parsley from the stems and put them on a cutting board to be finely minced together with the garlic clove.

In a bowl, add all the ingredients, minced meats, parsley and garlic, egg, cheese, soaked bread, salt, and pepper.

Taking about 3 tablespoons of meat from the mixture, start rolling within the palms of your hands until you get a good round shape. Make medium meatballs, so not too big, not too small. Make about 10 to 12 meatballs.

Pour oil in a frying pan, and arrange all the meatballs around. Fry them until lightly brown, then turn off the heat and keep all aside.

Beef Tenderloin (Braciole) in Tomato Sauce

Braciole is thinly sliced, tender strips of steak rolled together with cheese and breadcrumbs, then fried and slow cooked in a rich tomato sauce. Slow cooking the rolled meats in sauce is really what braciole is all about.

Total Time: 1 hour, 15 minutes
Prep: 15 minutes
Cook: 1 hour
Servings: 8

Ingredients:
2 pounds flank steak, thinly sliced
½ teaspoon salt
¼ teaspoon pepper
1 cup grated Parmesan
½ cup grated provolone
½ cup Italian breadcrumbs
½ teaspoon garlic powder
1 teaspoon dried basil
5 tablespoons olive oil
4 cups tomato sauce

Preparation:

In a medium-sized bowl, mix together the garlic powder, cheeses, breadcrumbs, and dried basil. Set the mix aside. Lay the flank steak on a clean surface and pound flat with a meat tenderizer. Sprinkle with the salt and pepper. Evenly distribute the breadcrumb filling among the flank steaks, then roll, beginning on the short end, all the way up like a jelly roll. Tie the rolls closed with butcher's twine to secure the braciole.

Pour the olive oil into a large pot and heat over medium-high heat. Sear the braciole rolls for about 30 seconds on each side, just to brown the meat quickly.

Add the tomato sauce to the pot and lower the heat to low. Cover and cook the braciole for an hour, basting the rolls occasionally to ensure they do not dry out.

Serve hot along with the sauce!

STEWED OCTOPUS

This recipe for Southern Italian stewed octopus with white wine and tomatoes originates in Puglia, near the heel of Italy's boot.

Octopus requires long, slow simmering, so keep the temperature low and give yourself plenty of time. This unusual dish is especially good made with baby octopus that you can find frozen in Asian markets, but you could use any octopus.

Serve with crusty bread or a big pasta, like ziti or penne, for a special weekend meal or a casual summer dinner party.

Total Time: 90 minutes
Prep: 15 minutes
Cook: 75 minutes
Servings: 4

Ingredients:
1 (1-pound) octopus
4 tablespoons olive oil
4 cloves garlic (finely chopped)
1 cup white wine

1 cup crushed tomatoes (canned or peeled, chopped fresh tomatoes)
1 teaspoon chili flakes
1 teaspoon salt
2 tablespoons honey (or sugar)
2 tablespoons capers (optional)
2 tablespoons fresh dill (chopped)
4 tablespoons fresh parsley (chopped)
black pepper (to taste)

Preparation:
Bring a large pot of salty water to a boil. Toss the octopus into the boiling water, return to a boil, and cook for 1 to 2 minutes, then remove. Discard the water. Cut the octopus into large pieces and sauté in olive oil over medium-high heat for 2 to 3 minutes. Add the chopped garlic and sauté for another minute or two.

Add the wine and bring to a boil over high heat. Stir well and let it cool down for 3 to 4 minutes. Add the tomatoes and chili flakes and bring to a simmer.

Add about a teaspoon of salt and the honey or sugar. Mix well, cover the pot, and simmer for 30 minutes.

At 30 minutes, add the optional capers, half the dill, and half the parsley. Check the octopus—sometimes small ones will be tender in just 30 minutes.

If it is still super-chewy, cover the pot again and simmer for up to another 45 minutes.

When you think you are about 10 minutes away from the octopus being done, uncover the pot and turn the heat up a little to cook down the sauce.

To serve, add the remaining dill and parsley and black pepper to taste.

Accompany with bread or pasta, either hot or at room temperature.

ABOUT THE AUTHOR

Marco De Sio is a former award-winning journalist who received a 2021 James Madison Freedom of Information Award from the Society of Professional Journalists. He was born and raised in California. His father was the only one of seven children born in the United States; the rest immigrated from Italy to New York.

In 1991, while on a Rotary International exchange trip to Brazil, Marco was taken by his hosts to a secret Masonic meeting held at midnight. Masonry is one of the world's oldest fraternal orders, accused of being a cult with covert rituals and secret handshakes.

Ten years earlier, in 1981, the author was riveted when a former monk unsuccessfully hijacked a plane, going from Dublin to London, in a bid to force Pope John Paul II to release the Third Secret of Fatima. A little more than a week later, the pope was shot.

In the summer of 1974, Marco visited Fatima, Portugal, specifically the site where the Virgin Mary visited three shepherd children fifty-seven years earlier. The children were given three secrets, two of which were revealed in 1941. The Third Secret of Fatima was supposed to be released by the Vatican no later than 1960, but it wasn't. Why not?

Marco first witnessed the splendor of a pope being selected by the College of Cardinals in 1978, when white smoke announcing the selection of Pope John Paul I emanated from a chimney placed atop the Sistine Chapel. Just thirty-three days later, the new pope was dead. How? Why?

Marco's family has ties to the Italian-American Mafia. His late uncle was a numbers runner in New Jersey for the Italian lottery. Gamblers placed bets with his uncle at a mattress shop. Another late uncle—a fisherman and union organizer—fled New Jersey after making trouble for the Mafia at the Port of New York.

As a boy, Marco worked as a dishwasher at a Catholic retreat center.